Beauty Among Ruins

BEAUTY AMONG RUINS

J'NELL CIESIELSKI

THORNDIKE PRESS
A part of Gale, a Cengage Company

GALE
A Cengage Company

Copyright © 2021 J'nell Ciesielski.
The lyrics in chapter 16 are from *The Braes of Balquhidder,* a traditional Scottish song from the 1700s.
Thorndike Press, a part of Gale, a Cengage Company.

LIBRARY OF CONGRESS CIP DATA ON FILE.
CATALOGUING IN PUBLICATION FOR THIS BOOK
IS AVAILABLE FROM THE LIBRARY OF CONGRESS.

ISBN-13: 978-1-4328-8744-5 (hardcover alk. paper)

Published in 2021 by arrangement with Thomas Nelson, Inc., a division of HarperCollins Christian Publishing, Inc.

Printed in Mexico
Print Number: 01   Print Year: 2021

Linda.
For believing enough in the magic of words to take a chance on this wide eyed writer with nothing more than a simple story and hope to offer.

GLOSSARY

a ghràidh: my dear

Àrd-Choille: high wood; the place where the clan would gather in times of war and decide what was to be done; MacGregor clan war cry

auld: old

bairn(s): baby/child, children

bannocks: biscuit/corn bread

barmy: crazy, foolish

bawbee: Scottish coin of small value

baw-faced: chubby face

beasties: animal, critter

bens: mountains

Bi samnach, tha mi seo: "Be calm now. I am here."

bonny: attractive, fair, excellent

bothy: small hut

brae: hillside

braw: good

burn: creek

canny: careful; clever

7

ceilidh: informal dance
Chan fheudar an t-eagal a bheth oirbh: Fear not
clot-heid: clot head
conies: rabbits
crags: steep, rugged rock with cliffs
creepie: three-legged stool
croft: small tenant farm
crowdie: Scottish cottage cheese
dinna: do not
dram: small portion of something to drink
dreich: dreary
drookit: soaked
fae: for
fash: vex; fuss; worry
fête: elaborate celebration
Gàidhligh: Gaelic
glaikit: foolish, giddy; fool
haggis: traditional Scottish dish
hie: to go quickly
Hogmanay: Scottish New Year celebration
Ifrinn an Diabhuil: son of the devil
kelpie: a water sprite of Scottish folklore that delights in or brings about the drowning of wayfarers
ken: to know
laird: lord
leannan: sweetheart
loch: lake
lolly: candy

8

luaidh: darling

madainn mhath: good morning

mayhap: maybe, perhaps

midge: tiny fly

mo bhean bhrèagha: my beautiful wife

mo chridhe: my heart, my love

mo maise: my beauty

parritch: porridge

Sassenach: English person or Lowlander

sgian dubh: small knife

shied: to throw

skelloch: to scream

smoor: to smother, subdue; to bank a fire

sporran: pouch worn in front of kilt

stad: to stop, halt, pause; whoa

'S e do bheatha: you're welcome

stramash: disturbance, smashup; fight

tae: to

tam: Tam o' Shanter; woolen cap

targe: a light shield

tarn: small steep-banked mountain lake or pool

tartan: a plaid textile design of Scottish origin consisting of stripes of varying width and color usually patterned to designate a distinctive clan

thaisce: my treasure

thick-heided: thickheaded

uisge: whisky water

wame: stomach, belly
wheesht: hush

PROLOGUE

May 1914
New York

Creeping through the back door, Lily Durham slipped across the black-and-white tiled kitchen and checked the hallway before scurrying up the stairs to the main floor.

Moonlight washed over the parquet walnut floors that the white-tied men and shimmering-gowned women of New York society had glided across earlier in the evening. The last bash of the season before the wealthy retired to their summer homes in Newport had been quite a feast for the eyes and ears. No expense was spared to bring in the most fashionable delicacies and highly acclaimed musicians on the Eastern Seaboard for a party that reeled in extravagance as the epitome of society's merriment.

And a complete bore compared to the hullabaloo offered in the servants' hall. What

11

girl wouldn't seize the chance to toss off her pinching satin shoes and kick up her heels for an hour of unrestrained frivolity?

Lily took off the lacy white maid's cap and skipped up the sweeping carpeted staircase. Her feet ached after all the running around, but nights like this were worth blistered heels and pinched toes. The summer was to bring nothing but hot days and evenings filled with boring card games.

She tiptoed down the hall, careful to avoid the squeaky places lest someone wake up and demand to know why she was returning after all had gone to bed. Sliding into her room, she eased the door shut behind her and sighed with relief. Not a soul was wiser to her midnight rendezvous.

"I sent you to bed over an hour ago."

Gaslight flooded the room. Still dressed in her ruby-red silk gown and glittering diamond earrings, Mrs. Durham stood as still as a marble statue in front of Lily's vanity.

"Oh, Mother." Lily flung the maid's cap on her feather pillow before flouncing down on the bed. "Can't we talk about this tomorrow? I feel much better prepared for battle after a good night's sleep."

"Don't take that tone with me, young lady. Where have you been? And dressed like a housemaid?"

"The servants would have recognized me in a ball gown, and those who do know my face were good enough to keep it to themselves lest they spoil the fun."

"If your father had seen you —"

"Father never notices me unless there's a chance to snag the latest eligible bachelor." Lily untied the apron she had borrowed from the maid's closet and leaned over to unbuckle the black patent shoes. "You can tell him I tried tonight, but Vincent Astor is recently taken, and Jakey won't inherit his trust fund for a number of years."

"That is it!" Mrs. Durham stamped her dainty foot on the thick, white carpet. Her sharp aristocratic nose flared red. "I have tried and tried, but you push us too far. I hoped your debut into proper society two years ago would settle you down to the matter you were intended for: making a suitable match. No man will take a girl who laughs too much as a wife, and before long they'll pass you over completely for a girl of more tender age."

"Eighteen is hardly in danger of spinsterhood."

"Your frivolities will bring nothing but shame on this house."

The shoe slipped from Lily's cold hand. This speech had sent a quiver through her

13

heart many times before, but tonight something was different. The finality in her mother's voice shot fear straight through her.

"Am I really so shameful to you, Mother?"

Mrs. Durham didn't blink. "Tomorrow Abigail will pack your trunks. You're going to stay with your cousins in Hertfordshire for the summer."

"England?" The coldness reached Lily's head, pushing in on all sides until her thoughts whirled together like a blizzard. What about her friends here? What would she tell Robert after he promised to take her for a ride in his new Renault? How could she survive in England? The English were so cold, so humorless, so bland. Everything that sent her tearing in the other direction. "I refuse to go."

"You do not have a choice." Her mother picked up the jar of powdered rice on the vanity and puckered her lips with distaste. "And know that if you attempt a dramatic confrontation in hopes of persuading us otherwise, your allowance will be cut off without another cent. Perhaps a few months in England will see you develop a bit of self-control." She put down the jar and dusted her hands clean. "One can hope."

"So that's it? You'll just ship me off to be

14

someone else's problem? I'll land on your cousin's doorstep and say, 'Surprise! I'm here to live with you.' "

"I wrote her over a month ago. They're expecting you by the end of next week."

"You've had this planned for over a month? Was I to wake up one morning and suddenly find seagulls flying outside my stateroom?"

"Your father and I do not need to inform you of every decision we think best. One day a husband will handle such responsibilities. Until then, you do as we say. We have given you every luxury and yet you continue without a responsible thought in that too pretty head of yours. Sneaking along dark halls dressed as a common maid." Mrs. Durham, the high society party planner of the season, pressed a hand to her mouth, unable to go on.

Standing, Lily walked to her armoire and flung the door open with numb fingers. The bottom board where her rows of shoes ordinarily smiled up at her was empty. Abigail had started early. "Thank you for letting me know exactly where I stand in this family." She shut the door and laid a hand against the smooth wood. "Perhaps you'll find some small pride for me from a distance. Absence makes the heart grow fonder. Or so they say."

"I shall write to Cousin Hazel when I think it's time for you to come home." Her mother glided to the door, hand pausing on the polished doorknob. "Use this time wisely. It's for your own good."

Lily spun and smiled with brittleness pricking her heart. "Shall I find a husband while I'm there? A lord, perhaps? That should make Father happy."

"Their gentry is still recovering. It may take a few generations for them to regain their power after that last boat of debutantes, like Cousin Hazel, rescued them. As much as your father would love to have a title in the family, it's best to wait until you return before we consider those prospects." Mrs. Durham paused, the ice briefly cracking on her face. "I have tried, Lily."

"I know, Mother. But we always seem to try for different things. Perhaps one day we'll get it right."

The door shut. Lily took a deep breath and turned back to her armoire to finish what Abigail had started. If her mother wasn't shedding a tear, then neither would she.

CHAPTER 1

April 1915
Laggan, Scotland

If only the snobs on Fifth Avenue could see this.

Lily Durham ducked her head back inside the car window, careful to prevent the pheasant feathers on her hat from being crushed against the glass. Sprawling green hills, lush woods, and a castle with diamond-paned windows and towers spiraling high into the blue sky were enough to vanquish any qualms she'd had about leaving gentle England for the wilds of Scotland.

"Are you sure this is a hospital? It's like nothing I've ever seen."

"A convalescent home." Her cousin Elizabeth — Bertie, as she corrected Lily at their first meeting almost a year ago — adjusted the wire-rimmed glasses on the edge of her nose and flipped a page from the folder in her hand. "Wealthy families are opening

17

their homes for the returning soldiers to recuperate without all the sterilization of an actual hospital. According to our introduction packet, the MacGregor estate is the oldest and largest in Lanarkshire County."

"Does it say anything in there about handsome soldiers?"

Bertie's nose disappeared into a paper crease. "Yes, right here. There will be at least three to every nurse. No more than fifty patients at a time to ensure proper attention is awarded each."

"You put your face any closer to that and you'll have ink marks on your forehead."

"You asked about the Tommies."

Lily snatched the papers from Bertie's hand and stuffed them back into the satchel tucked between their feet. "What I want to know can't be found from scribbled statistics."

Bertie rolled her eyes. "Oh, you mean the color of their eyes, the charm of their voice, and whether or not they'd make a good dance partner."

Lily grinned and hooked her arm through Bertie's. "Precisely. And I'm finding the best dancer just for you."

The barest smile floated across Bertie's lips. "You know I can't dance. Don't make me remind you of what happened at that surprise birthday party you threw for me last summer."

"The important thing was that you stayed upright. Besides, your mother's couch looks much better with a punch stain on it."

"She doesn't think so." The smile faded from Bertie's face as they rounded the last bend in the drive. Two bandaged men in wheelchairs sat under a large, shady oak tree. A nurse bent over one of them, tucking a blanket around his remaining leg. "I don't know if any of the men here will be up for dancing. They need quiet and fresh air."

"Sitting in a silent room staring at white walls may heal the body, but it doesn't heal the soul."

"Don't let the matron hear you say such scandalous things. They don't like nurses who talk about anything other than proper bandages and crutches."

"Good thing your Red Cross nurses denied me to join their ranks, and yet you dragged me along anyway."

"I couldn't stand the thought of leaving without you." Bertie squeezed her arm. "I'm so glad your mother is allowing you to stay so long. I thought with the war starting she would demand your immediate return to America, but it's so dangerous now to be sailing out in the open waters with those German U-boats lurking around."

Lily turned back to the window. The late-afternoon sun shot between the trees in a dizzying effect of light and dark, catching her thoughts somewhere in between. Her mother had written at the end of the summer, asking Cousin Hazel to extend her hospitality in hopes of Lily experiencing more of what the gentle English countryside had to offer. But as the gentleness disappeared with the declaration of war, Lily allowed herself the smallest hope that her parents would demand her return at once. It wasn't until after she had written to tell them of her volunteer work in Scotland that they had replied. And it was only to state their relief in knowing she would be much safer there than farther south in England.

"You know Mother. She only wants what's best." Lily turned back to Bertie. "And what's best is I'm here to help you get into trouble."

"That's not why we're here."

"Perhaps not, but we do have off days."

The Renault glided to a stop in front of the thick front doors. Bertie grabbed her satchel, stuffed to the brim with folders and books on nursing, and vaulted out before the chauffeur could throttle down the engine. With a quick fluff to her hair, Lily followed.

Despite New York society's determination to always appear unimpressed, she couldn't help staring in awe at the enormous castle that devoured the sky at this close range. Weathered gray walls scaling four stories high stood formidable as giants, harsh and rugged from years of challenging the elements that threatened their stance. Rounded towers with conical roofs guarded each corner, with a rectangular tower rising from the middle like a crenellated crown.

"I'll get lost in a place like this."

"Needs a good scrubbing." Having grown up on a sprawling English estate complete with Thoroughbred stables and garage house, the effect was lost on Bertie. "Then again, Kinclavoch is close to four hundred years old."

"I thought you said this place was called MacGregor."

"It's the MacGregors' estate." At Lily's confusion, Bertie sighed. "Kinclavoch Castle is home to the family MacGregor and by which the lord and master is titled Lord Strathem."

The British and their stuffy titles.

The massive brass stag head knockers shook as the front door swung open. A thick woman in a blue cotton chambray dress, starched white apron with a red cross, and prim nurse cap stepped out.

Her close-set eyes swept over them with shrewd appraisal. "I'm Matron Strom. Are you my new girls?"

Bertie stepped forward and inclined her head. "How do you do? My name is Elizabeth Buchanan, and this is my cousin, Lily Durham."

Lily flashed a smile. "It was a long trip, but we're delighted to finally be here."

Matron Strom raised a sparse eyebrow. "Delighted to spend the spring in the glorious Lowlands at this magnificent estate, or delighted to charm your way through the injured and haunted boys inside?"

If the woman thought to intimidate her with barbs, she was in for an unpleasant surprise. Lily's mother had given her a lifetime of practice. She smiled even brighter. "Whatever I am called upon to do, I am at their disposal."

"How magnanimous is the American spirit. Mixed with British sensibility, it should prove an interesting combination. Get your bags and come inside."

"Might we have a footman to help?" Lily called as Matron Strom turned back to the house. "We brought a trunk and a few cases."

"You were instructed to bring only one suitcase." The woman's colorless lips pinched at the corners. "Do you always have difficulty following instructions?"

Lily bristled. "Of course not, but I could hardly fit my nightdress in one suitcase. How are we expected to fit an entire change of clothes in one?"

"The same as every other girl here." With a click of her shiny black pumps, the matron marched through the door. "Get used to lifting things. You're going to work now."

"Not very friendly, is she?" Lily took one of the suitcases the driver pulled down from the luggage rack and slung it over her shoulder. Bending down, she grabbed one handle of the trunk.

Bertie took the other side of the trunk and lifted. "Talking like we're here on a lark doesn't start us off on the right foot."

"I know we're not here for a lark, but we don't have to keep a sour face the whole time either."

Inside it was difficult to keep anything on her face but awe. Gleaming mahogany floors opened up to a three-story great hall. Light filtered through the high-arched windows and scattered over the blue-and-gold rug and dark wood furniture. Oil paintings of kilted men with swords drawn and storm-ravished moors lined the walls. Centuries of masculine strength gazed upon all who dared enter, but a cold stillness hung in the air. As if the life were sealed behind the beaten stones.

"Ahem." Matron Strom stood at the bottom of a carved stone staircase. Her broad forehead creased with displeasure. "If you're quite finished ogling the surroundings, I'll take you to your room and then show you to your stations."

Lily's lungs strained against her corset as they trudged to the top of the fourth floor. Never in her life had she climbed so many stairs. Across the sagging trunk, Bertie's pink cheeks puffed in and out. Matron Strom looked ready for a marathon.

"This way." She turned left and then down a long maze of hallways and doors. The carpet gave way to bare floors and walls as the air grew closer. Stopping at an unadorned door near the end of the hallway, she turned the handle and stepped in. "You'll find everything you need, and if you do not, then you simply do not need it."

The narrow room had two metal-frame beds, a small dresser with a pitcher and basin, an unvarnished wardrobe, and a high window framed with yellow muslin curtains. Servants' quarters.

"Well, this is . . . darling." Lily set her suitcase down on the foot of the bed before testing the mattress with a bounce. "Good springs."

Matron Strom's eyebrow spiked. "Put your things away neatly. I give unannounced inspections, and a failure will earn you bedpan duty for a month. You'll find your uniforms in the wardrobe. I expect them clean and without wrinkles at the beginning of each shift."

Bertie opened the wardrobe and pulled out one of the uniforms. Nodding in satisfaction, she glanced back in the closet. "Are we to wear our own shoes or are they assigned as well?"

"Funds are limited, which is why you were instructed to bring sensible footwear." Her unblinking brown eyes sliced to Lily. "If the pretty silver buckles you brought pinch your feet, don't complain on my time. The men here are our priority, nothing more."

"Precisely why we're here." Bertie laid her uniform across the bed and dropped a hand to Lily's shoulder as Matron Strom continued to glare at her. "Both of us."

"We shall see." The matron paused in the doorway with one last warning. "The castle has a total of one hundred and eight rooms, only thirty of which you are allowed in for hospital, sleeping, and eating purposes. Stay out of the north wing. It contains the family's personal rooms, and they have requested we respect their privacy. Twenty minutes and I expect you properly dressed and downstairs ready to work."

As the door closed with a solid *click,* Lily pulled out a red velvet pouch holding her silver-handled brush, comb, and hand mirror. She peeked in the mirror and frowned at her blotchy cheeks. She'd need to summon her stamina if she was to trek those stairs again. "I've heard Scotland has mystical beasts, but I didn't expect to battle a dragon our first day."

"She's one of the most experienced nurses in the country." Bertie shrugged out of her blouse. Knowing they'd be without a lady's maid, she'd insisted on bringing clothes they could dress themselves in. "During the Boer War, she bandaged an entire unit using two of her petticoats and a horse blanket."

"You told me the men are here mainly to rest before returning home." Lily slowly pulled the pearl pin from her hat as apprehension prickled. "I failed the wrapping course when you signed us up for that first

26

aid lesson."

Bertie slipped the crisp white apron over her head and tied the strings at the back. "Well, I passed, so if you have any complications, I'm here with you. Unlike the dragon, as you have so fondly dubbed Matron Strom, I don't mind your questions."

Lily's anxiety faded as it always did with her cousin's encouragement. Plucking the feathered hat from her head, she tossed it onto the flat pillow. "Why did you not introduce yourself as Lady Elizabeth?"

"Titles don't matter so much here."

"Your father won't agree to that."

The smile of anticipation Bertie had worn all day slipped. "He's not here."

Reginald Buchanan was not a man given to easy laughter and warm hugs. Though affable and courteous, he had the distinct air of being fed with a silver spoon. With his legacy and wealth firmly placed on the shoulders of his son and heir, Reggie, he didn't hold much aspiration for Bertie beyond a suitable marriage.

"No, he's not." Lily took the nurse cap from the bed and pinned it to Bertie's chestnut hair. The richness of it turned her eyes to warm chocolate. "And neither is mine, so let's not allow them to spoil our bit of fun."

The corners of Bertie's mouth perked up. "Agreed. Do you mind terribly if I slip out early? I'd like to ask Matron Strom about the new procedures for facial reconstruction Dr. Gillies is performing."

"You and I have entirely different definitions of what constitutes a good time. Go if you must."

"Don't be late." Bertie fished a moleskin notebook and pencil from her satchel and tucked them into her apron pocket. "I'd rather not smell you after a month of cleaning bedpans."

With Bertie gone, Lily quickly slipped out of her satin blouse and burgundy skirt and wriggled into the plain uniform. The scratchy material caught against her silk chemise and smelled of bleach.

"No wonder she's such a dragon. Wearing this all day." She pinched the blousy material around the ill-defining waistline. "Good thing Mother warned me away from finding a rich Englishman, though I don't know a man who could resist this look."

Not that there were many lords left to pick from. Nor magistrates, doctors, or dockworkers as all the men of eligible age and decent health had marched off to fight the German army. Thank goodness America had the sense to stay out of it.

Cinching her apron to give a little more shape to the unflattering dress, she grabbed her cap and skipped out the door. A few left turns and three identical hallways later, she had not a clue where she was.

"Where is that painting of the horses?" She looked up and down the hall and frowned. "Or were they cows?"

The paneled oak walls stood unadorned and silent on the whereabouts of their artwork. Unlike the shined floor downstairs, the wood boards here were scuffed. The alcoves were bare of antique furniture. Stillness clung to the air. As if the breath were cut off.

"And no wonder." Grabbing the dark-blue damask drapes, Lily peeled the heavy material back from the window. Dust motes swarmed the air, angry at the disturbance of their untouched folds.

"Ack." Lily batted a hand in front of her face to ward off the dust storming in her nose. Using the corner of her starched apron, she scrubbed a hole through the grime to the windowpane beneath. The sunlight beyond skipped over sprawling green grounds and a winding river.

She inched closer to the window. Mountains — no, crags they called them here — rose in the distance above sweeping fields of purple flowers. Twice a week she'd taken strolls in New York's only claim to greenery, but Central Park was a laughable speck compared to this. Her eyes drifted down to the manicured lawn surrounding a freshly painted paddock fence. At least the horses had a nicely cared for home.

"Are you lost?"

Lily jumped, banging her forehead on the glass. She spun around to find a man with the most striking cerulean eyes boring into her. He was tall with burnished wavy hair combed to the side without a hint of fashionable pomade, and an angular jaw bristling with a full day's growth of whiskers. He held a light wood cane next to his left leg. A black-and-white border collie sat on his right side.

Lily rubbed her throbbing forehead. "I didn't hear you behind me."

"Clearly." The soft burr of his deep voice reverberated in the heavy air. "Are you lost?"

"Lost in the dust." She smiled as dust swirled around her head again. "Must be the maid's year off."

"Here to replace her, are you?"

"Replace?" Lily's laughter bounced around the empty hall and skidded to a halt on the straight line of his mouth. "Heavens, no. I wouldn't know the first thing about cleaning drapery. I'm a nurse, or at least I took training to be one, though I won't claim expertise in that either."

A long, blunt finger tapped against the top of his cane. "Are all Americans so modest?"

She refused to let the man's cool tone ruffle her. Those unblinking eyes were another issue. She turned her smile to the dog happily wagging his tail. "I was looking for the main stair and seem to have taken a wrong turn somewhere between the Rembrandt and a deer head, though which one I couldn't tell you. After the fourth set of mounted antlers I lost count. Wouldn't happen to have a map would you?"

"No."

How about a sense of humor? Leaving the stoic English behind, she had hoped their neighbors to the north would know how to crack a laugh. Apparently the stiff upper lip ran the length of the island. "Well, if you'll excuse me, I need to find the main hall before that dragon hunts me down."

"Matron Strom."

"I'd steer clear of her if I were you. I was sure I saw smoke curling out from behind her ears."

"I've never noticed this curling smoke. Mayhap it's you who provokes it."

31

"Absolutely not. But honestly, how can one pack her entire belongings for an indefinite trip into one tiny suitcase?"

"She has her rules." He tapped the top of his cane. "Like the one to keep out of the family's private wing."

"Is that where I am?" Running a hand down the damask drape, Lily fluffed it to pool in gentle folds on the floor. Though old and worn, craftsmanship winked in the silk threads. "Not a surprise. I always end up exactly where I'm not supposed to be."

"I find that hard to believe. You seem at ease here. Stirring up dust and opening windows that were clearly closed for a reason."

"No doubt to cover up the bareness of this wing."

He moved closer, the tops of his shoes crossing into the light from the window. "Or the family wishes to keep their property private."

"More like forgotten. From the layers of dust and unvarnished floors, I'd say they abandoned this place long ago."

"There is a difference between abandonment and keeping it from the public's eye. A line I wouldn't expect an American to acknowledge."

Lily bristled. "Yes, we prefer to barge in

unannounced. Oh wait, that's a trait we seem to share with you. For such a private space, might I inquire why you're creeping around up here? And don't tell me you're lost too. You hardly look the type of man not to know precisely where he's going."

Square of shoulder and thick of chest tapering to a trim waist, he wore dark pants tucked into boots and a white linen shirt with the sleeves rolled back to expose tan forearms. A vitality, consequential of a life spent outdoors, exuded with each breath he took. Not the whimpering manner of a man accustomed to skulking in unfamiliar dark passages.

"I do know where I am at all times. Unlike yourself."

Leaning forward, he took the edge of the drape where Lily had let go. Sunlight spilled across his face, highlighting the straight nose and full curve of his bottom lip that had yet to ease into any expression resembling pleasantness. How did he manage to own the most mesmerizing shade of eyes without any trace of warmth in their clear depths?

Her palms prickled. What kind of man cornered a woman in a dark hallway? The kind who deserved a poke in the eye, that's who. Why hadn't she kept her hatpin? She flicked a glance down to his left leg. Her silver-buckle shoes could whack a kneecap hard enough for an escape. She eased her foot up.

"Down that hall, two lefts, another short hall, and a right." He yanked the curtain closed, shadowing himself once more. "If I were you, I'd hurry. Matron Strom has a rather useful job to keep nurses from running late more than once."

He limped away, his cane *thwacking* against the floor in measured strides.

"Um, thank you," Lily called to his retreating back. Incorrigible, ill-mannered, and with the humor of a brick wall, he was the last kind of man she'd dreamed of meeting in a darkened corridor. At least he'd given her directions back to the main hall, where she didn't lose her way once.

Her elation at not taking a wrong turn turned to dismay as she hurried down the last flight of steps. The dragon stood still as a statue with her hands behind her back at the bottom of the stairs. "You may as well stop hiding up there and come down. I heard those silver buckles jangling."

"I wasn't hiding." Lily kept her chin up as she hurried down the steps and met the matron's withering glare with all the dignity her social-climbing mother had instilled in her. "I took a wrong turn, actually a few wrong turns. I apologize for the inconvenience, but I can now begin my duties."

"Oh, can you? How delightful."

"Mrs. Strom, I realize —"

"Matron."

Lily took a deep breath to suppress an eye roll. The working class certainly never tired of throwing around titles when they had one to use. "Matron Strom. We've gotten off on the wrong foot, but let me assure you that —"

"The only assurance I need from you is that you can follow orders. *My* orders and not any fuzzy little ones that come into that pretty head of yours." Her chin notched up, the light catching on three short gray hairs perched there like dying flower stems. "We're not in America anymore where you may do as you please."

"Obviously you've never met my mother or her iron fist."

"Until such a blessed introduction I have a special job for you." The gray hairs bounced as a tiny smile cracked the woman's lips. She pulled a clean bedpan from behind her back. "One month of scrubbing these should keep you on time in future."

Lily grasped the pan and turned it over. A groan stretched up her throat. How on earth did one go about cleaning such an accessory?

"Mayhap her sentence could be shortened on my account, Matron."

Lily craned her neck up as the deep burr filled the hall. The gentleman from the shadows peered down from the landing. Even from a three-story distance, his cool stare was enough to rankle her. "Thank you, sir, but I don't need your intrusion."

One dark eyebrow lifted. "And here I thought you were the intruder upon my dusty old drapes."

"*Your* drapes?"

Matron Strom stepped in front of Lily. "Lord Strathem, my deepest apologies. The girl is new and won't bother you again."

Lily's mouth fell open. *Lord?* Of all the people to insult, it had to be the one under whose roof she would be residing.

"She was quick to inform me of my shortcomings as caretaker. Something I shall have to remedy in my spare time." With a slight nod, he disappeared.

Lily's fingers curled over the lip of the pot, her nails straining against the porcelain. "Is he always so pleasant?"

Matron Strom snapped back to her. "Lord Strathem is a gracious host as long as we stay out of his way — which you have managed not to do in less than an hour since arriving. That earns you an extra week of scrubbing duty. Get started."

Turning on her heel, the matron marched across the main hall without a backward glance. "Stay out of the north wing, princess."

"Not to worry," Lily muttered. "The last thing I want is to see that man again. And that's saying something when I have a bedpan in my hands."

CHAPTER 2

"My answer is no. As it was last month, as it was last year, and as it was six years ago." Alec MacGregor brought his fist down on top of the antique walnut desk, smashing the rag newspaper's headline, "The Dying Class of the Masters and Their Fading Palaces of Old." "Kinclavoch is not for sale."

Unperturbed, Richard Wright stared at him from the other side of the desk. "I'm offering you double from last year. This estate cannot continue its expenses as if it were still the golden days when landowners held all the power."

"Don't talk to me about expenses as if you know what a house like this requires." Robert the Bruce, Alec's border collie, growled at his feet.

"I know it requires income you do not have and servants whose numbers are decimated after running away to fight the war."

Alec curled his fingers into the hackles raised on Bruce's neck. "They did not run away. They proudly signed up to fight for their country and with my blessing."

Wright's narrow eyes slid to Alec's cane resting against the desk. "Of course, but the fact remains that Kinclavoch is struggling and I'd like to help."

"Like you helped the Duke of Monroe and the Sinclairs? You turned Willowick House into a hotel for rich Americans and tourists from the Continent and dug up Lord Duncan's prized hunting grounds for coal excavation. Macbeth himself is said to have hunted stag and grouse there while he was High King of Scotland."

Wright shrugged and traced the sole of his expensive shoe with one long finger. "They signed of their own accord. I merely turned foundering estates into modern-day profits. I'm certain Macbeth would understand."

"Is that what you'll do here? Dismiss the servants, kick out the tenants, and till up the earth to erect iron monstrosities that clog the air with black smoke?"

"I'm a businessman not a philanthropist."

The urge to pick Wright up by his lapels and hurl him through the window shook down Alec's arms. He crossed them over his chest to maintain control. "I believe business should be conducted for the betterment of the people."

"As do I, but where you will hold on to the last thread of this outdated lifestyle, I will sever it to start over fresh. It may hurt in the beginning, but in the end it's for the best."

To sever Alec from his beloved homeland was akin to severing bones from his body. "These lands have been in my family for five hundred years — given to the MacGregors by James IV when we helped quell civil unrest with the English before his marriage to Margaret Tudor. I will not be the man to let it slip between my fingers."

"It slipped before you ever took the reins."

Wright's words gutted him like a knife in an old wound. Six years ago Alec's father died and left him a legacy of debts — gambling, women, bad investments, lavish purchases. Old Man MacGregor was enthralled with living beyond his means and left his family to suffer the consequences.

Pain seeped into Alec's left knee. Standing, he turned to the window before Wright saw his grimace. The most unbending newspaper owner in London, the man was known for seizing the weak by their necks and wringing until he got what he wanted. After snapping up the stale *London Herald* and turning it into the most read rag in the country, the man set to expand his empire by buying up old family homes. For some reason Kinclavoch was on the top of his list.

The pain wrapped around Alec's knee and squeezed. He pressed his palms flat on the windowsill to keep from reaching down to massage the muscle as it cramped up his thigh. "There are families who have worked this land for generations. The men are expecting to come back to jobs once the war is over. They are my responsibility."

"A bleeding heart only drags you down."

Alec turned, perching a hip against the windowsill to take the pressure off his bad leg. "A condition you've never suffered from."

"You don't get to my position by making easy choices, and you certainly don't stay at the top by considering every unfortunate beneath you. This is business, plain and simple."

"It's not to me."

"If you'll forgive the expression, that is your misfortune."

"So you keep reminding me."

"Only in hopes that you will one day soon see reason and sell." Wright tilted his head to the framed picture of Edwina Mac-

41

Gregor, Alec's mother, hanging between the two massive bookshelves. "If not for yourself, then think of your mother and sister. Accept my offer, and they can continue the lifestyle to which they are accustomed. They should not suffer because of your pride when the bills roll in and the debt collectors pound at your door."

"I'll thank you to leave my mother and sister out of this."

The door creaked open. Alec's stocky, kilted butler pushed into the room carrying a tray laden with tea and biscuits.

"You're a wee late, Guthrie," Alec said, relieved at his unusual promptness. "Mr. Wright was just leaving."

Wright unfolded his long body from the wingback chair, a tight smile playing on his thin lips as he glanced down at the now smudged headline of his paper on Alec's desk. "You have my card should you change your mind."

Alec couldn't stop the delighted curl of his lip. "Actually, we ran out of kindling last month. It came in handy. Along with the rag you print and call news."

"At least they didn't go unused." Reaching into the inner breast pocket of his immaculately cut Italian wool jacket, Wright pulled out a new stack of cards and handed one to Alec. "In case you need more kindling."

Alec took the card and tapped it against his palm. As soon as the fire was made in the morning, he'd add it to the pile. "Good day to you, Mr. Wright."

"A pleasure as always, Lord Strathem."

As the door closed Guthrie shifted back and forth with irritation. The tray balanced precariously in his hands. "Ye'll be wanting this or no?"

Alec's stomach curdled as the aromatic steam curling from the white teapot wafted around the room. "Do you have nothing stronger?"

Shaking his head, Guthrie placed the silver tray on the desk. "Only the boozers drink while the sun still shines."

"I'm sure it's nightfall somewhere in the world."

"Aye, but it ain't here. I can have Mrs. Moore brew some black coffee while we wait, if that's what ye be wanting."

Alec scrubbed a hand over his face. No beverage could fix what ailed him. Unless it carried a few thousand-pound banknotes.

"He badgering ye again?" Guthrie pulled a flask from his leather sporran and poured two drams of golden *uisge* into one of the teacups. After swirling the whisky around

43

he tipped back and downed the contents in one gulp. "Think he would've learned by now."

"Thought we were waiting until nightfall."

Not bothering with the pretense of tea this round, Guthrie tipped his flask to his lips and gulped down another dram. "Ye're waiting. I'm an auld man who doesna have many years left."

Wright's card weighed like a brick in Alec's hand. Its cool surface and sharp corners a perfect representation of the man. And a perfect reminder of the pride that would drive the Lord of Strathem to the grave. "He's relentless."

" 'Tis not right turning folks out o' their homes what's been there fae hundreds o' years. Some lands even been given tae them by the Bruce."

At the mention of his namesake, Bruce's black ears perked up. Alec grabbed a biscuit from the tray and tossed it to him. "As detestable as it is, it's perfectly legal for them to sign away their property."

"They're weak." Guthrie jabbed a stout finger in Alec's direction. A fierce light ignited in his dark eyes. "They're no ye."

Alec turned back to the window. The view of mythical rowan trees and rolling green bens under a wild, open sky did little to ease the frustration gnawing his insides. How much easier it would be to sign over his problems. Never to have to sell another painting or piece of heirloom furniture or his grandmother's pearls to keep the debt collectors off his front step for one more month.

That American woman's accusation of abandonment rattled in his head. Hiding, bah. Wealthy socialites with the world at their feet could never understand the gossip dragging behind him like a ball and chain. He'd done his best to shield his sister and mother, but there was only so much protection he could provide within these cold walls.

At least he'd managed to keep the stables in working order after the army confiscated his entire stock. All but two suffering from colic. His gaze drifted over the freshly painted white walls, the weather vane drifting back and forth on the eastern breeze, the neatly stacked hay bales waiting to be shoveled into the stalls. The trail of loose hay zigzagging across the yard.

Alec frowned. He'd raked the yard himself only that morning. "Have you been out to the stables this morning?"

"No. Something amiss?"

Opening the lower desk drawer, Alec

pulled out his ivory-handled pistol and checked the shot. He grabbed his cane and headed for the door. "Probably nothing."

"If I ever see my lady's maid again, I owe her a lengthy apology." Lily added the freshly scrubbed pot to the growing stack. "If I can look her in the eye after this."

At least she'd found a good use for her dancing gloves. Peeling off the elbow-length black satin gloves, she rocked back on her heels and pressed a hand to her aching back.

She'd spent all morning of her second day at the castle on her knees, emptying, draining, scrubbing, and drying bedpans. Much to the amusement of the other nurses in their pristine caps and aprons, their pinched noses high in the air as they strolled by, pushing the wounded patients in their wheelchairs. Under their fluffy white bandages the men burned bright pink with embarrassment and murmured their apologies for creating such a task for her. As soon as Matron learned of the sighted indignity, she ordered Lily around the back of the house and safely out of view — and stench — of the men.

She did her best to laugh at her new circumstances despite the gouge to her pride. But she'd never been told she was too undignified for polite company before. Then again, she was in the land of stuffed shirts.

"Of course it's you."

Lily stiffened as a large shadow loomed over her. Speaking of stuffed shirts, the lord and master himself. "Yes, it's me, and I'll thank you to let me get on without distraction."

"You're making a mess out of my yard."

"A mess? Hardly. My dressing table looks worse after a long night at the theater." She glanced at the discarded hay scattered around before turning to him. And screamed. "Good gracious! Is it really worth shooting me?"

Surprise flitted across his face as her words ended on a cracking sob. His dog whined next to him. "I'm not going to shoot you."

Terror pounding in her heart, Lily threw her hands up in front of her. "Then what are you doing with that?"

"I thought you were the conies ransacking my hay again." He shoved the pistol into his waistband and gestured to the piles of dirty hay. "Easy mistake."

Lily clutched her throat, her eyes wide in search of the beasts. "Conies. What is that? A rabid animal? Matron Strom never

47

warned of those when she sent me out here. Unless she thought these would protect me." She nudged the bedpans with her toe.

"I doubt you need protection against rabbits."

Relief swelled. Her eyes dropped to the gleaming ivory handle sticking out from his trousers. "You were going to shoot rabbits?"

"They're a menace to my crops and take all the hay from the horses. On the upside they make a fine meal. And they give Brucey a braw chase." He ruffled the top of the dog's head.

"You kill them for eating your food, then eat them for supper. The irony."

"Aye, you're in Scotland now. Nothing goes to waste."

So that's where his sense of humor went. Just a by-product of his country. Pushing slowly to her feet, her sleeping legs buckled. Lord Strathem leaped forward and caught her around the waist. Her face smashed into his chest.

"I know you're a city lass, but rabbits are hardly enough reason to leap into my arms in broad daylight."

The masculine scent of fresh-washed cotton, soap, and outdoors drifted into her throbbing nose. Looking up, she caught a flicker behind his brilliant blue eyes. "If I didn't know better, I'd think that was an attempt at a joke."

"Poorly executed."

"The important thing is that you tried. Next time add a smile. It'll make you so much more pleasant to look at. That, and don't stand next to a pile of bedpans. It diminishes the effect."

The corner of his mouth pulled up. Like the tiniest crack in a mountain. "I'll keep that in mind."

The strong arms wrapped around her flexed. Dressed in dark trousers, a deep-blue vest, and crisp white shirt with the cuffs rolled back to expose muscled fore-arms, he was the picture of a country gentleman. Handsome in a formidable, ready-to-shoot-something-at-any-moment sort of way. The pins and needles from her legs tingled up her spine. She quickly pushed away before they went to her head.

"Do you always carry a gun when walking around your house?"

"Not of late." He reached down and picked up the cane he had dropped when lunging for her. "I was told that with delicate ladies coming from soft London it might be prudent to tuck it away."

"I suppose with such restrictions your cane comes in handy." As soon as the words left her lips, she wished she had the dexterity to kick herself. "I'm sorry. Sometimes my mouth moves faster than my ability to stop it."

Deep, intricate carvings flashed as he twirled the cane. "Not the first time your affliction has surfaced. At our last meeting you called me a shut-in."

Her embarrassment burned deeper. "I'm sorry about that too. I never would have said it if —"

"If you'd known who you were talking to? Nurse Durham, if there —"

"Aide Durham, but I prefer Lily."

"All the others are called nurse."

"All the others passed the nursing course."

His burnished eyebrows flickered in brief surprise before dismissing the sensation. "If there is something you have to say, I want to hear the unvarnished truth." The cane spun to a stop, his fingers curling over the top. "I detest lies hidden behind good breeding and polite smiles."

"However do you navigate social circles?"

"I don't."

Lily laughed as she imagined him sulking in a corner like a child forced to sit quietly at church. Bruce yipped as if joining her joke and trotted over to rub his head under her hand. "Yes, your charming charisma would overwhelm those faint hearts that swarm drawing rooms."

"Precisely why I hide behind my drawn, dusty drapes."

"Oh my. Two jokes in one day. Pace yourself, sir, or I'll begin to think you have a sense of humor buried deep inside after all."

He shook his head, sparking russet in the dark curls. "I've been accused of many things, but never a sense of humor."

"Every person has one. Just takes the right time and thing to coax it out. Venture beyond your drapes more often and it'll get easier. Or better still, keep them open."

His head dropped to study the cane in his hand. Muscles flexed in his forearm. " 'Tis not so simple."

"I never believe people when they say that. Situations are simple. It's the people who twist them up."

"I believe it's circumstances that warp people."

"What circumstance brought the lord of the manor to close his windows and allow dust to settle on the bare floors?"

"We have a war on. Times are tough, or have the papers not reached across the pond yet?"

"I don't know what they're reading back

home. I've been in England for the past year visiting my mother's cousin's family."

His head jerked up, eyebrows pulled together. "Why have they not demanded you return to the States where you're not at war?"

Because they don't want me. Bruce whined, drawing her fingers to the spot between his ears. "They feel it's safer for me to remain on solid land with the U-boat attacks threatening the coasts. Besides, the war will be over by Christmas."

"That's what they said last year."

"Well, I'll keep my fingers crossed."

He snorted. "You Yanks and your eternal optimism."

"Do you have something against it?"

"Not against, simply no use for it."

"That's an awfully dreary sentiment, but I suppose I should expect nothing less in the land of eternal rain and gloom."

As if her words pricked the heavens' ears, the gray clouds gathering on the horizon rolled closer with an ominous growl. Wet earth prickled her nose.

His gaze tilted up to the sky, a slow curl pulling at his lips. "Don't insult the national weather, lass. We Scots take great pride in the bleakness."

She met his eyes, clear and blue as the

morning sky. "Ah, that's it. It's your national pride to blame for those drapes."

"Here you are. I was beginning to wonder if you'd run off." Esther Hartley. Tall and all limbs, with raven hair and skin as pale as bone china, glided over the yard like a cat. "Matron Strom needs you to finish here and come to the kitchen."

Lily sighed. "New shipment of potatoes?"

A perfectly placed smile of compassion slipped across Esther's lips. "I daresay." Her liquid dark eyes slid to Lord Strathem. "Hello, Alec. Out to check on your horses? I hope you don't mind that I gave Appin an extra brushing this morning. I find it soothing before the house wakes and daily routines begin."

Her daily routine of clipboard holding. Nurse Hartley had perfected the art of keeping busy without actually doing anything. Elegant and polite, she reminded Lily of the dozens of high society girls swarming the New York ballrooms each year. Each told she was the belle of the ball her entire life until she collided with other belles. One would think such an encounter would knock the wind out of their satin petticoats, but it only seemed to spur them on in the cutthroat pursuit of society's pinnacle.

If they only knew how boring their silly

little games were.

"Is something the matter, Aide Durham?" Esther's tone was smooth as honey, but her eyes flared with annoyance.

Lily swallowed her laugh. "Of course not. I'm only happy to hear that the horses receive as much attention as the wounded men inside."

A snort rippled in Lord Strathem's throat, which he immediately cleared. "Aye, I do appreciate the thought, Miss Hartley, but your help is needed inside. Don't let me keep you from it."

"It's no trouble," Esther said. "Perhaps on my next afternoon off we can give them a good stretch of the legs on the moor."

Lord Strathem shifted his weight, leaning on the cane. His fingers tapped the top. "I prefer to run them myself."

Esther's smile didn't falter despite the not-so-subtle hint. "Of course. Aide Durham, the kitchen, if you please."

When would these British girls learn that long gone were the days of acting like queens shouting orders from their thrones? If they cared to remember their history lessons, they'd find the last time an English throne dared to order about an American they got into a war. And lost.

"Tell the Matron I will come as soon as I

finish here," Lily said in her best imitation of her mother before the servants. "Oh, and would you mind taking this clean stack back inside? Matron wanted them returned right away, and I don't want to track my muddy feet across the floors."

Esther's lips shook from the strain of smiling. "She won't like it, but I'll tell her." Draping her apron over her hands and arms, she gingerly gathered the pans into her arms. Scrubbed squeaky clean, the porcelain basins still caused her nose to wrinkle. "And hurry. The men will need their lunches soon. Goodbye for now, Alec."

"Miss Hartley."

As Esther's skirts swished back to the house, Lily sighed and patted Bruce on the head one last time before tugging her dirty gloves back on. "As much as I hate to admit it, I do have to get back to cleaning these. Strange how when I thought of spending a quiet time in the genteel English country-side I never envisioned" — she gestured to the bedpans spread out before her like a carpet — "well, this. But I did find a use for my gloves, so that's something."

"Your optimism astounds me."

"At least something does. I'd hate to see you go through life without a spot of excitement, even at the expense of my once lovely gloves."

He eyed the dainty accessories covering her from fingertip to elbow. "Did no one tell you dancing gloves were unneeded up here?"

Lily smoothed the edges of the satiny material over her arms until there wasn't a ripple left. She wasn't bowing to a waltz, but old habits were hard to break. "Maybe."

"And you chose not to listen."

Turning her back on his patronizing tone, she rammed her fingers together, snugging the gloves into place with more force than necessary. "Maybe."

"Women and their frivolities."

Sinking to the ground, she grabbed a fistful of hay. "Do you not have someone else to antagonize? Or shoot?"

"As a matter of fact I do." Tipping his cane in salute, he started back to the house. Clouds rumbled closer. "Rain's coming. You don't want to be caught out here when it breaks."

"Your concern is noted." How could he dance on the verge of charming one minute before leaping straight to boorish the next? For a man with a cane, he certainly was nimble.

Movement flickered from a third-story

window. A pale woman dressed in black stared down at her. Lily smiled and offered a small wave. The woman's slender hands grasped the heavy drapes on either side of the window and slowly pulled them shut.

Chills prickled Lily's arms.

CHAPTER 3

"*What* are you doing?"

Lily's fingers fumbled with the ends of the linen as she double knotted them and Matron Strom stomped to a halt next to her. Lily greeted her with a self-satisfied smile. "Rebandaging Lieutenant Portely's leg, as you instructed."

"I instructed you to take Lieutenant Portely's temperature and bandage Lieutenant *Porcher's* leg."

Lily's smile fell. "Oh." She looked back at Lieutenant Portely. "Whyever did you let me rebandage your leg when it was a temperature check you required?"

"How often does a fellow get such a pretty girl fussing over him? After a year in a filthy trench with hundreds of smelly men, I'll have my leg wrapped all day just to have you come over and smile at me." He grinned and tossed her an unabashed wink.

"Mr. Portely, you are too terrible for words."

"It worked, didn't it?"

"I suppose it did." She laughed and patted him on the knee. Rising from the chair, she met Matron Strom's glare with what she hoped was her most conciliatory look. "I apologize for misunderstanding, but their names are awfully similar." Matron didn't blink. The woman could outstare a mirror. "I'll see to Lieutenant Porcher's leg now."

"Nurse Hartley is attending him, but there is an insurmountable pile of bed linens in the music room in dire need of folding. I believe your fine hands are up to the task."

Across the room Esther bent over Lieutenant Porcher with a soft smile on her lips. Sunlight streamed through the large window next to the bed, bathing her pristine apron in dazzling light. She blinked up at Lily, raking her with a delighted smirk.

Lily threw her shoulders back. "I'll get right to it." She walked away, muttering under her breath. "And I won't need a stream of sunlight to make that laundry stack spectacular."

Nearly two hours later she wasn't feeling anything close to spectacular, but she had managed to make a dent in the mountain of freshly washed sheets and blankets.

"If becoming New York's social planner doesn't work out after the war, you can always put your newfound talents to domestic work."

Lily lobbed a satin pillowcase across the table at her cousin. Bertie had walked in looking for scissors, but Lily had cajoled her into keeping her company. "Only if Nurse Hartley doesn't beat me to it. She could dance a cotillion all night, then skip down to the scullery for potato peeling. No doubt the skins would fall to the floor in perfect curls."

Bertie scoffed. "She tries too hard. All the *nouveau riche* do."

Lily's fingers stilled over a flower-embroidered top sheet. The unfamiliar sentiment of doubt niggled at the back of her mind. "Is that what you think of me? That I'm trying too hard?"

"All Americans are new money, so we forgive certain behaviors, but she's English. Trying to oil her way past the class boundaries is vulgar."

"The English don't appreciate people trying to better themselves?"

"Of course we do, as long as it's within their own station."

Lily snorted. "And here I thought the Astors held the corner on snobbery."

Bertie looked up, pushing her spectacles back on her nose. "Who?"

"Oh, just another simple family daring to scale the social ladder. I think they stand a good chance of making it."

"Americans have their own way of climbing the ladder, and so do we. Nurse Hartley is attempting the tried-and-true method of marriage to none other than our host."

"Lord Strathem?" Lily grabbed a blanket and shook the creases out. "I doubt a pile of bored rocks would want to marry him."

"If they wanted a title and estate they would."

Titles, land, money. Growing up as Philip and Mary Durham's only daughter, she had wanted for nothing. Gowns, jewels, furs, balls, and rubbing shoulders with the East Coast's finest families was a simple Saturday night in her glittering world. But it was a gilded cage. One that dictated her every move, word, and dance partner.

With her own eyes she had witnessed that once the suitable matches were made and the dowry secured, the pretense of love vanished like a dream. Unlike her parents, she wanted to stand in the same room as her husband without growing a headache.

She grabbed a pillowcase and snapped it in the air. "What about love, attraction?

Does that mean nothing in a marriage?"

"Perhaps to a modernist like you." Bertie's brown eyes twinkled with magnified mischief behind her glasses. "Brilliant blue eyes and wide shoulders like the set on Alec MacGregor don't hurt either."

Lily poked her finger in each corner of the case so they stuck right side out. "I don't recall saying anything about his shoulders or that his eyes are brilliant. Your glasses must have been smudged."

"Brilliant or not, he certainly knows how to maintain a sense of mystery."

"Unsociable is more accurate." Yet he offered his guests the plush couches, oriental rugs, and warm fires while resigning himself to dusty drapes and drafty hallways. Weren't fine lords supposed to wear ermine and order their servants to perform menial tasks?

Lily fingered the cotton seam. "Do you know anything more about him? What kind of man opens his home to strangers all the way up here in the Highlands and then refuses to mingle with them?"

"We're in the Lowlands. Did you not study that map I gave you?"

"Was it in the packet of papers you shoved under my nose?"

Bertie sighed. "The MacGregor family is one of the oldest names in Scotland. The seventh lord was said to be a great art collector, and the current Lord Strathem has an eye for horseflesh. Beyond that . . . you can ask him the next time he catches you doing something you're not supposed to. Which, knowing you, will not be that long in waiting."

"Come with me next time. It'll do you good to take a wrong turn once in a while."

"Then who would be left to steer you back in the right direction? Or in our case, to the storage cabinets." Bertie picked up her finished stack and piled them into Lily's arms.

Tucking the precarious tower under her chin, Lily crossed the parquet floor to the armoire that once held leather-bound folders filled with sheet music. Chopin, Beethoven, Mozart. The maestros had been cleared out in favor of storage space, much like the room itself. The blue-watered damask walls were hidden behind rows of fluffy white towels, rolled bandages, blankets, blue pajamas, carbolic lotion, and Lysol swabs. A piano, pushed into the corner and draped with a thick white cloth, was the only reminder of what this beautiful room once represented.

Lily nudged open the armoire door and frowned. "There were seven blankets in here last night. Now there are only five."

"Perhaps they're in use. The Scottish morning air brings a chill to the men's bones."

"No, they were all collected for washing." Perching the folded sheets on her hip, Lily wiggled her hand between the stack of towels on the top shelf and reached far back in hopes the blankets were squished behind them. "Whew. That cedar smell is getting strong again. I need to refill those lavender sachets before —" Her fingers brushed something soft and warm. "What on earth is — Ahh!"

A mouse shot out as Lily stumbled backward, dropping the sheets. The mouse jumped to the floor and scurried under the door leading to the hallway.

Bertie rushed over, grabbing tumbled sheets from the floor. "Disgusting creature. Do you suppose he's eaten the blankets?"

"Highly doubtful he could have a full stomach and jump like that." Pressing a hand to her stomach, Lily took several deep breaths to bring it back down to its proper place after leaping into her throat. By golly if she was going to let a furry little squeaker cower her like a child. She marched to the door.

Bertie clutched the tangle of sheets to her

chest. "Don't go out there. He's probably waiting on the other side of the door."

"I'm not giving that creature the opportunity to sneak its way up to our room to make a nest out of my pillow. His reign of terror ends today."

Without the first clue of what to do once said terror was found, Lily wrenched open the door and stepped into the hallway. To the left, voices sounded from the library-turned-recreation room with accusations of cheating at a game of table tennis. To the right stretched a long hall ending in a diamond-paned window and two doors. The perfect escape for a rodent.

Her clicking heels echoed off the bare walls, drowning out the pounding of her heart. She'd never chased vermin before, and she'd certainly never killed one. Her pulse skipped. Perhaps she should have looked for a broom before starting her hunt. A broom could muffle the sound or feel of crushing something beneath it. Sweat prickled her palms. Where was a cat when she needed one?

Her hand slipped on the doorknob. Drat her nerves. Swiping her palms on her apron, she turned the knob again.

"The Fragonard is her favorite," came an unfamiliar man's muffled voice.

"Does she care for it more than a roof over her head, or does she plan to use the painting for shelter? Sell it." The thick burr stopped her cold.

Lord Strathem. He sounded more sour than usual, and no wonder if he was selling his paintings. Sight unseen, Lily's mother would give her eyeteeth for that Fragonard.

"She willna be happy aboot it."

"She hasn't been happy for six years."

Lily's fingers tightened on the knob at Alec's heavy sigh. Whoever this was, she seemed to weigh him down like a ton of bricks. After living under her mother's roof, she knew the burden of unhappiness all too well.

"That still leaves us four hundred pounds under for the month. I ken ye dinna wish to think aboot it, but that piano —"

"No." Lord Strathem's answer reverberated through the door.

"Viola will understand."

"She won't need to. The piano stays."

"Yer stubbornness is admirable, Alec, but it'll break us if ye're no' careful."

"My stubbornness is the only thing keeping us afloat. Wright would have us sunk and drowned by now."

Lily's hand fell away, shame flooding her at having caught his private conversation.

66

He had said his circumstances were complicated, but selling his possessions trotted the same path as desperation.

Sadness wrapped around her heart. This beautiful old home filled with treasures and memories of generations past stripped to its bones and its owner struggling to keep it from falling apart. Next time she'd take care from kicking sand in his eyes. Unless he pointed another gun at her.

She edged away from the door. And stopped dead cold. The mouse sat still as a statue in the middle of the hall, its long whiskers twitching as his dark eyes watched her every breath.

"I'm not afraid of you." Her whisper bounced off the walls like a firecracker. Clearing her throat, she shoved her thundering heart back into her chest. "I'm not afraid of you. Do you hear me? I'm not going to live in fear of you curling up in my hair at night after you've chewed your little rat teeth through my good shoes."

Her eyes darted around for something to trap it — or hurl at it. Stretching her shaking fingers over to the small table under the window, she tapped the flower-painted vase closer to the edge.

"Apologies, Lord Strathem. I realize you're losing belongings faster than you would like, but I do this for the sake of all."

The mouse's whiskers stilled, then twitched as she lifted the vase high out in front of her. She rocked forward and the mouse streaked down the hall and disappeared around the corner into the library.

"You can't hide from me! I *will* find you!"

"Miss Durham, what are you doing?"

Lily jumped, the vase tumbling from her fingers. Lord Strathem caught it with one hand before it could crash to the ground.

"I . . . There was a mouse." She flung her finger in the direction her enemy had scurried. Alec's mouth twisted with bored disbelief. Her hand dropped back to her side. "Sir, I beg you to stop coming up behind me."

"Then cease doing things to demand my attention."

"Maybe you should stop assuming that everything demands your attention."

"If it happens within my house or on my land, I have every right to give it my attention." He set the vase back on the table with a thud. "No matter how irritating the matter."

"What's going on out here?" A short man with thick shoulders and dressed in a drab kilt stepped around Lord Strathem. Lily had seen him about the castle but had never been offered a proper introduction. His dark eyes widened in surprise as they unabashedly swept Lily from head to toe before swinging back to the master of the house. "Or is there a problem? Because from the look o' things I'd best be saying no."

"Seems we have a new houseguest, Guthrie," Lord Strathem said. "A mouse."

Guthrie grunted. "Cleaned 'em out o' the stables only last month."

"Then one escaped. Probably smelled the extra rations for the men in the kitchen."

Guthrie slapped his bare knee. "Fire take that cat for not doing its duty. Gotten lazy eating all the grain out in the barn. Told ye we should've gotten a new one last year. Didna I tell ye?"

"Aye, you did, but it's too late for that now."

Guthrie slowly scratched at the peppered whiskers covering his chin. "Suppose I should go after the ratten meself."

"If it's not too much trouble. I know you had half an apple to finish."

"He darted in the library," Lily offered.

"Good day tae ye, lass. No more tae be afraid o' with me on the trail." Guthrie gave her a toothy grin before stomping down the hall, his kilt swinging about his hairy legs. "I ken where all the hiding spots be."

Lily couldn't stop a smile as she thought of him crouching in the corner to wait for the mouse to come by. He'd spring out with kilt flying and scare the creature to death. "Quite a manservant you have there."

Leaning against the doorjamb, Lord Strathem crossed his arms over his chest. The rolled-up sleeves strained against his forearms. "My butler actually. Surprised?"

"I would think mouse hunting beneath a butler, but I can see Mr. Guthrie is not a typical white-gloves man."

"No, he's not."

"Seems more of an outdoorsman," she prodded.

"Aye, seems so."

She waited for more of an explanation, but the butler was to remain as much a mystery as his employer. For now. Reaching for the skewed vase, she turned it back to display the artistic roses and hyacinths. "You have a fine collection of art in this house."

"Fine enough to lob at rodents."

"I did apologize for that, but you weren't here to hear it." *Unlike everything I heard from you a moment ago.* She traced a finger over the curving petals on the pink rose. "I would've cleaned it up before you could notice. Seems my forte of late."

A thick burnished eyebrow spiked. "Cleaning or hiding things from me?"

"I never hide things. Requires too much energy." A string of coarse words bellowed from the library. "I think your man found the mouse, judging by the curses."

"Guthrie only curses in Gaelic. Those are threats that are best done in Scots for the more extensive vocabulary."

"How imaginative." Lily turned down the hall. Thumping and scraping punctuated the shouting. "Are you coming?"

"Guthrie can handle the situation."

"Doesn't sound like it." She stopped and turned back to him waffling in the doorway. "Are you sending me in there alone because you're too afraid of a little mouse?"

"No."

She tapped her foot, waiting as indecision warred across his face. Finally his shoulders squared back.

Brandishing his cane that had been hidden on the other side of the door, he hurried behind her. "Should come in handy."

Lily's stomach squirmed at the thought of such handiness but it immediately vanished as they stepped into the library. Books littered the floor, the golden-stitched corners of the long, red oriental rug were flipped over, and silver candlesticks were overturned on top of the enormous fireplace mantel.

Two patients stood beside the tennis table, their paddles frozen as their eyes darted around for the moving furry target. Two lieutenants with broken arms crouched in the green velvet club chairs flanking the fireplace.

Guthrie, the man of action, hauled a step stool to the towering walnut bookcases. "Scurried up here. Wee coward."

"No, he didn't." The captain waved his paddle to a roll top desk in the corner. "Went that way."

One of the broken-armed men shook his head. "Couldn't have. I saw him jump into that potted plant."

His companion snorted. "What's a mouse going to do in a plant? He slipped under the door on his way back to the kitchen."

Lily tightened her apron strings. "Did any of you actually see him?"

They all nodded fervently. "Yes."

"All right then." Marching over to the fireplace, which was large enough for two grown men, she plucked a poker from the stand. "Let's find him and be quick about it. I need to serve lunch in an hour."

"Miss Durham, what do you think you're doing with that? Go back to the kitchen or the cupboard or wherever you were. I'll handle this." Lord Strathem brushed past her to run his hand the length of the mantle behind vases and pictures.

"He terrorized me first. It's my obligation to return the favor."

"Let the wobbler do it, Aide Durham." The lieutenants smirked. "Maybe that cane'll come in handy for something after all."

Lord Strathem's back went rigid enough to snap. His knuckles whitened over the top of his cane as the other men joined in the snickering.

She'd made a nurse's promise regarding the welfare and care of these men, but by golly if she didn't wish to knock them about with common decency from time to time.

"I daresay he'd be doing a great deal more than cowering on a cushion like the rest of you childish lot. Come. I need each of you to look under your chairs and the tables around you. The mouse can't escape so many pairs of eyes." She touched Lord Strathem's arm. He jerked as if she'd stung him. "Lord Strathem, perhaps you and I can search the drapes. Our specialty, as it were."

"Aye." He gave a brisk nod, then whirled to the tall windows across the room.

No sooner had they pulled back the second heavy velvet curtain when a bloodcurdling screech cracked the air. Nearly jumping out of her skin, Lily spun around in anticipation of the infamous blue-painted, warrior Celts dropping from the ceiling.

Guthrie stood in the center of the room with arm raised and eyes focused on a spot ten feet in front of him. A knife was buried deep in the floor, its black handle still quivering from impact.

"You'd better have a good reason for stabbing my floor," Lord Strathem growled.

"Aye. Saw him, I did." Guthrie yanked his knife from the floor and drew the flat of the blade across his kilt as if wiping away the remains of a slaughtered foe. "Nicked his tail."

"Did you see where the rest of him went?"

"Out that way. Toward the stairs."

Lord Strathem rubbed at the scowl creasing his forehead. "We'll never be able to track him up there."

A mouse running around in the house was on Matron Strom's list of undesirables, right next to starvation and the Huns barging in the front door. Somehow the blame for the rodent's escape would work its way back to Lily. Not that she needed the old dragon's approval, but she certainly didn't want a rat pawing her hair at night. Nor the men's. Those poor boys had been through

74

enough torture.

"What if we had proper bait to lure him out? I have a tin of cookies upstairs that my aunt Hazel sent. Not my favorite with raisins, but maybe it'll think otherwise. Back in a minute."

Running to her room, Lily grabbed the full tin of cookies and hurried back down the hall. The tin was as heavy as when it had arrived three days ago. Why did Aunt Hazel think they needed so many, especially when neither of them liked raisins?

Turning left, her foot stretched out for the stairs and found only another hall. She spun around but found the surroundings unfamiliar. Not again. Nearly two weeks in this place and she was still lost. On her next afternoon off she ought to draw a map.

Feeling certain the stairs were back behind her, she turned around and retraced her steps. A muffled noise caught her ear. She stopped, listening. The slow, unmistakable staccato of someone crying tumbled from down the hall to her right. Probably one of the nurses licking her wounds after a run-in with Matron.

No, not a nurse in this gloomy part of the house.

Somehow she'd wandered back into the family's personal wing once again. Lily tiptoed away but the cries pierced her heart. The tin of cookies weighed heavy in her hands as a hiccup interrupted the crying. The master of the house wouldn't like it, whether for disturbing his lair or running late with the bait, she didn't care to ponder. She pivoted, marched down the hall, and stopped in front of the door where the sobbing broke through. He could dislike it all he wanted. No creature should make such pitiful sounds alone.

Summoning her courage, Lily knocked on the heavy oak door. The crying stopped. Blankets rustled. She slipped on her brightest smile and pushed into the room.

It was a bedroom done in pale-green wallpaper with a massive four-poster bed positioned between two large windows closed with thick drapes. Spindly furniture dotted the room with lanterns and candles sitting on the flat surfaces, casting their yellow light to every corner. In the center of the bed, sitting like a terrified sparrow, was a pale young woman with dark hair floating over her thin shoulders, dressed in a white gown.

"Hello there." Lily stepped farther inside. Her lungs choked from the pent-up candle vapors. "What a lovely room. How I would adore to have such drapes in my room.

Muslin does nothing for blocking out the morning sun, though I'm usually awake by the time it breaks the horizon. Who knew the world could start so early?"

Tears glistened on the girl's cheeks as she clutched at the bedcovers in her lap. She couldn't be more than fourteen or fifteen years old. Her wide eyes dropped to the tin.

"Would you care for one?" Stepping to the foot of the bed, Lily pried off the tin lid. The sickly sweet smell of raisins and vanilla assaulted her nose. "Whew! Can't say that I do, but my preference runs for extra sweet, and these simply don't make the cut."

The girl blinked her wide eyes. "Who are you?"

"Lily Durham, though some insist on calling me Aide Durham."

"What do *you* insist?"

"Lily."

A ghost of a smile flickered across the girl's drawn face. "The American."

Lily snapped her fingers in dismay. "Drat. I was hoping you wouldn't discover my secret."

The smile blossomed. "I heard tell there was one among us. Don't worry. I won't let on."

"Thank you, but I think that cat is out of the bag." Lily rattled the tin. "Sure you don't want one?"

"They're not good for my constitution. Or so I'm told." The girl swiped at a tear rolling off her chin. "Given the choice, I prefer sweet like you." Sitting up, she straightened the hair curling over her shoulders and smoothed the blanket across her lap before carefully folding her small hands. "I'm Viola MacGregor."

Most likely the same Viola Alec had spoken of in his study. Same wide eyes, smooth brow, and tilt of the chin. She must be his sister. He'd fought to keep the piano for her, though the frail thing looked barely able to lift a hand to the keys.

"A pleasure to meet you, Viola." Lily snapped the lid back on the tin and tried not to inhale as a final puff of raisin leaked out. Between that and the candle smoke, it was a miracle Viola hadn't suffocated in the stuffy room. Lily tugged at the collar of her starched dress as the air closed in around her. Too many times to count she had been locked in her own dark room. Best way to cure a wayward child, Mother claimed.

"I don't receive many visitors." Viola threaded the top sheet between her long fingers. "Did you get lost?"

Alec had asked the same question, but instead of his growling bark, Viola's delicate lilt coaxed sweet concern. What made the poor child cry?

"I'm afraid I did get a bit turned around." Lily ran a hand down one of the posters at the foot of the bed. Blooming thistles were beautifully carved all around like a climbing vine. "I was contemplating drawing myself a map so I can break the bad habit. At least that would be one down, and Matron Strom would have to find something new to yell at me about. She probably has a list at the ready."

Viola's reddish brows drew together. "She doesn't care much for you?"

"Order and starch are her companions, neither of which I have in abundance."

"Aye, but you seem to have smiles, and sometimes that is what is needed more than a clean apron."

Her kind words wriggled through a crack in the newest barrier Lily had constructed to ward off Matron's fiery darts. It was an old wall, reinforced over years of assault by those who thought her little more than a pretty, useless distraction with nothing of consequence to contribute beyond a hefty inheritance to the marriage market.

Her zest for life exasperated Mother, and Father barely gave her a passing thought beyond what dynasty he could marry her off to. Stoic and proud, they rejected her laughter as a grievous flaw in character and took every opportunity to curb it. The more they tried molding her into an obedient creature, the thicker she built her walls to defend against the hurt.

Why could they not accept her as she was? Why could they not see that a life of endless duties suffocating in a passionless marriage was not a course she wished for? Would someone ever care enough to scale her defenses and set her free?

"Strange how they teach nurses to heal the body but so often forget the spirit. What those boys really need is a — rat!" Lily clapped a hand to her head. "Oh no. I forgot what I was supposed to be doing."

Viola's brow wrinkled. "Lads need a rat?"

"Your brother will be furious. I'm surprised he hasn't stomped up to retrieve me." Lily turned for the door. "I'm so sorry to barge in and rush out, but there's a crisis I must see to."

"If it's a crisis, Alec is more than capable —"

"I'm sure he is, but I'd rather not give him the opportunity to crow about it."

"Will you visit again?"

The hopeful desperation in Viola's voice pushed aside Lord Strathem's warning of

80

staying out of the private wing. Surely at his sister's invitation he wouldn't object. "Nothing could keep me away."

Her objection met her on the stairs with a scowl. "Where have you been?"

Lily moved to brush past him, but he blocked her path on the next step. She tapped her foot with impatience. "Retrieving the tin of cookies to lure our rodent out of hiding. Why are you not downstairs watching for it?"

His eyes flicked down to the package in her hands, then back to her. "Bruce already got it."

Ever the loyal shadow at his master's heel, the border collie stepped up next to Lily and licked her hand with a whine as if in apology for his superior skills.

Lily scratched behind his ears. "All right, boy. I forgive you, but next time allow me to help because I don't know what I'm to do with these now."

Prying off the cookie lid, she held it down for Bruce to sniff. He whined and scooted back behind Alec's protective stance.

"Trying to kill my dog?"

"No." Lily sighed and recapped the obnoxious raisin cookies. "My aunt is."

CHAPTER 4

Cold rain sliced down the back of Lily's neck. April showers were purported to bring May flowers, but in Scotland they summoned deluges to drown out anything but the hardiest of plants. Her eyes watered from staring so long, desperate to peel back the downpour and see the ambulance trundling up the driveway.

A telegram had arrived the previous day announcing the impending arrival of new troops at ten o'clock. At precisely 9:50 a.m. Matron Strom had lined up the nurses in the great hall for inspection. Eight minutes later she marched them out the front door to wait with umbrellas ready for their newest patients.

Lily tilted the umbrella as the rain curved sideways. Why they would appreciate a parade of fifteen drowned nurses was beyond her, but come rain or shine each man received a reception fit for the heroes they were.

She leaned over to Bertie. "Do you suppose they were made to swim?"

"I don't think even the ducks are out today." Whipping off her rain-speckled glasses, Bertie rubbed them on a dry portion of her apron. "Though what that says about us I couldn't tell you."

"Dedicated. And waterlogged." Lily wiggled her toes to stoke feeling back into them. Was the word *warmth* never used in this country? "Hate to think what my feet will look like later tonight when I finally peel off these soggy stockings."

Bertie held up her glasses for inspection and frowned at the fibers of cotton clinging to them. "At least you brought more than two."

"Not so frivolous now, am I?"

"You are when they're silk."

Lily took the glasses and gently blew off the stubborn fibers that Bertie couldn't see and placed them back on her cousin's nose. "The cotton ones itch and catch on bandages. Yesterday I walked around with a roll clinging to my ankle before Nurse Sheridan noticed it trailing me like a limp tail."

"Yes, that wouldn't happen with silk." Bertie sighed wistfully. She inched closer, bumping her umbrella into Lily's. "One pair and I'll iron your blouses for a week."

"Two."

"Two? That's ludicrous."

"For French silk?"

"French silk stockings . . . ." Bertie's lips curved with imagined delight. A luxury of elegance. One never knew its worth until forced to live without it. "All right. Two weeks."

Lily grinned. Back on Park Avenue she'd never given a second thought to stockings. If she ever caught a snag, her maid was there to hand her a new pair. Once in Scotland, she'd had to dress herself, clear her own plate, and fetch blankets for sleeping men. No one here cared if her hair was properly pinned or if she was talking to the most eligible man at the ball. It was as if her corset strings were cut and she could breathe for the first time.

Bertie poked her in the side. "What are you smiling about?"

"Never did I dream of spending my days in a soggy country eating turnips and haggling over French silk. Kind of fun, isn't it?"

"When Reggie and I were still in the nursery, our nanny thought it great fun to have us plant a small vegetable garden. She

84

had grand visions of teaching us about life cycles, and seeds, and the differences between fruits and vegetables. I'm afraid we were a great disappointment as we spent most of the time lobbing said produce at each other in mock battles."

"Who won the battles?"

"Me, mostly, but I think he let me win. Until the day I hit him with a smashed turnip. He threw so many tomatoes at me that my skin was stained orange for a week." Bertie's lips flitted in a smile. "If it were only as simple as throwing root vegetables at one another these days. Now we've grenades to contend with."

Lily squeezed her cousin's arm. "Reggie is far from the front line with a cushy job to make all the other boys jealous. He'll be back in no time at all to rub tomato juice in your hair."

Bleep, bleep, bleep!

Lily squinted down the drive. The cold wetness was starting to affect her mind if she thought she could hear anything beyond the rain pounding against the castle's stone walls behind her.

Bleep, bleeeeep!

Matron Strom stepped in front of the line of nurses and clapped her hands, wiggling the umbrella propped against her shoulder.

"Ladies, straighten up. Our patients approach."

The auto rounded the last bend of trees, its sleek black corners distorted by the slanting rain. It veered to the left, then back to the right. *Bleep, bleep!* The wheels twisted left again as it screeched in front of the house, spraying pebbles over Lily's and the other nurses' legs. *Bleep! Bleep!* The entire frame shuddered as the motor ground to a halt. Steam choked out from the hood.

The hairs prickled on the back of Lily's neck. No ambulance carrying wounded men drove like that.

The driver stumbled out, his face white as flour, his long, shaking fingers curled as if still gripping the wheel. His mouth moved, but no sound came forth.

Matron Strom hurried forward to shield him with her umbrella. "My dear man, there is no need to act hysterical over a little rain. The road conditions are less than ideal, but next time —"

"K-kidnapped," the man gasped.

"Pardon, sir? I did not hear you beyond the stammering."

"Kidnapped!" Eyes wild, the driver grabbed the matron's shoulders. "Come out from nowhere. Tried to stop 'em."

Lips pinched white, Matron Strom tore

herself from his grip and ran to the back of the ambulance, flinging open the doors. The driver winced as her questions to the remaining men pierced the air. Tearing his cap from his head, he dropped it in the mud and slid to his knees.

Lily rushed over to him and covered him with her umbrella. "Take a deep breath. It will be all right."

"It won't." His voice cracked as he drove his hands into his hair, pulling it. "Ain't never lost a man on my watch. It's my responsibility to see 'em safe, but he had a gun."

"Who had a gun?"

His lips clamped shut as he slowly swung his head back and forth. Lily pulled a frilly hankie from her pocket and knelt beside him. She dabbed the rain streaks from his cheek.

"Sir, can you tell me who had a gun?"

"Why aren't the men being taken inside?" Lord Strathem's voice roared over the rain. Gravel popped beneath his boots as he marched out the front door. "Why are you all standing around in the rain?"

"A man has been taken." Despite the sudden turn to horror, Matron Strom's voice was as calm as if she were ordering Sunday brunch. "By whom or for what reason is unknown."

Stopping in front of the driver, Lord Strathem's cane stamped the ground. Thunder loomed on his face. "Who did this?"

The driver hunched farther over, rubbing his hands on either side of his face.

"Who did this?"

Lily glared up at Lord Strathem. "He's shaken enough without you shouting at him." She turned back to the trembling man and softened her tone. "What's your name?"

"F-Fred."

"Fred, can you please tell us what happened? If we're to find the man, we need as much detail as you can give us."

Swiping a hand over his mouth, Fred took a deep breath. "I met the train right at nine thirty. Never been late and I always keep a clean back for the boys. No good traveling in a seat that ain't been swept."

Lord Strathem's cane ground into the gravel. Lily could almost hear his teeth grinding too. She ignored him. "Did you recognize the kidnappers? Which way did they go?"

"They jumped out of the bushes just past Baker's farm. Had their faces covered so I couldn't see 'em. Nearly didn't with all the rain." Fred's head lifted, the shaking fear in his eyes stilling to malice. "Wish I had.

They'd be meat for the flies."

Queasiness tangled in Lily's stomach at the thought. "That certainly would've taken care of them, but they're still on the loose. Do you remember the direction they went?"

Fred's head sagged again into a shake. "Was raining so hard . . ."

Lord Strathem tossed his cane to the ground and squatted in front of Fred, grabbing the mumbling man by the shoulders. "Pull yourself together so we might have a chance of finding these men before it's too late."

The hankie fell limp in Lily's cold fingers. "Too late?"

His eyes cut to her with unblinking certainty. "They didn't kidnap the man for a garden party. Which way, Fred?"

"East, toward the river." Fred rocked backward on the wet pebbles and buried his face in his arms. "Poor Captain Gibbons. Lost he is."

Grabbing his cane, Lord Strathem pushed to his feet. Lily surged in front of him. He ducked before she knocked him in the head with her umbrella. "Your people skills are far from useful. You've frightened him from saying another word."

"Civility isn't needed in a manhunt. He told me everything he knows." Rain sliced down his face unheeded and soaked into his shirt, outlining his solid shoulders. "I suggest you return to coddling him before he catches cold. Guthrie!"

Guthrie appeared with the smell of wet wool clinging to him. "Aye, I heard him."

"Alert the constable, then round up every available man. I want these kidnappers found before sundown."

Pinpricks of trepidation tapped down Lily's spine. "Shouldn't you wait for the authorities?"

Yanking a small knife from his boot, he ran his thumb down the blade, then slipped it back into his boot. "No."

Lily shook her head in disbelief. "Of course not. Why would you?"

"Your opinion is not needed in this matter. Assist Mr. Fred into the house." Having collected and ushered the other two men from the ambulance into the care of the waiting nurses, Matron Strom set to tidying up the loose ends. "I'll prepare a first aid kit for you to take should Captain . . . em, the wounded man need it."

"Captain Gibbons," Lily offered as she took Fred by the elbow and pulled him up on wobbly legs. "Careful, Mr. Fred, or you'll take us both down again."

Matron Strom's eyes flashed with silencing ice as she flicked her gaze to Lily before calming herself to address Lord Strathem. "Should Captain Gibbons require assistance at the scene, you need to be properly prepared."

Lord Strathem shook his head, spraying more water drops. "I'll find a stick if he needs a splint, or a belt or set of suspenders for a tourniquet."

"Lord Strathem, this is not a battlefield," Matron Strom said. "We have the proper materials and strong-stomached nurses to apply them."

"I won't be dragged down or held responsible for a stumbling woman out in the woods."

Matron Strom drew herself up to her full height, which stopped just below his neck. "My nurses do not stumble, and if you refuse to take one then I shall not be held responsible should one strike out on her own in search of the patient. The men's care is our priority."

"Above personal safety?"

Lily held her breath. It was like watching two hardened ice cubes smashed under a rock. Who would crack first from the pressure?

After an eternity of not blinking, Lord Strathem's jaw shifted. His gaze swung to

Lily. "Stay far back unless you want to get shot. That river has swept off more than one unsuspecting person."

Lily's mouth dropped open. *She* was to find a gang of robbers and set a man's broken bones in the woods in the middle of a thunderstorm? Surely he was jesting. She'd only practiced tourniquets twice before, and each time her "patient" had complained of not feeling her leg for the rest of the day.

Before she could explain that Captain Gibbons was better off without her, Matron Strom motioned Esther over. "Nurse Hartley will accompany you. Go put on your sturdy boots and mackintosh and take one of the kits from the storage room. Hurry."

Esther's knuckles curled white around her umbrella handle, but she nodded and dashed off. The rain had not left one strand of frizz on her head. Lily's shoulders sagged. Despite her bumbling skills, why couldn't she display the same amount of confidence when a man's life hung in the balance?

"Miss Durham, take the driver inside and have the cook pour him a wee dram." Lord Strathem's voice cut through the sheet of water straight into her as if he sensed her lack of direction. Before she could find hope in it, he turned to Matron Strom. "Get back inside and don't let anyone out. They took once, and I don't doubt they'll come looking for more."

Rain slashed against the window like a hive exploding with angry wasps. Any minute now the glass was sure to shatter and the water flood in and drown them. Lily backed away, bumping the back of her legs against a bed.

"Quite a night out there, eh?"

She turned and smiled at Lieutenant Stoles, who gazed sleepily up at her from his pillow. One of the men — boys, really — witness to the kidnapping. "I'm sorry for waking you."

"Wasn't sleeping. Appreciating the rain without mud and shells going off over my head."

Pulling up a low stool, she sat next to him. "We promise no mud or shells here. Unless you want to splash in puddles tomorrow."

"Would the matron allow that? I saw steam coming out of her ears when she found a carrot touching the ham slices on the lunch trays."

"She does have rather high expectations, but it's only because she wants you to have the best care possible. That means no cross-contaminated food."

"It's not the boiled leather I've been chowing down on for the past year. Can you imagine tinned beef and powdered milk for months straight? After a while, the rats and worms creeping down the trenches are tempting for a meal."

Looking into his sweet, round face, her heart heaved with sadness. How many of these boys dug themselves to inhumane depths because of this war? She tucked the woven blanket around his legs.

"As long as you're with us, you won't have to worry about those things. Good food, fresh air, and clean clothes will have you back on the road to full recovery in no time."

He cocked his head and studied her through the dim light of a nearby lamp. "Aren't you going to ask me about the kidnapping?"

"Not unless you want to talk about it."

"It's just that everyone else in here, well, it's all they want to talk about. The nurses, the matron, even a kitchen maid who sneaked up here. All of them want to know the dirty details."

"I don't care for dirty details. It convolutes the truth, and truth is much more interesting than whatever tidbits are stirred up by gossip."

Wind whipped through the trees, tearing leaves from the branches and flinging them at the windows. Lily twined her fingers together and squeezed. Lord Strathem, Guthrie, and Esther had been gone for hours. They should have returned by now.

The boy's brow scrunched together. "Ma'am, are you all right?"

Rain whipped the opposite direction. Lily twisted her bloodless fingers in her lap. "My goodness. It's really coming down out there."

Thump. Thump.

Lily leaped from her chair, ready to defend her patients from sudden attack.

"Ma'am? I think it was the front door."

The front door. Taking a deep breath, she reassured herself that the kidnappers had not returned for the rest of them. Surely kidnappers wouldn't knock.

Standing, she pushed the chair under the table and pulled up the blanket to Lieutenant Stoles's chin. "Don't want you catching cold. Excuse me a moment."

Waving to gain the other nurse's attention from across the room, Lily motioned that she was stepping out. The massive wooden chandeliers had been dimmed to light the great hall in deep shadows, warming the armor to bronze and weaving over the

95

tapestries to highlight the gold-and-silver threads.

Muffled voices came from behind the closed doors of the entryway. The latch clicked open and the doors burst inward, ushering in angry protests.

"Ridiculous to have her there in the first place! She could have broken her neck." Lord Strathem's cane punched the floor as he stomped in. Rain dribbled down his long gray coat, leaving puddles behind each footstep.

Guthrie waddled in carrying a muddied Esther. "Could've happened tae any one o' us, Alec. The lass slipped is all."

"But it didn't. It happened to her, and now we've lost hours in catching those men."

"They're most likely holed up like rats until the rain stops. Best we take a wee rest and start again come morning."

"Alec, I am so very sorry for causing such an unnecessary problem." Esther brushed a muddy lock of hair from her forehead. A leaf fluttered to the ground. "I was trying so hard to stay out of the way that I didn't see that root sticking up."

Lord Strathem yanked the checkered wool hat from his head and ran a hand through his hair, splattering water over the floor.

Turning, he started for the stairs but stopped when he spotted Lily hovering near the potted palm. "What are you doing up?"

"I'm on shift and heard the door. I thought you were the kidnappers come to take the rest of us." Her poor attempt at humor fell flat on the tension suffocating the hall. "Captain Gibbons is still missing."

His gaze flicked to Esther for the briefest second. "Aye, he is. We'll join back up with the constable at daybreak. Guthrie, take Nurse Hartley upstairs."

"I can make it," Esther protested. "Mr. Guthrie, please put me down. The fuss is really unnecessary, and Matron Strom will be none too happy to find gentlemen in the nurses' wing no matter who he is."

"And I'll not leave you to drag yourself up the stairs only to roll back down." Angry blue lightning flashed in Lord Strathem's eyes. "Get her upstairs." He marched to his study and slammed the door without a backward glance.

Hours later the familiar cadence of his walk prickled Lily's ear as she signed over her duties to the nurse on the next shift. He and Guthrie were leaving again. Lily walked into the front hall and spotted the field kit sitting next to the door where she had placed it after checking the supplies. Most likely they wouldn't need it, but if they did . . . She glanced up and down the hall. Not a soul to be found, and Matron had buried herself under paperwork and filing after Captain Gibbons was reported missing.

If Guthrie or Lord Strathem fell, or if they found the captain in a bad way, they had nothing and no one to help them.

Heart pounding, Lily grabbed the kit and dashed out after them.

CHAPTER 5

"Constable Simpson said he'd take his men south and cover the area from there to Baker's farm." Alec pointed to the slanting hillside covered in thick pine. Bruce wove ahead, nose to the ground. "We'll take the riverbank and search for prints."

Guthrie ground his toe into the muddy earth. "Rain might've washed 'em away."

"Aye, but it would also slow them down. With that and hauling an injured man, they couldn't have gotten far." Alec scanned the woods surrounding them. Each tree and twist of grass as familiar to him as the back of his hand. One of the few things from his youth that had yet to be strangled by bitterness. "Mayhap they holed up until the downpour stopped."

"Plenty o' places for that 'round here. Donnegal's Cave, the Craven Tops, Hollow's Beck."

Alec shook his head. "Gibbons has a

busted leg. Impossible to make those steep climbs." Stiffening pain crept up his own leg. Rain always brought it on. Most days he was able to ignore it, but the early morn chill wrapped around his muscles and squeezed its icy fingers until they touched bone. "*Tannasg* Tarn is close enough."

Paling, Guthrie crossed himself thrice, spun around, and spat on the ground. "Dinna speak o' that place. 'Tisn't right tae in the fair break o' day."

"Bah, superstitions."

Guthrie pointed a thick finger in his face. "Highlands truth, lad."

Alec smacked the wagging finger away from his nose. "Of course. What was I thinking, that ghosts and spirits don't exist?"

"Have a care tae not speak such things in their presence. Might have a real problem on our hands."

"I'll be sure to watch my words when we arrive."

They slogged through the wet trees, the smell of musty bark thick in the air like a wool blanket left out to dry after the rain. Only Bruce seemed to delight in the outing, chasing squirrels through the leaves. Boots squishing in the mud, Alec scoured the forest bed for footprints.

With so many fallen leaves and the deluge

overnight, any evidence was likely to have washed away. He drove his cane into the mud. Gibbons was out here somewhere, and as long as Alec remained Lord of Kinclavoch, the man fell under his protection. He'd rather sell his soul than have another failure notched in his worn belt.

"Earth smells turned this way." Guthrie hunkered down, fingers splayed on the mud and nose twitching.

Alec didn't bother trying to discern storm-churned dirt from people-churned dirt. If Gibbons or the attackers had touched even one blade of MacGregor grass, Guthrie could track them. Old codger had the senses of a bloodhound.

"Which way?"

Guthrie pointed up a small rise ahead of them and down. *Tannasg* Tarn. Pain fastened around Alec's calf as he trudged up the slope, leaning heavy on his cane. Confounded leg! Always wanting to give out at the least convenient times.

"All right there, lad?"

Alec jerked upright at Guthrie's voice close behind him. "Aye, aye. Ground's slick is all."

"Good time fae a rest. We've been at it all night."

"No." Bruce whipped around, alert at the

sharpness in his master's tone. Alec stopped and turned back, shoulders sagging. "Apologies. This weather pulls out the worst of my temper."

Guthrie's eyes flicked to Alec's bad leg. "Forgot the ointment this time?"

Nodding, Alec absently rubbed his thigh. Never content to aggravate a mere portion, the old injury had a tendency to spread its malevolence along the entire limb. Twelve years since he'd been thrown from that horse, and not a day went by without pain. The doctor did everything he could to set the bone right, but the break failed to heal entirely. Years of faithful service had left Guthrie the only man brave enough to mention it — the only man who still looked him in the eye without judgment, without questioning why Alec didn't don a uniform for king and country.

Cresting the top of the slope, he gazed below into the carved-out basin. Filled with damp leaves and bracken, the moist earth was dissected with slim rivulets of water trickling from the tree roots standing as sentinels around the upper rim. The roots broke down through the dirt, gnarling together like curtains to form little hollows beneath the towering elms.

Perfect to tuck away in until danger passed.

A branch cracked behind them. Alec leaped behind a tree. Robert the Bruce followed and stood at his master's feet with hackles raised and a low growl in his throat. Drawing the pistol from his belt, Alec cocked the hammer and steadied his arm at his side. Close by, Guthrie did the same. Footsteps drew closer, slipping over leaves and squishing in the mud. He frowned. They were too unsure and light to be a man's.

Sweat prickled the back of his neck as the air built in his chest. Another branch snapped. His finger brushed the side of the trigger. Just a few steps more.

"Confounded mud. Does it do anything but rain in this country?"

Alec's finger slid off the trigger. Grinding his teeth, he jammed the pistol back into his belt and stepped out from behind the tree. "Daft woman! Don't you know how dang —"

"Ack!"

Something lumpy hurtled at his head. He dodged as it sailed past his nose and tumbled down the gulch. "Are you trying to kill me?"

Paleness drained Lily's cheeks. Cowering

behind a bush, she pointed to his pistol. "Are *you* trying to kill *me*?"

"I would if you were the kidnapper," Alec said.

"Clearly I'm not."

"How was I supposed to know with you clomping around like stags in the rut season?"

"I have not a clue what that means, but coming from you I'm certain it's an insult." She smoothed a hand down her damp apron. Leaves clung to the hem of her filthy skirt. "I can also assure you that I never clomp. My mother saw to that with fiendish pleasure."

Alec bit back the string of curses building in his throat. "What are you doing here? It's dangerous, and I don't have time to look after some helpless woman."

Her eyes narrowed at the word *helpless.* "You forgot the first aid kit. I thought Captain Gibbons may be in need of it. Or you or Mr. Guthrie should you find yourselves in less-than-ideal circumstances. Dangers afoot, as you said."

"You've delivered it, so see yourself back to Kinclavoch."

"And should you run across Captain Gibbons with a disturbed femur or gushing laceration, do you have the faintest idea how

104

to bind it?"

"A wee scratch won't gush." He had no idea what a disturbed femur was, but surely he didn't need a kit to pop it back in place. A quick binding with a belt would suffice to get him back for the matron's ministrations.

Lily plunked her hands on her slim hips, her shapely form accentuated by the clinging wet skirts. "Have you nurse's training?"

Have you? Scrubbing a hand over his face, he rasped his palm on whiskers he'd forgotten to shave in exhaustion. "I don't have time for this. Hie yourself back to the castle before you twist your ankle and I've wasted another search dragging another lass from the mud."

"Do you always wake up on the wrong side of pleasant?"

"Only as much as you test the patience of saints."

"Och, Alec. Nay need tae carry on so. The lass is only trying tae help." Guthrie lifted shaggy brows in his manner of proving a point. "Besides, ye ken it's too dangerous tae go back alone. Praying we find the good captain, her skills may be needed here."

"Does Matron Strom not have need of you elsewhere?"

Red rushed to Lily's cheeks as she turned her attention to the mud covering her shoes.

"Oh . . . well, she was busy at the time."

Alec threw his head back and stared at the sodden green canopy above. Bruce whined next to him. "You didn't tell her you left."

"She asked not to be disturbed unless it was an emergency, and if I'd taken longer to seek her approval I might never have found you in all these trees. I did not wish for you to be without supplies."

Sincerity shone from her large green eyes. Darkened from clouded skies above, they glimmered like gems at the bottom of a shallow loch. His throat constricted. An inexplicable urge to draw her close and study the conflicting tides within those eyes nearly overcame him. Nearly.

Guthrie clapped him on the shoulder, jostling him aside in the same motion. "He may be a wee thick-heided tae understand, but I'll appreciate a bonny lass worrying about me any day and twice on Sunday."

Lily beamed, grating Alec's taut nerves all the more. He spun around and eased down the slope into the tarn. "Stay if you must, but keep out of the way."

Furling green bracken brushed the tops of his boots as he made it to the bottom. Tiny raindrops collected along the frilled leaves and rolled together like glass marbles. He scanned the area, noting the unbroken stems, the undisturbed sides of the streams crossing the ground before swinging to the tree roots coiling above him.

"If the kidnappers holed up here for the night, we're bound to find something in the hollows under the trees." He looked back up to Guthrie and pointed left. "You take that side, and I'll look over here."

Guthrie didn't budge. His lips pressed into a pale line slashing across his tanned face as he slowly shook his head back and forth. "Nay. I'll keep watch here."

Alec leaned against his cane. He hated relying on its support, especially outside the seclusion of his room, but the long hours wore down the aching muscles to their last ragged cords. "No spirit has yet to grab me from the beyond. 'Tis safe enough."

The old man crossed himself. "Dinna be tempting them, lad."

"Not tempting anyone or anything, but I can't —" A cramp arced up Alec's calf and straight into his thigh. He gritted his teeth and waited for it to pass. "We'll get out of here faster with two of us searching."

Lily looked between them, confusion knitting her smooth brow. Suddenly a beatific smile parted her pink lips. Patting her nurse's cap as if it were a tiara in a ballroom, she laced her arm through Guthrie's. "I need to retrieve my kit, but as you can see it's all the way down there. Would you be a dear, Mr. Guthrie, and allow me to use your strong arm? I'm so terribly clumsy and would hate to twist my ankle on a slippery leaf."

Alec watched in bemused shock as the grown man — well into half a century of years, veteran of several military campaigns, and specialist in every Gaelic curse known to the ancient Scots — melted to parritch. Guthrie's flat mouth pipped up as bright red spotted his cheeks.

Rolling his shoulders back, Guthrie patted Lily's fingers. "Hold tight and I'll bring ye safely down, lassie."

"Thank you, Mr. Guthrie. You're the first true gentleman I've met in this wild land."

"Aye, 'tis a land o' fierce men, but ye'll never find a one more honorable than a Scotsman."

Inching their way to the bottom, Lily released his arm and picked up her kit. She brushed the wet leaves from the strap and wrinkled her nose. "Goodness. The smell down here is a bit, ah, earthy. What is this place called again?"

"*Tannasg* Tarn," Alec said. " 'Pool of the ghosts.' It's said to have been created by the dropping tears of a giantess long before man inhabited this land." The ancient story from childhood rolled out of his mouth before he could stop it. "One thousand. A tear for each bairn she lost. Their souls are said to be sleeping here."

The smile slid from Guthrie's face as he spun around and crossed himself. To her credit, Lily looked less convinced of the absurdity. *"Tannasg."* The Gaelic word rolled perfectly from her mouth. "You Scots certainly have a silver tongue for stories."

"My father told me that one when I was a lad." The unguarded memory hit Alec quick as an arrow. Sharp and cutting, burrowing into the deepest part of him that he wished never to feel again. The less he had to think about Father, the better. He'd had enough of the old man's mistakes staring him in the face day after day. "Faerie stories. Naught more."

Pivoting on his heel before she provoked more unbidden words from him, Alec marched to the farthest tree root and examined the ground beneath it. Nothing. Squatting, his knee buckled and dropped down in the quagmire. Hang the blasted leg and the never-ending trouble it caused. Gritting his teeth, he glanced behind him to ensure Guthrie and Lily remained occupied on the far side. His man pointed to a long line of mushrooms sprouting up a tree while she nodded in deep concentration at his every word.

Bruce brushed his soft head against Alec's shoulder. Alec patted the dog's side in reassurance. " 'Tis all right, boy. Give it a moment, aye?"

Leaning his cane against the sloping dirt, he pushed his thumbs into the throbbing muscle and worked it up and down. He'd never find that missing man if he kept stopping to nurse his old wound. Or converse with some unwanted female.

Though Lily Durham seemed to embrace all facets of life, Alec would never suggest that life as a nurse was her true calling, but she gave it her all in her own unusual manner. Never had he imagined he'd find a proper lady cleaning bedpans in her evening gloves. The corners of his mouth cracked up. She'd felt so warm and soft when she'd fallen against him. The thrill of a woman's touch had surged in his veins after such long depravation. No reasonable woman wanted to be seen on the arm of a cripple.

His mouth flattened. She wasn't a nurse, and she didn't belong in the untamed lands of Scotland. And she certainly didn't belong anywhere near him.

"Find anything?"

He spun around and found a pair of green eyes hovering over his shoulder.

Lily smiled brightly. "Sorry. Didn't mean to startle you."

"Then why do you creep around so?"

"I'm not —" She shook her head, slipping errant strands of blonde from her crooked cap. "No sense in arguing. Again. Mr. Guthrie has the task well in hand — well, nose really. I thought only bloodhounds could smell so close to the ground. I came to see if I might be of some use here with you."

"You cannot."

Hurtful disappointment flashed across her face, drawing her eyes down. If he were standing, he'd kick himself. He'd never been much good with women. He preferred stables to drawing rooms, and long solitary walks to dancing. Still, Highland bleakness was no excuse for boorish rudeness.

He shifted to let her see into the carved-out hole. "Not much to find here."

"What's that?" Laying her hand on his arm, she leaned forward and pointed. "Over there."

Heat charged through his jacket sleeve where she touched it, searing his skin and flooding his veins. It rooted him to the spot, but he felt nothing beyond the tether connecting him to her. For an instant he thought of reaching down to ensure the realness of her delicately curved fingers but quickly rejected the impulse. He'd given up the dream of a loving wife and happy family long ago, but the warmth surging in his blood was too bold to ignore.

He mentally shook himself. Lasses like her weren't interested in settling down to domestic duties. At least not yet. A rundown castle turned hospital offered nothing to appease her bright disposition, yet in every instance he'd found her making the most of the situation. Irritating idealism.

"What's irritated you now?"

Alec snapped his attention back in place. Unfortunately that meant her anxious face. Ignoring her question, he quickly looked to where she had pointed. "A clue mayhap."

Plucking the object from the sticky mud, he cupped it in his palm. A gold button from a soldier's uniform.

Lily's fingers bunched his sleeve material as she leaned closer to inspect it. "Did Captain Gibbons leave us a bread crumb?"

More than relief, the button weighed like lead in his hand. "Seems so."

"Odd to bring an invalid down here in the rain, knowing how swampy it would get.

Probably had to drag him, poor man."

Alec frowned and scanned the rim surrounding the tarn. "Guthrie. Have you found anything?"

Trailing the upper rim again, Guthrie shook his head. "Not a scratch to be seen."

A scratch. Alec pushed to his feet, shooting needles down his leg. He grabbed for his cane and missed.

"Careful now. I don't need another injured man to worry about." Lily swooped down and picked up his cane. She brushed her thumb over a stallion's head he'd carved into the handle, a faint smile curving her lip as she held it out for him. "Besides, you're too heavy to sling over my shoulder."

An added wink reeled him speechless. His hands fumbled as he took the cane, then stepped around her before his face flamed red. *Take hold of your senses! You're no laddie anymore.* Grabbing a tree root, he ran his hand all the way up until it connected to the trunk. He tried several more gnarled roots until his fingers brushed narrow gashes. "Guthrie! Here."

Guthrie raced over and knelt to examine where Alec pointed. "Aye. Someone's been scratching here for sure. And just here, the trunk's rubbed like something scraped by it."

"A body?"

The older man rubbed his chin, creating more wrinkles down his leathery neck. "Mayhap. Or the person was tryin' tae claw his way back up after fallin' down."

"I found this." Lily appeared next to him and opened her palm. A tiny bit of spun white froth sat in the center.

Alec frowned. "What's that?"

Her troubled green eyes met his. "It's from a bandage. And just here, on the end, is blood."

CHAPTER 6

"You really don't know where else to look?" Viola clutched the bedsheet around her, her face pale in the early morning light.

Lily stretched open the second set of drapes. Dust motes whirled around her like a disturbed cloud. "The police want sole responsibility for searching and have asked that no one else go out searching in case the kidnappers are looking for more to take."

"Heavens, what a thought." Viola shivered under her knitted shawl. "Poor Captain Gibbons. Are you sure those were clues he left behind?"

"That or he lost them in a scuffle with his keepers." Lily dragged the window up, fingers straining as it resisted against the years' worth of dirt caked in the track. A light spring breeze flew in and swept out the candle smoke as she went around the room to blow out the candles. Finally it looked like a bedroom and not a nun's prayer closet. "All I can say is that it must have been an act of desperation to take them to that place."

"You're a brave one to go there. The *Tannasg* Tarn isn't for the faint of heart."

"Disbelief in superstitions is hardly a call for bravery."

"Alec told me you chased after them."

"Chased? Hardly. They forgot the first aid kit. Never enter any situation without one, or so Matron drills into us."

"According to my brother a gun and knife are the only things needed."

"With which he almost shot me."

Viola's eyes popped wide. "He didn't tell me that."

Lily snorted and sat on the cushioned bench under the window. "I imagine there are many things he doesn't tell you. Talking to him is like going to battle with a brick wall."

"He does have an off-putting gruffness, but not always." Viola's eyes dropped to the bedcover. "Much of late bears heavily on him."

Hazy clouds hung low over the mountains in the distance, the thick sheath of trees rolling down its sides like a dark-green carpet. Untouched land as far as the eye could see,

116

all under MacGregor protection. For such vast richness one would never suspect the owner was pawning off every last item he owned to keep his head above water. Each day she noticed a new painting or vase missing, a ring of dust the surviving reminder of the once splendor. What had brought them to such ruination?

"Lord Strathem —"

Viola's gaze jumped up. "Please don't call him that. He hates it. It sounds too formal and restricting."

"I thought the aristocracy prided itself on formalities, especially with rank. My cousin's father, Lord Reginald — no, no, that's his name . . . Lord Fowley. There are so many names, but then they aren't titles, and I'm so confused when to use what and when."

"The blue bloods do like their titles, but we're not as touchy about them here in Scotland. We've more important things to think on."

"Like killing things and trying not to get eaten alive by mosquitoes?"

"Precisely, though they're midges. Fierce wee beasties, they are." Viola grinned. The effect rescinded the dullness from her eyes and sparked a life that was missing.

Lily patted the seat next to her by the

window. "Come sit here."

The girl's grin quivered to uncertainty. "I better not. My allergies are rather sensitive near open windows."

And they weren't from all the dust gathering in the stuffy corners? "The breeze is freshest here. Should we find a hint of pollen, I'll throw a blanket over your head and roll you back to bed. What's life without a bit of daring?"

Viola hesitated for a moment before peeling back the bedcovers. She swung two painfully thin legs over the side of the bed and settled bony feet on the threadbare rug. Hastening to cover the frail sight, she smoothed down her nightdress and pulled the knitted shawl tighter over her shoulders. She grabbed the carved poster closest to her and pulled herself to standing.

Lily's arms tensed, ready to spring forward as Viola tottered the four steps to the window. Only when she finally sat down did Lily relax again.

"Let's tie this nice and snug. Wouldn't want you to catch cold all the way over here." She gathered the pale-pink ribbon from the shawl and tied it into a bow under Viola's chin.

They sat in silence as the minutes ticked past on the porcelain clock above the fireplace. Brown-and-white birds flitted by, their wings stretched out and curling in as they swooped toward the roof. Tall green grass swayed on the lawn stretching out to a thicket of trees; beyond shimmered a river of dark blue. Lily breathed in deep. How different this was from New York, or anything she had seen in the States. Not long ago, she imagined nothing more fascinating than the fashion parading down Fifth Avenue. What a difference a little fresh air could do for the imagination.

Viola sighed and leaned her cheek against the window frame. "I never tire of this view."

"You're lucky. The only sight from my room is a road cutting through a valley. And that's only after I stand on a chair to peek out the tiny glass rectangle. I'd like to see the lake."

"The Spey River feeds into the lake, though here in Scotland we call it a loch. It sits on MacGregor property, but Alec opens it to the local village for trout fishing just like our ancestors did. Many of the locals would've died during the Highland Clearances after the Battle of Culloden if they hadn't been able to fish there. You should have Alec take you. It's his favorite fishing spot."

Lily's stomach knotted at the thought of

spending more time with Kinclavoch's surly owner. After nearly shooting her in that pit of sleeping spirits, he'd welcomed her presence like the plague. Growling at her and recoiling as if a harpy had latched on to him when she grabbed his arm to keep from hurtling over a root.

She traced a sliver of peeling paint on the sill. Men never reacted like that to her. Then again, they shrank away like boys in the shadow of Lord Strathem. While the good-time Charlies of New York shined their shoes and oiled their hair, Alec hunted kidnapped soldiers with nothing more than a long knife and a manservant old enough to be part of the earth's cooling crust. He was a rough visage of masculinity, like bark fortressed around a proud tree, rugged and unpolished with no need to tailor his clothes so they might define his shoulders and muscled calves at best advantage. A mended jacket and worn boots couldn't hide the strength filling out every muscle of his body. A fact she was finding far too distracting for her own peace of mind.

She flicked off the paint chip with her nail. "He has more important things to do than escort a city girl out to the country. You take me."

Viola shifted, pressing her knobby knees

together as she tugged the hem of her nightdress over her exposed, white feet. "I'm not good at outdoor things."

"Neither am I. My idea of experiencing nature is strolling past botanical paintings at the Metropolitan." She playfully bumped Viola's shoulder with her own. "We could help each other move past our fears."

Dark hairs swayed over the side of Viola's face, hiding it as she shook her head. "It's not so much a fear as a condition."

The textbook image of a frail frame, wanness, unsteadiness of feet, and protruding kneecaps flipped through Lily's mind. Bertie had gone through every medical journal and book in her father's library prior to their nursing courses. She'd shoved them under Lily's nose when she finished one and moved on to the next.

Childhood diseases had been the highlight of two evenings. Viola's skin was as untouched by the sun as the day she was born, the mark of a true society lady, but even ladies needed vitamins from the sun. Or so Bertie's book claimed. Perhaps there was a similar book in the downstairs library Lily might consult for Viola's symptoms.

"What about a stroll in the garden after my shift? There are some beautiful flowers there — heavens if I know their names —

121

that are simply glorious in the late-afternoon sun."

"No. I can't go outside." Viola's words bit with the sharpness of her brother's tone. She raised a trembling hand to her cheek. "The flowers sound beautiful, but I'm afraid I can't. I'm sorry."

Stiffness hung over them like a suspended knife, cutting through the friendly ease they had shared moments before. Once more her overeager mouth ruined things. Would she never learn to keep it shut? "That's all right. We can find something else to do."

Viola sat silently for a long minute until she finally turned to look at Lily, the softness once again in her eyes. "What do you have in mind?"

Lily scrambled for something that didn't involve being outside. "I was thinking of setting up a game in the great hall to —"

"What is *he* doing here again?"

Lily followed the direction of Viola's furrowed brow. A fashionable Rolls Royce glided down the drive and curved around to the front of the house. She leaned farther out the window as the shiny fenders disappeared around the corner. "I didn't know they made those in green and silver."

"When you're Richard Wright, you get anything you want."

Lily mentally tucked the name away. Mother was always looking for such new connections. "Who is he?"

"A newspaperman. He owns the *London Herald.*"

"How fascinating. We once had William Hearst to dine, a bit eccentric, but very entertaining stories. Perhaps Mr. Wright has come for stories on the soldiers recuperating."

"If he has, it won't be from any bout of patriotism or goodwill. Last week he printed an interview from a war widow that spun her heartache into exploitation of her husband's final moments." Viola sighed. "Whatever the intention behind his frequent visits to Kinclavoch, I can say without doubt that it's to fill his own pockets."

A brisk knock sounded before the bedroom door swung open and Lord Strathem — Alec as he seemed to prefer — strode in. "Vi, it's time for your med— What is she doing here?" His eyes narrowed on Lily, then cut to his sister.

"*She* is visiting a friend," Lily offered, jerking his attention back to her. "In case you're unsure of the reference, it's when one person enjoys the company of another."

"The family wing is forbidden."

"Is it? I must have missed the locks and

bars. Perhaps it's their day to be polished." She cocked her head to the side, daring him. "I was invited."

His eyes moved to his sister. For the briefest of seconds the cold, blue steel softened. Though sheathed in iron, tenderness was not lost on him. "Come away from the window. You'll catch cold."

Shaking her head, Viola smiled. "I can smell the heather readying to bloom. You should take Lily to your spot to see it."

The affection vanished from his eyes. He crossed the room and withdrew a small brown bottle of cod liver oil and a spoon from the top drawer of Viola's bureau. "Aide Durham has more than enough on her hands caring for the soldiers, and that outing is a good stretch of the legs to get to. I doubt she's brought the proper hiking shoes."

Ignoring his incivility, Lily smiled brightly. "Alas, only my dancing heels."

Still not looking at her, he poured a spoonful of the straw-colored liquid onto the spoon and held it out to Viola. "Back in bed. I don't need you to wear yourself out."

Viola swallowed dutifully, then made a face and turned away from him to stare out the window. Vitality had eased into her sullen cheeks. "A few minutes more. Please."

His palm twisted over the carved horse's head on his cane as his wide chest expanded on a deep breath. Holding it for several warring seconds, he finally allowed it to ease out. "A few, mind you, *thaisce.*" The icy blue eyes snapped to Lily. Crossing the room, he pushed the door open wider and swept his arm to the hall. "If you please, Aide Durham."

As she stood to follow, Viola grabbed her hand. A sad, sweet smile parted her lips. "I truly am sorry about the garden flowers. Promise you'll go see them and then come back tomorrow and tell me about them."

Bending down, Lily brushed a kiss over her cheek. "Promise. Tomorrow, if not sooner."

Out in the hall the less agreeable Mac-Gregor took her elbow and pulled her down a corridor lined with heavy drapes drawn tight over the windows.

His fingers tightened on the back of her arm, pulling her to a stop. "Are you incapable of following any kind of rule?"

"Are you always so rude or has living behind closed windows left you with the inability to interact with a degree of civility?"

"Both."

Lily sighed. "I had every intention of staying far from your private matters until I got

125

lost again and heard a noise that day I came to look for our mouse bait. Rather than leave a person in distress, as I'm sure you'd prefer, I went to offer assistance and met your lovely sister."

His thick burnished eyebrows drew together. "What sort of distress?"

Tightly controlled panic edged his tone. He would strangle Viola with his overprotectiveness if he wasn't careful. The poor girl had tasted freedom from that open window's breeze, and Lily wasn't about to stifle it. "It was a loud thump from her dropping a book. We chatted for a bit and she asked me to visit again, which I was only too happy to do except for the candle smoke and stale air."

"Something else you were only too happy to remedy by throwing open the windows to chill her to death."

Lily pried at the vicelike fingers bunching her sleeve. An hour's worth of ironing gone to waste. Matron wouldn't be happy. "If you think that, then you've overlooked her newfound rosy glow. Why is she closed up like a leprous monk?"

"My sister's condition is none of your affair."

"Squirreling her away in a depressing room isn't going to help. She needs fresh air, flowers, and blue skies."

Indignation flared in his eyes. He released her, dropping his hand back to his side. "An expert, are you? She has every available care and medication. She's defied doctors' expectations for years by living so long."

Brushing past him, Lily yanked open the thick brocade drapes. Dust flew into her mouth and up her nose. Coughing, she unlatched the window and shoved it up. It took a few good tugs before it finally groaned into lifting. Light spilled into the hallway, illuminating the nooks and crannies that had most likely been left in darkness for far too long. "Then you've missed the point of living. A soul needs rays of sunshine to thrive. No more cages wrapped in speeches of sanctuary."

Leaning her head out, she gripped the stone ledge as feelings of old bubbled dangerously to the surface. She'd heard renditions of this speech from those who claimed to have her best interest at heart. It was the reason Mother and Father had given her when they packed her up over a year ago and shipped her off to distant relatives in England. So she might learn responsibility and self-control.

Her fingernails dug into the cold stone. More like suffocate to death from all their rules and expectations. It was no way to live, certainly not for her, and certainly not for any poor creature she saw relegated to the same fate.

Alec moved next to her. His masculine scent of washed cotton and blue skies drifted to her nose. "You meet my sister once —"

"Twice."

A disgruntled sigh rattled in his throat. "Twice you've met my sister and now you presume to know all the answers. The American ability to know everything defies logic."

Ducking her head back inside, Lily bumped it on the window frame. She winced and rubbed the throbbing spot. "Why do you hate Americans so much? Is it because we won the war?"

His eyebrows slashed together. "No. You fought against the tyranny of England, our common foe. It is your naïve optimism that disturbs me."

"We put aside our differences with our foe long ago, as I believe you did. Everyone is getting along now. They even signed a few treaties if I remember from my history lessons."

"Some wounds never heal."

Scots and their pride. Though she'd only

been in the country a short time, she'd heard the stories of the infernal messes it stirred and the depths to which they would go to protect it. She'd never been among men so prideful, so stubborn, so hardheaded — nor so brave.

Alec stared across the vast land of his forefathers. The wide greenness of it, the deep blue of water and sky, the wild tumbling rocks, and the untamable wind that bowed to no master. Longing fissured through what had always seemed a complacency with her life to reveal the underlying cracks of loneliness.

How would it feel to belong to such a land? To grow here with roots firmly embedded in the soil? Certainly Lily was proud to be American, but she never felt entrenched to the land as one might here. Growing up in New York it was difficult to feel anything beyond the cement under one's shoe. Here one could walk on the same sod undisturbed for centuries, a tangible binding from past to present.

Alec's grip tightened on his cane, whitening his knuckles. Just as they did every time his leg pained him, though he tried to hide it. History, land, or injury. Pride had many layers. And she had trampled on more than one of them since arriving.

"Please allow me to visit Viola again. I promised to tell her about the flowers." Alec's mouth flattened with indecision as brotherly love and concern warred against each other. Lily pushed on. "I promise to shut the windows and draw the curtains to her convent should she be overwhelmed by the novelty of having a sunlit room."

A muscle ticked near the vein in his neck, the course of blood strong and steady beneath his tanned skin. A deep breath filled his lungs and stretched the fine white cotton shirt across his wide chest. "You may visit."

Lily squealed with delight. "Oh, thank you! Thank you! I promise you won't regret it."

"I already am."

"You'll rethink your opinion after you see the dresser overflowing with thistles and heather — those are the flowers you have here, correct? — instead of those drippy candles that light only depression."

"Aide Durham —"

"Lily, please."

"You may visit, but do not bring on a kerfuffle by changing everything." Alec snorted. "What's the use? You're going to do what you want no matter what I say."

"Only because I'm right. Just you wait. Before long you'll wonder how you ever could have doubted the opportunity." Elation lifted her to her toes to kiss him on the cheek.

Shock rippled across his face. His eyes widened. His lips parted into an uneven line. A warm, rugged breath ruffled over her nose, eyelashes, and the loose hairs sweeping around her forehead. Confusion collided with uncertainty in his eyes.

Accustomed to his collected reserve, his wavering unnerved her.

Suddenly he was standing much too close. Like standing before the Woolworth Building on Broadway. She could gain no sense of her bearings due to his towering presence drawing her sole focus. Though often shivering in its cool, gray shadow, her heart skipped to warm her throughout.

His confusion ebbed into questioning, then acceptance, then into something innately male and primal. Blue gaze darkening, it dropped to her mouth as he shifted a hairsbreadth closer. She leaned in for encouragement as what had started as a simple act of thanks turned to daring. One kiss to prove that a beating heart lay beneath his unrelenting exterior and she could walk away feeling truly accomplished at having discovered it. And yet, despite the handful of boys who had kissed her in her parents' garden, not one of them drew her in as if by an invisible cord like this. *Alec.*

His lips returned to a firm line as self-control reined him back in. "I have every reason to doubt until you give me cause otherwise, but I look forward to the challenge."

As if thrown into a cold river, Lily's pulse stopped short, then sputtered to claim the surface again. Had she just been rebuffed? "I-I . . . A challenge. Then you shall have it."

"And what challenge might that be? We have enough hardship around here without a stranger adding to them." A tall, painfully thin woman dressed head to toe in black glared at Lily from a few feet away.

"To boost the morale of Kinclavoch's occupants." Not the least bit ruffled by the woman's appearance, Alec indicated Lily next to him. "Mither, this is Miss Lily Durham. She's one of the medical personnel here."

"I know who she is. Her speech gives her away as the American we have hovering under our roof, but what is she doing *here*?" The woman pointed a bony finger to the floor. "This is our private quarters."

"She's been invited here for special advisement that I've given consent to."

Mother and son stared at each other, neither willing to give ground or break first. Lily's eyes darted between them like a table tennis ball.

After several dragging seconds, she could stand the silence no longer and offered her best smile as an olive branch. "Mrs. MacGregor, what a pleasure to meet you."

The woman's pointed chin nudged up. *"Lady Strathem."*

"Pardon?"

"Until my son finds a bride worthy of the title, I am still lady of this house."

Lily's smile faltered. "Apologies. The titles here still pose a little trouble for me, including the military ranks. Last week I called a first lieutenant a second. He eventually forgave me when I brought him an extra helping of bread pudding." Like a glacier in the dead of winter, Lady Strathem's face didn't crack. "What beautiful grounds you have."

"They were when my husband was alive." A thin, dark eyebrow winged as she glanced at the grimy windows. "These days things have fallen into disrepair."

Alec's gaze dropped to the floor. Did his mother not see how deeply her words barbed him? Was she unaware of the prized possessions he'd sold off to keep the decrepit roof over her head? The weight of the tension, vibrating like a plucked violin string, settled in Alec's clenched jaw.

"I still find them beautiful. New York has nothing like this, and certainly not such immaculate stables. It must take a great deal of dedication and know-how to keep them and the occupants in such well-standing."

Alec's gaze lifted to Lily's. Surprise shifted in the blue depths. His shoulders straightened. "Excuse us, Mither. I believe we have company just arrived."

Lady Strathem's black eyebrow spiked. "Wright." Alec nodded as a look passed between them that gave no well wishes to their visitor. "The man has always been persistent in lost causes. He should have learned no means no a long time ago. Instead he's chosen vindication."

"What lost cause is he vindicating?"

Pursing her lips tight, Lady Strathem brushed past them. The lack of answer turned Alec's mood fouler as he and Lily continued their descent to the great hall.

"There you are, MacGregor." A cold smile tilted the man's thin lips as he strode across the foyer to meet Alec and Lily at the bottom of the stairs. "Nurse Hartley was just telling me she hadn't seen you all day, but it appears you've been otherwise detained. I

134

hardly blame you for such company."

When their host made no polite effort for introductions, the man turned to Lily with a short bow. "Richard Wright, at your service."

Lily offered a polite smile as his clove aftershave stung her nostrils. "Lily Durham."

Recognition sparked in the dark-brown eyes. "Ah, the American."

"My reputation precedes me once more."

"You're in Scotland now, Miss Durham. Not much goes unnoticed, and as a newspaperman I have eyes and ears everywhere."

"I'll keep that in mind next time I require the latest gossip. Oddly enough, you don't sound local to Scotland."

Something flickered across the man's face, but Lily didn't dare call it emotion for such a tightly etched expression. "Dorset is my place of birth, but I've long considered Scotland a second home with old ties of friendship often bringing me back." His eyes drifted up the staircase, then cut to Alec. "Speaking of which, I haven't seen your mother in some time. I trust she's well."

Alec crossed his arms over his chest. "Well enough."

"We go way back, she and I. And your father."

135

Alec's cane tapped impatiently against his side. "What are you doing here, Wright? It's only been two weeks since your last unexpected visit, and why are you bothering Nurse Hartley?"

"Nurse Hartley was kind enough to open the door when I rang."

"It's not her job."

"I suppose it's not, but I'm certain you'll forgive her. Women are much too pretty to be angry at all the time."

"You still haven't stated your reason for being here. Again."

"I came to see if I could sweeten my offer for you." Wright passed a slim hand over his slicked-back strawberry-blond hair. "May we adjourn to your office to discuss business matters?"

Alec's cane twitched over the top of his knee-high leather boots. Worn and creased, they barely noticed the additional scratches. "My answer hasn't changed. You have nothing with which to entice me."

"You've yet to hear my offer."

"I'll listen for as long as it takes you to walk out the door and step into your auto. I've no time to banter inconsequential dealings."

Pivoting on his heel, Alec strode through the front door. Wright's jaw clenched as he settled his black homburg atop his head and turned to Lily with a stiff bow. Lily stared at the front door as it slammed shut, leaving her as last person standing in the social muck that had transpired seconds before.

One year she'd been on this island, and she thought she'd come to understand its inhabitants as well as she could. She'd grown accustomed to the watery brew at teatime, beans on toast, and even Bertie's cold dismissal of any writer or poet not British. Then she came here and found a wholly different breed.

Lily rubbed a hand over her eyes and turned for the dining room to begin her shift of laying out plates and cups for supper. Dark paintings of past Lord Strathems stared down at her passage. Arrogant, brash, proud to the point of breaking before bending, suspicious beyond reason, attack ready at any given moment, and fierce. And that was only the current master.

Sighing, she turned into the spacious room. Its walnut walls gleamed in the candlelight. Grabbing a tray of bowls, she placed them around the oblong mahogany table. Alec had wanted to kiss her. She'd seen the desire spark in his eyes, but he held back. Was he afraid she wouldn't let him? Or did a moment's hesitation find her less than enticing?

A bowl hit the table harder than intended. Who did he think he was? The Almighty's judge here on earth? Did he have such a high opinion of himself that he considered it beneath him to kiss her? She slammed another bowl to the table. He was a bad-tempered Scot who lived in the middle of nowhere exciting. She was probably the first girl to stand close enough for longer than two seconds before running away in terror from his growl. Of course he didn't know what to do. *Next time — no! No next time.* What was she thinking?

Grabbing spoons from the side table, she slid them next to the bowls. If he wanted to play high and mighty, then so be it. She had more important things to think about than Lord Alec MacGregor and his beckoning lips.

"Why are you not sending out more men to search for Captain Gibbons?" Alec fumed in the middle of Laggan's police station, gathering all attention to him like angry gray clouds whipping into a hurricane. He didn't bother acknowledging anyone beyond the squinty-eyed mole excuse for an inspector in front of him. "Or is such a task beyond the aptitude of your force?"

The inspector stared up at him from behind the protection of his battered little desk. With his oiled black hair parted in the dead center and combed to each side, he adjusted the round-framed glasses on his nose as if he could see better than the squint allowed. A mole if there ever was one.

"Lord Strathem, as I have told you before, we are doing everything we can for the missing person."

"Captain Gibbons. And he's not simply a missing person. He's a soldier in his majesty's army who has been wounded in service to our country. Instead of receiving proper care at the convalescent home, he was dragged out into the mud, broken and bleeding, and taken who knows where or if he's still alive."

"I understand your frustration —"

Alec landed both fists on top of the desk and leaned forward. "Do you? Because if you clearly saw the situation you'd ken well I'm beyond frustration. A man was kidnapped on my lands and as such is my responsibility to see him found."

Having scooted away at Alec's sudden closeness, the inspector inched his way back to the desk and straightened a lopsided pile of folders. A water ring and biscuit crumbs marred the top one. "You have been advised to allow our police forces to complete the investigation without further involvement on your part."

"If you were doing your job, I wouldn't have to involve myself."

"The last thing we need is you leading a search party of your own only to have you kidnapped. Or destroying potential clues. Inadvertently, of course."

"Clues. Such as the bloody bandage I brought in from the *Tannasg* Tarn, the one your team seemed to have missed? Is that the kind of clue you mean, Inspector?" Alec took a hard breath through his nose. How did this so-called inspector ever pass his exams? If this was an example of his sleuthing abilities, the county was in trouble.

"A stroke of luck, though I have no doubt my men would have found it."

"Before or after the body?"

It was the inspector's turn to let out an exasperated huff of his own, slipping his glasses farther down his nose. "Lord Strathem, I ask again that you return home and leave the investigation in my hands. I shall send for you if anything further is discovered. In the meantime, please only contact this office if you hear more from the kidnappers. Ransoms are often required in situations such as these."

A lesser officer inched toward the door, encouraging Alec out. Alec wouldn't leave until he'd finished saying the very thing that had been eating away at him. "Do you not find it odd that no ransom has been demanded? Or why a wounded soldier was kidnapped in the first place? As far as we know the captain is of a comfortable but by no means wealthy situation. It leads me to believe this kidnapping has a more personal intent than extorting money."

"All of which is under police investigation." Pushing from his chair, the inspector scuttled around his desk and beckoned Alec out the door. "Good day to you, Lord Strathem."

It wouldn't be a good day until Gibbons was found and the reason behind his kidnapping discovered. Alec could not call himself worthy of the title laird unless he ensured safety for all on his land.

His resolve rested uneasily as he leaned low over Appin's neck and galloped back to the castle. The wind tore at his hair while heavy horse hooves thundered deep in his chest, but not nearly loud enough to drown out the unanswered questions churning in his head. Truth be told, it wasn't merely the kidnapping grinding his agitation to a fine point. Rather a certain woman lacking points due to a series of finely sculpted curves.

Alec had come close to kissing Lily. Desire, quieted for too long, had stirred in his blood when she turned those full green eyes on him. Tilting her face up to him, she'd waited, her mouth begging for his touch, and it took every shred of self-control to resist. Life was complicated enough without a woman tangling it up. Especially a flighty, pampered one. With skin of creamed milk and hair of spun golden wheat . . .

He slammed closed the door of his mother's sitting room, having arrived home with no sense of calm.

Mither gasped. "We've enough problems without you rattling the panes down. Expensive to replace, you know."

"Aye, Mither. I know it." Alec knew the cost of every window, rug, vase, stone, screw, and nail in the house. Day after day was spent agonizing over which precious piece of his family's heritage to tear off next. Bits of his home lost forever. Next to go would be the few tenants whose families had farmed this land for the past six generations. Soon he'd have nothing left but the clothes on his back. He'd give them gladly if it meant Kinclavoch could stay in Mac-

Gregor hands and the tenants on their farms. "I saw the inspector today. He's no further along in the investigation than he was last week. I think he's satisfied in calling it a murder case and moving on."

"As you should. Police matters are none of our business."

"They are when the crime was committed on our land. As laird —"

She stabbed the material in her hands with her needle, drawing a welt of red thread through the snow-white fabric. "As laird it is your responsibility to see to Kinclavoch and those who reside within it."

"That's what I'm trying to do."

"No, you're off seeing to a perfect stranger when your duty is to your family first."

Alec flexed and curled his fingers. He should have stayed out riding longer to cool the blood thrashing in his veins. Its severity only increased with this conversation. "My duty is to all on MacGregor land. Stranger or not, the captain is under my care."

"He's under the British Army's care. Allow them to handle their missing persons."

"The English are inept at the simplest of tasks, much less a manhunt in the wilds of Scotland. I'll not rest until he's found."

"Waste of time."

The proverbial bucket of cold water to the

143

face that was his mother. He'd long ago grown accustomed to her freezing sting, but it didn't stop him from trying to make her see beyond her own sour moods. He dropped into a low cushioned chair opposite her, wishing he could drain his mind dry for relief from its tormenting thoughts.

She spiked a sparse eyebrow at him before dropping her attention back to the needlework balanced across her black velvet knees. "No need to break my chairs with all your flinging about."

"Mayhap if you didn't prefer such spindly chairs." Pulling the *sgian dubh* from the top of his boot, he pressed the tip of the small blade into a smooth spot on his cane and let it mark where it willed.

Mither slipped the needle through the stretched canvas for a second rose petal. Always roses. " 'Tis proper for a lady to have a sitting room and be surrounded by her own fine things as your father said so. Of course, my own parlor was taken from me by those soldiers you let in, forcing me to retreat to the old nursery. If my friends ever saw me like this . . . What would your father think?"

Six years since Father drank himself straight into the loaded end of a pistol, and she refused to lay aside her mourning.

Those who'd called themselves friends gave her up long before that. No respectable woman of society wanted to be seen entering a house of debt with tattered morals.

The tip of the knife slid up in a long, narrow line. "Homes are opening all across the country to give these men a place to rest. Sacrifices must be made."

"Have we not given them our finest livestock, our best horses save two, and the best vegetables from our garden? Must they force us into the shadows of our own home too?"

"These fighting men need everything we have to offer even if that only means a bag of grain and a clean pillow to rest their heads. It is our duty to give what we can" — the blade nicked into his cane: his blasted, bloody, cursed cane — "since we cannot contribute in other ways."

"And what precisely is Richard Wright offering as contribution?" A disgruntled noise passed her lips as she jabbed the needle into the canvas once more. "Why must he insist in trespassing on our goodwill every week?"

"He's a horse with a bit between his teeth."

"Well, he needs to spit the bit out. Mac-Gregor lands are not for sale." She bent her head back to her task. Afternoon light peaked through the lacy curtains and settled into the gray strands of hair winging over her ears. "Your father never would have allowed such a horror."

Alec squeezed the knife handle in his fist. Lachlan MacGregor had certainly done everything he could to send his family careening down a detestable path. A few more unlucky hands at cards, another mistress, or more crate loads of booze and they'd have been sunk for good. Shame snaked through Alec at the swell of relief he'd felt the day Father died.

"I'll see us through, Mither."

"Your Father . . . He tried so hard to do his best." She bit her trembling lip as the shaky words came out. "No one ever thought so, but I saw. I knew his heart was good."

Agitation burned up Alec's chest like bitter bile at her blind loyalty to the husband who'd lacked the strength of character to uphold the simplest of marriage vows. Her love was strong enough to conquer any and all flaws Lachlan MacGregor might have possessed, even beyond the grave where her memory shaped him as the husband he could have been instead of the man he truly was. It was nothing short of an obsessive poison she had deluded herself with rather than face the painful truth that she had never been truly loved in return.

Alec could never walk on water for her like she thought Father had. Miracles were for saints and those desperate enough to think the Almighty cared about them. "Heart won't matter when the bank forecloses and the leeches come to call. Wright is the worst scum of the land, but he won't be alone for long."

"He should have learned his lesson on the finality of no long ago, but it seems not."

The knife stilled in Alec's hand. "You and Father had a friendship with him. Did it sour?"

"For my part. He wouldn't let things go. Still can't, it seems."

Was that the reasoning behind Wright's determination to buy Kinclavoch? Because of an ancient grudge? "Each time he calls he asks after your welfare." Alec studied his mother's expression, waiting for any hint of reaction.

Mither had mastered the timing of concealment for her feelings and when to let them spew. Offering him nothing, she jabbed her needle into another bright-red rose petal.

CHAPTER 7

"Are you sure you don't need anything else?" Lily stuffed the pillow behind the sergeant's back.

He shielded his eyes from the midday sun and grinned up at her. "Lap is awfully cold. Could use a bonny lass to sit on my knee and warm me up a bit."

"I have something even better." Lily pulled the tartan blanket from under her arm and tucked it around his legs, making sure to keep the edges from the wheelchair's spokes. "There. Snug as a bug."

The corporal sitting in the lawn chair across from him laughed. "Nice try, Sergeant."

Bertie wedged a small round table between the men and set a game of backgammon on top. She held the corporal's chair steady as he swung his remaining leg underneath the table. "Glad to see you chums in high spirits, and I hope it continues no mat-

148

ter the victor. Unlike last time."

The sergeant pointed a scabbed finger at the corporal. "He cheated."

"A superior skill never sinks to cheating, Sergeant, but I'll give you a few lessons as you're in sore need of them from yesterday's thrashing."

As the men hounded each other, Lily and Bertie walked a few feet away and settled on a tartan blanket of red and green. The green nearly matched the carpet of grass rolling before them down to the blue ribbon of water slipping around through the thicket of birch and rowan trees that had spread wide their limbs to welcome the full throes of spring with leafy delight.

Lily tucked her legs close to her side so the silver buckles on her shoes peeped out just below the hem of her dress. Still not a favorite with Matron Strom, but Lily suffered from the discomfort of standing in them for ten hours straight to give her horrid nurse's outfit a touch of pretty. She shifted position as the corset dug into her hips, but it offered no relief.

"This corset needs to come off."

Horror escaped Bertie's lips as her head swiveled to the men surrounding them on the lawn. "It is not time to undress. How can you suggest such a thing with male ears all around?"

"I can barely move in this thing, much less breathe."

"You've worn one your entire life."

"Not while bending over and scrubbing floors."

"The maids do all that and still wear one."

Lily reached around to her back, desperate to scratch through the dress and yank at the too-tight strings. "For such a champion of basic human rights, I cannot believe you defend this polite form of torture."

Bertie eyed her over the top of her spectacles, nose thinning as her chin tilted down. "It is part of our proper dress."

"Proper dress, my foot. A notion invented by those too boring to have fun." Lily tugged at the steel band gouging into her hip. "No one can have fun in a straitjacket."

"Our mothers would disagree."

"My mother wouldn't have a word to say if she saw me lounging on the ground without a chaise in sight. She'd faint before she could get out a single outraged syllable." Lily swung her legs in front of her and leaned back on her hands as a low breeze brushed the faint scent of honeysuckle under her nose. Her skin tingled at the first touches of sunlight in weeks. Sunny days were few and far between, and she refused to ruin the glorious occasion with thoughts of Mother.

"Mine would have more than enough for both of them." Sighing, Bertie reached into her pocket and pulled out a creased envelope. She carefully pressed it against her knee and rubbed her palm over it to smooth out the wrinkles. "I've had a letter from Reggie. He says the correspondence office is busier than ever with the German U-boats circling like sharks in the Mediterranean and the Dardanelles campaign proving a stalemate that borders disaster."

Lily glanced over at three soldiers near the house, reclining in chairs. A breeze stirred the edges of their standard blue hospital robes, nudging the collars open, but not one lifted a bandaged hand to adjust them. They hardly spoke beyond a whispered thank you or a single grunt when their burned limbs were bathed. "To believe the papers, your Tommies are down there enjoying ice cream socials."

"Poor chums. Most tell me all they'd like is one bite of food that doesn't taste like rancid dirt." Bertie squinted as she scanned the letter. "Yet Reggie's been to more than one commanding officer's charity gala that boasts stuffed mutton, butter rolls, and fruit cakes."

"He should make it his mission to stuff as much as he can into his pockets and send it out into the trenches. Maybe this war will end faster with good food in the boys' bellies."

"Seems he's too busy playing patty fingers with a colonel's niece for that. The Honorable Joan Dawson."

"Honorable, my, my. I'm sure your parents are over the moon about that."

Bertie brushed at the dark-brown hairs slipping down her neck. "Delighted that the bloodline is nearly secured. Next box to tick is marrying me off so I'm not the spinster sister hiding like some troll under the grand staircase."

Lily smiled. "You'd make the prettiest troll I've ever seen. I'm sure not even the Honorable Joan has your beautiful brown eyes."

Bertie snorted. "Whatever color hers are, I doubt they're hidden behind glasses."

"What's the harm with glasses? You have silky brown hair, lovely eyes the color of melting chocolate, and a figure that can fill out a ball gown better than anyone I've seen. The good Lord had to give you at least one affliction or it wouldn't be fair to the rest of us girls."

"You're being kind."

"Someone has to since you aren't to

yourself. And it's no kindness when it's the absolute truth."

Refolding her brother's letter, Bertie slipped it back in her pocket and smoothed down her skirt. "Do you really think I have a shapely figure?"

Lily rolled to her side and propped herself on her elbow. "I tried on that blue velvet gown of yours, the one with the cream underskirt and bow on the back, and it hung on me like a potato sack. Do you know how many handkerchiefs I would need to stuff into the bodice to round it out?"

Scarlet flamed Bertie's cheeks as she smacked her leg. "Shh! Someone will hear you."

"Good, maybe we'll spark interest. One of these boys is bound to be a decent suitor for you."

The blush burned down Bertie's neck, bright red against her starched white collar. "We are here t-to nurse the mind and b-body. Medicinally only."

"A sweet smile can go a long way toward healing the unseen places within the spirit." Lily winked at her. "Give it a try sometime, and you might just surprise yourself."

Bertie bristled like a pine cone. "And turn into Nurse Hartley? No, thank you."

"Polite, efficient, and teacher's pet hardly

make for a coquette. Unless you find ice alluring."

"She's had a keen interest in Lord Strathem for years. Ever since her family took a second home in the neighboring county ten years ago. Been after the title of Lady of Kinclavoch ever since."

"And here I thought you weren't given to rumors."

Bertie shrugged. "This is a small island. Everyone knows everyone's business, especially if there's a title involved. There are only so many of them to go around and triple the number of females vying for them. Besides, she calls him Alec. In public. Only a woman staking her claim does that."

Lily rested her elbows behind her and leaned her head back, allowing the warm sun to bathe her face. "She needs to change tactics as it's apparent witty repartee isn't going to secure the man."

"Her father will provide a large enough dowry to cover any shortcomings of personality. Even a Scottish one in a pinch, though I daresay our lord in resident seems immune to feminine charms."

Other than her simpering smiles, it was doubtful the proper Miss Hartley had invited Alec for a kiss. Which meant he'd never had the opportunity to turn her down.

Lily's fingers curled into the tassel around the blanket's edge. Unlike his refusal of her. "Why do you say that?"

Shrugging, Bertie plucked a blade of grass. "He's hardly seen around the estate, and when he is, he seems to prefer brooding by himself."

"I believe he doesn't want to get in the way."

"The men whisper about him. Say he's cowering away in shame for not fighting."

Lily bolted upright. "Those sorry, good-for-nothing gossips! Do they expect him to crawl through the trenches with his cane? He's opened his home to them, and they have the gall to slander him for cowardice? If they knew what he's doing to —"

She bit her lip to hold back the venom. Bertie would never repeat a confidence, but it seemed dishonorable to lay out the man's ruinous circumstances, especially when she herself wasn't supposed to know about them.

Bertie studied the grass between her fingers, each slender green vein highlighted in the sun. "Has he told you what happened to make him carry it?"

"Why on earth would he tell me such a personal thing?"

"Because every time he's spotted, you're

never far."

"He's not some mythical beast like that loch monster the locals are always going on about, nor am I the trailing fisherman trying to cast my line for him. Coincidence, nothing more."

Irritation swelled at her need to defend him. She didn't want to think about him, had tried oh so hard to focus on everything but him, but Alec MacGregor was not a man to be put off. Unless it was interest in kissing her.

Bertie tossed the grass in the air and swiveled her head like an owl to stare at Lily. "My dear cousin, something more is afoot than coincidence after half the stunts you've pulled with him. If Matron Strom knew you sneaked up to his sister's room, she'd have you on bedpan duty until the end of the war."

"It's not sneaking when I have Viola's invitation to be there. Besides, what I do on my time off is hardly any of the dragon's affair."

"She'll make it her affair, especially when it goes against the rule of not entering the family's private wing. Invitation or not."

"Viola is kept in there like a frail bird. No fresh air, no sunlight, and suffocating on candle smoke. It's no way for a young girl to live, and I'm going to help her."

Bertie's dark eyebrows winged up. "How? By throwing her a coming-out party?"

"A party! Why didn't I think of that?" Delight tickled Lily as the possibilities soared through her head like dozens of colorful ribbons. "It's exactly what we need to liven up the mood around here. Matron wants us to act like we're in a tomb, but we're not. We should smile and laugh from time to time. Otherwise, what are those boys fighting for?"

"Ever the champion of fun."

"The serious things always have one. Why not the entertaining things as well?" Leaping to her feet, she yanked Bertie up next to her. "Ask nicely and I'll let you help me."

"Golly gee. Can I?" Bertie rolled her eyes. "Don't forget the minor detail of asking Matron for permission."

"Leave the dragon to me. If I could convince Mother to let me go sailing with Jim Hollows unchaperoned, then a party will be a slice of cherry cake."

Grabbing the blanket, Lily folded and tucked it haphazardly under her arm. Their charges were more than ready to return to the house after each losing a game and were too riled up to call it a fair draw. Heated vows were exchanged to thoroughly beat

157

the other on the morrow as Lily and Bertie pushed them back to the terrace where a buzzing crowd had gathered above on the blackened stones.

"What's all the hullabaloo?" Bertie called to a fellow nurse squished between two men on crutches.

"A ship's been sunk by another U-boat. The *Lusitania* off the coast of Ireland. British and American lives lost." The nurse held up a copy of the *London Herald* with its great black headline: "One Thousand Souls Perish. Will the Coward America Finally Fight?"

Cold swept through Lily like frigid wind from a glacier. Every week they heard of a new battle won and lost, while each Sunday produced a list of casualties and lives cut down in the line of duty. Each headline wrapped around their hopes of a swift war like a black cord, cinching tighter until the very air was stifled with despair. But to hear of her own countrymen dying . . . She clenched a numb fist to her breast as her breath settled like lead in her lungs.

The sergeant poked the corporal in the arm. "God rest those mates, but tie me up in a haversack and beat me with a willow whip if it ain't a blessing. Bound to get those Yanks in the trenches now."

The corporal nodded eagerly. "We'll have the war over by Christmas for sure."

"All right there?"

Lily jumped, banging her head on the bed's wooden footboard.

"Sorry, miss." Lieutenant Stoles, the ruddy-cheeked bed occupant, blushed a deep red that burned to the tips of his ginger hair.

"No, I'm sorry. My mind was a million miles away." She adjusted her now lopsided nurse's cap and jabbed the hairpins back in place to keep it steady. Images of those poor torpedoed souls drifted back to the dark corners of her mind where they had kept adrift ever since the terrible news broke nearly a week before. She patted the edge of the bed. "What can I get for you today? *Robinson Crusoe? The Count of Monte Cristo?*"

His eyes swept her trolley filled with books. "Nothing today."

"Can I fix your pillows for you?"

"Thank you, no. Nurse Hartley got them into just the right spot last night, and I'm afraid to move them again."

Lily eyed the stack of pillows supporting his lower back. "I'm sorry for the cot. With the gas victims coming from Ypres we've had to double up the rooms. I believe some of the patients will be healed enough in a few days to be shipped back — I mean, discharged — and a bed should be available for you."

"It's all right. We know that once we get a clean bill of health, most of us will get shipped back to the front. Only the lucky few get to go home from here."

"Are you ready to come down to breakfast this morning, or would you like to continue with a tray?"

"A tray if it's not an inconvenience."

"Certainly not. You may take as long as you need until you feel up to sitting at the table."

"It's not sitting at the table that bothers me." Anxiety worried Stoles's lower lip as he fiddled with the top bedsheet. "It's the other men. They don't know what to make of me."

Lily eased back the edges of the curtain that had fallen over the foot of his cot and pushed open the tall window to allow for a better view of the stables below. "What do you mean?"

"Never mind. I'm sure you've got more important things to do than mind me."

"Lieutenant Stoles, you are the most important thing to me right now." After pulling around a straight-backed chair from next to the walnut armoire, Lily sat and took his hand between hers. "Please tell me."

His Adam's apple worked up and down as his stare roved beyond the grounds outside the window. Finally he swallowed hard. "They think I'm a coward for not stopping them."

"Stopping who?"

"The kidnappers. If I'd had more guts, I could have stopped them from taking Captain Gibbons."

Compassion swelled as she squeezed his hand, forcing him to look at her. "You were prostrate on a stretcher when you arrived. There was nothing you could do for the captain no matter how much you may have wanted."

Wetness crowded his lower lashes. "I should have done *something.* I'm a soldier, his brother in arms."

"War brings out horrible situations, but you can't blame yourself for the abhorrent acts of terrible men."

"He's dead because of me."

A chill shook down her spine. The entire house had whispered of the likely conclusion, but there was no definite proof to give up now. "No, we don't know that. The local authorities are doing everything they can to find him and bring those responsible to justice. Lord Strathem himself stalks the grounds for clues of where they might have taken the captain."

Stoles swung back to face her, eyes wide and anxious. "Does he?"

"Yes, I've even accompanied him on one outing. By mistake of course, but his search is relentless to find even the tiniest of clues."

"And did he? Find anything?"

She desperately wanted to give him the reassurance he sought, but the constable had warned them from false hope. Not to mention Matron would have her by her silver buckles if she worked the poor man into a frenzy. "Only a small piece of bandage and scratch marks."

Tossing the covers away, he rolled to his side. He gasped in pain and fell back against the pillows. "Blast this bruising. Pardon the language. Please help me up. We must return and search for more clues."

Lily scooted from her chair to stuff him back under the blankets. "You're not going anywhere. As I said, the local authorities have this in hand and we'd only be in the way."

"Li— Aide Durham."

Lily turned at the familiar gruffness. Alec

hovered in the doorway, fingers strangling his cane. "A word."

"Certainly."

Alec glanced around the now silent ward. She noticed the men's gazes rake over him, their eyes like pokers burning into him with disdain. Alec's knuckles whitened. "Outside." Without gracing his order with a please, he turned on his heel and left.

Given no choice, Lily followed to find him waiting just outside the room. The floors had recently been mopped and the towering windows cleaned. The faint scent of bleach hung in the air from laundered sheets. Why, even the fern she'd recently taken to watering had finally perked up on its pedestal in the corner.

She took in every detail with great interest except the one that blazed over her. Alec's stare. She felt it, knew the heat of its unwavering severity and the depths to which the blueness plunged. The last time she'd stood so near those depths, she'd nearly tumbled headlong into them. Until his rejection had whooshed her back to the cold surface.

"Inform Stoles that the inspector will be here tomorrow morning for more questioning."

"He told them everything he remembers."

"It seems they have a few more questions."

Lily sighed. "If it helps bring Captain Gibbons back sooner. Please be quick. The lieutenant tires easily."

"I'm not — You inform him."

Lily's head snapped to Alec. Uncertainty wavered against his impenetrable armor despite the tense set of his shoulders. She'd spent hours equally dreading and anticipating their next meeting after that disastrous rejection of a kiss. After all, it wasn't a situation she was commonly acquainted with. Shame told her to hide but wounded pride demanded indifference, to scoff in his face as all proper debutantes were trained to do. So close to him now, she could rally the strength for neither.

"I'm sure Lieutenant Stoles would appreciate the message coming from you."

"I'm certain he would not."

Alec's fingers were bruising purple from his grip on the cane, as if he could squeeze out the whispers from the next room. Whether spoken aloud or not, they followed the lord and master around his own castle with accusations and distrust in the hushed undertones. He'd chosen to hide and it had turned him into a lurking beast.

Lily softened, all vestiges of shame and

pride disintegrating into flecks of dust eager to be swept clean. "We can tell him together."

The corners of Alec's mouth pulled down, but something shifted behind his impervious mask of self-control. A crack appeared in the well-plated armor he bound himself in. "Aide Durham —"

"Lily."

The fingers wrapped about his cane eased back to their normal color as he shifted his weight to his stronger leg. "Despite your contrary insistence, the men have no need to communicate through me. All is best that way."

All wasn't best that way, but forcing Alec to give public speeches wouldn't alleviate the root of the problem. It would only drive him further into his comforting darkness that festered doubt. A place that too often beckoned her.

Lily's gaze swept to his cane. The beginning of an intricate swirl looped up the side. "New carving?"

His eyebrows sharpened, then softened as he studied the line. "Aye. Uncertain of what it's to become, but it'll tell me when the time is right. It always does."

"Has it ever told you to create something you didn't want to?"

He looked at her. The light shifted once more in his eyes, drawing Lily back to that moment of drowning in deep blueness. It stretched between them for a breath of wonderment before snuffing out.

Alec's hand clenched. "Inform the lieutenant." He strode away, back straight and cane tapping in a severe march. Lily's heart outpaced it by a gallop.

"What are you doing out here?" Esther stood at the bottom of the staircase, hands on hips and lips pinched tight. Like an agitated swan, she glided across the hall and stopped inches away from Lily. "You are supposed to be on the third floor this morning."

Lily took a step back to keep from bumping the woman's nose and matched her haughty glare. "Matron reassigned me."

"I didn't realize reassignments included the lord of the house."

If Lily hadn't been trained at the elbow of New York's most razor-sharp hostesses and their cutthroat daughters, she might have claimed ignorance at such a barb. Instead she smiled. "Lord Strathem had a message for one of the patients."

"Well? What is it?"

Lily shook her head. "I was asked to deliver it. Confidential."

Esther's dark eyes shimmered like silt at the bottom of a volcano readying to explode. "From now on, *I* am to speak to Lord Strathem. Your efforts to steal him away every time Matron isn't around are pathetic."

"If you must know, he sought me out."

"Always think you're so clever, that a simple smile will send the men trotting at your heel. Alec MacGregor will never come at your bidding. He's meant for greater things among his own kind." Esther leaned forward, leveling her eyes to Lily's. "And I shall see that he has it."

CHAPTER 8

The last line in the journal smeared under Alec's hand. Grabbing a nearby cloth, he dabbed at the inky mess. Paper was expensive these days, and he had no wish to waste what remained of his limited supply, even if it was only for his insignificant scribblings.

They had started as lists of tasks needing to be done around the estate, then grown into detailed notes. The bound journals lining the shelves of his quarters now contained his most private thoughts and deepest longings. Pieces of himself he would not dare breathe aloud lest they, too, be wrenched away from him. He bled himself dry on the paper as it absorbed every ounce of his heart without censure. The pen moved with the beating of his pulse, the ink a river of his blood, and the smooth pages a captive to his soul.

Alec dabbed once more at the splotchy ink and jerked his hand away from the bold

L staring back at him. His entries had become littered with the *L*-word. Lily pushing the men's beds closer to the window so they might observe the garden butterflies. Lily singing a ridiculous song called "Happy Birthday" before apologizing for the lack of cake. Lily offering dance lessons in the library where the men were supposed to be reading. Lily back on bedpan duty.

The woman had taken to filling his pages and his mind. Every corner he turned he expected to find her wandering lost again. Her laughter danced on the ragged edges of his conscious, daring him to emerge from his fortification of loneliness.

Grunting, he flipped the page and flattened the crease with a defiant smack of his palm. He unscrewed the cap of his fountain pen and jotted down the items that should fetch a decent price to count against their debts.

Knock. Knock.

"Enter."

Guthrie stamped into the room, his face twisted like a gnarled tree root. "Best be coming down tae see this."

Alec frowned as he grabbed his cane and pushed to his feet. "What's she done now?"

"No the lass. An ambulance with police escort."

169

The entry hall clattered with shrill voices jumbled in confusion. A small group of nurses clustered around the front door while others scurried about and patients peeked from every doorway.

"What's going on here?" Alec cut his way through the chaos.

No one paid him any mind as the front doors banged open and a man was carried in on a stretcher.

"Bring him in here." A rock among the pandemonium, Matron Strom directed the stretcher bearers to the sitting room. "Everyone back to their stations and patients to their beds."

As quickly as it had come, the wave of confusion receded to leave Alec and two policemen in the hall.

"Found him out near the ridge next county o'er," one of the men said. "A hunter in the eastern woods came across a bothy sunk low in the ground. Dog kept scratching at the door, and when the man opened it he found this here lad."

"Captain Gibbons," the other said.

Alec rocked forward. "You found him?"

The first policeman nodded. " 'Bout the only thing we got out o' him. Mighty shook up. This was the closest hospital we could get him to."

"His captors?"

The man shook his head. "We're still searching, but it seems they didna tend to their captive much. Mayhap once a day to make sure he was alive. Inspector'll be calling on the morrow to take the captain's report."

"If Gibbons is as shaken as you say, I doubt he'll be recovered enough for an interview."

The policeman shrugged. "Orders and protocol."

Questions burned to be asked, answers demanded for such a horrendous incident to happen on his land. Justice must be sought.

Now was not the time. Alec shook each of their hands. "Thank you, gentlemen. Matron Strom will look after the man from here." He motioned to Guthrie standing behind him. "Guthrie, a wee dram to chase the chill from their bones."

Guthrie waved them down the hall to Alec's study. "Follow me, if ye will, lads. A few drops of Glenavon's finest and ye'll be feeling finer than a toad squatting on a shroom."

Alec moved to the sitting room doorway. He dared not take a step in as this domain had long since passed from his hands to that

171

of the British Army, and they had no use for him. Matron Strom had set up a divider in the far corner to shield Gibbons from the curious eyes of his fellow patients. Ripping material and stifled moans came from behind the curtain as nurses bustled around carrying hot water and towels.

"Why are there no sheets on this bed?" Matron Strom whipped around the curtain with thunder billowing on her brow.

Esther appeared at Alec's side, her starched shirtsleeve brushing against him. "Oh dear. I hope she's not in trouble again. That girl never seems to learn."

Without asking, Alec knew precisely who Esther meant. He pulled his arm closer to his side.

"Aide Durham!" Matron Strom's bellow silenced the room. Lily dashed through the door connecting to the library and skidded to a halt in front of the matron. "Why is this bed not made?"

"I did make it, Matron. This morning as you instructed," Lily said.

"Then explain to me why it is not prepared for Captain Gibbons."

Lily's cheeks flushed pink. "I . . ." Her gaze skittered across the room and landed on Alec's for the space of a heartbeat before sliding to Esther. Shoulders straightening,

Lily turned back to Strom. "I'll remake it at once."

"Not necessary. Nurse Buchanan will take over from here. You're reassigned to scrubbing duties."

"Scrubbing what?"

"Anything that requires a bristled brush. You are excused."

With the grace of a dethroned queen, Lily left the room without looking at anything. Or anyone. Poor lass. She didn't have the manner of things, but she tried in her own ways. Unfortunately, those fell flat at Strom's dictates. Alec gripped his cane, refusing the desire to follow her. What would he say? Sorry your life hasn't better equipped you for service?

Alec frowned. " 'Tis a wonder about Gibbons's bed after being made already this morn."

"Perhaps one of the nurses didn't think Durham had stripped the used ones yet." Esther patted her pristine cap as sadness painted her face. "It wouldn't be the first time Durham has shirked her duties with hopes of Matron not finding out. Such a shame when these Tommies need all the care we can give them, but then, what can you expect from an American? Safe in their own country with an ocean keeping them

173

from harm, they have not an inkling of what it means to sacrifice for a greater cause."

"Perhaps then it is your Christian duty to inform Miss Durham of her selfish ways while setting yourself as the prime example of hospitality."

"I do try so to make everyone feel welcome here in our home." Red stained Esther's cheeks as her eyelashes dropped. "What I mean is, we've done all we can to make Kinclavoch feel like a home away from home for the men. I think it helps to know someone here cares about them despite their injuries." Her hand dropped lightly to his resting atop his cane and squeezed.

Esther's words salted the gaping wounds he'd tried in vain to scab over. He'd carried them so long it was difficult to remember what it was like without them. What it was like to walk through the village without stares and whispers. As the war broke over their shores, the whispers turned to open taunts and people waving white feathers. Coward. Scrimshanker. He'd tried for a commission, but the officers had turned him down, and soon, too, did the enlisted. No need for a cripple in the trenches. So he did what he could for the war effort by offering Kinclavoch as a place of rest, though Alec himself found none of it.

He turned away, breaking her grasp. "I'm certain the soldiers appreciate your concern."

"Not only the soldiers, Alec. If you should ever need anything, I'm here."

Esther's voice floated after him, snatching at Alec's peace of mind. His needs. What did anyone know of those? The world took one look at him and consigned him to pity. A wretched sentencing if ever there was one.

He needed out. Needed air.

Storming out the back, Alec cut his way across the ground to the stables. The gloaming cast its shades of blue, purple, and gray in a fading blanket that stilled the air for the approaching night. It was always his favorite time as the world slowed to a soft hum after the bustling of day, and he clung to it with desperate abandon.

Darkness seeped into the stables, but Alec had known every cobbled stone, every patch of hay and line of stalls since he was a lad roaming the sacred space of his sanctuary. Appin and Sorcha poked their noses out of their stalls, their ears turned forward in anticipation. Alec muttered an apology in passing for his lack of treats, which earned him a snort from each horse. He stopped at the back of the stables and flung open the doors. Cool air rushed in and swirled with the warmth of hay and horseflesh. Alec closed his eyes and inhaled deeply, willing the familiar scents to calm his pounding thoughts. He sniffed again. Rain wasn't far off.

"Alec?" Esther.

With great effort Alec opened his eyes. "I've a mind to be alone just now."

"You're alone too much of the time. It worries me."

"I find solace in the practice."

"Perhaps you've not found the right person to confide your troubles to. I see them wearing on you day after day. Long gone is the carefree young man I met at the Laggan clan gathering. I remember telling Daddy I didn't wish to witness men tossing trees about and playing tug-o'-war, but he insisted I learn the local customs since we were to have a second home in Scotland." Her footsteps shifted softly against the stone floor. "He was right. I've come to adore this place as if I've always belonged. Yet it troubles me to see you carry the worries you do now."

"People grow as do their responsibilities." Alec braced his arm against the door and stared across the wide expanse of grass stretching like an emerald carpet to the far woods.

176

"Yes, the caretaking of Kinclavoch has become a great responsibility, and I do so hate seeing you bear it alone." She stepped closer. A perfume of powder and vanilla wafted under his nose, snuffing out the scent of cool grass. "You needn't put on a front with me. Our families have known each other far too long for that. I've seen the vases and pictures disappear from the galleries. Only last week the acquisitions manager from Sotheby's came by to see the Queen Anne mantel clock kept in the study."

Alec spun to face her, every nerve on edge. "How did you —"

"I'm a woman. I notice details. Especially those regarding you." She rested her white hand on his sleeve. "Please let me help you."

"I don't know what sort of help you imagine I need, but circumstances concerning Kinclavoch are mine alone to deal with as laird."

"Every day there's a new leak in the roof. The grounds are barely farmable. Your family is relegated to a tiny corner of this once glorious house. Is that fair to them? To yourself? We can make it great again."

We. A word tangled with possibilities and scathing disappointments. The few times Alec had allowed himself fantasies, he'd pictured a wife, bairns, and a comfortable home to grow old in. In boyhood he'd devoured picture books of courageous knights and Highland warriors. Always did they have a faithful love awaiting their hero's return home. It's what Alec had always dreamed of finding. But no woman he'd met wanted the dilapidated package he had to offer now. He tried to hold the collapsing pieces together, but year after year, more crumbled to dust through his fingers. Watching Mither and Viola sift through the debris tortured him. How could he bring a wife into such decay with nothing of worth to offer her?

Esther's hand slid up his arm and curved behind his neck. "I hear you walking the corridors at night. Such a lonely sound. It fills my heart with an ache of longing. No man should walk alone without a woman to rely upon. Lean on me, Alec."

Tilting her face, Esther pressed her lips to his. Soft and small, they beckoned him to take command.

He should want this. Esther was beautiful, rich, well sought-after, and moved in the highest circles of London society. The kind of woman who would make his life infinitely more comfortable and his financial standing secure once again, along with being a genteel mistress guaranteed to restore beauty to Kinclavoch. But her gentle insistence did nothing to stoke the fire of desire long smoored within him. It felt wrong standing in the vulnerable darkness with her pressed familiarly to him.

Alec stepped back. "Apologies."

A dreamy look shimmered in Esther's dark eyes. "For what? I've been waiting years for you to kiss me."

"I never instigated such an action."

"Always speaking your mind. Such a refreshing change from the mindless prattle one usually hears around gentlemen, but then you're not like other men, are you?"

Refusing the bait of her curved lips, Alec turned his back and braced his arm against the doorframe once more. "Best be returning to the house. Matron Strom'll not want you caught outside after dark."

Either oblivious to his mood or refusing to relinquish the moment, Esther sighed and moved closer. "The house is a lonely place. A shell compared to the glory it once reveled in. The balls, the shooting parties, the ceilidh dancing, women in silk gowns and evening gloves, men in white ties."

"Those days are gone."

"They don't have to be. You and I can return Kinclavoch to her rightful place as jewel of the county. To her destiny. The one you and I can build together."

"Wartime has no need for frivolous jewels. Sacrifices are what's required."

"Not if you marry well. A sizable dowry, like the one my father is ready to settle on me, would set the lords Strathem up for generations to come. You'd never have to sell another vase to make ends meet. As Lady of Kinclavoch I'd make sure you never go without again."

Fighting to control his frustration at her persistence, Alec dug his fingers into the wood. "No."

Esther blinked widely as the first hint of uncertainty wrinkled her brow. "No? You want to keep selling your family portraits for scraps? I admit some of them are hideous, but my taste —"

"No, Esther. No more." Clenching his cane, Alec stormed from the stables.

Lily clapped a hand to her mouth and crouched lower in the hay. She'd never been witness to a marriage proposal, but she sincerely hoped they weren't all as blighted as the one she'd just overheard.

Alec's footsteps had faded away. Lily could imagine him taking his frustration out on each step of dirt beneath his boots, stomping it down and daring it to protest his mood. Poor man. Selling off pieces of his home, his history, his legacy simply to keep the roof from collapsing on their heads. With no one to help shoulder the great burden he tore himself inside out to alleviate. What could have led to such dire straits?

Esther muttered a few unladylike words before retracing her steps down the corridor toward the stalls where Lily hid. No, she wasn't hiding. Hiding meant guilt, and taking refuge for a moment's peace was not an action to be found guilty of. It was hardly her fault Alec stumbled in here of a same mind. Or that Esther followed. Despite the reasoning, hunkered in a horse stall after overhearing that monstrous speech was not a place Lily wished to be discovered.

Yet at that precise moment the horse decided to step sideways and flick its tail in Lily's face. She jumped, banging into the stall door.

Esther's eyes snapped to her. A tumult of emotions flashed across her pale face until finally settling on a disdainful sneer as she stepped closer to the stall. "Hear everything you wanted to?"

Lily picked hay from her apron and met Esther's glare over the low door. "I was here and quite alone before your little interlude. Speaking of which, did you hear everything *you* wanted to?"

"Alec MacGregor needs me. He simply doesn't know it yet. A fault I am patiently endeavoring to correct."

"Lord Strathem is many things, but a problem in need of solving is not one of them. If there are issues at hand, he appears to prefer handling them in his own way."

Esther's lip curled. A tigress in starched petticoats. "Quite an expert you've become on our resident lord and master. Tell me, are all the American girls in search of a titled husband as knowledgeable of their target as you?"

"I wouldn't know, but then I've never had to throw myself at a man to get his attention." Spoken with the precision of a socialite's cutting blade, the cattiness soured in Lily's mouth. "Pointing out a person's shortcomings is a cruel blow, no matter the person's rank and title."

"You know nothing of our ways, of what it takes to keep them in hand so they do not die out with every spin of the world."

"Perhaps not, but pride is the same in any land."

Esther plucked a piece of hay from Lily's shoulder and snapped it between two slender fingers. She flicked the pieces at Lily's feet. "Stay away from Alec MacGregor."

CHAPTER 9

Lily ducked out of the stables and raced across the yard as rain pelted her. After Esther left, she'd had no desire to return straightaway. The horses — being the good company they were — had cajoled her into a lovely scratching session while patiently listening to her long list of self-woes. Promising to return in the morning with apple slices, she became aware of the downpour outside. And she was without an umbrella.

Avoiding the front door lest the dragon be on the prowl set to devour her at first sight, Lily sloshed around to the kitchen door. Locked.

Bang! Bang! Bang! "Hello? Someone!"

Nothing. She hurried around the side of the house with feet sliding in the mud. A light poked through the drizzling darkness. Lily moved toward it like a moth to its comforting beacon. Where there was light there was help.

A door materialized. It swung in when Lily pushed the handle and she bolted inside. The room wasn't much warmer, but at least it was dry. Shutting the door behind her, she pushed aside the sodden hairs plastered to her face and looked around. Dark wood walls and floorboards glowed like rich oil under the single lamp. Books stacked on shelves lined the walls while a large map detailing the estate hung behind a massive desk carved with age.

Alec's study.

Lily took a tentative step farther into the room, fearful of disturbing the quiet sanctity that seemed to cling to the very grains of the space. How many times had Alec paced this floor, wearing grooves into the wood while weighed down with decisions? His presence lingered, capturing Lily on all sides and drawing her to the center of its mystery.

Her eyes roamed to the desk. Ledgers were stacked high on two corners with a tally sheet between them. Gas bills. Overdrawn bank notes. Bills of sale for two Vermeers. An unopened letter from Richard Wright.

Sadness rippled through her heart. "Oh, Alec. We live under your roof never knowing the ravages you crawl through just to

185

keep it propped up."

Smoothing a rumpled paper, her hand brushed a solid object beneath. A flat piece of wood no bigger than her hand with leaves carved into it. The flower had yet to take shape, but it would no doubt be a beauty under his skilled hand. Lily smiled and carefully placed it down as the words written on the paper beneath caught her eye.

Green fields of longing. Crown of bitter thorns. Hope resurrected.

Lily glanced at the door, then back to the paper. It wasn't right to read another's personal words without invitation, but then again, creativity often hid itself behind modesty. A most highly overrated trait. She tugged the paper out and read the last lines.

When the eyes of Heaven look down upon us, what do they see? Braes of green and seas of crashing life? No. Gone are the days of past where hope once trod. Bones lie crushed in the earth and the sea roils with the blood of fighting men. Where will this misery find its bitter end? When can the spirit reach once more for the goodness it so longs for? The drum beats of war with a steady pulse, ever growing stronger in its rage, but still the heart remains strong.

"What are you doing here?"

Lily jumped. Alec glowered in the doorway. "I-I was locked outside. Your study was the only door open."

"So you barged in?"

"I do apologize, but it was either drown or risk Matron Strom finding me out beyond hours. She'd be forced to concoct another hideous form of torture for me, though by now you'd imagine she would have used them all up."

Alec moved into the room. Waves of anger rolled off him like heat to stifle the shrinking space. "I fail to see how that led to you dripping wet behind my desk."

Lily glanced down at the ring of water around her feet and winced. "I'll clean that up right away, but I couldn't help admiring your wooden carving with the tiny leaves. You must spend hours studying them to replicate such intricate details."

Alec's narrowed gaze dropped to her hand and the paper she still held. "What do you have there?"

"Did you write this?" Lily held the paper up. Questions whizzed through her mind for the reclusive soul who dared to bleed himself so effortlessly by ink and pen. "It's so beautiful that I couldn't stop reading."

"It's not yours to read."

"I know it isn't, and it's terribly wrong of me to snoop, but words like this shouldn't be hidden. You have a true gift."

He stopped on the other side of the desk. Lamplight pooled in his hair like rich mahogany but receded into his eyes with the deepest of winter's chill. "You have a talent for venturing to places uninvited. Get out."

His coldness speared across the desk, causing Lily's bones to shiver. "Please stop shutting yourself away. Your words echo with such loneliness —"

"Your sentiments are not wanted." Nostrils flaring, Alec ripped the paper from her hand and crumpled it in his fist.

"Oh, please don't do that." Lily reached out to stop him, to stop his voiceless words from going unheard.

"Get out." He dropped the wadded ball on the floor and flung his arms across the desk, scattering papers. "Get out!"

Tears flooding her eyes, Lily ran from the room.

CHAPTER 10

" 'While one is broiling a steak one cannot be designing a dance dress, but if her whole mind is on that steak for the time being she will be able to cook it properly.' " Lily clucked and turned the page of the *Ladies' Home Journal* she read under the dim pool of lamplight. No need to worry about rustling pages with all the snoring men on the other side of the privacy screen. Most of the nurses abhorred the night shift, but she had come to find it peaceful. Not to mention fewer interruptions from the dragon. "I'm not certain of that, Miss Mary Pickford. Honestly, she thinks she knows how to write an article because she's a famous actress. Why do we have cooks and seamstresses but for these tasks?"

Bertie shifted on the stool opposite the bed and peered over the rim of her spectacles. "Because not everyone has a domestic at their bidding."

"Well, they should. Ah! Look. 'The Pavlovana. The first of a new series of social dances by Mademoiselle Anna Pavlova complete with pictures.' From the looks of this you'll run the risk of twisting your gentleman into knots but have a jolly good time doing so. What do you say, Bertie? Give it a go?"

"Certainly not. I prefer a waltz if I'm forced into such an undesirable situation as dancing."

"A waltz, yes, how dignified and graceful and boring and English. Where is the spontaneity of fun when you're reduced to moving in a box?"

"I don't require fun outside of a box."

"You do, only you're too modest to admit otherwise." Lily turned her attention to Captain Gibbons, who lay quietly on the bed between them. He was still much too thin from his kidnapping, but color had returned to his cheeks despite his inability to sleep most nights. She and Bertie often sat with him to keep his mind from the nightmares stalking the precious few winks he did manage to catch. "Can you not see our Bertie twirling about to the new Pavlova steps?"

Gibbons leaned up on his elbows and twitched his trim mustache. "Is this Miss

Pavlova qualified to give the general masses instruction on dance steps?"

"I'd say so." Lily angled the magazine for him to see the woman gracing the pages. "She's a Russian prima ballerina made most famous by her dance *The Dying Swan.*"

Gibbons squinted hard, then nestled back against his pillow with a stifled yawn. His eyelids drooped to close. "Too skinny."

"All that leaping on stage helps keep the sweets off, I suppose." Lily flipped the page and scanned the dozen pictures of well-decorated rooms. " 'Looking into Other Women's Homes. Every woman loves to see what the other woman is doing to make her home more attractive.' I don't find that one attractive at all. Too much fringe on the settee."

Bertie snorted. "Haven't you had enough of looking into other people's rooms?"

Lily rattled the magazine and held it up to block Bertie's patronizing gaze. "I never should have told you about that."

"You didn't have a choice when you crashed into our room crying and wrung out like a dog under the soaker." Reaching across the bed, Bertie curled a finger over the magazine and tugged it down to reveal Lily's face. "Have you spoken to him?"

Lily shook her head and looked away. It

had been over a week since that scene in Alec's study, and she'd not seen him since. Not that she wanted to. A scathing mixture of wounded pride and humiliation swamped her night and day. Running into an unsuspecting Alec as she was wont to do would only put her further down the hole of shame. A hole she'd dug herself.

"I wouldn't know what to say to him if I did."

"Start with an apology. That generally helps clear the air."

"I did apologize. He was rude enough not to take it."

"And you were rude enough to intrude on his personal things." Bertie placed a hand to Gibbons's forehead in the practiced way of temperature taking as he drifted asleep. "What kept you so fascinated?"

Lily had not told her about the carving or writing. It was too personal, too vulnerable to share lest the fragile words flake from their painstaking pages and scatter to the indifferent wind. Lily had peered into fragments of Alec that he kept secret from all others. Exposing them to the curious light of onlookers would be an unforgivable break of trust. He had so little of it to begin with.

Avoiding Bertie's searching gaze, Lily tossed the magazine on top of the medical books she'd been hunting through for conclusions about Viola's symptoms. Who knew there were so many diseases chronicling weakened muscles and tiredness? From malaria to the common cold. "Nothing much. A few drawings of the estate."

"I find it rather difficult to believe that Lord Strathem would scold you over a simple sketch of the building in which we all abide."

"His ways are not always straightforward. Scottish and all that."

Gibbons coughed and rolled to his side with a troubled snore.

Lily gathered the blanket around his exposed, bruised leg. "I wish the captain could remember something. Any bit could help us capture the horrible men who did this to him."

Bertie smoothed a hand over her sleeping patient's brow, eyes softening behind her glasses. She never could resist a creature in trouble. "He may recover his memory once his body has had time to heal. Traumatic experiences can put a strain on the mind."

"The police did nothing to help, grilling him as they did."

"Badgering a man until he breaks down is shameful. I told Matron to bolt the door the next time they came with questions."

Footsteps pounded in the main hall and skidded to a stop outside the door. Alec MacGregor flew into the sitting room with hair askew and jacket cast off. He scanned the room and stopped on Lily. A current sparked between them, molding Lily to her chair.

Alec wove through the rows of sleeping men to reach her. "I need you. Come with me."

Under any other circumstances Lily may have fainted away at such a romantic command. One look into Alec's frantic eyes told her that moonlight and roses was the furthest thought from his mind. "What's wrong?"

"It's Viola."

Lily sprang off her chair. Bertie grabbed her arm. "You've already got two strikes against you. If Matron finds out you've been in the family wing again, she'll dismiss you for certain!"

Lily slipped from her grasp. "I have to, Bertie!" she said and rushed away.

Alec guided her up the back stairs, avoiding the other nurses on night shift, nearly sprinting through the twisting hallways of the family's private rooms until they burst into Viola's. Shrouded in smoking candles, the girl writhed on the bed with painful moans.

Alec crossed to the bed and grappled his sister as she twisted near the edge of the mattress. "Viola! That's enough now. Calm yourself before you're hurt, *a luaidh.*" His gaze shot to Lily. Pain pleaded in his eyes. "She won't stop."

Right. Swallowing back her own fear, Lily settled on the other side of Viola and gently stroked her clammy hand. "Hello there, darling. What's all this fuss about, hmm?" She patted Viola's arm. The wet material clung to the girl's damp skin. "No wonder. You're drenched through your nightgown. Alec, be a dear and open the window."

Alec didn't budge. "The night air will chill her to death."

"Or the smoke in here will choke her to death."

A moment of battling wills and Alec finally conceded, his mouth set in a grim line. Flinging back the suffocating drapes, he opened the window. A cool breeze ruffled in to chase out the heavy smoke.

Lily rang out a cloth in a basin of water next to the bed and draped it over Viola's feverish brow. "There now. Isn't that better?"

Viola's thrashing ebbed to shivering

quakes. Her gaze roamed unseeing about the chamber. Dark hair plastered to her bony cheeks, her chest rising and falling on barely a puff of breath.

"How long has she been like this?" Lily asked quietly.

"Years. Mither is usually here to help, but she's taken laudanum tonight, and well . . ." Alec squeezed the back of his neck, the skin reddening under his fingers. His eyes softened on Viola. "I can always calm her after a bit, but tonight she didn't want to give up the struggle. I didn't know what else to do."

"Perhaps Matron Strom —"

"No. I'll not have Viola exposed to the judgment of others despite their best intentions. Besides, Dr. MacLeod has taken care of us since we were bairns. A diet of broth, lemon water, cod liver oil, and bed rest is his prescription."

Lily moved the hair away from Viola's neck. The cool air pebbled her exposed skin. "A prescription that doesn't seem to be helping." She mentally flipped through the medical journals she'd taken to reading before bed, but the diseases and supposed cures blurred in confusion until one swam to the forefront. Rocks? No, something more English sounding. Cricket? Rickets! Her qualifications were severely lacking when it came to a proper diagnosis, but certainly the book's suggested treatment was better than cod liver oil. Anything was, for that matter. "Vitamin D is said to do wonders for poor constitutions."

"I didn't realize you were so well versed in medicine."

"Then why did you come for me?"

The hardness fractured from Alec's face to reveal the deepened fissures of strain beneath. "I could think of nothing else to do."

The confession set a match to the kindling of rifts between them, catching them into purifying fire that burned away the lingering resentment to naught more than cinders. The ash swirled momentarily between them before being swept away on a cool breeze.

For the first time all week, Lily smiled. "Glad to hear I'm your last resort." Alec didn't return her smile, but he didn't quite frown either. An encouraging sign. "If you'll be so kind as to step out for a moment. I believe a change of clothing is required."

Alec left and Lily quickly shimmied off Viola's sweat-drenched nightdress and replaced it with a cool cotton one with purple ribbons at the scooped neck. She opened the door and found Alec pacing. "You can come in. Hold her in the chair

197

while I change the sheets."

Scooping up his sister, Alec sat on a nearby chair and held a much quieter Viola on his lap. She curled into a ball, tucking her feet against Alec's leg.

"Let's see. If I were a pair of sheets, where would I be?" Lily tapped a finger to her chin as she scanned the room and stopped on a wardrobe tucked in the corner. She pulled out a set of clean if somewhat musty sheets and an embroidered pillowcase and placed them on the trunk at the foot of the bed, then began stripping the mattress.

"I'll do that." Alec started to rise and set Viola in the chair, but Lily waved him down.

"Nonsense. There's no reason why I can't see to this chore myself. One of the few things I've learned since coming here. Hospital corners still elude me, but why nurses insist you sleep strangled in a strait-jacket is beyond me. I prefer to kick my feet about." Lily yanked, tucked, smoothed, and stuffed until the bed was in the best order she could manage. She turned back the corner of the downy cover and patted the dimples in the pillow. "Your magic carpet to dreamland, my lady."

Carrying Viola, Alec slipped her beneath the covers and pulled them up to her chin. Or tried to. The left side only reached her shoulder.

"What's a magic carpet?" Viola's voice was thin as a silk thread, ready to snap at the slightest pluck.

"It's a magical rug that can whisk you anywhere you wish to go in the entire world. It's from the book A *Thousand and One Nights.* My favorite. Would you like to hear the story?"

Viola nodded. Lily picked up a silver brush from the nightstand and sat on the bed, stroking the soft bristles through the girl's dark hair. "Once upon a time in a faraway land filled with spices and secrets . . ."

Lily melted into the words, the story as alive in her memory as the first time she'd heard it. The room spun with flying carpets, a golden lamp, and Arabian nights filled with diamond stars. As the story ended, she blinked, only to find herself back in the bedchamber now chilled from the open window.

"The end." She shivered.

Alec rose from his position on the other side of the bed and retrieved a wool blanket woven in MacGregor colors, which he draped across Lily's shoulders. His hand brushed the side of her neck as he withdrew. Her gaze flew up to his. Red flushed the skin exposed by his open collar. He spun around quickly and closed the window, bracing a forearm to the side of the glass as he stared into the darkness.

Viola's hand closed around Lily's, drawing back her attention. "Another."

"I'm afraid that's all I can remember."

"Then tell me of New York. Is it true you have no trees?"

Lily laughed and moved a hand to her neck where Alec's touch still lingered. An unintentional brush, but oh how it pressed to her skin, seeping down to trill in her blood. "We have trees, but they're mostly confined to spaces called parks. It's a glorious Sunday afternoon to stroll through one. Some are only a block or two long, but it would take nearly all day to cover Central Park's grounds by foot. In the summer you can listen to music at the pavilion and skate on the frozen pond in winter. I was never very good at that. My legs prefer to wobble while balancing on a knife edge."

"Alec can teach you." Viola yawned. "He's ever so patient and graceful."

"Men don't care for being called graceful." Alec growled from his post by the window.

"Well, you are." Viola yawned again as her eyelids fluttered closed. "Lily sees it too."

Not knowing how else to deal with that

declarative insight, Lily laid the brush aside and checked Viola's pulse as she'd seen Bertie do. Steady and even. She breathed a prayer of relief as she stood. Hopefully the poor dear would find peace from her ailments in sleep.

"Alec?"

He came to the bed at his sister's call. "Aye?"

Lines creased Viola's forehead like crinkles in parchment. "It won't come back, will it? I'm safe now?"

Leaning over, he pressed a kiss to her forehead. *"Bi samnach, tha mi seo."*

His steadying touch smoothed the drawn lines. Turning on her side, Viola pulled the cover over her shoulder and promptly fell asleep.

"She rests easy after these episodes. Wakes bright as rain in the morn."

"Do you sit with her all night?" At his nod Lily pulled the blanket tighter over her shoulders and settled in a chair. "Then I hope you won't mind the company."

Without a word Alec sat in the chair on the other side of the bed and pulled a block of wood from the nightstand's drawer, then a small knife from his boot. The edge of the blade glided along the wood with a throaty scratch, curling away brown slivers that spiraled to the floor. The wood piece was dwarfed in his hands as he cradled it like a glass egg, deftly turning it this way and that, the shape almost eager to form at his bidding.

Lost in fascination, Lily leaned her head against the chair back. What silhouette did his mind desire, or was it simply following the lines predestined in the grain? He once told her the wood would reveal itself in its own time. A lock of dark hair, oiled bronze in the candlelight, slipped over his forehead, breaking the fierce lines of concentration. Perhaps tonight she had seen the bark crack with a strength raw and pulsing beneath. Time would tell, indeed.

Alec gathered the pile of spent wood shavings and tossed them into the dying fire, then replaced the whittled wood block back in the drawer where it would rest until he was called to another night's vigil. His bones ached from sitting all night but slipped easily into mobility after years of quick risings.

Crossing the room, he peeled back the heavy drapes to reveal a gray-washed morning glowing on the horizon's fringe. Light filtered into the chamber with sleepy resistance, stretching its shadowy limbs across the floor and touching to life those still lost in silent slumber. It swelled over Lily's chair and burrowed into her hair, loosed from its pins sometime during the night. The blonde strands paled to silver. Alec curled his hands to his sides to thwart the temptation of combing his fingers through them.

Lily had fallen asleep faster than anyone he'd ever witnessed. Including Guthrie after a night wetting his tankard at the Thistle and Horn. Long, thick, black lashes rested against her smooth cheeks and one hand was tucked under her chin. Pink lips softly parted. Peaceful as a new bairn.

Snorting, Lily turned over.

Peaceful except when she did that.

Pulling out his pocket watch, Alec squinted at the numbers. Nearly six. The nurse shifts would be rotating soon. He needed to get Lily out of there before Matron Strom noticed she was missing.

How did one go about waking a sleeping woman? Guthrie favored slamming things until the sleeper was startled awake, and Viola was a light sleeper with no need to wake.

"Miss Durham." Why was he whispering if the point was to wake her up? Alec cleared his throat and tried again. "Lily."

Her eyelashes didn't so much as twitch.

"Lily." He touched her shoulder.

Yawning, she arched her back and stretched widely. "Hot chocolate and toast with jam this morning, please. Thank you, sweet." She reached back and patted his hand. Her fingers curled around his wrist and plucked at the wiry hairs. With a gasp, her eyes flew open. She launched out of her chair and whirled to him with cheeks flaming. "Oh, I'm so sorry. For a moment I thought I was back home with my maid coming to wake me."

"Sound much like her, do I?"

"She has a rather deep voice for a woman. Her father was a well digger from Maine, which I believe contributed to it."

Silence settled and the memories of last evening leaped to fill the void. He had grown accustomed to Viola's episodes — small seizures Dr. MacLeod called them — until last night when he could no longer settle her alone. She'd been in danger of hurting herself and he'd been frantic. His mind had cleared for a split second amid the chaos, a pinprick of light flashing in the storm. Lily. She'd come without hesitation. They owed her a great deal. *He* owed her a great deal.

Alec cleared his throat. "I want to thank you for last night —"

"I was only too happy to help, though

204

little I did."

His chest tightened in failure. "You calmed her when I couldn't."

The sunlight shifted on her face, washing away the playfulness of youth she so often wore. "Give yourself more credit, Lord Strathem. You'll find your accomplishments greater than you realize."

"It's Alec." She'd called him by name when the moment of reliance was upon them. Now in the early stillness of morning before the world took on the harsh sophistication of rules and expectations, he wanted to hear her say it again.

"You have a distaste for stuffy titles." Viola blinked sleepily up at them from where she lay on the bed. "Something else you both have in common."

Flushing pink, Lily's gaze skittered from him. She fluffed the blanket at the foot of the bed. "Viola, how are you this morning?"

Viola looked at Alec, a thin line puckering between her brows. "Was it terribly bad?"

"It lasted a wee bit longer than usual, but we managed." He looked to Lily and she smiled back, releasing the tightness suffocating his chest.

"Managed what, or dare I ask?" Their mother's voice screeched into the quiet calm. She stood in the doorway with a shawl pulled tight about her like a shroud. Deep purple bowed under her eyes. The effect of laudanum. She pointed her chin at Lily. "What is *she* doing here?"

"Miss Durham is a nurse. It should be fairly obvious."

"I don't want nurses here. This is our private wing. If something is required, you are to send for me or Dr. MacLeod."

Anger boiled inside Alec. As many times as they'd been over this, she never understood. "Dr. MacLeod has offered what help he can, and you were otherwise detained."

Mither clenched her widow's shawl tighter, pinching white the skin around her neck. "That doesn't change the fact that a complete stranger —"

"She's not a stranger. She's my friend and welcome to visit me anytime." Viola pushed into a sitting position. Gone was the whimpering of last night. "Now if you'll all excuse me, I'd like to get dressed."

"Let me help you."

"No. Thank you, Mither. I should like to try myself this morning."

Mither's lips pressed into a pale line. Glaring at Lily as if she'd brought the pox on them, she left the room, shoving the door on her way out.

Lily twirled the blanket from her shoulders

as if to dissipate the lingering strain and tossed it on the chair. She reached for the brush on the nightstand. "Are you sure you wouldn't like some help? I could do your hair."

With a tired smile, Viola shook her head. "I'm fifteen. For once I'd like to wear something not resembling a doll's frock all day. You'll come back later, I hope. I'm eager to hear another one of the Arabian tales."

Lily laughed. "I should be delighted to give it a valiant go. Surely there's a copy in your vast library." Leaning over, she kissed Viola's cheek and walked out the door.

Viola grabbed Alec's hand and whispered. "Be kind, brother." At Alec's frown, she nodded toward the door Lily had just disappeared through. "Something's thick as parritch in the winter between you two. A kind word will take you further than growling."

So much for thinking he'd hidden it well. "Now who's spinning tales?" Grabbing his jacket from where he'd tossed it hours before, he started for the door. "Concentrate on tying your hair ribbons and leave me to my own habits."

She shied a pillow at him that thumped harmlessly on the floor behind his retreating heels. "Your habits are what lead you into gloominess."

"More like quiet solitude."

"Perpetual loneliness."

Viola's words latched on to his chest, and try as he might to shake them free, their bonds wrapped tight, cutting off his rebuke. Others saw loneliness as something to fear and ward off at all cost, even to the point of sacrificing their own sanity. He protected his solitude with the might of a fortress long since constructed out of necessity.

Rounding the corner, he found Lily pivoting between two hallways.

"Are you lost again?"

"Not this time, surprisingly. I'm trying to decide which staircase Matron Strom is less likely to be guarding this early in the morning."

"The back." Retracing their steps down the private staircase winding along the back of the house, Alec led her through a series of corridors and out a side door that opened to the gardens. "I could use a bit of fresh air. Join me?"

"I'd be delighted."

The stagnant air bottled inside faded as the crisp morning breathed life around them. The crystalline beauty of nature unperturbed slowly roused from night's slumber. Leaves dipped under the delicate weight of pearling dewdrops, and the sweet smell of wet bark and new blooms wafted through the mist carpeting the grass and the gravel avenue down which they strolled.

Covering over eighty hectares, trees of all variations formed a periphery border. Bushes and flowers planted in neat boxlike shapes were laid out along the central avenue and its diverging pathways in a more formal configuration with each section providing its own theme. A wooden table carved from a single oak stump in one set, an arbor of twisted vines in another, and a fountain that had long since run dry in still another. Red, purple, white, pink, and yellow blossoms exploded amid the greenery in a riot of color.

"I've never been an early riser, but this could convince me otherwise. It's breathtaking." Eyes wide and unblinking, Lily gazed at the sweeping scene with awe. "I've never seen so many colors in one place. Your own paradise."

Alec had forgotten to see it as paradise — in fact, he hadn't thought of it as such since he was a lad climbing the rowan trees as they burst to fiery red in autumn. The caretaking of ownership now only afforded him a view of the expense and maintenance he could no longer afford. Gazing about, those old feelings of carefree youth and love for this place pushed past the fret of expense and burrowed into his soul.

"Look at this!" Lily dashed into an area bordered by rhododendron and azalea and knelt in front of a small grassy knoll with wee ceramic mushrooms scattered about.

" 'Tis a fairy mound." Alec squatted next to her and plucked one of the mushrooms chipped with red-and-white paint. "Viola and I painted these as children. For the fae when they crept from their underground homes. I'd hide and wait for them to come out so I could catch one and take it inside for her to see."

Lily touched a squatty mushroom with black spots. "Did you?"

"Caught a toad once."

"At least your efforts didn't leave you empty-handed."

"No, but our governess wasn't at all pleased about finding the slimy creature in her bed."

"You horrid little boy!" Lily's laughter spilled into the air, unrestrained and carefree as the wind across the moors.

"She deserved it for making us wash in frigid water with ash soap to cleanse our souls and keep Auld Hornie at bay."

"Perhaps she did deserve it then." The conspiratorial hitch of her eyebrows whittled away at the distance spanning between them. If he were an honest man, and Alec liked to think he was, he might admit to not minding the shrinking proximity.

Lily stood and brisked her hands up and down her arms as the mist crept over her toes and through the thin cotton of her rumpled uniform. Alec slipped off his jacket and placed it around her shoulders.

Her wee face popped above the folds of wool, green eyes dark against the grayness. "Seems I still can't acclimate to your Scottish weather."

" 'Tis a hardiness we're born with." Though not all. Some were made to suffer no matter the strength in their hearts. The all-too-familiar ache tightened around his heart once more. "You were a true comfort to Viola last night."

"She's a sweet girl. I want to help however I can. As long as your mother doesn't eat me alive."

Alec jammed the ceramic mushroom back into the ground. "My mither is a complicated case of depression and longing for things that will never be again. She had no reason to speak to you in such a way."

"Handling spear-tongued mothers is a

particular specialty of mine. I know well how to fend them off before they draw blood." Lily drew the collar of his jacket up around her neck. "My own mother has high expectations. Sadly, I do not often reach them."

She turned down the path where the moss grew thick between gnarled rosebushes and silver-tipped birches. Shoulders hunched forward and chin tucked down, she appeared to be holding together the cracking vestiges of a confident shell. A shell Alec recognized all too well from the bits and pieces he'd tried to cobble together for himself.

Lily stopped at a statue depicting the infamous Rob Roy MacGregor. Alec's several times great-grandfather. He was missing an arm now but had managed to carry on wielding a sword flecked with springy lichen.

"What did you say to Viola last night? In that other language."

"*Bi samnach, tha mi seo.* Be calm now. I am here. It's Gaelic."

"The same thing Guthrie says when he reaches for his flask."

Alec picked the lichen covering the sword hilt and rolled it between his fingers. "Aye, his usage is a bit more colorful than what my gran taught me."

"You don't speak it often. I've only ever heard you a few times."

"It's not spoken often if at all as the auld ways find themselves dying out. Gran came from the MacDonalds, the wildest of the clans far up in the Highlands. She was determined that we would learn our ancestors' tongue. The Scots do love their words."

"So I'm learning." The lightness dropped from her tone. Their peace suddenly faltered.

Guilt had eaten him alive since the night he'd confronted her in his study. He hadn't been the least bit surprised to find her there as the woman had a habit of wandering into the least acceptable of places, but he'd been unable to control the snap of fury at seeing his writing in her hands. Words that had poured from his tormented heart and meant to be read by no one. Writing was an exercise in purging the burdens of his mind, not for the examination of others. Anger had burned away all responses of civility and he'd struck without thinking.

Alec cleared his throat, girding himself for the no-longer-avoidable task at hand. "The other night I shouldn't have spoken as I did. My day had gone from wretched to unbearable. Then to find someone meddling through my personal papers was an insult to my acquired grievances."

Lily rounded the statue, tracing a line down the sett pattern in Rob Roy's kilt. "I am sorry for looking through your things. My curiosity often overtakes my sense of propriety."

"Curiosity killed the cat."

Her gaze snapped to his with eyebrows sharp as arrows. "I beg your pardon?"

"No, what I mean to say . . ." A dull ache knotted at the base of his skull. Confound the woman for always muddling his thoughts. "While you shouldn't have been in there to begin with, I'm willing to move past the incident."

"How gracious of you."

"Would you rather I carry the grudge?"

"Believe it or not, I'm among the very rare number of women who don't like to remain sour over the past."

"Good. Then we agree."

Lily crossed her arms and cocked her head to the side. An unfathomable look glinted in her eyes. "You haven't had much practice in apologizing, have you?"

"That's what I've been doing." The knot shifted higher until the entire perimeter of his head throbbed.

She stepped toward him, into his pulsing space of frustration, and dropped her hands to her sides. "No. You've been talking about doing away with cats and how this past week's awkwardness has been due to me."

"It is because of you. You should not have read my papers!"

"And you shouldn't have acted like such a beast!"

Alec bowed up for a stinging retort, but her truth punched him square in the mouth. The air sizzled, charged by their hurling bolts of accusation. Alec dared not move lest the friction surge again and char everything in its path. Once upon a time he might have relished such a burn to singe his opponent, but the opponent standing before him now held a unique position. She was right.

He took a step back, away from the current she charged through him. "My conduct was less than that of a gentleman and host. I apologize most sincerely."

Lily stared at him until the cracks of pressure twined about his head once more. Then she flipped her hand through the air and strolled away. "I'm willing to move past the incident."

He stood dumbstruck at her cheek until she tossed a wink over her shoulder. With

215

that, the tempest roiling between them dissipated like fog into the clear sky of the unburdened. Alec caught up to her as she started down a new path dappled with a tangle of late-blooming roses and hyacinths. Trellises arched over them in botanical embrace. Lover's Lane. Pushing that thought out of consideration's reach, new questions flooded his mind until at last he could keep them at bay no longer.

"What did you think?" He winced. Desperation did him no favors.

"Heartbreakingly beautiful." No feigning, only a simple understanding of his meaning. "You have a gift, Alec."

He plucked a leaf from a hanging vine as something unfamiliar yet not unpleasant bloomed in his chest at her praise. "I wouldn't go that far. The paper doesn't judge, nor does it cry foul when the words go astray. My thoughts are too often heavy, but the pen never buckles under the weight." The intimate confession startled him, yet regret didn't rear its bitter head. Lily had a way of plucking words from him as easily as pebbles from a flowing burn.

"It's good to have a confidant in matters that burden us. All matters, really."

She smiled, and before he had time to doubt her words, he smiled back. "Aye."

"There you are, Durham." Their quiet refuge split with a deafening crack. Matron Strom cut down the center of the garden with the grace of a torpedo closing in on its target. Alec and Lily were the sitting ducks.

Lily paled, her fingers nervously working the top button of Alec's coat. "Matron Strom. I can explain —"

"Save your breath and pack your bags immediately. You're dismissed from service."

CHAPTER 11

Rain splattered on the window outside Alec's study. He gritted his teeth. Of all the times his knee flared up, this was the worst. Turning from the steely gray sky, he leveled a glare on the sole recipient of his foul mood. "You cannot dismiss Miss Durham."

To her unnerving credit, Matron Strom stood resolute as one of the gargoyles guarding the northern tower. "As I told you before, the nurses are under my care and supervision even while we remain under your roof. You have no authority in such matters."

"Everything under this roof and on these grounds is under my authority."

"Not according to the contract you signed with his majesty's royal army. While the estate itself falls under your hand, the medical equipment and personnel are under mine. There is no debating this."

Leave it to the English and their insufferable rules to lord over common sense. "Li—Aide Durham —"

"*Miss* Durham. Aide was a glorified title for her. She was only allowed in because Lady Elizabeth's father is a generous donor." Matron bristled with intolerable contempt.

"*Aide* Durham was performing a service to my sister, whom you understand has complications."

"Of which I sympathize, but rules are rules."

All patience gone, Alec thumped his fist on the desk. "*I* placed the rule of none entering Kinclavoch's private wing, therefore it is within my right to forfeit said rule at my own discretion."

"Miss Durham abandoned her post in the middle of the night. I will not tolerate disobedient actions. It is akin to a solider deserting his post."

"My sister required immediate attention."

"Then you should have sent for me."

"I'll not have my sister terrorized by your rough handling that's better suited to the trenches." There it was again. The emergence of the beast Lily had accused him of. Alec spun to face the window. Seize and fire his temper. What kind of man was he if he couldn't control his own crippling weak-

219

nesses? He should have argued for Lily immediately in the garden, but she'd left without a backward glance. Without so much as an utterance in defense of herself. By the time he'd limped back inside, her car was disappearing down the driveway.

Alec pressed his hand to the window. The cold pane battled the heat of his palm, the glass's ambivalent coolness drawing out the pulsing fever that charged his entire body and simmering it to a more wieldy state. There was none to blame except himself. In desperation he'd begged Lily's help and doomed her to the repercussions of such a reckless plea. His only thought had been for Viola. Lily had saved them from the brink of madness, and this was how her unselfish kindness was repaid. He owed her everything.

Behind him, Matron Strom drew in a breath that whistled through her stub nose. "Rules are rules, Lord Strathem. If I allow one exception, where will it end? Leave without asking? Tea gowns in place of uniforms? Ice cream socials in the library? The precedent will ensure anarchy."

"If you think anarchy will arise in the form of an ice lolly, then perhaps you are not as equipped to handle this position as you thought. A fact I'm certain your superior would very much like to be aware of." Dropping his hand from the glass, he turned to face the woman. If this was the path he was forced to take, so be it. He would deal with the guilt of manipulation afterward.

Her sparse eyebrows slanted over her eyes like steel shields. "I am the most qualified person to run this hospital."

"This is a convalescent home. *My* home. I am entitled to the last word. I will not allow you to punish Aide Durham for something I required. Is that clear, madam? If you disapprove of my home and how I run things, I will inform army command that they may find a new address of care."

The grandfather clock ticked through the maddening silence as the rain drove on without restraint like a drum never reaching its crescendo.

"It seems you leave me no choice," Matron said at last.

"But I have. Take Aide Durham back under your firm grasp, or I will hire her myself and she will have free rein under my employ. A thought that sends chills skittering down your spine, no doubt." He had no means with which to hire any help, but the matron need not be privy to that fact. Though it did offer an amusing prospect with Lily flitting about the castle under no one's submission but her own.

As easily as the thought came, a wave of guilt washed it away. Taking Lily from the nursing ward would deprive the men of their much-needed care. True, most of them were long out of danger and merely required quiet days of peace for their recoveries, but medical hands were in short supply this far north.

"You have been given free rein since coming to Kinclavoch, and never once have I interfered. Until now when the blame lies entirely at my feet. Take your rancor out on me if you must, but not Lily."

Matron's eyebrows tilted, not as shields but as blinders on a horse, narrowing her focus. "She means a great deal to you."

The nerves pinched around Alec's knee, buckling his leg before shooting up to stutter his heart. He retreated behind the defense of his desk before Strom's observation could lay him out flat. "A great deal to my sister."

"It's a shame you're not in our trenches on the front lines. That bark would send the Hun scattering. In any case it has served Aide Durham well. I will allow her to return, but only on probation. One more broken rule and she'll be out on her pretty ear for good."

"Agreed." Conditional, but a victory nonetheless. "I also ask that you grant her freedom to visit Viola when she is free to do so."

If the squatty matron stood any straighter, she'd crack her spine. "Anything else, my lord?"

"Where has she gone?"

"The train station. To catch the ten o'clock."

Alec glanced at the grandfather clock ticking sadly in the corner. Nine thirty. He'd have to hurry. Brushing past Matron, he strode into the great hall as it echoed with the men shuffling to their morning activities.

Mither blocked the front door with a forbidding scowl.

"You cannot do this." Her black hair was scraped back into a severe twist, tugging back the corners of her eyes. "It is undignified for the Lord of Strathem to chase after some uppity strumpet!"

The rustle of voices died. No doubt firmly attentive ears strained at each doorway. More witnesses to the feckless MacGregors.

Guthrie materialized holding out a mackintosh for Alec to thrust his arms into. "Have a care with the name-calling. You've done enough damage by seeing to the lass's dismissal."

Mither's brow crinkled. "I've naught to do with that."

"How else would — Never mind. It matters not."

"If you insist on this spectacle, at least send your manservant. That's the only good he brings." Mither waved a dismissive hand in Guthrie's direction.

Never ruffled by an insult, Guthrie held out a sagging hat to Alec.

Alec took the hat and settled it atop his head. "I'll not send someone else to do what is my duty."

He stalked to the door and yanked it open. Rain fell thick and fast, colliding in puddles of marbled gray. Appin stood saddled and ready, his great hooves pawing the muddy ground.

"Have the fire ready. The lass will nay doubt be cold on our return." Alec slammed the door behind him and strode out into the deluge.

Lily pulled out a crumpled hankie and pressed it to her wet cheek. A few brave souls ducked under the cover of the train station and hustled into the cramped waiting room. She had no desire to sit inside and parade her puffy eyes to their curious whispers. Like a wounded bird shaken from its gilded cage, she wished to suffer her disgrace alone.

How foolish she'd been to believe she was creating an acceptable place for herself here. Scotland beckoned her to its unrestrained wildness asking for nothing in return, all the while stealing her heart with no thought of returning it. Not that she wished a return. Unfastening her heart from behind its sheltered walls and offering it to the heather had gained her freedom of self and a confidence of belonging she had lacked on the carefully paved streets of New York. No longer was she required to stage herself as the perfectly reticent lady of society to fluff a patient's pillow or hold a soldier's hand as his bandages were agonizingly changed. They merely asked her to stand at their side providing a sense of comfort. Little could she comprehend how much comfort it had brought to her as well.

How quickly that sense of comfort turned on her with ferocious humiliation.

She glanced at the clock hanging over the waiting room door. If only the train would hurry. Each second was agony. Impatient shame wanted her gone from this place as quickly as possible. She had always found a solace of sorts in distance. Problems never loomed as large nor as hurtful the further behind she left them, and then they faded into a passing memory. Could she fool herself again this time?

The rain shifted, drifting mist across her face. Its coolness swept her cheeks and dotted her hair with tiny glass beads. The scent of heather and wet sheep chased the breeze on wet heels. Once she may have wrinkled her nose at such bucolic scents, but now it swept her back to green fields, an ancient castle, and walks in a dewy garden. A place that existed in the stillness of time. A place that conjured Alec.

Tears washed over her face. She didn't tell him goodbye. A few hours ago she'd walked among the flowers of early morning with him. The day was fresh and without guile as social propriety had yet to rouse itself, leaving them unfettered to its demands. A barrier had broken between them, shifting them into an unfamiliar and unguarded territory. Alec's formidable wall of stoicism had cracked, and she'd glimpsed the untouched splendor beneath. A quiet strength without the customary sharpness bade her into its respite. Vulnerability wove between them, drawing them together with delicate strings — none more fragile than when he'd asked her opinion on his writing. There was the heart she'd deemed beat within him all along. Would she ever see its likeness again?

Tweeeeet! Tweeeeet!

The approaching train's whistle split the air. The mighty black beast chugged into the station, its great wheels grinding against steel with sparking hisses. It ground to a stop with one last bellowing heave. Smoke belched from the stack and poured over the platform.

"All out for Laggan!" The conductor hopped off the back of the train and ambled down the walkway as passenger doors swung open. He stopped in front of Lily. "Where to, darlin'?"

Lily smiled as another tear threatened to escape at his soft brogue. Not quite Alec's deep intonation. How she'd miss the accent. "Hertfordshire by way of Edinburgh."

He pulled on his drooping mustache. "Fine lady such as ye should be sittin' inside, no' out fightin' the dreich."

"I don't mind. It may be my last time to enjoy the Scottish weather."

"Up visitin' yer dearie at the castle, were ye? Aye, many a poor lad's passed through here and his family comes tae see him on the mend. Always best when the *leannan* comes."

The sweetheart. Lily squeezed the hankie

227

in her hand and turned on her ingrained, polite smile. Familiarity was easier to hide behind. "Should I summon the porter to bring my trunk?"

"Dinna fash o'er that. See yerself tae first class now. Nay sense in gettin' drookit afore the trip's started. Wet clothes be a great bother on these long rides." Smiling kindly, he moved down the platform.

With one last glance at the silver clouds swirling in the east far above Kinclavoch, Lily gathered her case of personal items and walked to the first-class cars. A man stepped from one of the compartments, knocking the case from her hand.

"Apologies, miss." He bent over and retrieved her case. Straightening, his eyes narrowed on her. "Pardon me, but have we met? I never forget a face."

Tall and slender as a shark's fin, Richard Wright was even more imposing up close. Lily accepted her offered case. "We met briefly at Kinclavoch. Lily Durham."

His light eyebrows raised above keen brown eyes that missed nothing. "Ah yes. The American nurse."

"No longer, I'm afraid. Though I was never a nurse. More of a glorified scrubber and trolley pusher."

"Is that so? A shame to lose your attentions. The brave boys need all the help they can acquire."

Lily stiffened at the painful reminder and turned the conversation as skillfully as etiquette lessons had taught her. "Do you have business at the castle?"

"The return of the infamous Captain Gibbons. His survival story would make quite the splash for my newspaper."

A shark indeed. The smooth, silky kind that glided along the bottom of the sand waiting for an unsuspecting foot to step on him so he could take a bite. Heat steamed from Lily's collar. "The man has been through a horrendous ordeal. I can't imagine that plastering him all over the front page of your papers for people to gawk at would ease his troubles."

"Trouble sells."

"As does mudslinging with your insidious jabs at Lord Strathem." Lily pointed at a sodden copy of yesterday's *London Herald* on the bench with a bald-faced lie for a headline: " 'Lord Strathem Behind Kidnapping Conspiracy? Why the Royal Army Never Should Have Entrusted the Tommies to His Care.' That article accuses him of plotting the kidnapping for ransom money to pay his debts on Kinclavoch."

Wright merely shrugged. "It is but one

theory floating among the public's opinion. Another is that he hoped to have his position as lord revoked and the soldiers transferred elsewhere. It is unsafe for them to remain under the roof of a scoundrel who would use them for his own profit."

"Lies. His reputation will be ruined."

"So be it."

Lily's anger boiled. "Once you've smeared Alec's name beyond repair, there will be nothing to stop the army from removing the Tommies. Where will they go then? All those wounded men without a safe place to go or kind people to care for them."

"I didn't realize you spoke for the patients. Now that you're leaving." A light glinted in his eyes. A hook sharp with bait.

Lily tilted her hat, blocking the poisonous hook. "I don't speak for them, only for their interests as one who has spent time with them."

"My apologies if I seem callous. The country is hungry for news, for a connection to the boys in the trenches. This is the kind of story that solidifies the bleeding hearts in opposition to the enemy."

She'd like to solidify her hand across his face. Of all the arrogance — to use a haunted man's pain for emotional blackmail at the price of a newspaper. Gobbled up one day and tossed out with the fish bones the next. Alec would have more than a few choice words on the matter. A defender to his marrow. Lily's heart pinched at the thought of him.

Tweeeeet! Tweeeeet!

The conductor walked back down the platform, gesturing people from the waiting room. "All aboard!"

Mr. Wright's focused gaze never left Lily. "Will you remain in England or travel to America, Miss Durham?"

"Hertfordshire. My uncle has an estate there." *One with a lot of clout and money who would think nothing of trampling you beneath his prize racehorse if your newspaper comes sniffing around. I'd volunteer to ride the beast.*

"A wise decision. After the sinking of the *Lusitania* no ships crossing the Atlantic are safe from German U-boats, though it may be just the thing to get you Yanks into the action. We need all the allies we can acquire down in the trenches."

"You should go to work for the war office, Mr. Wright. Nothing like a few thousand souls exploding on the water to strike up the fighting spirit."

"The newspaper is my war office." His lips cracked into a cool smile. "If you are ever in London, do look me up." Touching his

231

somber homburg hat, Mr. Wright moved off the platform and ducked into a waiting black automobile.

Lily shook off his odious presence and stepped into her private train compartment, shutting the door behind her with a resolute click. It was spacious enough with velvet seats worn from years of service. Placing her valise on the opposite seat to deter other passengers from welcoming themselves into her desire for solitude, she sank wearily onto the bench. Bertie should be warned about Mr. Wright's intentions. Lily reached for the stationery tucked in her bag, then slowly withdrew her hand. No. The concerns and patients of Kinclavoch no longer belonged to her. Despite her best efforts to prove she was worthwhile, she wasn't needed.

Alec had needed her.

Wild with desperation, he'd sought Lily out. He'd trusted her to help his sister when he couldn't manage alone. No one had believed in her like that before.

The stale air closed in around her, suffocating and taunting. She drew the window down and stuck her head outside. Rain caressed her face in soothing jabs of cold. What a terrible fool she was going on about a man she barely knew. They'd shared a few moments together and even more arguments. Hardly anything to lay a claim on.

"Marriages are often contracted on less. A title and money can make up for any short-comings."

Lily jolted at her mother's voice prodding the back of her mind. "Who said anything about marriage?"

" 'Twasn't me, miss. Though I'd be willing to give it a go," said a man passing by.

Lily shook her head. "Another time."

The man tipped his hat and moved along.

Overhead, the heavens breathed a sigh of relief and the rain gentled to silver mist. Alec always limped more in the poor weather.

Stop it! He is no longer your concern.

It was time to return to a life of ease where no one counted on her for anything. No responsibilities to be had, no expectations beyond those of a charming adornment. The knowledge left her hollow.

The engine growled forward. Black smoke collided with the soft rain in swirls of dirty gray. Lily pulled her head back inside, watching as the train station slipped by, growing smaller in the distance. Back at Kinclavoch the men would be about their morning exercises confined to the library until the skies cleared, and Alec . . . Lily twisted her hankie . . . Alec would most

likely be prowling about in his study delib-
erating about which heirloom to sell off
next. If only she could have helped him.

A dark cloud streaked next to the train
several cars back. Odd. Shouldn't the mist
be falling away, not racing forward?

"Lily!"

Lily frowned. Surely that splotch wasn't
calling to her. Oh golly. The lack of sleep
combined with that morning's humiliation
wasn't doing her any favors. The cloud
formed into four long legs. A head with flaring nostrils. Appin? A rider materialized
with coat flapping. The determined shoulders were unmistakable.

"Alec!" Leaping off her seat, Lily grabbed
the emergency cord and yanked. Brakes
screeched. She pitched forward, sprawling
across the seat. Righting herself, she thrust
her head and arms out the window. "I'm
here!"

Alec spurred Appin faster and pulled up
sharply beside her compartment. Bright
blue eyes outshone the cloaking gray mist
as rain droplets rolled off the brim of his
hat and splattered down his raincoat. Lily's
heart tripped. "What are you doing here?"

"I've come to fetch you back."

"B-but I was dismissed."

"A mistake that's been righted."

Lily stared at him as thoughts of all manner collided in an inextricable tangle. "You did this?"

"I may have added a word or two, but your own merit cannot go unaccounted for." The tired lines furrowed around his eyes and mouth eased, and the mask of determination he always sported slipped to a vulnerability she'd seen only once in him, silhouetted by candlelight. "You're needed too much."

Lily tucked her arms back inside and gripped the windowsill to stay the purely joyful urge to vault straight through it.

"What's all this now causing my train to stop? Ye there, back away." The conductor clattered down a set of metal stairs and jumped to the ground, walking toward them.

Alec nosed Appin around. "Apologies for the interruption, Seamus. One of our nurses tried to bolt, and I've come to take her home."

"That ye, Lord Strathem? Aye, well, do what ye must but be quick aboot it. I've a schedule tae keep." Seamus cocked his cap up his forehead and squinted at Lily. "She looks too fine a lady tae be boltin'."

"I didn't bolt. I was tossed out on my ear, trunks waiting for me at the front door."

235

Matron Strom had personally thrown all of Lily's belongings into the trunk, probably kicking it down the stairs, before she'd snagged Lily in the garden. Lily had begged permission to say goodbye, but the door had slammed in her face and the car whisked her away.

She rolled the memory out of her mind. Her second chance was at hand — no use sinking into the mire of the past. "Speaking of my trunk . . ." She gestured to the baggage compartment.

"Dinna fash. Best hand me the ticket and I'll see to them." Seamus reached for the ticket in her offered hand.

"Thank you, Seamus," Alec said. "I'll send my man down to the station to collect them later."

"Seems ye've the better deal in this collecting business." Chuckling, Seamus waved the ticket at Lily and stomped toward the baggage car.

Alec guided Appin closer to the train. *"Stad."* At the command the horse stilled and Alec dropped the reins, then scooted back on the saddle. He turned to Lily and held out his arms. "Down with you."

Lily hesitated, eyeing the distance between them and the precision required to fall neatly into him as the train was elevated several feet above the ground. Not to mention how close it would put them together. She'd had her fair share of close encounters with men on the ballroom floor during the daring fox-trot, but this was likely to be something straight out of a dime novel.

Opening the door to her compartment, Lily sat on the edge and dangled her legs over the side. "You should know this is highly unladylike and bound to end with my face in the mud."

"I'll catch you. Besides, you're never to see these people again. Most likely."

"Well, I am in Scotland. I might as well embrace the opportunities presented to me." She pushed off and collided into his chest. Alec maneuvered her into a sideways position tucked neatly in his lap.

Lily patted her crooked hat into place and grinned. No face in the mud. "That was jolly good fun."

Alec gathered the reins and clucked for Appin to move. "Don't you Yanks jump on horseback all the time?"

Mystified passengers pressed their faces to the train windows as the pair rode by.

"Contrary to popular belief, not everyone in America is a cowboy. Just as not all Scots paint themselves blue and streak into battle."

"Only on special occasions." His warm breath mingled with the cool mist on her face, sending a shiver through her.

It's only the rain and not the fact that a Scotsman rode up on horseback to rescue you from a train in the most romantic scenario possible. Lily lifted her eyes to his. The bright blue dimmed, like sapphires caught in the fading glimmer of candlelight. She longed to drift into the glow and curl herself around the warmth. His head lowered and the warmth tugged her closer.

Tweeeeet! Tweeeeet! The train chugged into motion.

Alec blinked. The warmth evaporated.

"Here. Put this on." He pulled the additional mac Guthrie had packed from his saddlebag and whipped it around her shoulders.

With a twinge of disappointment and some effort to maintain her balance, Lily pushed her arms into the sleeves and tugged it closed over her soggy chest. "A little too late for this."

"Aye, you're drookit for certain, but nay use in turning you into a fish."

"There's that word again. I need to start carrying around a notepad for my Scottish vocabulary collection."

"A long list that'll be."

"But entertaining." Lily swayed easily with the motion of the horse as they ambled away from the tracks and started down the road to Kinclavoch. Trees towered on either side, their leaves dark and dripping with raindrops while the heavy smell of watered earth hung low in the air. When had dirt smelled so lovely?

Alec's arms boxed her in, his flexed muscles solid through the dark fabric of his raincoat. Heat flushed her cheeks. She looked away, at anything that didn't revert her straight back to his strong arms slipping so easily around her waist. To keep her from falling off, Lily reminded herself.

"I suppose I shall have to find a way to pay you back for having me reinstated. Box of chocolates. Monogrammed cravat. Gold-dipped riding boots."

His knee twitched. The injured one. "I was the one who begged you away from your duties and asked you to step beyond Matron Strom's boundaries — boundaries I set in place myself. You've a compassionate heart and should not be punished for it."

"Why, Lord Alec MacGregor. Is that a compliment I hear from you?"

" 'Tis no a compliment when it's the truth."

The man was a charmer whether he realized it or not. His not recognizing the worthy trait made her admire him all the more. And this admirable man had come for her. Immeasurable gratitude tightened her throat. It was an unfamiliar sensation, but then again, she'd never been the recipient of such a selfless act.

Lily leaned back a fraction of a hair, touching her shoulder just to his chest. "Thank you, Alec."

" *'S e do bheatha.*" The corner of his mouth tugged, and — did she imagine it — his arm brushed the small of her back. "You're welcome."

CHAPTER 12

"Golly gumdrops!" Lily dropped the linen napkins on the grass and snatched the newspaper from Bertie's hands, scanning the entertainment article.

Bertie grabbed at the paper to no avail. "I was reading that."

"She's here. Entertaining the Tommies."

"Who are you talking about?"

Exploding with excitement, Lily flipped the page around and shimmied it in front of Bertie's spectacles. "The First Lady of the American Theater. I wonder if she'd come here."

"Not another one of your half-cooked ideas."

"Whatever do you mean by that insulting comment?"

"Like the time you wanted me to sneak backstage with you when that Houdini chap toured London." Kneeling on the blanket they'd spread beneath an ancient rowan tree

241

bowed low with dark-green leaves, Bertie pulled a plate of triangular cucumber sandwiches from the picnic basket and set it next to the basket of summer red apples that added a splash of color to their rationed samplings.

"I merely wanted to discover where that elephant disappeared to."

"Or the time you 'lost' a bracelet at the races just as the royal entourage was passing by."

"The Prince of Wales turned out to be every inch the gentleman I thought he would be. He had quite the time skirting around all the frilly Ascot dresses to retrieve it for me, though I can't image what those roving hands will get up to when he's full grown." Lily brushed off thoughts of Edward with a slight frown and brightened. "This time would be different. The boys need cheering up. Think how wonderful it would be for a grand entertainer to come and perform for them."

"How do you expect someone as famous as *her*" — Bertie jabbed a finger at the delicate face gracing the paper — "to make her way to the wilds of Scotland for a song and dance when all of London society is clamoring for her attention?"

"Ethel is an old friend of the family. She

sings for Mother's birthdays while her brother Lionel sketches. She won't turn down this rallying opportunity. Besides, Ethel is an American. She'll pull through."

After folding the newspaper and placing it back inside the basket, Lily picked up the napkins and arranged them delicately around the circle of empty plates. It had taken nearly two weeks since her dismissal and subsequent train rescue to gather the items required to make a splendid party and then another week for the rain to curb its enthusiasm for its Scottish dreariness. At last the day — in all its milky, sunlit glory — was upon them.

She'd wasted no effort in planning the perfect picnic as a thank-you to Alec for reinstating her at the castle. She'd even spent most of the morning cutting the crust off the tiny triangles of bread for an added touch of refinement. Despite the limitations rationing brought to their choice and quantity of food, she wasn't about to give the war the satisfaction of forfeiting a perfectly set table, er, blanket.

"And Matron Strom? How precisely do you plan to gain her agreement?"

Matron. The only rain cloud on an otherwise clear, blue horizon of possibilities. "I'll cross that bridge after E has confirmed. It'll be difficult to refuse an actress who is already on her way."

"Better to do and ask forgiveness later, eh?"

"My tried-and-true method. I'll go to Laggan now and send a telegram to E's theater." Standing, Lily placed her netted hat atop her head and jabbed a pearl hatpin through it.

"You don't have time. Remember you wanted to cut the apple slices into rosettes before your guests arrive in less than an hour?"

"We'll do without the rosettes. Alec will think they're too fussy anyway. Ten-minute walk to town and ten back. Plenty of time before the guests are due to arrive."

"Lily, I really think —"

"Don't sample the tarts before I return. There's only one for each of us. See you soon!"

It was a brisk walk to the village with a mellow, buttery sun high in the sky. Thank goodness after all that rain. Her hair appreciated the reprieve from what could only be deemed unsightly frizz. On the pleasant side, it did provide a fashionable poof, and she no longer had to comb the hair from her brush and roll the strands into those ghastly hairball rats.

Laggan slept along the winding shores of the River Spey, nestled snugly in the arms of the Monadhliath and Grampian Mountains. Its handful of shops clustered along a single thoroughfare, their gray-and-white stone walls hunched together like cheery old men who were only too happy to pass the centuries in one another's company beneath their slanting roofs and puffing chimney pipes. Clumps of heather sprouted here and there at the corner of the buildings, standing tall and proud against the occasional wind that might brush the tiny blossoms from their proper homes atop the green stalks.

Lily crossed the grassy square plunked in the middle of town where a towering monolith, dedicated to the MacGregors who fought in the Jacobite Rebellion of 1745, stood. White cockades and roses were scattered around the base. Symbols for Bonny Prince Charlie, the local chemist had informed her on her first trip to the village. How strange to think that her own country was still in its infancy when Scotland had been fighting wars of rebellion for hundreds of years.

Stepping into the post office, Mr. MacGregor, a sprightly man with puffs of white hair, popped up from behind the counter.

One of the many MacGregors in the area being of the same clan lineage. *"Madainn mhath."*

"Madainn mhath." Lily beamed in pride despite her awkward return of the greeting. She'd always had an ear for languages, something about being able to express herself in several different ways, but Gaelic had proven the most challenging yet. "I'd like to send a telegram, please."

The postmaster nodded as he searched behind the counter for a pencil and paper. "Yer Gaelic be comin' along just fine, lass. I see ye've been practicin'."

"Guthrie has been teaching me, although I'm beginning to question what precisely. Last week I told Mrs. Grierson at the bakery thank you for the scones. Her face turned red and I thought she was going to slap me across the face."

"Of all the Badenoch region, the *Gàidhligh* language has survived the longest right here in Laggan, ye ken. Proud we are fae ye tae be learnin' it. Our own American *Sassenach.*"

Lily beamed with pride at being included in the village's claim to fame, though they were quick to let her know that she in no way competed with their most illustrious claim — that of Rob Roy MacGregor — of

246

which she proved most understanding.

"About my telegram." She rattled off a quick message to be sent to Ethel's theater in London. The postmaster's eyes grew rounder with each word until he jotted down the final STOP.

"I trust we can keep this between us. Wouldn't want to ruin the surprise." Lily pulled out twice the amount owed and pressed it into Mr. MacGregor's waiting hand.

He tapped the side of his nose and dropped the coins in his till. "A braw time that'll be fae the lads."

"Remember, our secret." Lily waved goodbye as he punched the dotting mechanism that would cross the cables from the wilds of Scotland to the posh Queen's Theatre and straight into Ethel's hands.

Stepping outside, she envisioned the grand event whirling before her mind's eye. A stage with lots of lighting. A few of the men could start the show with novelty acts of playing piano or performing card tricks. A sketch maybe, followed by a rousing song or two. And finally for the *pièce de résistance* none other than the goddess of American theater herself.

Now. What to tell Alec? She'd need an argument ready and in pristine order for when he said no.

"You're in quite the hurry." Richard Wright's voice stopped Lily in her tracks. He stood in the doorway of the building she was passing. Faded gold letters marked it once the home of the cooper. "I'm beginning to think our meetings serendipitous."

Hardly. The man was forever skulking around. "Back in Laggan so soon? Dear London must miss you from all your absences."

"Something in the fresh air here calls to me."

With his pale skin, shiny tipped shoes, and manicured hands, it was difficult to believe he'd had a lungful of fresh air in his oiled life. "Seems it keeps calling to you. Your newspaper must not require much attention."

"On the contrary, my newspaper is my life. Its efficiency is due to me hiring the right people, buying their loyalty and time, which allows me to see to advantageous ventures further afield. Come. See for yourself." He swept an arm to his open doorway.

"I'm afraid I have a prior engagement."

"I insist." Looping an arm around her back, Wright drew her into the building.

It was a decent-size place with large lead-paned windows lining the front. The wooden floor creaked with each step and empty shelves lined the walls. A mop bucket and a broom sat unused in the corner next to a crate with a cloth thrown over it.

"My northern office for the *London Herald*. What do you think?"

"You're moving your office here?"

"Opening a new branch. My *Herald* is fast becoming Britain's top paper, and I won't rest until it does. Then someday the world's source for news."

If one could confuse salacious gossip and detrimental scandals with news. "Why Laggan? Edinburgh or Glasgow seem the more likely candidates in which to establish yourself."

"There are often other factors — personal, let us say — in my decisions. Not to mention the convalescent home is ripe with riveting stories for my paper." A hungry light gleamed in his eyes. "Do not trouble yourself with business dealings, Miss Durham. Only delight in the knowledge that fashions of London, Paris, and New York will soon be at your feminine fingertips with each Sunday edition."

Lily turned her head, feigning interest in the mop bucket so she wouldn't roll her eyes in Wright's face. Certainly she adored a detailed article on the latest lace fringe, but being told that was all she was to adore was insufferable. Her gaze drifted to the crate, catching on a gild frame around a painting of a woman with dark hair and strong cheekbones. Only one person she knew had cheekbones like that.

"Is that Lady Strathem?"

"Her father had this commissioned when she turned sixteen and was presented at court to Her Majesty Queen Victoria. Edwina was a lovely girl. Destined for great things. Until she chose wrong and threw it all away with both hands." His own hands clenched and unclenched as if to steady him. "Now, as I was saying about the Sunday edition —"

"Is that a Raeburn?" Lily's eyes narrowed on the painting propped next to Lady Strathem's portrait.

Wright's gaze snapped to the painting and then to her. "I believe so. I instructed my secretary to purchase a few paintings for me. This is what he came back with."

Lily crossed the room, her skirt stirring up dust, and pulled back the edge of the cloth. Her stomach flipped. "Was this not hanging at Kinclavoch?"

"Perhaps one like it. This came directly from Sotheby's."

"There was only one ever painted. My mother is a great patron of the arts, and while I don't share the same passion, I've read many articles on the subject."

Wright crossed the floor in two long strides and yanked the cloth back over both paintings. "You must be mistaken. A fault forgiven as your feminine senses cannot see the shrewd differences."

"I believe I can spot a fake when I see one."

"A good eye on you, lass." Alec glowered in the doorway. Dressed in navy and rich brown, his squared-off shoulders blocked out the sun trying to squeeze in behind his towering frame.

Lily's stomach flipped for an entirely different reason. "Alec. You're supposed to be at the river."

"Your note stated eleven. I'd time enough to stop at police headquarters and see if they'd found more evidence in the kidnapping case. Unfortunately, the mystery remains." He strode inside, his seething presence swallowing up the already stale air. His cane thwacked the floor as he stopped next to her and glared at Wright. "If you're looking for Old Man Malloch, he retired some time ago. Difficult making barrels and the like with arthritis. You can take your business to Dalwhinnie."

Wright's cool demeanor slipped into place. "As a matter of fact, I spoke to Mr. Malloch last week when I signed the contract buying this place from him." His lip turned up in what some might consider as a smile but on him was a devious trap.

Knuckles whitening atop his cane, Alec hissed through clenched teeth. "You bought this place? Here? In Laggan."

"I did."

"Is the newspaper trade finally souring your wame? Needing to take on an honest living now? You've hardly the hands of a man accustomed to working with them."

Lily leaned closer to Alec. "I don't believe Mr. Wright to be a man who sullies his hands with actual work. He keeps his far less agreeable talents of defamation to the printed page."

Wright inclined his sleek head. "Miss Durham is quite right. I leave such menial tasks to those with no other options of betterment. This will be a new office for my ever-expanding *London Herald*. We're to be neighbors after all."

"You're not welcome here," Alec snarled.

Wright shrugged a slender shoulder under his immaculate suit and moved over to a leaning desk stacked with fresh papers. He tapped them into a neat pile with the tip of his finger. "The deal is done. At quite the bargain, I might add. Land is cheap here."

"Don't think to call on my door for a cup of sugar."

"I doubt you have a cup to spare. Next time I call will be to buy that pile of crumbling stone from you."

The muscles in Alec's neck strained against his white collar. "This world will burn before you have Kinclavoch."

"Your father threatened similar words once upon a time, though I could hardly make them out through his drunken slurring."

"I'll not suffer a slander to the MacGregor name. Least of all from a snake like you who can't lift his head beyond the dirt through which he crawls."

"You'll not suffer? Those sound remarkably like fighting words. Perhaps the closest you'll ever come to battle, hmm?" A sneer twisting his thin lips, Wright flicked his gaze to Alec's cane.

A growl rumbled in Alec's throat. The warning sound of an animal preparing to attack. Fist clenched tight on his cane, he started forward. "I've been waiting a long time to thrash —"

Lily slipped her hand around Alec's arm,

neatly stopping him from his own stubborn stupidity. He had the right to punch Wright on his weaselly nose, but that would mean blood everywhere, and they were late enough to the picnic.

"Gentlemen, must we ruin this glorious morning with insults and violence?"

Muscles tensed under Lily's hand. Alec took a steadying breath and dropped his shoulders. "Miss Durham is right. I'll no longer subject her to your loathsome presence." Turning on his heel, Alec guided her to the door.

Holding tight to his arm lest he renege on his acquiescence, Lily smiled over her shoulder at Wright. "We'll be sure to send you a welcome basket. With rat traps."

Appin waited patiently for his master outside. His dark ears pricked forward as Alec approached and took the reins. Glancing at the saddle, then over to Lily and her fashionably slim skirt, indecision warred across Alec's already tense face. "Care to walk?"

"Of course." Lily would agree to parachuting with pantaloons if it meant keeping his anger at bay. His temper wavered more than a kite in the winds, and she had no desire to get caught up in its gusts. Not with scones and jam waiting.

Alec said not a word as they set off at a clipped pace, his long legs eating up the ground with Lily scampering to keep up. The village fell behind to the cooling reprieve of the woods. The rustling of leaves and scurrying creatures in the brush quieted as if nature itself sensed the brewing storm in its midst. Thunder loomed across Alec's brow. Any second now lightning would bolt from his eyes and sear the nearest tree. A shame it wouldn't be Richard Wright. If anyone deserved a good blackened searing, it was that bullying man.

Alec grunted, drawing her attention. He leaned heavily on his cane as his steps stomped and jerked. Lily stopped walking. Absorbed in her own pity, she'd failed to notice his. "On second thought, might we ride? I don't wish to be late for our rendezvous."

The tiniest line of relief eased around his mouth. Dropping Appin's reins, Alec slid his cane into a specially designed holster attached to the saddle. He grasped Lily around the waist and lifted her to sit sidesaddle as if she weighed no more than a doll, then stuck one foot in the stirrup and swung up behind her. Just as they had sat when he rescued her at the train station. A few more times of doing this, and she'd be akin to a novel heroine.

Alec's arms slipped around her to brace her from falling off. "Next time remind me to saddle Sorcha for you. This is becoming a habit." At the click of his tongue, Appin set off with Lily and Alec swaying in rhythm to the steady motion.

Sunlight filtered through the towering boughs, casting golden rays onto muted green as they touched upon bark and leaf in the subtleness that only nature could conjure. How peaceful it was here. She once thought the shops of Fifth Avenue were paramount to her happiness, but this place with its quiet simplicity breathed into an untouched part of her, startling her senses to life.

"Where might I purchase rat traps?" she asked.

Alec shifted against her. "Neish carries them at the mercantile, but Guthrie can take care of — No. You can't send Wright traps. Much as he deserves it."

"Then what do you suggest?" Lily swiveled to look up at him.

Alec ducked as her hat grazed past his chin. "A bloody nose."

"Ah yes. Which I prevented you from distributing."

"You did."

"Well, I agree. That would have been much more satisfactory in the moment."

"Aye, it would've been."

"Especially since he owns a portrait of your mother's coming out." Her mistake was immediate and slapping a hand over her mouth did no good in calling back the words.

Alec's arm squeezed around her. "You saw this?" At her nod he was quiet for a long moment. The muscles in his arms and chest bunched with tension. "He regards my mother with too much familiarity."

Lily offered a noncommittal noise. Presenting details on the lingering look Wright had given the portrait was out of the question. Alec was likely to wheel the horse around, gallop back into town, and trample the newspaperman to death.

Alec craned his neck to see past her. "Would you remove your hat afore it takes my eyes out?"

"A lady does not remove her hat outdoors."

"Would the lady prefer to drop off a cliff because I can't see two steps ahead of us?"

Reaching up, Lily pulled free the hatpin and removed the blinding piece of fashion. She quickly patted her hair into place. Hats were notorious for flattening an otherwise elegant updo, hence the remaining on top of one's head to disguise the damage done. "Why is there so much animosity between the two of you?"

"He's a slithering snake, and I detest the monstrous things except from the muzzle end of a rifle."

"Reason enough, but I detect a deeper root to this festering relationship."

Alec sighed heavily, ruffling the loose hairs around her ear. She resisted the urge to touch them. "He and my father were class-mates at St. Andrews. He came around a few times when I was younger and my da not so full of drink. The years went on and their conversations turned to disagreements and then to arguments. It ended one night with my mother running out of the room crying with Wright fast on her heels. My father tossed him out." He wove the reins between his fingers, the leather straps rub-bing against stained callouses. "I thought him gone for certain until he showed up at the funeral. Then came back a week later with an offer for the estate."

"Did you throw him out?"

"I was armed at the time. Didn't need to." At Lily's gasp the corner of Alec's mouth ticked up. "Was out shooting pheasant. Most likely the blood from cleaning them scared him off."

Lily shook her head in amazement as the image played vividly in her mind. "Why do you suppose he desires Kinclavoch?"

"He's been buying up many of the faltering estates in the county for years." Agitation rippled through Alec. "Kinclavoch has seen better days, but I'm none so desperate to consider his offers. The castle is my family's home, and I'll do everything I can to keep it that way."

"It's admirable of you to stand firm. Fighting to keep what's yours."

"I feel it's all I do of late. Fight. Yet the battle rages on with no difference to me or any other man's struggles, not when the world spins on the pointed finger of the few in power. There was a time when men acted in honor and not in the interest of their bank accounts — when integrity was prized above all. Those days are long gone." He sighed with the weight of a dying dream. "Kinclavoch was entrusted to me to safeguard. I'll not let her down. No matter the sacrifice."

She didn't know why, but pride surged through her at his declaration. Such words were often left to the margins of literary works from master pens of eras gone by. When kings and knights and warriors roamed the pages recounting their deeds of heroism. Men like Alec MacGregor didn't exist, at least not anymore. But here he was, living, breathing, and duty bound to protect all under his charge. A rare man indeed.

"You ken there's a dimple when you smile to yourself."

Smile widening, Lily threaded the veil of her hat between her fingers. Accustomed only to arguing with him, she found their easy banter danced close to familiar territory. Never had she imagined flirting with the cantankerous Lord Strathem. Nor had she imagined coming dangerously close to enjoying it. "I was just thinking how different you are from the men I know in New York."

"Different."

"You tell me the truth whether I wish to hear it or not. You never allow me to have my way all the time as social politeness dictates."

"A barmy notion to ease the female ego."

"No spatterdashes, cloying aftershave, or boring conversation about how many yachts you stand to inherit along with Newport homes."

"I've no yachts to entertain you with."

"I'm beginning to find I enjoy horseback riding rather than sailing."

"Are you now?" His low voice rumbled in her ear, skittering nerves beneath her skin. They pooled pleasantly warm in her lower back just where his arm brushed her.

"Unlike so many others you challenge me to rise above expectations, to form well-based opinions and stand firm in them. To not be another empty-headed ornament."

"Your stubbornness is not a credit I can claim. It was firmly rooted long before you came to Scotland."

"Claim it or not, but it's heartening to have someone imagine I can be more."

"You are more, Lily. You're like no other woman I've ever met."

Lily's nerves spiked, blazing to a frenzy that heated her throughout. Each part of her attuned to his nearness, his even intakes of breath fanning across her neck, the calloused fingers holding the reins, his unique smell of cotton, soap, and outdoors that curled around her like a welcoming blanket.

There was nothing rehearsed about Alec, nothing smooth. He was rawness in contained form. The ragged edges sincere in their simplicity. They grazed against the polished defenses of her heart, cutting open slivers and seeking entrance. Dare she allow him entry? Dare she reveal her own rawness and insecurities?

She lifted her eyes to his, searching for an answer.

Dark auburn lashes swept down to shade his eyes, deepening them to a fathomless blue. They pulled her toward him like ripples on a pond, ringing all around her. Her hands trembled in her lap even as her eyes grazed his lips in eagerness. All sound faded and the only tangible existence that remained was the breath of space between her and Alec.

The light shifted in his eyes, unearthing flames of desire. "Lily." He breathed her name like a prayer. One she hoped to answer.

Laughter pealed in the distance.

Alec's gaze snapped over Lily's head. His eyes narrowed to arrow points. "What is *she* doing here?"

Momentarily dazed by the disappointing change of expectations, Lily turned in the saddle to see her picnic set up next to the river. It was the prettiest picture she'd ever hoped to create as smiling faces waited to greet them. She turned back to Alec. "Surprise!"

All elated hopes were doused under his scowl. So much for answered prayers.

CHAPTER 13

"You brought my sister out here?" Alec leaped off Appin's back as anger snuffed out the tender notions he had seconds before.

Unable or unwilling to admit her error, Lily blinked down at him from atop the horse. "I did. As a surprise."

"I don't care for surprises."

She slid off the saddle in a flurry of fine wool and lace, landing neatly in front of him. In a flash she repinned the frothy hat at what was probably intended to be a fashionable angle atop her blonde pile of curls. "Well, you should. They're jolly good fun when you allow yourself to enjoy them."

"Not when it concerns my sick sister." There Viola sat on a blanket spread wide under a tree next to the river with a heavy shawl tied around her thin shoulders. Bertie sat next to her as they arranged strawberries in a bowl. Didn't she realize Viola could catch her death sitting so close to the open water? Alec moved toward them.

Jumping in front of him, Lily braced a hand against his chest. Her touch was like a heated iron. "Before you go stomping over there to terrorize what should be a lovely outing, I want you to look at Viola's face. Truly look at her outside the sickly confinement of shut drapes and ghostly nightgowns." Her eyebrows inched up, daring him.

Never one to back down from a challenge, especially not when he was in the right, Alec pushed down his instinct and looked at his sister. A full smile stretched her mouth, a most welcomed sight he'd not seen since she was a wee lassie. No tremors shook her bones, nor did she whimper in pain at the soft breeze whispering across the grass. She looked happy. A lump stuck in his throat.

Alec grunted. "She could still catch a chill."

"There are a mountain of blankets and two hot water bottles in the wagon for such an occurrence." Lily folded her hands in front of her. The spot where she'd touched him now felt cold. "I was looking through a few of Bertie's books and found symptoms like Viola's. Some studies have proven that sunshine and fresh air can help strengthen the sufferer."

"Dr. MacLeod says she suffers from a weakened immune system. That she was born with it."

"Has he ever mentioned rickets?"

"The poor man's disease?"

"It has nothing to do with one's wealth and more with a lack of vitamins and bone calcification. I haven't had time to look up precisely what that means, but all the sources agreed that fresh air and sunlight were the most important methods to correct the suffering."

For years he'd watched his sister suffer, each cough and tired blink of her exhausted eyes breaking his heart all over again. He couldn't bear the thought of lifting her hope when it was naught more than another disappointment in disguise. "What if you're wrong?"

"Viola is miserable. She's living a shell of a life. If a bit of air and sun can make her feel better, isn't it worth trying?" Lily cocked her head to the side. Sunlight filtered the decorative holes in her bonnet, spotting her translucent skin with light. "If it doesn't work, I give you full permission to yell at me. Later. I won't have you spoiling our lovely picnic."

He wouldn't mind standing there a wee

longer to argue with Lily if only to watch the dark-green rims of her eyes recede to a pale starburst at the center. On the other hand, the longer they remained the more likely he was to forgo the actions of a gentleman and kiss her as he'd come so close to doing on the horse. "One chance."

Beaming like the sun itself, Lily laced her arm through his and turned around to wave at the waiting party. "Hello! We're here!"

Robert the Bruce bounded toward them, first jumping at Lily, then finally gracing his master with a sniffy greeting before racing back to the blanket. Faces of warring excitement greeted them as Viola and Bertie settled their attention on Alec, waiting to see what he would say.

"A pleasant morning to you both, ladies." Alec bowed low at the waist.

Relief washed over their faces. "Good morn."

Alec's initial anger lifted. It was such a small thing to bring happiness to another, but he was grateful he'd been given the opportunity, reluctant though he was.

"And a pleasant morning tae ye, m'laird." Guthrie strolled from around the wagon dressed in his finest kilt. Which equated to one without whisky stains.

Alec eyed him thoughtfully. "Your best

kilt. It's not even Hogmanay."

Guthrie took Appin's reins from Alec and hobbled him near a patch of grass. "Nay, but 'tis the same in my mind on this day. Thanks to the lass." He ran a hand over his slicked-back hair and gestured to Lily.

Blushing, she knelt on the blanket and picked up a jug nestled among the triangular sandwiches, strawberries, bannocks and jam, and shortbread cookies. She poured yellow liquid into glasses and passed them around before holding hers aloft.

"My banquet for each of you. It's not much and rather late in coming, but my appreciation goes far beyond the simple bounty I lay before you today. You see, I wouldn't have made it very far without the generosity each of you has shown me, and so I thank you. To dear ones" — she saluted Bertie — "To new friends" — she tipped her glass to Viola and Guthrie, then turned to Alec. The pink on her cheeks tinged red. "And to you. I thought all was lost until you came to the train station that morning. You've given me hope."

It was the last thing Alec had expected.

His knee buckled.

Many things he was, but not often enough a giver of hope. After surrendering such virtues himself, how could he offer them to another? Yet here Lily was commending him for acts deemed more worthy to others.

"Don't look so surprised, Lord Strathem." A smile played about her lower lip.

"My actions didn't warrant such grand gestures."

"Kindness always deserves recognition."

Precisely why he'd fought to keep her at Kinclavoch. No! Heat flushed up his collar. Not her per se but her post as a nurse, er, aide. Lily saw the good in others, yet she seemed oblivious to the same qualities within herself. She'd whirled into their lives like an orbiting sun, bringing warmth and light. Alec had tried to crouch beneath his gray cloud of obscurity, but her rays had drawn him out most unwillingly. Yet he could not find it within him to banish himself from the lingering light. He edged closer to the blanket. Closer to her.

Guthrie coughed. "Might we get tae drinking now? If ye're done sharing the looks."

Lily blinked and looked away, breaking the trance that drew Alec. She smiled brightly and lifted her glass. "Cheers!"

Alec saluted with his cup and sipped. And nearly spit out the lemony sourness.

Lily pressed her fingers briefly to her mouth and bravely swallowed. "A bit more sour than I expected, but I suppose that'll be the sugar rationing. Doesn't make for good lemonade."

"We brought coffee, as well." Bertie held up a thermos in apology. Lily tried to smile, but the corners of her mouth didn't perk up as they usually did.

" 'Tis no so bad." Alec took another sip. His mouth puckered in response. "If you swallow fast."

Lily laughed, a true sound this time, and set her cup down with a dust of her hands. "Enough of that. Who's hungry?"

The food was nothing grand, but Alec was filled more than he had been in years. The easy chatter and laughter danced around him, coaxing him to join in, but habit kept him relegated to observation.

"You're smiling." Alec started at Viola's voice so close to his ear. "A sight I haven't seen in a long time."

"We've not much to smile about of late." Alec turned to her. "You look cozy as a lamb's ear."

Viola wormed farther down into her wool blanket. High color dusted her cheeks. "I was seven years old the last time I sat under a tree. It was warmer than today, but there was a chill in my bones that I couldn't shake."

"Do you need another blanket? The hot water bottle?" Alec started to stand, disturbing Bruce from where he napped between them. "A moment and I'll fetch it."

Viola laid her hand on his arm. "No chills haunt me today. In fact, my bones haven't shaken once."

Alec forced a nod despite the dreaded knowledge of coming winter. The war would be over by Christmas, they'd said. That was a year ago with one Christmas down and another on the horizon with no end in sight. Kinclavoch was miserable but durable in the cold as they'd managed to keep the family rooms somewhat warm from the wood he and Guthrie chopped. This year they would have to manage for the recovering soldiers and nurses as well. Another item of worry for his ever-growing list.

A leaf fluttered from the boughs hanging overhead and swayed gently to the ground. Alec picked it up and examined its green body tinged gold along the ruffled edges. "Seasons'll be changing soon enough."

"If Mother Nature approves, I'll hang on to summer a few weeks more if only to spend more days like this out of doors."

"It's too much too soon. If your body is overtaxed —"

"How can I tax myself by sitting here?

Alec, I can breathe. It's as if the sun has kissed my sickness away."

"Let us hope that is the truth of it."

Viola tucked away an errant strand of dark hair. She'd woven a yellow ribbon through the plait curving over her shoulder. Lily wore a matching one around her hat. "You were angry seeing me here today."

" 'Twas a surprise and no mistake."

"As intended." Smugness flitted across Viola's face, then softened to sincerity. "Lily may be grateful for all of us today, but this picnic is truly for you. She agonized over it for days."

Alec didn't move lest he give away the uptick in his heartbeat. "You know this how?"

"Because I had to listen to every suggestion while she helped walk me up and down the hallway. Her initial plan involved a piper, streamers, and a three-tier cake."

"She's been walking you along the corridors? Your strength —"

"My strength is gaining due to our daily exercises."

"You might have told me."

"And ruin the surprise? Brother, my stature and weakness may lead you to believe otherwise, but I'm a child no longer."

"I hear a certain American in those words."

"Go gentle with her. She's trying so hard. Things aren't as easy as she makes them appear. I feel in some ways she, too, is struggling to hold herself together."

Alec tore the stem from the leaf. Best to change the topic before that revelation had time to settle in a place he preferred to keep closed. "However did you slip past Mither?"

"She locked herself in her chamber crying the walls down. It would've been her and da's twenty-fifth anniversary today."

"How about a game of charades?" Lily pulled a small sack from the picnic basket and passed it around. "Our gentlemen patients were kind enough to oblige me by writing down one- or two-word suggestions for our use. Rest assured that I will be as surprised as you to discover what they wrote, though we should be warned because I heard a fair amount of sniggering. Who would like to go first?"

Alec's gut clenched as the bag passed to his hands. Partaking in games was akin to crawling through thistle-laden bracken. He'd rather have thorns prick him all over than have watching eyes cast upon him, seeing the flaws.

The paper weighed like a boulder in his

hand as he read the unsteady script. *Marching soldier.* Of all the suggestions for him to pick. His heart rate kicked up. Sweat slicked his palms.

"No one?" Lily eyed them each in turn as no one volunteered. "Cowards. I'll go first and you can laugh at what a fool I make of myself."

Standing, she tilted her chin as if to ready herself and raised her arms to paw at the air. She bounced forward and back, still pawing, and shaking her head. Bending forward, she placed one hand on the ground and curled the other close to her chest with a most refined look on her face. Completing her stunt, she leaped to her feet. "Ta-da!"

Guthrie scratched his beard. "Was that it?"

"Yes. What else did you suppose I was doing?"

"Stretching."

"I am not repeating that performance so you'll have to guess something."

"Brucie when he begs for deer jerky?" Viola offered. Laying between her and Alec, Bruce perked his head up at the sound of his name.

"Good golly, was I that bad?" Lily laughed.

Bertie shook her head. "I thought you were a spider trying to climb a window."

"A spider? Heavens, I think I could have done a more decent job to one of those. No, I was a circus pony!"

Laughter ringed around the circle. How enjoyable they all made it seem to socialize in one another's company. Though Alec sat among them, he felt as though an impenetrable line blocked him from joining them. The line had been present most of his life, and he'd always found comfort in the emotional detachment it provided. Until now. The line began to shift, coaxing him beyond its safe obscurity to an exposure that left him vulnerable.

Heat flushed through his body, swelling his skin until his clothes clung like manacles. Any minute now the attention would turn to him. Scrutiny would be the gaping hole into which he would plunge. Distance was his only savior.

Standing, Alec grabbed the water jug. "Needs refilling."

The blood droning in his ears blocked out any replies as he walked away. His knee throbbed from the quick pace. Too late to turn back for his cane, he made his way down the slope to the riverbank of Spey. He dropped the jug on the pebble-strewn bank and knelt by the dark water. Cupping a handful, he splashed it over his heated face. The cold water stabbed his skin in welcome relief. He took a deep breath and fraction by fraction his heart calmed.

"That looks refreshing." Lily stood behind him. Lost in himself, he'd not noticed her approach.

"If you don't mind a chill." Alec moved to stand. "Come. I'll take you back afore they miss your company."

"They'll miss yours as well." Those green eyes cut into him sharper than any blade. Only the smile curving her lips kept the blade from plunging to the point of pain. "They're content enough with the strawberries, and I wouldn't mind sitting here for a while. Unless I've disturbed your peace."

"You don't disturb me." Unnerve at times. Frustrate to no end, but her disruptions were something to expect now. Like his knee flaring up in bad weather. The storm would approach and there was nothing he could do to stop it. Best to let it come and deal with the aftermath in due course.

"A shame you can't say that about all of our interactions." Lily bent over and brushed the somewhat flat stone next to him with her gloved hand before settling atop it. A few feminine flicks of her hand smoothed her skirts around her like a yellow lily pad.

"Is this your favorite spot that Viola mentioned?"

"No. That's beyond the ridge there to another bend in the river with the valley opening up below."

"It sounds lovely, although I could understand if this was it. It's very serene. Nature has an honesty that soothes the soul without the trappings of life. No restraints enforced here, only simple reminders of who we truly are. Of who we wish we could be."

"About the only place I find freedom."

"Do you not find freedom as the master of Kinclavoch?"

"Not always."

"But you love your home."

"Aye, but love of something often proves the most heartbreaking of difficulties."

"Overcoming the difficulties is what makes it all the more precious."

Alec grunted at her growing talk of feelings. "I apologize for my abrupt departure. Charades and small talk have never been a strong suit of mine."

"Never would I have guessed that." Winking at him, she picked up a rock and tossed it in the river. It plonked in the depths with a tiny splash. "Don't worry. Any shortcom-

276

ings you may have in that area my inane chatter can more than make up for."

"I wouldn't necessarily call it chatter. You always seem to know what to say."

"Do I? It's a ruse. Most of what I say isn't taken seriously so why not have fun with it?" She selected another rock and rolled it around in her palm. Her head dipped, her face disappearing beneath the wide brim of her hat but not enough to mask the low sigh. "I talk so others won't see the missing pieces."

The admission was a flaming arrow that struck true to his innermost self. It blazed bright in the darkened corners of his retreat, striking back loneliness until Alec had no place left to hide. Everything in him told him to remain behind his defenses, to keep his vulnerable spots protected from the all-seeing light. But he had no desire to struggle. Not now. Not with her. "And I keep quiet so they won't see the missing pieces."

Lily's head lifted. A look as he had never seen settled across her face, her green eyes sober as she gazed at him. It was unsettling to stare so openly at another as the closeness uncovered an intimacy not often allowed. Yet he found not exposure in her clear expression but understanding.

"Do you think you don't have anything

worthwhile to say, Alec? Because I believe you do. 'When a man's honor is at stake, he may only count himself a true defender in preparation of laying down noble sacrifices for the sake of his cause. In only this will he find freedom. Only in sacrifices for others will he find honor.' "

Alec snorted. "You quote my own words to me."

"You are truly a remarkable man, Alec MacGregor. I wish for others to see it as I do. To see you." She touched his cheek. Her gloves were soft and cool on his skin, compelling an urge to press his hand against hers to keep it there, but like a butterfly's wing it fluttered and released. "Your writing proves you have a great deal to say and others should count themselves fortunate to hear the beauty of your words."

"Poetry reading and speech giving are not my life's calling."

"No, but people need heart. They need to believe in something solid as this war shakes the very foundation of good beneath our feet, but they don't know who to listen to anymore. There is hope coming from the front lines. Little bits of humanity that the Tommies cling to when mortars explode over their heads in the trenches. Would it not be wonderful to share those scrapes of faith with a hungry population?" Lily turned to face him, her eyes bright with excitement. "Talk to the Tommies. Write their stories."

"No. You've read a few lines of rubbish and think me a writer. Those men deserve a pen worthy of their exploits."

"A pen like Richard Wright's?" With a slight raise of her eyebrows, Lily dusted her skirt in exaggerated strokes. "Wright is planning to interview Captain Gibbons and print his story for the newspaper. A 'shiny farthing' I believe is what he hopes to gain. No doubt he'll twist a few salacious details to sell more copies."

Alec grabbed a rock and squeezed. The jagged edges bit into his palm. "Has Captain Gibbons remembered anything more from his kidnapping? A clue as to who took him and why?"

"All good questions that you should ask him yourself. Or if you're too afraid, wait and read his account when Wright concocts what's sure to be a rag piece."

Why must she insist on turning everything back on him? "Captain Gibbons may do as he pleases in his own time, but Wright is forbidden to cross my threshold. He wants gossip, he'll find it elsewhere." He hurled the rock into the river. It hit with a mighty plunk.

"It wouldn't be gossip if you wrote the soldiers' stories. Their true stories with no embellishments, just their own words."

Alec shook his head in amazement. The woman knew how to drag out a point. "You're a canny one, are you no?"

"If that means clever, then I shall take it as a compliment as opposed to the warning you make it sound like."

"I stay out of the men's way and they stay out of mine. End of discussion." Standing, Alec offered her his hand. "We should return before Guthrie has a chance to eat all the shortbread."

Lily slipped her hand in his and stood. Her small fingers fit perfectly in his palm, the netted gloves doing little to barrier her warm skin from his. "Haven't you learned by now that the discussion is never truly over?"

Treasuring the feel of her hand in his for a moment longer, Alec turned them back up the slope to the picnic. "With you, I'm starting to."

CHAPTER 14

"There we was at Loos hunkered down not two hundred yards from the Hun trenches. All of a sudden this piper starts up from the Scot's division, and there goes those kilt swingers clamoring over the top." Corporal Dreymond, the newest resident storyteller, slapped his hands together. "We bust over the top to a flat field crawling with smoke and star shells. Me mate starts choking while I'm smelling something off — like that stuff my mother uses to clean the chamber pots. That yellow smoke lobbed from our own trenches."

Across the narrow aisle and squashed between two men on the small bed, Lily leaned forward. "Then what happened?"

Dreymond looked slyly around at his crowding audience. "The wind kicks back and the gas smoke whips at us instead of across no-man's-land to the Huns. Me mate — Charlie's his name — was there at Ypres

281

when those Jerries first used that death chemical back in April. Lost his sight for three days, so naturally he sees it coming for him again and he's having none of it. Charlie rips off his smoke and tube helmet and starts screaming."

Lily bunched the apron in her lap. "Poor Charlie."

"I'd no choice but to give him mine. Little good it did. Got a bullet in the head not a minute later." The corners of Dreymond's mouth worked against the emotion cracking his voice. "The gas took me then and I got dragged off the field. Blinded, coughing, chest pressure . . . the Sisters got me binded up and now I'm here with you fine folks for a bit of rest."

How horrible this war was. Cursing and striking down young men in their prime. Lily reached for Dreymond's hand and squeezed. "I'm so sorry for Charlie. You must miss him greatly."

"We've all lost someone on the line. Bound to lose more before this thing is over."

Next to Lily the man sporting a bandage over his handless arm harrumphed. "I hear command is checking hospitals to see what soldiers are fit to fight again. As if we haven't given enough, they're taking us from our sickbeds."

Dreymond's face paled. He knotted his hands together until his thumbs turned white. "It'll be over before Christmas. We was promised. Trenches aren't fit for humans." A hacking cough doubled him over.

Lily jumped to his side and placed a hand on his shaking back. "Please. You must calm down."

"Afternoon check." Matron's voice cut from the doorway.

"Scatter! It's the matron."

The men jumped back to their beds as if their trousers had been set on fire just as Matron Strom marched into the room. Her tiny eyes narrowed and nearly conjoined as her gaze stopped on Lily. The dragon stalked down the row of beds, her starched skirt whipping behind her like a tail ready to cut down anyone who dared to step in her path.

She stopped in front of Dreymond's bed. "What is the meaning of this, Aide Durham? The men are not to frolic between the beds."

"Don't get upset at her, Matron," Dreymond said as his coughing attack subsided. "She was shooing us back to our own bunks."

Matron's cycloptic eye returned to the customary close-set two. "Good, but it's time for you to take your afternoon walk."

Dreymond shrank back into his pillow and clutched the covers to his chin. "No. Don't think so, Matron, if it's all the same to you."

"It is not all the same. Your chart prescribes fresh air and brisk walks to stimulate your heart."

"My heart don't feel too good today. Like it's skipping out of my chest, not to mention the sun burns my eyes."

Matron shook her head at the golden afternoon light filtering through the tall windows. "Hmm. Soldier's heart. I've seen it time and again. They proclaim the damage resides in the body, but the true problem roots in the mind, young man."

Dreymond bolted upright, fear forgotten in indignation. "What're you talking about rooting in my mind? I'm the one who's been gassed."

The air vibrated as two strong wills tried their level best to crush the other through brute glares. But there were more effective ways of settling a match.

Sighing, Lily moved to stand next to the Matron. "Perhaps Mr. Dreymond is right. If his eyes are too weak, then the last thing we should do is torment him with the beauty of nature." She turned a sweet smile on the patient. "You wouldn't mind if Sergeant Rume took your place strolling with me among the last blooms of autumn? His legs are not so long as yours, and I do have difficulty in keeping to his shortened pace, but he more than makes up for it in witty conversation."

Dreymond swung his feet over the side of the bed. "Blast — Oh! 'Scuse me, ladies — If that pig snout is taking my place. Where are my slippers and glasses?"

"Here they are." Lily handed him the specially made dark-tinted glasses and allowed a tiny smile in Matron's direction.

The older woman refused to acknowledge the conspiracy. "I see you have things under control. I'll leave you to it."

Bundling up against the cool of late September, Lily walked arm in arm with Dreymond along the garden's central path. The roses, hyacinths, and rhododendrons had faded to a dusty gold, their sweet fragrances replaced by the musk of falling leaves and crisp grass.

"Spring has always been my favorite time of year, when everything bursts to life, but I can't deny the unique splendor of fall." Lily plucked a red leaf from the ground and twirled it. "The trees are as colorful as one of Lucile Duff-Gordon's newest fashion palettes."

"They all look green from behind these

glasses."

"Perhaps you should take them off. Your pupils have returned to normal. There's no need to wear the lenses any longer."

"I'll keep them on. Just in case." Dreymond touched the rim of the glasses as lines feathered his forehead. "They call us the lucky ones. The ones who ain't dead but got their leg blown off, eye taken out by shrapnel, or face melted off with one of those flamethrowers the Jerries like to use. Tell the good people of England to come take a look at us and see how lucky we are."

She'd never witnessed a wink of worry on his usually jovial countenance. The quiet change was more worrisome than the bodily damage he'd received. "But you're alive. Surely that's something to be grateful for."

"Would've been more grateful if Charlie were here with me. Now no one'll ever remember him and what he done. Most of us ain't afraid of dying, it's the horrors of what we see before that final bullet gets us . . . The waste of blood and bodies sinking in the mud, never to be remembered again."

They rounded a towering oak tree. Or was it a hawthorn? She never could tell the difference between trees. Alec had mentioned his ancestors planting rowans in some ancient Celtic tradition for protection.

"You must have more faith in people — Ahh!" Lily's foot struck something and she toppled forward. Strong hands clamped onto her legs, holding her upright. The blue eyes of her rescuer caused her heart to zip as he looked up from where he sat hidden behind the tree.

Alec.

"Thank you. Heels and grass are never a good combination." Lily looked down at Alec's outstretched foot, which her own foot had snagged, then up to the hands locked around her calves. Her gaze traveled slowly to his arms, to his shoulders, and finally to his face to share the precise moment of embarrassed realization. "Um, do you mind?"

Alec jerked his hands back fast enough to pull his wrists out of joint. Stuffing his knife into his boot, he grabbed his cane and pushed to his feet. "Didn't mean to hide there."

"Didn't mean to trample you there." He stood close enough for her to curve her hand over his shoulder if she so boldly chose. It had come so naturally while they rode on the horse, and if she were honest with herself — which she hesitated to be at the moment — she wouldn't mind being back on that horse with him. Lily locked her hands together to dissuade the temptation. "What are you carving today?"

Alec brushed his hand over the neck of the cane where it looked like the twisting of a stem with sprouting leaves. "Naught but to keep my hands busy."

And his mind from overworking itself, or so it seemed. Something was whirling behind that defensive countenance based on the amount of wood shavings speckling his trousers. Was he forced to sell another family heirloom, or had Wright paid another unsavory visit? No, if the latter, Alec would be dancing a jig after throwing that baggage off his property.

Lily smiled politely. "May I introduce Corporal Dreymond? Mr. Dreymond, this is Lord Strathem whose hospitality we are beholden to."

Alec gave a curt nod. "How do you do, Mr. Dreymond?"

"Lord Strathem." Not even the dark green–tinted glasses could disguise Dreymond's unabashed curiosity of Alec. "Never did I think to meet you. The boys inside think you're a ghost."

"As you can see, I'm not."

"Only, rumor is you don't want no one to see that busted leg. Lots of the boys got

288

busted legs. Some got no legs at all. How'd you get yours?"

Alec stiffened. "I fell from a horse when I was fifteen. The bones never set correctly."

"You ashamed? Don't mean no disrespect, but some of the lads are known to give themselves blighties to get out of the fighting."

"I do not hide behind my afflictions." Alec's jaw clenched hard enough to cut glass.

"Meant no offense, my lord. Some of 'em come in with such tall tales it's hard to know who's lying and who's merely survived Gabriel's summoning horn."

Lily knew that stance. Could dissect that straight, almost brittle line of Alec's shoulders to within an inch of its snapping point. The man hid away in shadow when he could create a light much craved by others. He merely needed to spark the flame.

And she had the perfect match. "The men have such wonderful stories to tell. Wonderful and tragic and hopeful. I'm honored to hear them. What good it would do the country to hear them all as well. Straight from the soldiers and the front lines. Don't you agree, Lord Strathem?" Ignoring Alec's death stare, she ignited the torch and passed it to Dreymond. "Do you know that Lord

Strathem is an astonishment with the written word? If he were to take down your stories and send them to be printed, why, the people of Britain could read for themselves what it means to live in the trenches. No political twists or personal agendas. Simple stories from simple Tommies."

"What, like that *London Herald* been printing? 'Huzzah for the Heroes.' How we all come back with medals and war stories to tell? All we want is to forget what we seen over there."

"You can help set the stories straight — as men who have been there with no embellishments needed."

The lines smoothed from Dreymond's forehead. "Do you think people are interested? We can't paint a pretty picture for 'em."

"I think people want honesty. The Tommies and the civilians both desire it so that no struggle is forgotten. Or men like your friend Charlie."

Dreymond peeled his glasses off. Red scarring webbed around his eyes, but the pupils now revealed a healthy shade of brown. "Could you really do that for us, my lord?"

Alec stepped back. "I . . . um . . . I don't think I'm the right man —"

"Here you are." Impeccably and unpleasantly timed, Esther glided up behind them, her starched white-and-blue uniform crisp against nature's warm shades of red and gold. "You shouldn't force the patients so far from the castle, Aide Durham. Weakened lungs can't handle the stress."

"Exercise is beneficial for a full recovery," Lily said.

"This appears more of a tête-à-tête than exercise. I'm certain A — Lord Strathem has more important things to do than give you a private tour of the garden." Esther smiled at Alec who in turn studied the top of his cane. Smile slipping, she rounded on the patient. "Come along, Corporal Dreymond. The army doctor has arrived for inspection, and I'm to take you in to see him at once. Aide Durham, help is needed in the kitchen sorting beef bully from the tinned meat."

"As appealing as that sounds, my duty is to Mr. Dreymond. I shall attend to the kitchen afterward."

"Matron Strom's orders."

Lily held back a groan of exasperation. The old dragon was fond of settling her with the latest element of torture, even if it meant overriding her current duties. Esther's perfectly angled eyebrows winged up in anticipation of another argument. A face full of bottled chicken would wipe the smugness right off her, but for the sake of appearing professional in front of Dreymond, Lily refused the instinct.

Lily transferred her patient to Esther's arm. "Come along, Mr. Dreymond. Nurse Hartley is going to take you back inside."

Breath hitching, Dreymond fumbled to put his glasses back on. "They're going to send me back to the front, aren't they?"

Esther latched her hand over his arm. "If the doctor deems you fit enough then you shall rejoin the fight for our glorious cause of king and country."

"I'm not ready. My eyes —"

Esther tugged him back down the path to the castle. "Come now, none of that, lest someone think you afraid to do your duty. Don't worry, I shall vouch for you if you're not fully recovered despite what others might say."

Lily sighed. "If that woman did more nursing and less floating around like a queen bee . . . Poor Dreymond. He's a sweet man, but his fear of returning to the trenches is overwhelming. Have the wounded not sacrificed enough?" She looked around to find herself alone. "Alec?"

His retreating form disappeared around a

hedge. Matron would have Lily's head if she didn't report to the kitchen posthaste, yet her heart tugged toward the bushes.

She caught up to him next to a dilapidated dovecote, the pigeons having long flown the coup for safer habitation. "Alec, wait —"

He whipped around so fast his cane nicked the top of her shoes. "You just can't help yourself, can you? Always thinking you ken best."

Lily stopped short, mouth popping open at his ferocity. "What did I do wrong this time?"

"The stories, Lily! The soldiers, the newspaper. You never asked if it was something I wished to do. You took it upon yourself to decide for me. What's worse is you dragged that unsuspecting corporal into the scheme."

Heat boiled off him, scalding what she deemed a sensible opportunity. "It's not a scheme."

"You're trying to manipulate me into a setup for failure."

"Manipulation requires directing someone to a place they did not know they wished to go. No one could ever accuse you of that." Lily softened her approach. "You could help them."

"Have you not looked around to see I have

my hands busy already?" As if cued, a slate from the dovecote roof slid off and crashed behind him. Growling, he squatted to gather the broken pieces. "One thing after another demands my attention."

Lily knelt beside him and picked up the smaller pieces stuck between the dying grass blades. "I understand you have hardships."

"We're managing." That jaw again.

"Alec. Your home is falling apart." She held out a handful of slate chips and softened her tone. "I saw the debt notes from the bank, and I know Wright has made you offers on Kinclavoch."

"I'll burn it to the ground afore he steps another foot in my hall."

"What a grand idea. Where would you, Viola, and your mother live then? Not to mention all the patients residing here. If you think to pack me back off across the Atlantic as target practice for the German U-boats, I will have something to say about it."

"You always do."

"Instead of selling your family's pictures and jewels, sell the newspaper stories of the wounded who come in our doors broken and desperate for hope."

His gaze snapped to hers. Blue flames seared into her. "I will not use the disadvantage of others to profit for myself."

"Wright certainly will. Not only will he expose the men and twist the stories for his own gain, he'll use the money to snap up the land around here in an attempt to suffocate you out. He's already made himself quite cozy in the village. I imagine he'll want to run for mayor soon enough. Mayor Wright, Lord of Kinclavoch, because the previous lord was too prideful to stop him."

"My pride is the only thread keeping this estate together." Slate smashed in his hand. Red swelled from his palm.

Pulling a hankie from her apron pocket, Lily took his hand and wrapped the cloth around the cut and pressed firmly to staunch the blood. "You're hiding behind it just as you hide behind that cane. So you have a bad leg, so what? It doesn't make you any less of a man."

"Tell that to women who throw white feathers at me on the train. Tell that to the men who whisper behind my back because I'm not in uniform."

"Their ignorance is not worth dwelling on. Shooting a rifle in the mud wasn't in the cards for you, but you've hardly been kicking your feet up. You've opened your home for the wounded. That's not the act of a coward."

Yanking his hand from her grasp, Alec

jabbed his cane into the ground and stood. "Don't speak to me as if you understand such things. The bonny American princess who's known not a day of hardship in her life. Was life too comfortable for you there that you needed to find a new thrill halfway across the world? Or perhaps events were no longer going how you pleased so you ran away. Life is a game to you and other people the pieces you move around to suit your whims. I'm not a piece to be played."

Lily jumped to her feet in defense. "I would never think to —"

"But you do. Your smiles. Always finding me when I wish to go unnoticed. Leaning against me in the rain. Never leaving me to my solitude even when I'm alone. Your attentions push me, pull me like a game piece across your playing board. To what end? So you may have your own say."

His words struck her like a hot iron, branding her with shame. Despite everything, he saw only selfishness and a childish pursuit to make herself worthy of understanding. The deterioration of Kinclavoch's pride called to her in loneliness. A kindred cry for acknowledgment that, discarded, would forever kill the spirit struggling to rise within.

Then she'd met Alec. Wanting only to pull

him from the shadows to which he kept. Never had she imagined he'd spark a light within her. One that twinkled with purpose and growing affection.

It now guttered under humiliation.

"How clear your perception of me is, Lord Strathem. I never have anything serious to say. I'm a frilly rich girl with too much time on her hands, so I'm left to cause mischief. That's why my parents shipped me off to England to begin with, that I may create trouble for someone else. How grateful I am to know I'm giving full potential to their expulsion. Now, if you'll excuse me. I have jellied animal parts to identify in the kitchen."

With a queenly sweep of her head, Lily walked away before he saw the imminent tears. They clouded her vision and amplified the boom of blood in her ears, muffling Alec as he called her name. She kept walking, each step distancing her from his fading voice. She rounded the tree where she had tripped over him. Wood shavings crunched under her feet. The tears fell and she raced back to the castle.

Bam!

The shot went wide as the covey of grouse sailed high out of harm's way and into the giant swallow of the descending sun.

"Ifrinn an Diabhuil!" Alec thrust another round into the rifle chamber and took aim.

Bam!

The birds flew farther away, their brown-and-white bodies disappearing into tiny dots over the red-and-orange treetops. Bruce whined at Alec's feet.

"If you think to do better, then do your part and flush them out." Bruce yawned and looked away. The latest notch in Alec's belt of regret. "Even you think I can't manage to do right."

He never should have let Lily walk away. He should have chased after her and told her what a thickhead he'd been. Told her he hadn't meant any of those wretched words. Told her that she was the only bit of loveliness to grace his drab world. He'd waited for her in the garden, paced the landing of the nurses' hall, and watched for a glimpse of her outside the patients' ward, but she never appeared. As the hours passed into days and the days into weeks, the walls mounted higher about him, closing him into solitary confinement.

She had been trying to help — with that irritating yet endearing arrogance she wielded without concern for probable fall-out. How freeing that must feel. His responsibilities sank too deeply to allow him a foothold out of the mire. Yet Lily was not free. Her effortless charm hid her own set of chains. Exiled from her home and sent across an ocean to a foreign country at war. Bravery existed in many forms, but never had Alec witnessed courage such as hers.

And he'd cracked it to pieces.

Shame tore at his so-called honor for exposing her innermost pain, yet he could not allow himself true regret for in that moment their falsehoods had been ripped away and they stood unveiled before each other. He saw it all. Her humiliation, insecurity, and longing for acceptance. Cries that matched the deep aching within him. Instead of drawing her close as he longed to do, he'd gnashed at her like a beast before she had a chance to pity his weaknesses.

Another pack of birds shot from the tall, dead grass. Alec shoved a round into the chamber and threw the rifle to his shoulder. He took aim and squeezed the trigger. Nothing. He tried again. The flock skimmed the tree line and disappeared into the sun setting on the horizon.

"Baw-faced, worthless piece of metal. Being the progeny of your ancestors, no wonder we lost the '45 to the bloody *Sassenachs.*"

"Who here be conjuring the sacred name o' our beloved rebellion?" Guthrie shuffled through the dry brush, his dingy kilt swaying over the weed tops. "Ye raise such a skelloch I ken where tae find ye a county o'er."

"Was hardly raising any disturbance. And what does it matter? I'm on the wilds of my own property."

"It matters because I taught ye tae curse better than that. Give me the gun. Ye've gone and jammed it good."

"I can take care of my own weapon."

"Nay need tae bite my heid off aboot it."

There he went again. Biting and gnashing. Always at the ones trying to help. He handed the rifle to Guthrie. With quick movements that belied his stubby fingers, the old man dislodged the angled cartridge and slid it back in slick as an arrow. Alec reclaimed his gun and the two sat in silence while Bruce lolled between their feet. A late October breeze tumbled from the east, lifting the barren heather stems from where they burrowed beneath fallen leaves of gold and red. Autumn was his favorite time of year, when nature gave its parting salute before settling in to a well-deserved rest.

The bushes rustled. Feathered bodies exploded into the glowing afternoon light.

Bam!

A plump quail faltered and twisted to the earth in death.

"Fetch, Bruce." Bruce shot off in a blur of black and white. He rooted through the brush, then trotted back, grinning with the fat bird cradled in his mouth. A bonny addition to the other two he'd bagged.

Guthrie took the bird and brushed the grass blades from its brown feathers. The faint scent of blood mingled with dirt. "It'll be a grand feast at the castle fae us tonight."

Alec reached for another cartridge in the ammunition bag. "I thought to stay out here a wee bit longer."

Guthrie eyed him from under shaggy eyebrows. He sat on the ground, unmindful of his kilt hiking up, and plucked at the bird's wing. "Hiding, ye are. From the lass."

"Quit your havering. I'm not hiding." He was. "Least of all from her." Precisely from her and the confusion of emotions she stirred in him.

"Gonna force me tae ask what happened between ye two?"

Alec swiped at the loose down floating to his sleeve. "Nothing happened."

Guthrie snorted and yanked out a tail feather. "Ye tell me that in the same tone she says and I dinna believe either o' ye. A lovers' spat, it was."

"No, nothing like that." It was and worse.

" 'Tis all right. I used tae have them all the time wi' my *leannan*."

That caught Alec's attention. He took in the man he'd known since he was a lad, the toad-like figure as familiar to Alec as his own shadow. The weatherworn clothes of a bygone time, the dark eyes squinted in perpetual suspicion. Alec could no sooner place him next to a woman than sitting on the Stone of Scone. "Since when did you have a sweetheart?"

"Afore the earth's crust cooled. She was none so bonny as yers. Wisps on her chin that tickled me when I kissed her." Guthrie flicked his fingers under his chin. A fuzz of down clung to his whiskers.

"Lily is not mine."

"Could be if ye tried harder."

"She'll not want me, not after the things I said." That dim light of hope that had flickered deep in the recess of Alec's heart flashed to consciousness. It had plagued him for months, leaping to awareness, then springing back to shadow before he could grasp its origin. Saying the words aloud, the light blazed to full formation in blinding truth.

"Ye're a man o' few words, that's true, but when they come they oft carry a sting.

302

Go tae the lass, fall on yer knees, and tell her what a clot-heid ye've been. Women adore that kind o' prostration."

"I hardly wish to be taking advice on the feminine nature from a crotchety old bachelor."

"As yer own methods are working so well." Guthrie held up the dead bird. Its head wobbled back and forth. "This o'er a golden beauty."

"It's not so simple. Her insistent need to meddle and prod at me, thinking she kens best." Alec swallowed against the words sticking in his throat. "She hit the truth of me and I chased her away."

"Pride, lad. At my age ye'll learn too late 'tis nay good carrying such a worthless burden."

"What's one more to me?"

"Aye, well . . . Make that two more." Dusting the feathers from his hands, Guthrie pulled a stack of letters from his jacket pocket and peeled off the top one.

A rock plunked in Alec's stomach as he tore open the envelope. "Past due payment required for interest on death duties. I paid the taxes off last year with the sale of the mill." He crumpled the statement in his hand. As if the death of the ruling lord wasn't cruel enough, the surviving family was forced to pay additional tax on the inheritance. "Where am I to find two thousand pounds? I own nothing worth that much."

"Ye do." Guthrie looked south to where Kinclavoch's central tower rose like a soldier's gray helmet above a thick swath of hawthorn trees. "No."

" 'Tis but a pile o' stone. Easy enough tae find another that doesna cost yer life's blood. We could make do."

This estate *was* the MacGregors' lifeblood. Alec would not be the one to sever the last vein and bleed them dry of everything his ancestors had worked to achieve. He would not be the failure his father set him up to be.

Shoving the missive in his pocket, Alec held out his hand. "Better get it all out now. Hand me the rest."

Guthrie thumbed through the stack. " 'Tis the only one, that was. The rest will keep." He quickly stuffed the others away.

Alec shifted the rifle to his other arm and waggled his fingers with impatience. If it was more bad news, he'd rather shoot his aggression out here than at the woodwork in his study. Guthrie slapped the stack into Alec's hand. New rationing requirements. The village paper proclaiming need for knitwear for the soldiers. And a note from the Queen's Theatre in London addressed to Lily. Why was she receiving letters from a theater?

He smoothed his thumb over the loopy *L*. Mayhap if Alec delivered the letter and begged an explanation of himself before she opened it, things could be righted between them. And if she rejected him . . . ?

"Best deliver these to Matron Strom. She'll see them to their proper place." Alec could have sworn he heard Guthrie muttering about pride.

Back at the castle, Alec promised to meet Guthrie in the kitchen to help clean the birds, then went in search of Matron Strom. He found her in the music room turned linen storage. Sadness swept over him at the sight of Viola's cloth-draped piano tucked in the far corner. A table lined with bedpans took its central place.

Matron kept her broad back to him as she counted off syringes in a cabinet. "What can I do for you, Lord Strathem?"

"Post came."

Turning, she checked off items on her clipboard before raising her gaze to him. The sparse eyebrows drew to a fuzzy line. "Is the delivering of messages not below the master's station?"

"When footmen and ladies' maids were once a customary part of life, mayhap. These days I've learned to enjoy doing things myself."

"A character trait I can admire." She took the messages and slowly tapped them against her clipboard. "Have there been any updates on finding Captain Gibbons's captors?"

"I'm afraid not." Alec ran a hand through his hair. "They grow wearisome of my continued presence at police quarters and have no substantial leads. If there are more clues, they grow stale with each passing day."

"I believe the greatest clues to uncover are found with Captain Gibbons himself, though his memory of the incident remains locked. For now. In time I hope it begins to reveal itself." Her scant eyebrows wriggled like aging caterpillars. "Might I speak frank?"

"I wish you would."

"Captain Gibbons's kidnapping is but one unfortunate addition to some ever-growing concerns." Flipping to the back of her clipboard, she pulled out a newspaper clipping and handed it to him.

"There is nothing so detestable as rumors, but for the sake of my nurses and patients I must ask. What is the state of Kinclavoch?"

A curse clamored to Alec's lips. Fire take Wright and his insidious paper. The matron's eyes watched his every breath. He chose his words with care. " 'Tis true the passing years have wearied Kinclavoch past her former glory. I give you my word that I will do whatever is required to provide a place of rest for those under your care. Mine as well." A ticking clock counted down to the exposure of his truth.

"Thank you for your assurance. I know you are a man of your word, and I have frequently reminded my superior and the army's Director of Hospitals of that fact. It seems a few newspaper articles have called into question your participation in Gibbons's kidnapping for your own profit. 'Rubbish,' I told them, from a salacious rag, but even so they are threatening to come to Kinclavoch for an inspection with the possibility of relocating the soldiers to safer accommodations."

Alec dug his fingers into the top of his

cane, the wood a smooth contrast to the coarse words pricking through his mind. "Richard Wright will do anything to ruin me, including framing me for a crime. Let the inspection come if it must. I've nothing to hide."

"I've told them as much but also thought you should be aware of our precarious situation. You would think his majesty's army had more important things to do than read a rag like the *London Herald*. Next he'll start accusing my nurses of foul play." Sighing, Matron selected the envelope with Lily's name on it and tore it open.

On reflex Alec reached for it. "Should that not be given to Miss Durham for opening?"

"Matrons are required to open all of their nurses' mail to ensure propriety and confidentiality."

"It's breaking confidence to open letters not addressed to oneself."

"It's for the sake of our patients. One loose-tongued nurse can feed the rumor pot and destroy the security we endeavor to create. I don't relish reading personal correspondence, but rules are rules." Her colorless lips pressed into a tight line as she scanned the message. Folding it in half, she marched to a door hidden in the wall and opened it. "Aide Durham. Come here."

Instinct told him to flee. He needed to face Lily, but not here. Not without time to formulate what to say to her.

"Stay, please, Lord Strathem," Matron said. "This involves you as well."

Before he could reply, Lily walked in carrying a tower of folded towels. "I just finished these, Matron, and am on my way to change the bedsheets upstairs."

"Put those down and explain to me the meaning of this." Matron wielded the letter like a blade.

Lily placed her load on the table. Her eyes met Alec's over the top of the towel folds. Shock widened her eyes before the pain of sadness shuttered them to a shadow of dull green. In that gaze flashed the regrets that had haunted him since their parting.

Emptiness echoed inside Alec, its taunt relentless as it begged release from her silence. He stepped toward her.

She spun away and took the message from Matron. "Ethel is coming!"

Matron's nostrils flared. "Precisely."

"This is wonderful news. Exactly what the men need to lift their spirits. They've been down of late, what with the changing weather. It affects their wounds more acutely."

"I'm well aware of seasonal implications

on recovery. What I want to know is why *she* is coming and why you thought you were excluded from asking my permission for such a thing. This hospital is not dictated by your theatrical whims."

"I thought it was a convalescent home."

"Might I remind you that you are on thin ice as it is, and I will not be subverted in authority."

"Subversion was not my intention —"

"I'm glad to hear you admit that."

"— secrecy was."

"Girl. I should have your buttons —"

"When I sent that telegram to E it was only to inquire if she had time in her schedule for a brief visit. I merely wished to know if it was a possibility before I brought the matter to you. After all, there's no sense in bothering you if her answer was no. Upon your approval, and only then, would I issue a formal invitation to her." Lily glanced down at the letter with half a smile. "I should have realized Ethel would take it as an open invitation."

Alec could keep quiet no longer. "Who is Ethel?"

Lily stiffened at his voice. "Ethel Barrymore."

"A person of the worst kind," Matron spat. "An actress. From America."

Alec couldn't tell if the profession or the country was what offended the stout woman more. "Is this Miss Barrymore coming to entertain the soldiers?"

Still not looking at him, Lily nodded. "As of right now, yes. Saturday next, which should be the first of November."

"Plenty of time to cancel," Matron said. "No doubt she can make up the disappointment with an afternoon matinee."

"Ethel isn't one of those types. She's respectable. The First Lady of the American Theatre."

"And that's where she can remain. Not pushing in on those needing peace and quiet, and she won't stop there. She has the gall already to begin making demands."

Lily frowned. "What kind of demands?"

"There in black and white" — Matron jabbed a finger at the telegram — "she explicitly says no honey of any kind may be served in her presence. No doubt she wants only sugar and will be disappointed to discover such a commodity is rationed at present."

"Ethel is severely allergic to honey. I'm certain that's the only reason she mentioned it, not to empty our limited sugar supply." Lily folded the note and tucked it in her apron pocket. "Besides, one missing lump

311

of sugar will hardly be noticed when she can offer such joy to the men."

Lily had a point. Not to mention agreeing with her could earn Alec a place back into her good graces. "Matron, if I might. Entertainment can have a far-reaching effect of rousing spirits."

Matron did a double take. "You are approving of this?"

"I am. And I ask for your consent as well. For the men, of course."

The woman stood silently for so long Alec feared he might have his own showdown with her. At last the vestiges of her hackles lowered. "Very well. One day only. Nurse Hartley will help you organize the event."

Lily smiled, but the happiness dropped as she caught Alec's eye. "Thank you, Matron. I'll write Ethel immediately."

Matron nodded. "Take this tray of glasses to be washed first, then replace the rolls of gauze. We have more missing by the day."

Lily took the tray and made for the door. Alec moved to go after her, but Matron stepped neatly in front of him. "I don't wish to take up any more of your time, Lord Strathem. We all run a tight schedule, and it doesn't do to chase after things that are only a drain on our limited resources."

"You have work to do. I shall see myself out."

As he turned to the door exiting opposite from Lily, Matron called her parting words. "It is best to stick with what we know. What is trusted will bring far more comfort than what glitters in the passing sun. I've no time for mending hearts."

"I've no intention of fracturing myself over spangles."

"It isn't *your* heart I speak of."

Alec clenched his cane and walked on, the lonely echo of his footsteps his only companion.

CHAPTER 15

"It's Gaudy."

Ignoring Esther's disdain, Lily stood back and admired her handiwork. It wasn't quite time for Christmas greenery, but the thick pine branches and crusty cones perfectly heralded the changing seasons into the library. Festoons of red tablecloths procured from a storage closet blossomed across the windows and doorframes in festive participation. Bowls of chrysanthemums and cinnamon sticks dotted the ceiling-high bookshelves. The sticks had somewhat lost the height of aromatic affability, but standing close enough might afford one a surprising whiff of holiday cheer.

"Where'd ye want this, lass?" Guthrie huffed in the doorway with Viola's piano. The girl had been so excited to hear of Ethel's impending visit that she'd offered her precious instrument for accompaniment.

Lily waved him into the room and pointed at the western wall. "Right over there, opposite the fireplace."

"All right, lads. Backs intae it." Guthrie and two patients, each missing one eye and referring to themselves as the Squints, pushed the piano across the hardwood floor. The wheels squeaked with each rotation until groaning at ease upon reaching their destination.

Left Squint wiped the sweat dotting his upper lip. "Phew! That beast is heavy."

Right Squint nodded as he stared down at his hard day's work. "Lucky this place has double doors to wheel it through. We couldn't all cram into the room we found her. Too many bedpans."

"By the window is a better place. Move it there," Esther announced.

"No, I prefer to keep the piano where it is," Lily said.

Drawing closer, Esther gave her best impression of a swan staring down at an insignificant bug. "I know this castle more intimately than you ever could or will. Why, it's practically a home to me. Best to leave the placement of things with me."

"Matron Strom left me in charge."

"For now."

Lily ignored her and walked around the

piano. The reddish hue of rosewood promised true beauty beneath a layer of grime. "I certainly do appreciate it, gentlemen. The performance will be so much more enjoyable thanks to your noble efforts."

"Got a player yet?" Right Squint asked.

Lily shook her head. She had begged Viola to play for the men at the show, but the girl had blushed to her roots and begged an excuse, saying she hoped to sit in the back without causing a disturbance to the true artist. "Not yet, but I'm hoping to —" *change her mind.* Alec's accusations taunted her. Always assuming what was best. Making decisions for others without their consent. He may not be in the same room, but his voice never left her. "I'm certain a talent will spring forth soon enough."

"I shall do it." Like a heavenly light meant to illuminate them all, Esther took her seat before the piano. Her white fingers floated above the keys as if awaiting divine inspiration to flow into them before touching the ivories. At her touch it emitted something close to a heavy sound rolling around in a barrel. Esther shot out of her seat as if offended. "Ugh. It's out of tune. I simply cannot play on this instrument in this state. A repairman must be called at once."

Guthrie tapped a black key. It tinked like

316

a sad bird. "Last repairman we had got his hands blown off in that campaign at Gallipoli. Churchill killed his own career wi' that disastrous plan. We'll no likely be hearin' much from that puffed-up jackanape again."

"Winston's mother, Jennie, was matron of honor at my parents' wedding," Lily said. "There was talk of setting a match between me and Winnie but nothing came of it. Thank goodness with his penchant for cigars."

Esther sniffed. "Another American added to the great British noble bloodline. Good heavens, you come over in droves. Perhaps we should run your stars and stripes up the flagpole at Buckingham Palace."

"And rob you of your quaint little country after besting you in the Revolution? That wouldn't be — what do you say here? — cricket."

Guthrie swiped a forefinger through the dust on top of the piano and gave it a close inspection. "Confusin' game, cricket. Shinty's more of a man's sport. Dinna hae tae wear all the white and fashin' 'bout it gettin' dirty." He wiped his hand across his kilt. "A repairman we need, aye. I'll be seein' aboot that."

He ambled from the room while Esther

rounded on Lily. "This is quite the feat you're toting to return to Matron's good graces."

"Matron has no good graces when it comes to me. I wanted to do this only for the men. Bad news pours off the battlefields every day. They need cheer, especially with the commander requesting more and more of them be sent back after they've recuperated."

"And what a magnificent party planner you've become. Why, with the quaint fêtes under your adept management, the nurses are allotted more time to care for our patients without distraction." Esther bestowed a patronizing smile on her. "Whatever will we do without your games when it's time for you to return to America?"

The barb at Lily's uselessness hit closer than she dare let on. "I have more important matters at hand than listening to your petty opinions. Excuse me." Lily brushed past her.

"The hospital reinforces consequences to those wishing to frolic instead of provide care."

"If you had the experience of training under my mother's hostess duties, you would know frolicking has no place in party planning. As far as consequences, my only concern is not having things prepared for

Miss Barrymore's arrival and only as it pertains to our patients. If you don't mind getting your hands dirty, there are a few more cinnamon sticks in need of a home. I have an extra pair of evening gloves if you prefer to cover up first. The dust and all."

"Your impertinence is insufferable."

"And your snobbery is tiresome. Here." Lily grabbed a box of pine cones and thrust it into Esther's arms. "There are more outside if you run out."

Esther looked ready to spit feathers. "How dare —"

"What is so urgent that you drag me down here?" Alec strode into the room with Guthrie clipping at his heels. Alec's frowning gaze swerved to the Squints staring openly at him. Right Squint leaned over and whispered to Left, who nodded in agreement. Alec's spine stiffened. Lily could sense him recoiling even as the invisible links of armor tightened their defense over him. His gaze jerked away and landed on Lily. He stopped dead still.

Lily's heart leaped to her throat.

Dressed in faded green trousers, a tweed jacket, and knee-high brown boots with his unruly hair curling around his ears, he looked like he'd come in from shooting something. A stag, a bird, a portrait of her.

319

Or Wright.

Lily had avoided Alec like a cat avoids water, but seeing him now swept in every tangle of emotions she had desperately tried to unwind herself from. She missed the blueness of his eyes, but it now cut her with shame. She missed his voice, though she now cringed at what accusations it might wield at her. Missed the still quietness that settled between them when the world threatened chaos. Would she ever find such peace again? Doing so would require a risk of rejection. She couldn't bear another. Not from him.

Esther spun around, a wide smile lighting her face. "Alec. Whatever are you doing here? Come to see the festivities for yourself?" She walked toward him, cradling the box of pine cones. "I was just about to arrange these. Don't you think they'll make darling additions around the room? I could use your help."

Guthrie brushed past her. "He's here tae see tae the piano."

"Aye, the piano." Alec said the words slowly as he continued to look at Lily.

His gaze held her captive, trapping them both in an impenetrable space all their own. Was she the greater fool for wishing to escape or stay? Escape would be the easier of the two. It's what she had done her entire life when a problem had risen its head to force introspection and change. Those were confrontations she never wished to make. Fleeing had served her well in the past, yet that dance grew wearisome. She wanted to stand still in the circle Alec's unmoving fortitude carved.

But his silence since that day by the dovecote, when they'd flayed each other with truth, told her everything she feared.

She dropped her gaze, breaking the spell.

"The piano." Alec's tone turned sharp. His boots thudded on the floor as he marched to the instrument. "What's wrong with it? And why is it in here?"

"Miss Durham wanted music fae the actress, but it's hittin' a sour note," Guthrie offered. "Fitz canna tune anymore less he's learned wi' his toes."

Flipping open the piano's bench seat, Alec rooted around until he found a burlap sack. He pulled out a tuning fork. "Never was the best with these, but I watched Fitz enough times. Viola should be here. She could tell me the accurate pitch I'm supposed to find."

"I can do that." Dumping her box onto a nearby chair — bouncing out several cones — Esther sailed to position herself at the side of the piano. "I have perfect pitch." She opened her mouth and out soared a note. "That's middle C."

Lily turned away. She couldn't stand to watch Esther's smirk of superiority as she leaned over Alec with a feigned interest in the strings. Lily had more important things to do. Such as fluffing the red curtains-turned-garland across the side table. The same red matching the MacGregor colors. A bold color to set in a kilt. Did Alec ever wear one? She threaded the smooth fabric between her fingers. He would look handsome in one. No, what was it they said here? Braw. He would look braw indeed.

Esther screeched higher. D flat, she claimed.

Dropping the kilt, er, garland, Lily gathered up the batch of white chrysanthemums and arranged them in empty potted-meat bottles, depositing them around the room. She was careful to keep her focus on the task, yet every sensation in her body hummed back to the piano. Or more pointedly, to *him*. As clear in her mind as the sun in the sky, she saw the brow furrowed in concentration, the corners of his mouth curved down in determination, and the large, capable hands twisting the screws to submission.

Esther's next note nearly broke glass.

Wincing under the auditory assault, Lily placed her last makeshift vase. They were missing something. Ah, the pine cones. Which had been conveniently abandoned near the piano.

Or inconveniently in her case.

She could either stand here and will the cones to float across the room to her, summon the Squints to fetch them for her, or respond in a mature manner and retrieve them herself. Herself it was. If Alec should happen to look up, then so be it. Just because they wavered at an awkward impasse didn't mean they should go on ignoring each other forever.

The piano tinked as she crossed to the chair. Each note sped up the cadence of her heart as Alec's nearness closed in around her. She reached for the pine cones that had jostled free of their container. Good golly, why were her hands shaking?

"Miss Durham."

Lily jumped at Alec's voice. The pine cone in her hand went flying. It bounced under the piano. Crouching, she ducked under the wooden body and grasped the runaway cone. A hand closed around hers.

"Lily." The sound of her name in that familiar lilt sent her heart careening off course. Alec's gaze, as blue and deep as the lochs, bored into her from where he crouched on the other side. "I need to speak with you."

"I need to speak with you."

Their words clashed over each other at the same instant. Alec's ruddy eyebrows lifted in surprise as a similar shock rippled in Lily. She hadn't meant to say that, but as soon as the words freed themselves from her mouth, a swell of relief stole through her. Seems they could ignore each other no longer. Thank goodness.

The piano strings thundered with disapproval. "E flat has been forgotten." Esther grabbed Alec's elbow and tugged him up. She shot Lily a look of acid.

"I'm no repairman. Unless we find someone suitable before the show, this is how it'll play," Alec said, dusting off his knees, which had become littered with pine needles.

"And leave the great Miss Barrymore without a proper accompaniment? For shame."

Lily gathered up her cone and stood. "Ethel can sing and act her way around a bad tune. She won't be shamed in the least. In the meantime perhaps I can make inquiries further afield for repairmen."

"There is no meantime." Matron stormed

into the room like a diva in the middle of act two waving a telegram. She bore straight down on Lily, gray chin hairs quivering. "Your actress friend arrives today."

"Today? No. She's supposed to come tomorrow." Without asking permission, Lily snatched the telegram from Matron's hand and read the announcement. A surprise, Ethel said. To spend more time with "the boys." "We're not ready. I haven't arranged her room. The chairs aren't set up. There's cinnamon dust all over the floor. The piano."

Esther placed a gentle hand on Lily's arm. "You run along and see to the room. I have everything in hand." She quickly scooped up the pine cone box and turned to Alec with a sweet smile. "Might I have your assistance? Perhaps we can recreate the same decorations your mother had up the first time she invited my family to celebrate Christmas at Kinclavoch. Such a warm time for all of us."

"I'll leave the decorations to more capable hands. The horses need tending." With a final glance at Lily, Alec marched out the door to seek his more preferred company.

Matron hauled Lily into the storage room and slapped a pair of sheets into her arms. "This is your responsibility. You assured me this invasion would cause no unneeded stress."

"It won't. It hasn't. Everything will be perfect by the time she arrives. I promise!"

"See to it immediately that our guest's chamber is readied." Surprising she didn't use the word *trollop* to clarify the designated status of said guest. Pulling a stack of envelopes from her pocket, Matron added them to the top of the pile of linens. "Your little surprise kept me from remembering to hand these over to Lord Strathem. His post. Slip them under his study door. Under the door, not waltzing in."

Lily hadn't waltzed in months, but it was of little use to point that out considering the hot water she was already in. Nodding obediently, she balanced the linens in her arms and traversed the corridor to Alec's study. The door was wide open. Oh dear. She was to waltz after all. Her feet stumbled to a halt in the entry.

Or not.

Papers, books, and trinkets were strewn about the room. Pictures hung from broken frames. The drapes were ripped from the rod that dangled precariously in front of the window. Swallowing her horror, she crossed the landmine of destruction to the heavy desk and stepped over the chairs that had

326

been knocked to their sides. A ledger lay open on the desk. Cold dragged its dreaded finger down Lily's spine. Pages were torn out, leaving bits of jagged evidence with neat pencil marks tallying the beginning of rows and columns. Expenses and debts of Kinclavoch for the past year. Gone.

CHAPTER 16

"My bet is on Wright."

Bertie's words stopped Lily dead at the top of the stairs. "You're saying that because you want it to be true."

"I'm saying it because it's most likely true. He despises Lord Strathem. You've told me numerous times."

"I thought you English were above such blatant accusations of guilt, reserving your disdain beneath civilized demeanors of ice."

"We allow it to melt out in times of duress. Keeps the ice fresh." Bertie adjusted her glasses back to the bridge of her nose after the walk upstairs had slid them down. "Has Lord Strathem said anything to you about the incident?"

Lily shook her head. Only yesterday Guthrie had walked in after her to Alec's study. He'd taken one look around, sworn in Gaelic, then told her to hie herself gone and not speak a word to anyone. He would inform Alec. Hieing herself as instructed, Lily had been unable to witness Alec's reaction to the unforgivable breach in privacy and destruction of his property, but it was one she didn't have to imagine. She'd experienced it firsthand not so long ago.

"Wright is a snake in the grass, but he seems more of a man to cover his tracks. Or better still, pay someone else," Lily said as they started down the long hall of the west wing with its faded wallpaper revealing missing artwork and rows of floor-to-ceiling windows she had hastily scrubbed. Unfortunately, she could only clean so far as her arm stretched, leaving the top window parts still coated in grime.

"Who's to say he didn't hire thugs to ransack the room? I find it odd that they ripped out pages. Why not take the whole ledger, and more pressing, why account numbers on expenses and debts? You said Wright wants the castle, not to become its banker."

"Perhaps he wanted to see how deep in the red Kinclavoch is. Or maybe it was creditors. I hear they lack all scruples to recover their payments."

"Aha!" Bertie snapped her fingers. "Hartley. She senses the competition closing in and decided to make her move. By knowing the estate's accounts, she would know what to hold over the master's head, thereby forcing him to capitulate to her marriage designs."

Panicking at how close her cousin's astute declaration came to Esther's bridal plans, Lily rushed to cover it. "Nonsense. Esther may preen too much, but ripping apart a man's personal study is beyond what her delicate nails would touch. She's the star nurse and Matron's pet. She's beautiful and wealthy and has no need to blackmail a struggling landowner into loving her. A girl like her could knock out the men of New York before they knew what hit them."

"The only thing she wants to knock out, as you so colloquially put it, is the title of Lady Strathem." Bertie's chin was tilted down, but her gaze shifted up through her glasses in that intelligent cock of the head that only a person wearing spectacles can achieve to perfection. "Your competition."

"That's ridiculous." Lily's footsteps muffled on the threadbare carpet running the center of the wooden floor. It was sparse but clean as several of the ranking officers were given private chambers along there. "Besides, Alec wishes to stand on his own merit. He has no intention on securing income by marriage."

"What do you mean by that?"

Overhearing Alec's rejection of Esther's blatant proposal out in the stables had remained a secret. For Alec's sake, Lily had no desire to gossip about what had transpired. If she had, inevitably her own feelings on the matter would have presented themselves. He stirred something far beyond attraction in her. Far beyond what simple words could describe, he spoke to a part of her she'd never fathomed.

"Lily."

Lily jumped from the window she'd found herself staring through. "Yes?"

Bertie's dark-brown eyes tuned her back to focus. "What did you mean by securing income by marriage?"

Hurrying to cover her blunder and the subsequent heat rising to her cheeks, Lily feigned interest in a burn mark concealed beneath her apron. She'd been daydreaming while attempting to iron the night before. "Only that it's not unheard of for marriages to occur under business arrangements. I believe your aristocracy thrives on such matches." She continued down the corridor while rearranging her thoughts from the distracting lord. "Besides, Esther was with me all morning arranging pine cones and cinnamon sticks. She didn't have time to destroy the room without Alec noticing before me."

"One can achieve anything by putting one's mind to it."

"Such as your mind wanting to condemn people without trial first?" Lily nudged Bertie's shoulder.

"Only those most likely of guilt." Her cousin primly shrugged.

"They can't be guilty unless we have proof of who actually committed the offense."

"I shall never understand the mentality of always needing to prove a point. It's quite exhausting." Bertie sighed with dignified exasperation.

"The sensation is new to me as well. Will you help me?"

"Of course I will. No one threatens my cousin's suitor and gets away with it."

Heat flushed unchecked to Lily's cheeks. "He is not my suitor!"

"I see the nurses are hard at work. Surely your patients need you downstairs, or are you too busy wandering my halls to attend them?" At the junction where the corridor angled off to a darkened portion of the wing, Alec's mother stood pale and tall as a Gothic ghost. The weak sunlight floating in through the arched windows lining the corridor touched the delicate bones of her face before scattering off. As if the light found the sharp structures too cold to linger upon.

Lily and Bertie smiled in unison. "Good afternoon, Lady Strathem."

"There's nothing good to be said of it. I've unwanted guests filling my rooms and an actress set to perform in my home." Lady Strathem practically spat the word. "God pray this war ends soon so we may all return to our peace." Snatching the folds of her black velvet skirt, she retreated into the dark hall from whence she came.

Flashing Bertie a look of relief from having escaped the woman's death stare, Lily knocked on the door to their left.

"Entre."

The Willow Room, so aptly named for its view of willow trees crowding close to the River Spey, floated in a décor of blues and greens. Bright spots of gold sconces flickering with candles flashed through the watery effect like sunspots on a pond. Sitting at the vanity like a floating lily pad was Ethel, dressed in a frothy gown of pink chiffon with matching heels.

"Ah, there you are, Lily." Ethel's large eyes found her in the mirror's reflection. "Help a girl out, will you? I've traveled without a maid before and can manage on my own most days, but this back button always gives me trouble."

Lily crossed to stand behind the great actress and quickly slipped the pearl buttons through their appropriate holes. Her fingers lingered over the smooth roundness with no eagerness to return to the drab yet functional ones on her uniform. She stood back and examined the two decidedly different figures in the mirror. Ethel in her perfumed finery of elegance. Lily in her turnip knapsack.

"Is this the latest fashion from New York?"

Ethel laughed, a silvery sound elongated to ripple across theater rows. "Hardly. It's from last year when froufrou trimmings were all the rage. American ladies have since turned to sturdier fabrics and silhouettes to show solidarity with the entrenched women of Europe."

Lily smoothed a hand down the coarse chambray fabric of her uniform and smiled with a pip of pride. It may have been ugly, but it didn't catch on the men's bandages. Perhaps it wasn't so terrible after all.

"Is that rouge?" Bertie whispered over a small pot sitting on the vanity next to a silver-handled comb and brush set.

Ethel picked up the pot and held it out to Bertie. "Would you care to use some? I had it specially mixed at House of Cyclax on

Bond Street in London after the props man broke my other one."

Bertie reared back in horror. "I could never."

"How stupid of me. Of course you can't. I've been so long in the theater I too often forget how respectable ladies are supposed to dress." Ethel laughed and playfully patted her own rouged cheeks. "Here I sit primed like a Saturday night special."

"You look beautiful, Miss Barrymore."

"It's only so I don't look dead sick to the folks up in the peanut gallery. I suppose you can take the girl out of the theater, but you can't take the theater out of her."

"Might I have your autograph?" Blushing, Bertie pulled a card decorated with ribbon from her pocket. One of the many she spent her off-hours decorating for the boys in Reggie's unit to send in care packages. "It's for my brother serving in France. He must be tired of all the mundane letters I send him. I'm certain one little word from you would send him over the moon. He always wanted to go on the stage, but family duties dictated otherwise. How I would adore to see him perform alongside a great actor such as yourself."

"Flattery, my dear, will get you everywhere with me. Especially if a handsome man is involved." Taking the card from Bertie, Ethel signed it with a flourish and added a kiss that left an imprint of stained lips. "Tell him if he ever sails to New York to come and see me. We can talk actor to actor."

Bertie hugged the card to her chest as if it were gold. "Oh, thank you, Miss Barrymore. This will mean the world to him. And me."

"My pleasure, dear." When she stood, Ethel's dress fell in shimmery waves around her as if the fabric had practiced its routine to perfection. Must be a technique taught in acting school. "Is it nearly time for curtains up?"

"Almost." Lily swept her arm to the door in the same way she'd seen the theater attendees do hundreds of times. "Your audience awaits."

Coming off the stairs into the great hall, they were immediately surrounded by a mob of adoring fans. Ever the professional, Ethel smiled at each of them as if he were the only man in the room and proceeded to answer each inquiry in turn. Bertie had slipped off to stand next to Captain Gibbons, who'd hobbled in on his crutch. Her eyes fluttered behind her glasses.

Wait. Was she flirting?

Lily shook her head in amazement. Wonders never ceased, though to work true magic she needed to tilt her chin down a touch. Lily made a mental note to offer a few pointers later and slipped around the grand staircase to check on the refreshments in the kitchen. The back corridor was dim after she'd taken most of the candles to fill in the library, but the turns had become familiar enough that she hardly took a wrong corner. Hushed voices stopped her.

"This is not the time." Lady Strathem.

"If not now, then when? I've been a patient man, but the passing years cannot wait for your pride alone." Richard Wright? What was he doing here?

"It is my heart and not my pride that rules this decision."

"Let go of the past, Edwina." Why was Wright cavorting with Alec's mother in secret? Lily inched closer.

"The past is all I have left to cherish. Do not ask me to give up what can never be yours. Not a second time."

"Life is full of second chances. Ways to right the wrongs."

"No wrongs have been committed unless you persist in this wasted plea. I told you no thirty years ago. My answer has not and will not change."

"Edwina, I insist —"

"Let go of me, Richard."

Lily rounded the corner. Richard Wright stood impolitely close to Lady Strathem with his hand circled around her wrist. "May I be of assistance?"

Lady Strathem broke the hold on her wrist and narrowed her blue gaze. "No, you may not. I have things well enough in order without interference."

What was it with the MacGregor family and their infinite accusations of interference?

Pulling her black lace shawl over her shoulders, Lady Strathem swept past Lily. A hint of dried violets trailed in her wake. Wright smoothed the front of his vest and made to go after her.

Lily stepped in front of him. "If Lord Strathem discovers your unwanted admittance, he's liable to shoot you."

Wright's lip curled back. There in the semidarkness the sharp angles of his thin face jutted out in harsh relief. "Broke, limp, and a suspected kidnapper. How far he's fallen in this world."

"He's still far above slithering from a rotten apple. The same cannot be said of you."

"You call it slithering while I refer to it as taking advantage of opportunities when others are too afraid to do so."

"Such as harassing women in darkened

corners? Surely the first time Lady Strathem said no wasn't meant to fall on deaf ears."

"That conversation is none of your business." His lips flattened to a bloodless white line.

"It doesn't change the fact that you are trespassing. Get out."

"Quite the lovely mouthpiece you've become for that boy. Falling in love with him, are you? Alec MacGregor is nothing more than a sinking ship."

"And you the torpedo to blast the fatal hole." It took everything in her not to react to the distracting mention of love Wright hurled at her.

"It is the way of progress. The old must be done away with. Forgotten and buried to make room for new possibilities. New chances resurrected." His gaze drifted over her shoulder to where Lady Strathem had disappeared.

"What has Alec done to make you want to destroy everything he stands for? Why can you not continue on your miserable little path without crossing his at every turn?"

Ghosts of the past shifted across Wright's face, the forms flitting between regret, desire, and anger. A life wasted in pursuit of that which he was never the victor.

"Strathem is a memory of circumstances that never should have been allowed to happen. A blot upon my destiny and all I was intended for. This pile of stone imprisons a ghost I want vanquished." Wright stepped closer, capturing her in his torrid scent of clove aftershave. "The current lord and his prideful stubbornness is the only thing impeding my success."

Lily had never had reason to fear another person, at least not directly and certainly not a presumed gentleman like Wright. She was wrong to lean on such naivety, for a well-polished shoe and rounded vocabulary was the perfect disguise of threats because it was where one least expected to find them. And that made him all the more dangerous.

"I hope he continues to impede you. With a scattering of buckshot," Lily said.

"An ill-advised move."

"Only if he gets caught. I doubt anyone in a fifty-mile radius would find him guilty after ridding the populace of an Englishman." Lily dropped her voice to a stage whisper. "They don't care much for your sort around here."

"Perhaps not, but Miss Barrymore does. I'm here at her invitation."

Lily's mouth popped open in a most

unladylike way. "I-I beg your pardon?"

"Miss Barrymore has agreed to do a feature story for my paper. I'm thinking of titling it *Barrymore for the Boys.* These sort of collaborations between the famous and the wounded are a huge hit with my readers." Wright's lip lifted in that irritating smirk again. Lily's hand itched to slap it off. "Of course, if Lord Strathem forces me to cancel the interview . . . I can't image that going over well in the press. He's on shaky ground as it is."

"Who said anything about canceling the interview?" Ethel's voice trilled down the corridor followed by the soft swishing of her gown as she walked toward them. "This will do tremendous good in lifting the morale of people not only in the country but around the world. The piece can encourage other performers to utilize their talents for good in places that need cheer."

Lily's resolve faltered at Ethel's heartfelt plea. As much as she detested Richard Wright and suspected him of foul play, she couldn't deny the much-needed encouragement this article would initiate. Nor would she ever allow Alec to face the backlash Wright would hurl his way if the interview failed to go forward.

Conjuring her most charming smile, Lily

placed a gentle hand on the actress's shoulder. "You're right, E. A piece like this could do a world of good. Mr. Wright was just telling me how he'll be unable to linger after your performance as he needs to return to London to get the story off to print as soon as possible." She flashed an icy warning to the snake. "I doubt we'll see him again."

"An assurance I in faith cannot make. Nor would I want to." Wright buffed his hand against his lapel, then offered his arm to Ethel. "Miss Barrymore. Shall we?"

"By the way, Mr. Wright, I forgot to ask," Lily called. "When was the last time you were at Kinclavoch?"

Wright's expression revealed nothing. "That I cannot recall."

"No? Was I wrong in thinking I heard you inside Lord Strathem's study not two days ago?"

"I never wish to correct a lady in public by claiming she is wrong, but in this case I'm afraid it's true. Two days ago I was in my London office." His thin lips tilted in mockery. "Would you care to wire my secretary for a copy of my schedule?" The tilt slid into a sneer before he turned and escorted Ethel away.

Insides raging, Lily held perfectly still until the unlikely pair twirled around the corner. Alec would be livid at Wright's presence, and she would have no one to blame but herself. There was no telling what he might do if he actually showed up to the performance. This was one instance where she was grateful for his self-exile.

Alec stood uncertainly at the back of the library. He waited for all eyes to turn on him, pronounce their judgment, and banish him from their presence. Heart pounding, he counted the seconds.

No one took notice. His breath eased out.

The drapes were drawn while hundreds of candles lit the room in a warm glow that sank richly into the wood panels. The air was spiced with fresh greenery and aged book pages in a unique spell of comfort that cast an enchantment upon all who entered. He'd sat in this room thousands of times over his lifespan, but never had he gazed in wonder as he did now.

He moved along the back wall, careful to skirt the crackling fireplace, while keeping behind the rows of chairs facing the stage at the far end of the room. One man stood juggling three balls while another tossed tin plates in the air, catching them deftly before hurling them skyward again, all to the thunderous applause of their audience.

Spying an empty chair on the end of the back row, Alec took a seat and leaned his cane against his leg. Laughter pealed as one of the juggler's balls bounced on top of the plate man's head. Alec found himself smiling along with them. When was the last time he'd heard the ring of laughter in this room? Or saw it come alive for a festive occasion?

On instinct he sought her. Only Lily had the whirlwind presence to create transformation in a matter of hours. A room, a castle, a routine, a person, a peace of mind. Nothing was out of bounds to her abilities. Least of all him. He brushed a finger over his cane where the carving of a single petal had bloomed. He'd held her at arm's length and yet her touch had reached the most concealed parts of his inner self, easing the pervasion of loneliness.

Peering over the tops of heads and bandages, he spotted the one he sought standing against the wall nearly obscured by shadow save for the light of candle bouncing off her golden hair.

Lily stared back at him in horror.

Alec frowned. Well, that wasn't the reception he'd anticipated.

Lily's gaze swerved from him to a figure near the front row, then skittered back to Alec. Alec squinted through the haze of candlelight as he made out the long head. The arrogant points of his shoulders and the vengeful tilt of his chin. Richard Wright. Alec's fists curled atop his knee. He'd warned that snake never to slither near Kinclavoch again. Apparently he needed a more physical lesson in listening.

Alec moved into the aisle. A one-eyed man popped up in front of him. "A message for you, my lord."

"Move."

"The lady insists." The man pushed a piece of torn paper into Alec's hand. "She insists you sit first."

Alec looked over the man's shoulder to Lily, who still stood with a look of horror but now with a pen clenched in her hand. An open book lay next to her on the side table.

Taking a deep breath, Alec sat and snatched the paper from the man. Page six from a copy of Sir Walter Scott's *Ivanhoe*. Fire take that woman for ruining one of his best editions.

Don't kill him! Ethel invited. I'll shove him out myself right after show!

Alec's fury slammed into Lily's pleading eyes. Every righteous bone in his body demanded the satisfaction of training a rifle to Wright's fleeing form as he raced down the drive, but he couldn't. Not with Lily looking at him like that. And not with all these men about.

Maintaining eye contact with Lily, Alec folded the page with a quick jerk of his fingers and shoved it into his front jacket pocket. She sagged against the wall and mouthed, *"Thank you."*

"Ahem."

Alec's attention snapped to the one-eyed man who'd taken the empty seat next to him. "What?"

"Do you wish to reply to the lady?"

"No." The man didn't move save his gaze, which traveled to Alec's cane, which had been knocked to the floor. Alec snatched it up. "Is there something else you need?"

The man shook his head even as his eye remained on the cane. "Only, I'm curious who made those markings. My old man's got a bum leg and he'd be right tickled to have a fancy stick like that."

"I made them."

"Is that so? Me and Right Squint — that's what we call ourselves, the Squints, for reasons you can see — were trying to decide yesterday what they were when you came in here to fix the piano. Right Squint claims they're naught more than shapes and lines. I said it had to be ancient Celtic runes, this being Scotland and all. I see now we were both wrong. A beauty you've created here."

"You weren't —" *whispering about me?* Like hooks never far from the surface, the old insecurities sank their treachery into Alec's eternal shame. Would he never learn that not all intentions were distrustful? He cleared his throat and tried again. "The task keeps my hands from restlessness."

The jugglers finished their act and bowed as a new man sauntered forward to sing a rendition of "If You Were the Only Boche in the Trench," a gory adaption of the more popular "If You Were the Only Girl in the World."

Squint leaned back in his chair and crossed an ankle over his opposite knee. A slipper dangled off his foot. "Never was much good with my hands. Always wanted to be a photographer. Seeing how different and alike we all are. The humanity and destruction within us all."

Trying not to focus on the singer's recounting of death and destruction in the trenches, Alec settled more firmly in his chair. "A picture is worth a thousand words."

"I had a few choice words when it cost

me my eye."

"How?"

"Bullet came right through the lens when I was taking a photograph of the trench. A fraction more to the left and I would've found my muddy earth box. Want to see it?" He rummaged in his pocket and pulled out a smashed cartridge, holding it out like a diamond for Alec to inspect.

Alec studied the talisman of death. Such a small thing to cause such horror. "I don't know whether to congratulate you or the sniper on such a shot."

"I've pondered the same myself." Laughing, Squint pocketed his treasure. "I'd been living in the trenches for over a year. My feet were toughed from the miles of marching while mud squelched in my ears. My prayers at night were to wake up just before the rats bit me so I might grab them and enjoy a good meal with my mates. One morning I was having breakfast with a man from Dorset. He turned to grab his canteen and took shrapnel to the head for his efforts when a shell exploded overhead."

Lily walked to the front of the audience with a smile beaming across her face. "And now, ladies and gentlemen, please welcome back to the stage our guest star. Miss Ethel Barrymore."

The actress swept to the piano. "Thank you. My, what a rapturous crowd. You remind me of a great speech I once heard on stage. Something that goes like this: 'Be not afraid of greatness. Some are born great, some achieve greatness, and others have greatness thrust upon them.'" She paused for dramatic affect. "What do you think? An accurate description of you brave men?"

Applause thundered to the roof. Nodding with satisfaction, the actress continued the Bard's famous lines. She had a beautiful, rich voice that resonated as if she were standing directly next to you without reaching an octave of shrill.

Alec found his attention turning back to Squint. "It must be incredibly difficult living minute to minute like that. Never knowing if it's to be your last."

"War. Acclimates you to things only a nightmare could drum up. Leads you to find a demon with fangs instead of a man staring at you from across no-man's-land."

Alec considered his words and the juxtaposition it posed between the normality of two worlds. The reconciliation between them was not something to come naturally but through a brute force of circumstance where one must bend to a will greater than his own. Yet human nature was resilient.

Where once a man might have scoffed at the use of rocks as a pillow, he may slowly find himself scraping together pebbles for a semblance of the familiar, though it may be far from his grasp.

"I suppose it's the acceptance of such things that aids survival," Alec said.

"I saw plenty of them, usually the newer ones who couldn't accept the reality. They were always the first to go."

"Did you not fear death?"

"A man wouldn't be in his right mind if he thought he could outwit eternity's calling. There were times when I prayed for death. A quick death, not the cruelty of starvation or drowning slowly in the mud. Bad way to go, that."

"Yet you were spared."

Squint dropped his foot to the floor and leaned forward on his knees. "I often wonder if I'm supposed to be grateful for that or not while my friends' bodies feed the worms. I needed a salvation if I was to live and they weren't. A camera became that. I photographed everything. Rat-infested trenches, barbed wire slick with blood, tree stumps where once a forest stood, mud craters with bloated bodies, and faces. Faces of death, of hope, of friendship, of loss. We lost everything that mattered over there."

His words rooted deep within Alec. All this time he'd thought he understood the sacrifices being made, the nobility in which the soldiers must armor themselves against the foe. How naively colored his notions had been when confronted with the rawness twisting over Squint's face.

"Your homes and families are kept safe because of what you've done. Such a sacrifice cannot be discarded as lost."

Squint's eye shifted to him. Pain filtered through the broken blood vessels. "What do they know of what we've done? Tommies send letters to keep their families hoping, but they'll never understand. Only the few of us who make it out alive do. Count that leg of yours as a lucky token keeping you out of the whole mess."

Snorting, Alec rubbed his knee. "A curse is closer to the truth."

"I was wrong a minute ago when I said only those of us who made it out could understand. Don't mean no disrespect, your lordship, but sacrifices come in all forms. I'd wager you know as much about that as the boys in the trenches."

Alec shook his head and gazed over the heads in front of him. Every one of them had earned their place while he sat among them as an imposter. "I doubt very much they'd agree."

"Ever ask them?"

Alec shifted with discomfort at the sudden turn of attention on him. "I'm not so vain a man to want comparisons."

"Pain is pain, festering in all of us. My photographs are proof enough of that."

Pain was pain, rotting like a disease kept hidden from pitying eyes. These men craved salvation from the nightmares they lived. The only way to banish a nightmare was to bring it to light. Stories like Squint's and those of his friends in arms deserved to be told with illuminating truth and their heroism celebrated.

"Do you have any of the photographs here?"

Squint wedged his finger under the bandage behind his ear and scratched. "My commander was able to salvage a few after I was shot and sent them to me at hospital. One of the nurse's brothers ran a studio, and he offered to develop them for me."

"I should be very interested to take a look."

Around them men burst into applause as Ethel finished a recitation from *Romeo and Juliet* and took a bow. "That's all there is — there isn't any more!"

"Encore! Encore!"

Smiling benevolently, Ethel took a sip from a cup on the piano next to her and turned back to her eager audience. "Now, for my last set I hope you don't mind me attempting another song. This one from your neck of the woods." She nodded to Esther. A tune cascaded from the piano keys in a memory that Alec had not conjured in years. Ethel sang.

> Will you go lassie go
> To the braes of Balquidder

Alec's gaze drifted to the far wall where Lily stood. Hands behind her back, she leaned against the wall with a dreamy sort of look washing across her face. Bonny she'd look strolling among the heather. He'd like to take her come summertime.

> Where the high — *cough cough* —
> mountains run — *cough cough* —

Ethel turned her head away and delicately tapped her chest. Smiling with reddened cheeks, she continued.

> And the bonnie blooming heather —
> *cough cough cough.*

Ethel swayed as her face and neck turned

splotchy red. More coughing wracked her body. She grabbed the piano for support, her hand clawing at her throat as her eyes rolled up. Toppling forward, she hit the ground unconscious.

Shouting erupted. Alec jumped to his feet and lurched toward the singer. Lily rushed forward, quickly followed by Matron Strom as Esther sat in place looking shocked. Amid the pandemonium Richard Wright rose to his feet and calmly took a small notebook and pen from his jacket pocket and proceeded to jot down something.

He circled slowly around the crowd surrounding the great American actress with pen flying over the page. He looked up, straight to Alec. And smiled.

CHAPTER 17

"If someone is trying to kill me, then they'd better try harder." Holding a small mirror, Ethel patted the red blotches marring her neck. They stood vivid and angry against her lacy white nightdress. "I've no intention of being snuffed out by an allergy to honey of all pitiful things."

The castle had spun into an uproar upon Ethel's collapse hours before. Matron Strom swept her upstairs for immediate treatment while the men droned around like bees stunned in smoke. Never one for tangling himself in hysterics, Alec had pushed his way through the crowd, seized Wright by the lapels, and dragged him out.

Lily gave a passing thought to follow, then thought better of it and grabbed the tainted teacup. A wisp of golden honey glistened on the inner rim. It was nearly impossible to find these days with rationing, unless one knew of the seedier places to obtain it.

Where had it come from?

"All I can say is how deeply sorry I am," Lily said. "My invited guest takes time out of her busy schedule to come do a good deed and she's poisoned while singing. If ever I shall send you another invitation, there will be no offense taken if you decline."

"Where would be the fun in that?" Ethel settled against the bed pillows and beckoned Lily closer. "How do you suppose it came to be in my cup?"

"It may have been an honest mistake. I told the kitchen staff of your request, but nurses go in and out of there all day. With all the hustle and bustle from your arrival and the performance, perhaps one of the nurses thought to help prepare your cup while the cook was otherwise engaged." Guilt stabbed Lily. She should have been the one to prepare Ethel's tea, but she'd allowed the day to distract her. "I'm so sorry, E."

"Nonsense." Ethel patted her hand. "Listen. From all my experiences on stage, honest mistakes aren't what bring the curtain crashing down. Almost always it's jealousy behind the mask of threats."

Jealousy. A horrid green-eyed beast that sank its claws deep into a victim and filled him with poison. Had the disease spread into the castle to rampage through Alec's study and ladle harm into innocent teacups? Fear prickled deep inside Lily. The incidents were too close together to be considered random acts of animosity. Their cruelty had been carefully plotted, but to what end?

Smoothing down the green coverlet over Ethel's lap, Lily offered a bright smile. "Get your rest as the doctor ordered if you plan on returning to London by Sunday."

Ethel returned her smile, though it dipped in sadness. "I've been around actors long enough to detect avoidance through painted-on smiles. Be careful, Lil."

With those words still ringing in her head, Lily bid Ethel a good night and carried the tray down to the kitchen. She hesitated at the corridor leading to Alec's study. Warm yellow light pooled under the closed door, bidding her forward. She could easily imagine him pacing as he contemplated the next item of worth to be auctioned off or how best to dispose of Wright without the local law enforcement taking notice. There was no possibility that what happened to Ethel would stay out of the papers. If Wright had managed to leave Kinclavoch intact after Alec was through with him, the story would be splashed across the *London Herald* by morning.

Her heart twisted toward Alec, but her feet carried her on. They may have approached a truce, but their rift had yet to mend.

Unlike all other times of the day, the kitchen was quiet with its stone walls and wooden built-ins bathed in soft light glowing from the burning fireplace. She set the tray on the long counter and pumped water into the bucket in the sink. The water splashed out icy cold and she chided herself for not taking time to heat it over the fire. Then again, those precious minutes could be used to get her to bed quicker and put this terribly long day to rest. She dipped a plate into the water, sucking in a breath as the cold numbed her fingers.

Plop. Plop. Plop.

Frowning, Lily followed the sound to a small puddle on the corner of the counter. Tracing the trajectory upward, she groaned in dismay at the wet splotch on the ceiling. A leak. One more repair to Alec's ever-growing list. Would he never find a moment to rest easy?

Footsteps sounded behind her.

"I'll be only a moment with these." Lily swiped a sudsy cloth across the porcelain surface. "If you need something washed, just put it there and I'll see to it."

The feet shuffled closer.

Lily glanced over her shoulder. "Was there — Oh! Mr. Dreymond. What are you doing here? You should be in bed."

Drying her wet hands on her apron, Lily rounded the worktable in the center of the room. "You know the kitchen is off-limits. If Matron catches you, we'll both be in trouble. Let me escort you back." She put her hand out to take his arm.

Metal glinted in his hand. "I'll not be going back."

A knife. And not the kind used to butter bread. Lily frowned. "What are you doing with that?"

"I'm not going back."

"Please put down the knife so I may help you back to bed."

"You've helped enough. Always getting your way with those charming words. It was enough to send me back, but I'm not going."

Her heart rate ticked up a pace as her mind raced. "Put down that knife. Now."

"I'll not be putting anything down until you tell them. Tell them no."

"Who are you talking about? Tell them no to what?"

He shifted from side to side. Sweat beaded

359

his forehead. "It's all your fault. You told those medics I was fit for duty again. Got my orders now to ship back. Well, they're not packing me off to a coffin. You tell them. Set them straight on how it's going to be."

A light pair of footsteps stuttered nearby.

"Aaaaah!" Esther's scream rattled the dishes. Whirling in the doorway, she raced down the corridor.

Sweat dripping down his chalky face, Dreymond clenched the knife tighter. "Now she's going to tell everyone. You're a nice lady, but what you did was bad. You shouldn't have talked to those doctors behind my back."

Pans dangled from hooks on the wall to Lily's left. One whack to his head and she might have a chance to escape. Blood drumming in her ears, she inched closer while keeping her eyes locked on him. "I did no such thing. The doctors who came to evaluate you made their own conclusions after thorough exams. If it were my choice, I'd keep every last one of you here. You must believe me."

The knife quivered in his hand and sadness filled his teary eyes.

"Drop the blade. Now." Alec blocked the doorway. Anger rolled off him like the great, heavy, black wings of an avenging angel.

Lily nearly cried with relief. All would be well as long as he was here.

Dreymond's head snapped up. Panic shook him from head to toe. "I-I'm having a talk w-with the nurse here."

"You've talked enough. Drop the knife."

Dreymond lunged for Lily. He clutched an arm around her while his other hand held the knife in front of her throat. "I d-don't want to h-hurt her."

"Then don't." A cry scratched up Lily's throat. She choked it back. Breaking down now would do no one any good.

Voices crackled in the corridor as sleepy-eyed patients and gawking nurses swarmed behind Alec. He didn't budge, blocking them like a fury-swept mountain.

"What is the meaning of this?" Matron Strom elbowed her way through the crowd, ducking past Alec and into the kitchen. Her eyes popped open at the spectacle, then snapped back to beady glints. "Unhand Aide Durham this instant, Corporal."

Dreymond trembled behind Lily. "I'm not going back. You can't make me."

"You are a soldier in his majesty's army. Act like it."

"L-leave!" Dreymond pressed his face to the back of Lily's shoulder. Hot tears soaked her collar. "Please. I d-don't want to hurt

361

anyone."

"Out. All of you." Alec's voice thundered with authority. Taking Matron's arm, he hauled her from the kitchen and slammed the door on her loud protests. He stood with his back to the door, arms crossed in defiance should anyone try to enter. Or leave.

Dreymond peeked over Lily's shoulder and sniffled. "Just m-me and the l-lady."

"I'll not leave her alone."

Lily breathed with relief. Alec's solid presence rippled across the room, wrapping her in safety. "You may speak freely in front of Lord Strathem. This is his kitchen after all, and I believe he means to remain by the door."

"If he puts down the knife, aye. Continue to hold it and I'll crack his head against the counter."

A strangled noise retched up Dreymond's throat. The blade slipped against Lily's throat. It stung like a paper cut.

Alec's stare narrowed to death.

He's going to kill him. The knowledge came swift and cold with not a second of doubt to spare. Pulse racing, Lily fought against the swelling tide of fright. "Mr. Dreymond. Nathan. It's all right to be scared."

"How w-would you know? You've never seen what it's like over there. The fear. I

362

won't make it out alive." Dreymond wiped his nose across the back of her blouse. Lily did her best not to flinch.

"I'm scared for brave men like you. I'm scared of the Huns crossing the Channel. And I'm frightened right now because my friend has a knife held against me."

"Friend?"

"Yes, and I'd like to do everything I can to help my friend."

A gentle sob escaped him. Weighed down by his despair, Dreymond sagged to the floor, clutching the hem of Lily's dress.

Quick as a flash Alec pushed Lily out of the way and grabbed the knife from Dreymond's trembling fingers, tucking it into the back of his waistband. "You dare to threaten the lady, in my home?"

Like a child without his teddy, Dreymond curled into himself and rocked back and forth. Lily's heart wept at the broken creature before her. Fear was a crippling master, chaining itself to one's deepest vulnerabilities to haunt the dark recesses kept far from the freeing light.

Edging past Alec's barricading arm, Lily knelt next to Dreymond on the cold stone floor and touched his shoulder. Fat tears rolled down his cheeks. "I d-didn't want to h-hurt you."

"I know you didn't," Lily said. Alec growled in rebuttal. She ignored him and pulled a mostly clean hankie from her apron pocket, holding it out to Dreymond.

The poor man reached for it, but his gaze skittered up to Alec. Whatever he saw made him withdraw his hand.

Lily reached up and took Alec's hand, pulling him down next to her. "Lord Strathem knows it too."

"Do I? The knife held at your throat would convince me otherwise." Alec grimaced and stretched out his left leg, rubbing his knee. "You've yet to answer me why I find you prowling about with a knife in the wee darkened hours, boy."

"I — she —" Dreymond looked frantically between them until settling on Lily. "The doctors should've known I wasn't ready. My eyes still need time to heal, but you told them the pupils had returned to normal. It's why you wanted me to take off the glasses."

Lily shook her head. "I wanted you to take off the glasses because you don't need them anymore, it's true. Never once did I speak to the doctors about you. Or about any of the men. The doctors keep their own counsel."

"Why do you blame Miss Durham?" Alec asked.

"Because I was told." Dreymond dropped his head into his hands and crawled his fingers across his scalp. "How else would they have known?"

Air hissed through Alec's teeth, his frustration building. "Who told you it was Miss Durham?"

Dreymond's eyes turned glassy as he stared off unseeing. "They want to kill me. That's it. They want me dead like all the others. Their bleeding voices never leave me alone." He pounded his hands against his head. The dull, sickening slaps echoed off the stone walls.

Alec grabbed his hands. "*Wheesht* yourself, man. It brings nay good stirring yourself up in such a way."

Dreymond blinked to refocus. A scowl twisted his lips. "What do you know of my sufferings? Sitting here high and mighty in your castle."

"I ken a wee bit of dealing with afflictions. I ken well the feeling of living as half a man while the world expects you to carry on. The burdens are heavier and the roads longer, but trudge on we do, all with the pain gnawing inside."

"Then why do you go on?"

"Because I must. As you must."

"Easy enough to say when you're kept far from the front lines." Dreymond's gaze traveled down to Alec's knee. "An injury that keeps you safe. My eyes weren't bad enough, but if they — the knife. Where's my knife?"

Instinctively, Lily inched closer to Alec. "What do you need the knife for?"

"They can't take me if my eyes are gone. I'll be safe. Give me the knife!" Dreymond lunged forward, driving Alec backward. The desperate man clawed around Alec's back. In one blurring motion, Alec flipped him over and pinned him to the ground.

Lily scrambled out of the way as Dreymond's legs flailed. "Mr. Dreymond! Please calm down. You're going to hurt yourself." Alec grunted as Dreymond twisted beneath him. " 'Tis his meaning. Get Guthrie."

Lily raced to the door and flung it open. Guthrie and Matron Strom barreled in. Lily slammed the door behind them on the shouts of protests and craning necks of the others gathered outside. Alec and Guthrie grabbed Dreymond by his arms, wrestling him still. Dreymond sagged between them as if the bones had dissolved from his body.

The only one to appear completely nonplussed by the scene, Matron assessed him

366

from top to bottom. "We'll take him upstairs to a private room."

"The Inverness Room is down a quiet hall. They'll be no one along there," Alec said.

"Very well. Bring him."

Crossing the room with Dreymond securely in tow, Alec halted next to Lily and touched the side of her neck. His brow creased. "You're bleeding."

Lily quickly covered his hand with hers. As if to hide it herself or keep his touch in place she didn't know. "A scratch."

The deep corners of his mouth pulled down as his hand lingered. His fingers curled slowly around the back of her neck, drawing out the enduring cold that the knife had branded against her skin. A multitude of emotions flooded his eyes. She recognized herself in the currents as they rushed forward to collide with her own tidal waves.

Matron opened the door and waved the men onward. Alec's hand slipped from Lily's. The skin on the back of her neck froze immediately.

Matron's beady stare turned on Lily. "I assume you'll have an explanation for this, but for now bring linens, a washbasin, and laudanum."

"Right away, Matron."

Hurrying to the supply storage, Lily gathered the instructed items into a basket and raced up the back stairs. The hallway was dark except for a single light glimmering under the bottom of a closed door. She knocked once. The door cracked open to reveal Matron's pale face. Behind her, Alec and Guthrie held Dreymond to the bed.

"Wait out here." Matron took the basket and closed the door.

Darkness settled, smothering the straight lines of wall and glass windows until they were nothing more than a trick to the memory, awaiting their time to be recollected in the day's light. It seemed an age as Lily paced the hall. The events of the past hour no longer seemed real, yet neither did yesterday nor the day to come as she hovered in the uncertain space between. If she could but fix herself to a solid point, perhaps reason would take hold to banish the unsettling events that had cast her adrift.

The door cracked open and a small figure slipped out, shutting the door firmly behind. Matron. "He's sleeping now."

Lily hurried to join her. "May I see him?"

"No. I'll not chance you being near him again."

Despite the nick stinging her neck, Lily couldn't forget the pathetic creature weeping at her feet. Nor the terror haunting his eyes as he silently begged her for reprieve from his nightmares. "He didn't mean to hurt me."

Matron's face wavered with the softest of hesitations. "My girl, whatever his intentions the fact remains that he threatened you with a knife. I will not allow my nurses to go near such harm again."

"He needs help."

Matron passed a hand over her face. Her work-worn hands seemed to brush more haggard creases into her skin in the blue light of night. "Shell shock. I've seen it before."

Lily had heard the men utter the word on the ward. A sentence arguably worse than a bullet to the heart. Those imprisoned by it became the walking dead, forever painted with targets of scorn. "They'll treat him as a coward."

"The doctors would customarily order a swift kick back to the front lines to confront his terrors like a true soldier, but in this case . . ." Matron tapped a finger against her chin, agitating the hairs poking out. "I've a doctor friend in Birmingham who's been trying new treatments for the more severe cases. I'll see what's to be done."

"The poor man. I knew he was frightened,

but they all are."

"I should have noted the signs. You did good to remain calm."

Lily nearly smiled. "Thank you, Matron."

"I'll put Nurse Dixon on duty here. You go to bed."

"Yes, Matron."

Matron padded down the hall with her uniform still in starched order, but a droop tugged at her shoulders. A crack in the dragon's scales that showed the tiny glimpse of a heart beating beneath.

Unwilling to retreat to the confines of her chamber and Bertie's forthcoming interrogation, Lily turned to the tall window and leaned her forehead to touch the cool surface. A gray film coated the glass, blurring the outside world. Once upon a time she might have retched at the thought of dirt smudging her skin, but tonight it didn't matter. If she thought of anything beyond the blur, she would shatter like the fragile glass, the hollow pieces of her scattering to the winds. She pulled her arms close, desperate to keep her pieces together.

Behind her, a door opened and hushed men's voices rumbled along the corridor. The window reflected two figures that stopped for a moment. The shorter one continued on while the taller, familiar shape moved toward her.

"Lily?"

Alec's soft voice cracked the quivering bits of her heart. Turning, she fell into his waiting arms and quietly fell to pieces.

CHAPTER 18

Crumpling the paper in his fist, Alec hurled it into the fire. The edges curled into orange flame and crackled to pieces. The title printed in bold black wording stared back at him as the fiery destruction crept closer to it: "Actress Poisoned: Accident or Intentional? Chaos at the Castle."

Wright had wasted no time in drumming up his exclusive story of horrors for the morning edition newspaper. Every detail was bloated beyond grotesque falsehood; claims were made that the patients feared for their lives, and the castle was painted as no more than a crumbling coffin. All while the laird himself fiddled like Nero at the burning of his empire.

"Ye could sue him fae defamation o' character." Guthrie grunted behind him.

The headline disintegrated to ash. Whiffs of inky black smoke filled Alec's nostrils. Bruce lifted his head from his spot stretched out on the rug and whined. "Aye, and see it dragged out in court to bankrupt me with money I don't have."

"Pistols at dawn?"

"A gentleman's notion. I'll not dignify him with such an offer. A horsewhip he's better suited for."

"We got one in the stable."

Alec crossed the study to his desk. Wadded papers littered the corner, their creamy surfaces dotted with inkblots and scratches. A nighttime's reprieve from the chaos clashing in his mind. It wasn't until the wee hours of morning when the blackness melted to gray outside his window and the first crack of dawn spilled across the desk that he could find the words of peace. Pages later, he'd tossed his pen aside, utterly spent in exchange for a quieted soul.

Until Guthrie brought in the morning paper.

"I should've thrown him out when I had the chance. It's no mere coincidence he was here the same time the world's most famous actress was poisoned." Or that it should happen so quickly after an unresolved kidnapping. "What if it's his plan to sabotage me? To smear my good name and that of Kinclavoch in order to take it from me."

Stretching from his slumped position in

the high-back leather chair, Guthrie braced his elbows on his bare knees. "That snake kens which way the wind blows. He'll blind ye wi' his fangs all the while his tail is rattlin' the poison. I'd bet my cleanest kilt he be in the thick o' this."

Considering Guthrie only owned two kilts, one his Sunday best and the other for every day, it wasn't much to bet on. "If only we could be certain. Find evidence."

"Och, 'tis easy enough. I'll slip intae his shop in the village and have a wee poke around."

"I don't have the money to bail you out if you get caught."

"Then I willna get caught."

Alec moved to the window. The pale sun had slipped behind a bank of midday clouds, bathing the landscape in a pearly silver and chilling the air. Winter was nigh upon them. Most years he took a Scot's pride in their readiness for the harsh season. 'Twas the christening of any with Scottish blood, but this year his pride faltered. How many more could Kinclavoch survive? "Whatever evidence we discover needs to be obtained the honest way. I'll not have it come back around to bite me for breaking and entering."

"Only if ye're caught," Guthrie muttered.

"My reputation, that of Kinclavoch, cannot afford to be caught. Between the poisoned actress, the knife-wielding madman, the salivating journalist, the creditors, and a leaking roof, I've enough on my plate. One more incident and we might not survive. What would become of the estate? My tenants? What of the hospital?"

"Our problems only increased since they set up here."

"Our problems pale in comparison to theirs." If only he could help them more. Alec turned from the barren grounds and sized up his man. Built of the earth from which he sprang, Guthrie's roots ran deep but didn't extend much beyond his soil of comfort. One was forced to dig deep before he'd sprout for you. "Have you not a patriotic bone in your crusty old body?"

"Aye, and they're stained blue and white. No the colors fae auld King George." Hauling himself from the chair as the subject of the English monarch always left him restless, Guthrie took a splinter of wood from his sporran and jammed it between his teeth. "Yer leg keeps ye from the trenches and so ye've insisted on a way tae do yer bit by helping them here, but lad, we canna help anyone if the estate falters."

All the more reason to return the estate to

working order. A thriving, well-maintained Kinclavoch was not only beneficial to him and his family, but to the Tommies under his roof as well. Alec cast a glance over his shoulder out the window to the braes rolling in darkened green to the steel sky. He could almost smell the cool air thickening over the trees. "A few years ago Lord Kinnifie made me an offer on my northern fields. I'll need to ride over there and estimate the value before I meet with him. The sale could settle the amount of death duties." And not much else.

Guthrie's bottom lip dropped. The piece of wood dangled precariously. "Ye vowed ne'er tae sell off the land."

"As you said, the estate cannot falter. A minor sell can prevent it. For a time, at least." The bitter words weighed with guilt on Alec's tongue. He'd done everything to move heaven and earth, but it wasn't enough. It was too vast a task, and not even his pride could bolster the load for much longer. He needed a new income of steady means.

"Mayhap ye wish tae think on it. The past few days, months really, havena been easy and the strain —"

Alec snapped. "Are you my man or my nursemaid?"

"Yer man always, m'laird."

"Then trust that the path forward has gathered beneath my feet for some time. This is not a simple whim of exhaustion."

Guthrie's expression shuttered to stone. "Aye." He bowed stiffly and turned for the door with a swish of his kilt.

Ears pricking, Bruce roused from his spot and trotted over to lick Alec's hand. Shamed by his more insightful dog, Alec called out to his old friend. "Will you take a dram with me when I return?"

Glancing over his shoulder, the scowl lifted from Guthrie's haggard face. "Aye."

The door clicked shut and the quiet ensconced Alec, broken only by the popping logs in the fireplace. His mind often craved silence with its endless possibilities unfettered by determined noise, but as the quiet settled his guard was lowered to usher forth thoughts he'd rather keep at bay. Wright. That Barrymore woman. Debts. Dreymond. Lily. That blade to her throat.

His heart had splintered in that moment.

Lingering shards dug deep, expanding in his veins and stretching against his skin. He needed out.

Grabbing his journal and pen, he strode out the side door to the stable with Bruce at his side. Fresh air filled with hay and grass and woods whipped through his hair, tempering the pressure within. But it wasn't enough. He needed the sanctuary of surrounding countryside.

"He's gone."

Alec stopped. Lily stood at the corner of the stable, arms crossed at her waist and no jacket covering her pink-and-blue dress. Like a spring flower in bloom much too late. He hurried toward her. "What are you doing out here? There's a chill." He slipped off his jacket and wrapped it around her shoulders.

She reached down to scratch Bruce's ears as he cuddled up to her leg. "I went to see Mr. Dreymond, but they told me he'd left. Was taken, rather."

"Aye. Matron Strom had no choice but to inform his command. An ambulance came this morning to take him somewhere he can be looked after."

She curled into his jacket. It swallowed her whole like a vulnerable doll. "Do you think he'll be in trouble?"

"For nearly killing you, aye." She blanched and looked away. Why could he not control his callous words today? "You did your best to help him, but his mind's been broken. There's naught you can do for him."

"Then I pray someone out there can."

"You've a tender heart, lass." He was now glad he hadn't beaten that glaikit against the stone floor, if only for her feelings. The world had shifted between them last night. Perhaps it was the flash of uncertain mortality or when she'd reached up to take his hand. Rumblings of an alteration set in motion beyond their own powers.

When she'd fallen, weeping into his arms, the pieces had slipped perfectly together as if they had been aligned from creation. He'd held her long after her tears were spent, content to breathe in the silence they shared in a moment no one could fathom beyond the two of them. It had taken every ounce of restraint to escort her to her room and bid her good night when he wanted nothing more than to hold her until night surrendered them to dawn's early light.

Tired circles smudged beneath her eyes, revealing a restless night much like he'd endured. His head too full and his arms longing for Lily, he'd sought respite in his study until the candles burned low over journal ramblings. If only he could offer relief to the turmoil he knew to be churning in her mind. "How fares your friend?"

Lily sighed and brushed an errant curl swinging over her ear. Her hair was looser today, as if she'd forgone the customary amount of pins to hold it in place. "She's determined to take the afternoon train back to London."

"Hie herself from this cursed place. Kidnappings. Poisonings. Threats in the kitchen. All we need now is a plague of locusts."

Sadness darkened the green of her eyes to wet leaves. "I'm so sorry, Alec. I've brought so many terrible things on you. Richard Wright never should have been here, and then for him to print those awful things about you in the paper. I wish now you had ignored my silly note and tossed him out on his ear."

Wright. Alec would catch him soon enough and expose his dark deeds to the world. In the meantime, he needn't burden Lily beyond her friend nearly dying. "Whit's fur ye'll no go past ye. What will be, will be, and what has been, has been."

"No good deed goes unpunished." Her sadness slipped behind a wee smile. "See? I can quote colloquial expressions as well as you."

Ever a ray of sun, ever seeking him behind the clouds where he wished to remain. If not for the Scottish practicality of self-deprecation into which he'd been baptized, he might allow her a winning chance.

He leaned a shoulder against the stable

wall. The rough wood caught at the fibers of his linen shirt. "There's much in the world to trouble ourselves with, but this isn't a burden I wish for you to carry."

"And I don't wish for you to carry it alone. I demand part of the blame."

"An odd request. Most are quick to turn the blame from themselves."

"Once upon a time I would've done just that without a second thought, but you make it rather difficult to be selfish. A saint of integrity you are. Besides, it's the least I can do after nearly providing two dead bodies in your house in the span of a few hours." She tugged the collar of his jacket to cover the thin scab on her neck.

"I've never felt such terror. Or rage." Gently, he pulled the collar down to reveal the bright-red line marring her creamy white skin and lightly ran his finger over it. "Or helplessness. I only wanted you safe, Lily."

"I was. Because you were there."

The shards having pricked him mercilessly disintegrated as her words whispered across his heart. "I'd like to show you something. Come with me?" He pushed off the wall, anticipating her refusal. "Unless you've work to do."

Smiling, Lily shook her head. "Matron

Strom ordered me to take the day off. Likely so I won't cause any more catastrophes. I'll fetch my coat. Don't leave without me!"

She raced back to the castle with his jacket flapping behind her. Alec smiled to himself. As if he could leave her behind when she'd fashioned a place at his side.

Ten minutes later she returned wearing a dark-blue coat trimmed in silver fox fur and a low-crowned top hat with black netting that swept across her forehead and back to her hair. His jacket looped over her arm.

Her gaze narrowed in confusion as he led Appin and Sorcha from the stable. "I knew I should have packed my riding habit despite Bertie claiming we had no more trunk space."

"A sturdy tweed would suit you better."

"Sturdy and tweed are not used in ladies' fashion." She handed him his jacket.

Her scent of fresh flowers whirled about him as he shrugged it back on. "I doubt the horses mind either way."

"You've brought two of them. Considering our history, I should think one enough."

Heat shot through him as the memory of their bundled rides raced between them, unseen but very much alive. Those had been under unusual circumstances. How could he justify such an action now without looking the proper cad? But having her cozied up against him was awfully tempting. "I . . . em . . ."

A light teased in her eyes as if she knew exactly what he was thinking and wasn't ashamed at having prompted the thought. "Help me mount?"

Taking a deep breath, Alec cupped his hands to bolster her foot and leaned over. "Up with you, lass. Afore I change my mind."

The view stole Lily's breath.

From their perch on the hilltop, or brae as Alec called it, the land sloped down to a thick stretch of trees, many bare-limbed with the onset of winter while the dark points of evergreens rose among them like sturdy soldiers. The tree line faded to a small meadow with a river winding its way through in a lazy ribbon fashion. On the other side, the meadow gave way to bushy firs that beckoned Christmas decorations as they stretched farther and farther away to lay as a crowning bough around three peaks of mountains capped with snow. Silver light gleamed all around this court of nature.

"This is your spot, isn't it?"

Alec shifted in his saddle and pointed. "Beyond the rowan and oak trees, come spring the moor will burst with yellow gorse and purple heather so thick you can walk atop it."

"I should like to try that."

"Then I'll bring you back." He swung off his saddle and gazed across the valley to the mountains. "Rob Roy MacGregor was said to have hidden in the Black Dwarf there for a time when he was outlawed by the Duke of Montrose."

"The Black Dwarf?"

"Aye, so called because come sunrise it'll be eclipsed in the shadow of *Mòr Ruadh,* Big Red, which bursts with the colors of the maple trees in autumn. A grand display it makes."

Lily smiled at his obvious pride. For a man so closed up in himself, nature opened him up in ways nothing else could. Here was his heart in all its beautifully intricate facets, mesmerizing her at each new turn until she'd fallen utterly and hopelessly for him.

The awareness had crept up on her like the changing of seasons when day by day one notices the air is not quite so nippy. One by one the buttons come undone on winter's coat until it's shed altogether. Slender grasses reach for the sky and flower petals unfold to the warmth, and without realizing it, spring has sprung. Her heart had burst to life.

"Winter is taking its first deep breaths now." Alec's *R*s rolled. "A different kind of beauty with ice and frost. Skies made of lead with swift changes of sleet and snow."

Lily raised her face to the sky as a chilled wind whisked by, filled with the scent of pine needles and crisp water. Her soul lifted with it and cast itself into the tantalizing wake. "I appreciate the weather's honesty here. It is what it is, and if you don't care for it, then you don't deserve to witness its brutal glory."

Alec looked at her, surprise and something else — pride? — kindled in his eyes. A deep blue color under the slate clouds, they held her enthralled. "Aye. You've the right of it."

Coming around the horse, he reached up and grasped her waist. She unhooked her leg from the sidesaddle and slipped effortlessly into his arms. They felt achingly familiar yet excitedly new at once. Resting her hands on his wide shoulders, she dared to search his face without rushing. The striking cerulean eyes offset by thick waves of reddish-brown hair. Red stubble spreading across his square jawline and around the broad mouth that was quick to scowl, but when it turned up, oh dear heart, did it make her soar. More than anything she wanted the corners of those lips to curl up just before they kissed her.

"Lily." His breath washed over her face.

Her pulse ignited. "Alec."

"There's something else I want to show you." He pulled away.

Lily blinked in surprise. Well, that wasn't what she'd expected.

Leaving the horses to graze, he led her to a fallen log that served as the perfect viewing bench for the surrounding heaven. The calm confidence from minutes before wilted away as he tapped his fingers against his knee. Lily smoothed her skirts to give him a moment of collection.

Finally, he took a deep breath, reached into his jacket pocket, and pulled out a leather-bound journal. His eyebrows lifted with uncertainty. "I wrote something."

His gaze bored into hers, as if willing her to understand. Lily accepted the book as the gift he offered. She flipped open to the first page. The inner workings of his mind leaped out at her in frankness with vulnerability crowded between the margins. The glories of Kinclavoch fading under debt. The estate rich with possibility but no funds to maintain it. His family pulled apart with only the cobwebs of what could have been stringing them together.

Tears wet the corners of her eyes. She blinked them away lest he think they formed from pity and trailed her finger across his words. Strokes of boldness, handwriting born of the straightforward lines of the man himself. "Oh, Alec."

" 'Tis not what I wish you to read." His hand brushed over hers as he flipped closer to the back of the journal. "Here."

A Tommy's Tale

Standing on the battlements of Artois, France, is a lone knight armed for battle. Not with shield and sword, but helmet and rifle. His charge is not on a white steed of medieval fields, but on blistered feet through pits of mud. No shining armor or trumpet fanfare. His remnants of glory are to be pried from the festering trenches with shells soaring high overhead to illuminate the fields of death awaiting him on the morrow. If there is one thing this soldier wishes his loved ones to know, it is this . . .

The words continued for two pages as the soldier's venture was captured not only in words, but also with heartache and hope. A story the world had never heard but needed to believe in. A legacy for everything worth fighting for.

This time, Lily didn't bother to blink away her tears. "This is wonderful."

At some point Alec must have risen for he stopped pacing. "I never wanted to be involved with the men here, didn't want them to see me and gain a chance to judge me." He looked down at his leg. There was no cane to lean upon today. "That day when you tried to get me to talk to Dreymond, I said terrible things to you."

"No. You were right to say those things. Thinking I knew best, I didn't take your feelings on the matter into consideration. I shouldn't have tried to force you. I'm sorry."

"Sorry for pushing me to do better? To be better? You struck me in a place I wished never to be discovered, and I lashed out because I knew you were right. I cannot apologize enough for my conduct."

"Seems we both acted the fool."

"Aye, though I think it's because we both see the potential in the other. At least I'm trying to give you reason to." His gaze dropped to the journal in her lap. "That lad sat next to me at the performance and told me about his experience. I couldn't get it out of my mind."

Lily gently closed the pages and smoothed her hand over the worn leather. "This story is incredible, and the way you've painted it . . . I've never read anything that touched the core of humanity the way this does. The country is hurting, but stories like this can help it heal, or at the very least, to understand. You have a gift, Alec."

"Do you really think this would be of service?"

Like bubbles of champagne, giddiness rose inside her. Pouring his thoughts onto paper provided release now to come full circle in offering the freedom of pen and ink to others' chaos. He'd found kinship in the pain, but instead of drowning in it, he and the soldiers drifted together in search of shelter.

"The wounded find catharsis in sharing their experiences. They don't feel as alone, and the people back home need to see what kind of men are coming back to them. You're giving them a chance to be better. I'm so proud of you." Unable to contain her joy, Lily jumped up and threw her arms around his neck and kissed him full on the mouth.

She jerked back in shock. "Oh dear! I'm sorry. I didn't mean to . . ."

She whirled away as the astonishment of

her brazen move engulfed her in heat. Had she come to the country to lose all sense of decorum? Never had she thrown herself at a man. Kissed a few, yes, but never lobbed herself at one like a common hussy. Then again, she'd never wanted to kiss a man as much as she had Alec. She'd become desperate for him in a way that made her feel utterly vulnerable, and the only cure was to reveal her need for him.

She whirled back around to face him with all the unflinching nerve her pounding heart could spare. "No. I'm not sorry in the least bit. In fact, I'm glad I did it. I've been wanting to for quite some time. And I think you have too."

"I've been wanting to kiss you?" His brogue thickened, dropping to a husky pitch as he moved toward her.

Blood rushed to Lily's cheeks, this time for a much different reason as the distance between them shrank to inches. "Don't deny it."

"Wasn't going to."

Spreading his hands over her cheeks, he met her mouth with an intensity long held at bay. He was light and darkness seeping into every crevice of her soul. Gentleness and boldness seeking her will as a match to his own. Lily wrapped her arms around his neck and pulled him closer so he might feel her heart calling for his. Alec was safety and comfort and exhilaration and fierceness, and he held her like a gem to be treasured.

His lips moved to her cheek, nose, forehead. With a spent sigh, he rested his forehead against hers. "I didn't realize how lost I felt until now, when I find myself in your eyes."

Lily cupped his cheek. The soft bristles scraped gently over her palm. "A man of few words, but what words they are."

"That may have been my romantic quota for the year."

"The year? Who else have you been spinning them on?"

"No one. I believe they've been saved for you." Frowning, he leaned back a bit and plucked at the netting covering her forehead. With decidedly sure movements, he pulled out her hatpin and removed her hat. "Now that it's off I'm not sure what to do with it. Only it was irritating my skin."

Lily took it and tossed it on the ground. "I never cared much for it."

"Mayhap a tweed next time." He brushed away the loose hair curling around her neck with a slow drag of his fingers that prickled butterflies down her spine. "Or none at all.

Your hair looks bonny all loose from the ride."

"My good laird, I may dare you into kissing me, but don't think for one minute that I'm one of those women who flaunts unbound hair."

" 'Tis a shame. I'd wager it rivals the sun in crowning glory."

She locked her fingers together behind his neck in fear of floating away with happiness. She couldn't remember ever feeling like this. If she had, it wasn't true. Not like now, in this moment. "Do you intend to sweet talk me the rest of the afternoon?"

Shaking his head, a devastating smile curved one corner of his mouth. "I've something else in mind."

After a great many more kisses with the glories of Scotland as their backdrop, they rode back to the castle. Guthrie met them at the stable.

"I'll be puttin' the bottle o' whisky back on the shelf fae the now." He took their reins and winked slyly at Alec. "Seein' how ye're busy, laird."

The tips of Alec's ears pinked. "Aye, that'll be fine. I'll give you a hand."

Guthrie shook his head and led the horses inside to their respective stalls. "I've things in hand withoot yer interference. Ye go on now and take the lass. I heard a motor 'round front but a few minutes ago."

"Must be the ambulance," Lily said, taking Alec's offered arm. He smelled of fresh air and horse. "Bertie said a new load of patients was due to arrive today."

"Mayhap you'll introduce me to a few once they're settled. If they're willing." He held up his journal.

"Certainly. I know a few others in the meantime who would be delighted to talk your ear off. A nice break for us nurses. There's only so many times we can listen to the tales of stale slingers in a flying mess, that is to say, finding food no matter how bad wherever one can. Golly gumdrops, I'm beginning to talk just like them."

Rounding the front of the house, Alec stopped her on the steps. "I'm thinking of sending them to the newspapers."

"The men? A splendid idea. Journalists can tackle them in no time."

A smile quirked his lips. A sight she was growing rather fond of creating. "The stories. For the nation to read. And I'm going to speak to Gibbons. Mayhap he's remembered a detail or two."

Others may not have seen the significance in his sudden bravado to speak to the soldiers, but she did. Filled with pride, she leaned up and kissed him on the cheek. "A marvelous idea."

Alec pushed open the front door and ushered her inside. A man and woman dressed in the height of fashion stood in the center of the entry hall. Trunks and luggage were piled on either side of them. At the sound of the door opening, they turned.

Lily gasped. "Mother! Father!"

CHAPTER 19

"Is this really the best they have to offer? This is a castle for goodness' sake." Mother circled the room with her arms drawn in as if afraid dust might set upon her burgundy traveling suit. Her nose wrinkled at a pair of crossed swords and targe over the fireplace. "Barbaric at that."

Taking in the rich walnut wood and thick damask drapery, Lily found it appropriate for a centuries-old castle standing stalwart against the harsh terrain. It existed as it needed to be, not renovated to a lesser shell of chintz and toile. "The country is at war, Mother. You can't expect the Waldorf. Besides, Kinclavoch was built in the seventeenth century. There's bound to be a bit of wearing in."

"An understatement."

Lily bristled at the need to defend the castle that had become her home over the past nine months, but it would do no good.

Mother would only cast her critical eye to something else. As usual, Father was not to be counted on for tempering the mood as he stood in his impeccably cut suit at the window staring out at the back garden.

Sighing, Lily sat on the edge of the massive four-poster bed that boasted an intricate twining of Celtic knots carved into the headboard. Alec's handiwork. "What are you doing here?"

"You cannot imagine our utter distress upon receiving news that our daughter, one of the most eligible young women on the Eastern Seaboard, had reduced herself and our family name to that of working status after sending her here for a period of maturing."

"I wrote you several months ago to say I would be working here."

"Yes, and you failed to mention the precise manner of your labor until Cousin Hazel was so kind as to fill in the details of what these convalescent homes were comprised of." Mother fluttered a hand as if still in shock by the news. "Rather than post you our displeasure, which we knew you would ignore, we came in person to take you home and save you from further embarrassment."

A resounding *no* shouted in Lily's head. She gripped the nearest poster to keep from jumping into a defensive stance. "I belong here. This is where I work."

Mother's artistically sculpted eyebrows winged up in disapproval. "The women in our family do not work."

"All right. I volunteer."

"Working with *men* in their beds."

"Patients."

"Who are men. Proper young ladies do not put themselves in immoral situations. No decent young man of good breeding and family will make an offer for such a wife."

Lily glanced at the ceiling. What help that might offer she didn't know, but it was better than rolling her eyes at her mother directly. "There is nothing immoral in nursing the wounded. All the women here are professionally trained."

"Then allow them to do it."

"We are doing it."

Mother pulled the pearl hatpin from her Watteau of matching burgundy and ostrich feathers and handed the creation to her waiting maid. "My dear, you are many things, but a professional is not one of them. Unless the men require dance partners or event planning, you are unneeded here. Stop playing games and allow the tired spinsters to do their duty."

Lily shot off the bed. "This isn't a game.

And they aren't spinsters. Well, perhaps a few are, but most are young women of society from good families. Did you know that the Countess of Carnarvon was one of the first to open her home at Highclere Castle for convalescing soldiers? And the Duchess of Westminster has sponsored a military hospital in Le Touquet."

"The British and their eccentrics. Nothing you need be part of."

"Mother, I'm helping. For the first time in my life I feel as if I'm doing something worthwhile."

Glancing in the gilded mirror over the dressing table, her mother fluffed the puff of golden hair atop her head that had been flattened by the hat. "Don't be so dramatic, Lily. You said the same thing the first night you wore your hair up for a ball."

"This is entirely different."

"The country is at war." Father's voice, low and even like running steel, silenced the room. He turned from the window. With the gray light silhouetting him and his hands clasped behind his back, he looked like the large oil painting of himself hanging in their New York dining room. All he needed was a dog at his feet. The sleek kind without the friendliness of Bruce.

A tiny well of hope sprang within Lily.

"Yes, Father. That's why my work here is so important."

"*This* country is at war. America is not. The safest thing is for you to come home and let Europe sort out its own problems."

The well sank as she scuttled to keep reason together. "Europe's problems may well become America's soon enough."

"Do not trouble yourself with politics. There are things beyond which you cannot understand." Pulling out a solid gold pocket watch, Father squinted at the numbers. "Teatime, I believe."

There was nothing new under the sun about this argument. Although it was more words than her father had ever spoken to her in a single conversation, they hit squarely to the hollowness Lily still carried. Months away from their cloying restrictions and given the chance to find her wings, she'd become a new creature. A creature with abilities beyond what was expected of her. Ten minutes in her parents' presence found her shrinking back to childhood insecurities of amounting to nothing more than an expensive trinket whose only purpose was to be observed and never allowed an opinion.

Mother turned to her maid who was busy setting up glittering bottles of fragrant perfume and powder on the dressing table. "Priscilla, go fetch the tea. If they even take the civilized custom this far north." Priscilla performed a perfect curtsy and left the room silent as a mouse.

Lily took a deep breath. Her parents thought her still a child. Snide remarks would only prove them right. "The men take tea in their beds or in the dining hall. Nurses take it in the kitchen if you care to join us."

Mother thrust a hankie to her mouth for the briefest of ladylike seconds. "I've never stepped foot in a kitchen. We'll take it here as well as our supper if the dining room is otherwise occupied."

"Mother, there simply aren't enough servants anymore to scurry about with trays full service. Most of them have gone to the front lines."

Knock. Knock.

Mother quickly folded her hands at her waist in proper hostess posture. *"Entrer."*

The door slowly opened and in walked Bertie balancing a tray full of tea accoutrements. "I heard tea was required." She set the tray on a small table, then smoothed the front of her uniform with a wide smile. The scent of warm brew, cookies, and jam wafted around the room to sweeten away the lingering must.

Lily could have clapped with relief. Bertie always added sturdy support in a moment of crisis. "Allow me to introduce my mother and father," she said. "This is Bertie."

Mother's stiffness went from hostess to welcoming relative with a smile. "Ah, Elizabeth. A pleasure to meet you at last. Your mother sent me a photograph when you were christened. You've turned into a beautiful young woman."

Bertie blushed. "Thank you, Aunt Mary. What a surprise to see you both here. I didn't think they were allowing civilian crossings of the Atlantic with the U-boats creeping around."

"Customarily, no, but we were fortunate to find a captain with sense in our plight."

Or open to bribery. There was nothing enough money couldn't solve, and Lily's parents had no qualms in using it to their advantage.

"How long have you planned your visit?" Obviously her cousin didn't feel the frigid waters of familial turmoil already in motion.

"We wished to return immediately." Mother cut a glance at Lily as she moved to inspect the tea tray. "Unfortunately, passage could not be procured for the winter months, so we shall have to endure until the waters calm and the ice is not as treacherous. We don't wish to run afoul of another *Titanic* fiasco."

No! "Whatever will you do until spring?" *Please don't say stay here.*

"Return to Threading Hall as guests of Lord and Lady Fowley. I hear there is to be a wedding then."

Bertie nodded. "My brother Reggie to the Honorable Joan Dawson. He proposed before he left again for the front. I haven't heard from him in weeks."

Adding a dash of milk to a cup emblazoned with the MacGregor crest, Mother then poured in the steaming tea. "I'm sure his mind is engaged elsewhere with a fiancée and wedding on the horizon."

Bertie looked down, but not before Lily caught the glimmer of tears behind her eyeglasses. She took her cousin's hand and squeezed. "He'll be all right," she whispered. Bertie squeezed back.

"Will you join us for tea, Elizabeth?"

"Thank you, no. I start my shift in an hour, and I've promised to try new leg exercises with Captain Gibbons. It's a new technique crafted by two women, Sanderson and McMillan, to help the wounded recover the use of their limbs. Speaking of which, I found this for you in the library." Bertie pulled a book from her pocket — how she managed to wedge it in there only heaven knew — and handed it to Lily. "About the ligaments and ointments we were discussing the other day."

Lily read the title. *A Modern Medicinal Way to Treat Aggravates.* She hoped to find something in it to help Alec's leg. Not to heal it but perhaps to alleviate the discomfort.

"Perfect. It'll go straight to the top of my reading pile." How long had this been sitting in the library collecting dust? Did Alec never peruse his own shelves? "I'm ready to return to rotation."

"I'll inform Matron Strom." Bertie smiled at Lily's parents. "A pleasure to meet you both." She slipped out of the room. The lucky duck.

Dipping a silver spoon into the delicate teacup, Mother stirred her brew. She arched an eyebrow in Lily's direction. "I hope you're not intending to wear that for supper."

Lily glanced down at her pink-and-blue striped gown. It was the height of fashion when she'd set sail from New York, but she had given little time to wearing it since coming to Scotland. A smile flitted across her lips. Perhaps if it were tweed. "We don't dress for meals here. Evening gloves aren't part of our uniform."

"Perhaps for those on duty, but as you are not" — Mother sniffed over one of the exceedingly rare cookies the kitchen had scrounged to obtain — "I expect you to join us appropriately attired."

"I'm afraid I can't join you this evening as I have a previous engagement. Lord Strathem and his sister, Lady Viola, have invited me to dine with them." It had been only an hour ago when she had parted from Alec after a stiff introduction to her parents, but she was already counting the minutes until she saw him again. And it would be so good to visit with Viola.

Father moved from his rooted spot. "Lord Strathem. Whom we met in hall."

"Yes."

Nothing stirred behind his secret-keeping mustache. "Rather young to be the owner of this estate. Why is he not out fighting with the others?"

"His father died some years ago, and he's been managing on his own, with a mother and sister to care for. An injury keeps him from the war."

"Why did you not have an escort when strolling through the front door with him?"

Mother's spoon clanked against the saucer. A sure sign of agitation.

Heat rose up Lily's neck as she recalled precisely why they didn't have an escort. "I . . ."

"You have grown positively wild in this country. No escort. No gloves. I see two freckles on your nose. Do not tell me you've been outdoors without a hat."

"I can't tell if you wish me to answer that or not."

Mother's pale fingers curled around the cup handle, threatening to snap the delicate china. "I dare not think it possible, but your cheek and disrespect have discovered new boundaries with which to propel themselves."

Lily flicked off the sharp dart of insult. Too long she had viewed her mother as the opposition to amusement, which had been bred out of polite society. Where once Lily had abhorred her mother's guardianship of the old ways, she now felt pity; the cold and stately tower her mother had built must be terribly lonely. "Scotland has changed me. It's offered a freedom I dare not find any place else. There are no constraints of what *should* be done, but rather what *must* be done, and there is all the difference worth noting."

"Forgive me if I fail to trust in your judgment on such matters. They have not proven sound in past experience."

"Enough, Mary." Father's tone silenced any rebuttals as he hooked his thumbs into his lapels. The stance he took when addressing an inferior at the bank. Or Lily. "Daughter, you have not seen your family in nearly two years. You will dine with us and see these people another time."

"Father, I promised —"

"You have caused us enough fret and headaches coming to fetch you. Do not compound another one."

Mother wedged herself between them and shoved a teacup and saucer into Lily's hand. "Tea."

Alec paused outside the small chamber that Viola had recently taken over as her sitting room. Her bedchamber was too confining, she said, which made his heart glad. Feminine voices within, one in particular, made his heart skip. He pushed open the door and took in the cozy scene of Viola and Lily curled up on a velvet settee with a light snow drifting behind them beyond the window.

"Two lassies plotting if ere I saw them."

Lily jumped as if to come off the seat, to

him he hoped, then quickly smoothed her uniform skirt to cover the action. "I came to give my formal apologies for breaking our dinner engagement last evening. My parents were rather insistent I join them."

"As you should have after all this time apart," Viola said. Her plaited hair was wrapped around her head in a coronet, showing off the fullness that had returned to her cheeks. Dr. MacLeod was still dubious about a rickets diagnosis, but even his old-fashioned notions couldn't deny the miraculous improvements a bit of sunlight had procured.

"I assure you, I'd have much rather spent it with you." Lily smiled at her before fluttering a gaze to Alec.

Crossing his arms, he leaned against the doorjamb to keep from sweeping her into his arms. Kissing her again was the only thing his mind could focus on, and her presence last night had been sorely missed. "I have business in the northern fields this morning, and later I ride to Laggan. Is there anything I might retrieve for you there?"

"What has you going to the northern fields?" Viola's brow creased sharply. "Lord Kinnifie."

It was a blessed day when his sister began to leave her bedchamber and explore the world once more. Unfortunately, it also meant she saw the true state of Kinclavoch. A state he'd avoided sharing with her. Until now. "It's sitting fallow and he's offered a good price."

"Alec, I love this place as much as you. This is our family's only home, wrapped in memories and history. We can't parcel it off as if it means nothing."

Her wide-eyed innocence gutted him. "You think I don't feel the same? Our options grow more limited by the day."

"Will selling land help? To keep our home?"

"Aye, for a time." The sale would pay off the death duties, but it wasn't enough to cover the estate's remaining debts. He'd be forced to sell everything he owned, including the shirt off his back, before that amount was paid in full. If only his shirts were worth more. And that was why he'd set up a meeting with Glengaryle's estate manager to discuss the former dowager's cottage for rent. It gutted him to think of leaving Kinclavoch, forsaking the blood and sweat his ancestors had put into each stone and blade of grass, but he'd be naught more than a selfish fool to put a legacy above his family's well-being.

He glanced at Lily and her ready smile.

How would she feel about a landless man? Lord Strathem he would remain, but no longer a laird without land. She was accustomed to the finest things money had to offer. He could not ask her to lower her expectations to accommodate the lower station in which he might soon find himself.

"Is the piano still in the library?" Viola asked. "I should like to practice this afternoon and play for the men come Hogmanay."

Lily's brow shot up in interest. "What is that? A barbecue of sorts? I didn't realize you had those over here."

Viola laughed. "It's the Scottish celebration of the New Year. When the Norse settled here, they mixed their tradition of the winter solstice with the Germanic Yule and the more Gaelic Samhain. We give gifts, dance, pour whisky, mayhap light a fireball, and partake in general merrymaking."

"Sounds wildly delightful."

The joy bursting on his sister's face seconds before fizzled to sobriety. "It was once. We haven't celebrated much in the passing years. A small family dinner is all."

Where no one spoke a word and their mother stared at the empty chair she insisted be kept in honor of their father. It was an evening of agony.

Lily shook her head. "That's a shame. I, for one, am curious to see Gaels torch things in the spirit of revelry."

"And I, for one, think we should start with music and leave the fireballs to the folks in Stonehaven. They're more daring in Aberdeenshire." Alec pushed off the doorjamb with a stern look. Leaving it to these two with Guthrie thrown in for kicks, Kinclavoch wouldn't have a scorched stone left to stand on.

"Speaking of daring, I better take my leave before I'm late to work. Matron Strom is said to have a room full of sheets ready for me to launder." Lily stood and kissed Viola on the cheek, then moved toward the door. "I'll be sure to clear the men from the library so you can have peace to practice."

Viola held her hand out as if to stop her. "Oh, please don't. I like to think they might enjoy a spot of music, especially with the snow coming down like it is."

"If you insist, maestro." Lily performed a perfect curtsy and walked out.

Keeping with the spirit, Alec gave his sister a short bow. "I'll see you this evening."

"Good luck, brother."

Alec shut the door and turned to find Lily waiting for him a few yards ahead at the corridor corner. The hall was lined with medieval-style windows, high and thick paned to keep out the temperamental weather. The gray light brightened by falling snow warbled its way through the glass to wash her features in pale tones. She was dressed once more in her plain uniform and silver-buckle shoes, and he missed the lovely dress from yesterday in which she had stood like a flower next to Mother Nature's bleakness. Even now the grayness could not hide her inner luster, like a pearl still caught in its shell. A half-expectant look amused her face as he walked toward her, his heart pounding with each step.

He stopped in front of her, close enough to see the green thinning around her dilated pupils. Just as they had yesterday when he'd held her. "I should very much —"

"Would you mind —"

They laughed nervously as their words tumbled over each other. Alec rubbed a hand over the back of his neck, desire knowing precisely what it wanted to do yet the awkwardness of a school lad bumbling it. "Ladies first."

"No. You, please."

I should very much like to kiss you. I haven't been able to stop thinking about you. May we walk to the hilltop again so my heart might confess its longing for you? "Have your parents settled in?"

Disappointment flickered across her face before she covered it with a civil nod. "Their first time in a castle. I believe they find themselves unaccustomed to its . . . charms."

"If there's anything they should require, don't hesitate to ask. I want them to feel comfortable during their stay."

Lily sighed and continued down the hall. "They intend to travel to Threading Hall, Bertie's family home, and wait for spring to return to New York."

"Leaving so soon. But why when —" Realization hit him like lightning ripping from the sky. "They want you to go with them." He should have known after their cold introduction and the high-handed manner in which they'd ordered Lily up the stairs after them. It wasn't right to speak ill of persons he'd only just met, but the tension they brought weighed enough to fell a mountain.

He swallowed against the rush of emotions threatening to undo his masked calm. "So you'll be leaving with them."

"I will not."

"No?"

"My parents can bluster all they like, but spring is a long time from now and I've work to do here. A lot can happen in the next few months." The staircase came into view where they must part ways. She stopped and turned to look at him. "Unless you want me to go."

"No." Unable to help himself any longer, he stroked her cheek as emotions held at bay bucked against the restraint. "No, I don't want you to go."

The teasing light in her eyes smoldered as her gaze dropped to his mouth, then dragged back to his eyes. Heat flashed in his chest yearning to break free and consume them both. They moved together, seeking relief from the flames.

Her lips were soft and yielding, yet burning with boldness that begged him not to hold back. How could he with her? She who shone so brightly into his soul that he craved nothing more than the light she brought him. He pulled her closer, one arm around her slim waist as his other hand brushed up her back and to the thick coil of hair pinned at the back of her slender neck. A shiver ran through her body as she leaned into him, thrilling him that his embrace could elicit such a vulnerable response. The satisfied pride of a man reveling in what his touch could bring to a woman, yet it was she whose powers could bring him to his knees.

Never in his lifetime or beyond could he have dreamed of such a woman with all her beauty for life and passion for goodness, but here she was settling herself into his arms as if she'd been waiting her whole life for him to open them wide and allow admittance. His lips curved in a smile, prompting hers to follow suit in matching sweetness. Aye, she fit him very well indeed.

Cupping his face, Lily leaned back, the smile still on her face. "Lord Strathem, you do make me weak in the knees."

Alec traced his thumb over her bottom lip. Red and plush, enticing a kiss once more. Again. And another. "As you steal from me the willpower to stop kissing you."

"And do you wish to stop?"

"No. Not when I've only just begun."

Footsteps sounded on the stairs. "Esther, it really is too much. Your dear father should not have troubled himself so."

Alec and Lily jumped apart before their lips could graze one final time as his mother and Esther stopped on the landing below.

"No trouble at all, Lady Strathem. The king gifted my father for his honorable service with two fattened geese, and we wish to share our blessing."

Like a beacon Mither's gaze narrowed upward. "Alec. There you are, skulking."

Steeling himself, he descended the stairs with Lily directly behind him. "Good morning, Mither. Miss Hartley."

Mither drew her black shawl tighter over her shoulders as her gaze swept to Lily. "Apologies, but I can't seem to remember your name."

"Miss Lily Durham," Alec offered.

"*Aide* Durham," Esther corrected.

Appearing unruffled by the frostiness that went beyond the snow outside, Lily smiled. "Good morning, Lady Strathem. I've just come from visiting Viola. She looks absolutely lovely. Her spirit seems to grow with each passing day."

"No doubt thanks to your encouragement." Mither cut her attention back to Alec. How frail she'd become. The widow's weeds dragged her further down to the shell of the woman he once knew. Could she not see how her determined lingering in the past affected them all? "Esther has informed me that we now have a fatted goose to enjoy for our Hogmanay meal. You needn't worry about hunting us a hare this year."

Alec nodded, not missing her familiar use of Esther's name while blindly forgetting Lily's. "A wonderful substitute. Please thank your father for thinking of us."

"You must join us," Mither said.

Esther touched a hand to the starched collar at her slender throat. "Oh no. I couldn't impose."

" 'Tis no imposition to grace our table if Matron Strom can bear to part with your invaluable services for one evening."

"I should like that very much. Especially since I won't be traveling to visit my own family. Our patients aren't afforded such a luxury and neither shall I allow it for myself."

"As much as I dislike their disturbance to our lives, I applaud your selflessness. In the meantime we will fold you into our family. After all we've known you long enough that we might consider you a part already. Family should be prized above all." Mither pointed a meaningful stare at Alec.

He ignored it. "If we're to make merry, I'll extend the invitation to Mr. and Mrs. Durham and Miss Durham." Alec turned to Lily, praying she'd not bow out and leave him dangling in the wind. "Your chance to experience a true Scottish tradition firsthand."

"How delightful," Esther said. "Of course we must invite them for a taste of Scottish hospitality before they whisk you back to America."

Alec frowned. "The celebration benefits

416

little to be tainted with rumors."

Gently swishing her skirt to the side so she wouldn't trip, Esther joined him on the step. Standing close enough for her starched sleeve to brush his arm. "Crossing open waters during wartime is a dangerous voyage. Surely they only took on the risk to remove their only daughter from further threat. After all, America has nothing to lose in this war, content as they are far across the ocean."

"You are correct in their concern, but they are also aware of my devotion in staying on at the hospital and cannot tempt me away." Lily smiled graciously. "We'd be delighted to join you. If you'll excuse me, my shift is about to start."

Alec did his best not to stare wistfully after her and the tender spot on the back of her neck where he wished to press his next kiss. One afternoon on the moor and he was losing all well-earned sense.

Lifting her dark skirts, Mither continued her ascent past him. "I'll go and see your sister. There's no telling what that American is filling her impressionable head with. If your father were —"

"She's good for Viola."

"Good as a cat in the cradle."

Alec swallowed his response. Her grief

417

forced others into misery, but he refused to go easily down that path. Nodding to Esther, he moved down the steps.

Her hand curved over his shoulder to stop him. "You've been avoiding me of late."

With good reason. Several reasons, in fact, and most of them centering around Lily and what she was coming to mean to him. A conscience of his heart. Esther, on the other hand, embodied a sense of logic to his circumstances. While she proved a safer path of stability, it was not one he was ready to consider. "Kinclavoch is a large castle with everyone about their own business."

"You work so hard. I'm hoping this Hogmanay feast will put your spirit to rights as we gather around the table with loved ones. A true family. A time to imagine how things could be, a fresh beginning."

"It's not necessary that you do —"

"But I want to. I care a great deal about you and seeing the home you love in such disrepair breaks my heart." Her soft white hand dropped to rest over his heart. "Watching your shoulders bow under the pressure, why, lesser men would have buckled by now, but not you. You are strong and capable, but burdens can only be carried for so long. A solid union would restore this castle and ensure future Lords and Ladies of

Kinclavoch to reign for generations."

He took a step back as the topic he'd been trying to avoid revisiting squared off. "Lords and ladies. A marriage, you mean."

"A dowry for a title. Marriages are made in much less agreeable ways and often between parties who detest each other. At least we don't have that hurdle."

She said it so matter-of-fact, as if the solution couldn't be simpler. In a way she was right. Most marriages were nothing more than business arrangements trussed up in gold bands and vows of love and obedience. He wanted more for himself than a bank account, and he certainly did not wish to view any potential wife as a means for his financial profit. When and if there was a new Lady Strathem, she did not deserve to be pulled into his current mire. No matter the competing temptation of his heart and logic.

"My situation is such that I cannot fathom a proposal of any kind at this time. I've put such notions from my mind. As should you."

"I don't want to, Alec." Her large brown eyes pleaded with him. She was a beauty with a gift for twisting a man's insides, but he had been stirred within by another.

"It's best if you do, Miss Hartley."

Her doleful eyes iced over. "And what's best for you? Selling off pieces of your home and land? To Lord Kinnifie of all people. He'll turn it to the ugly venture of pig farming."

"Where have you heard about Kinnifie and me?"

"His gardener is brother to our cook. Servants can never resist gossiping. Unfortunately the gossip has made its way upstairs and into the *London Herald,* where Wright has taken a special interest in running stories of Kinclavoch's incidents where the facts are barely legible beneath the sensationalism. The kidnapping, that actress being poisoned, but worst are the despicable things he's saying about you." She shivered as if Wright's name slithered across her skin. "Vile man. You should sue him for defamation of character."

Sue? With what money? All the charges Alec could summon against Wright in court would bankrupt him before a jury had enough time to scramble for evidence against the snake. While Alec had yet to find anything tangible connecting him to the mysterious events occurring around the castle, there was nothing against the law on slander in a rag paper. If that were the case, half the newspaper columns would be obsolete.

"Lord Strathem!" Matron Strom hurried

across the second-floor landing, skirts whipping about her ankles like agitated birds. "Your attention is required immediately." She hurried on without waiting for him.

Alec took the stairs two at a time. Pain knotted down his leg, but he ignored it and caught up to the older woman. "Is there a problem?"

"One might say that."

They rounded the corner into the east wing that had been assigned to the soldiers with more serious cases who were in need of quieter care. Several of them poked bandaged heads out of doorways at the commotion erupting halfway down the corridor.

Matron Strom stopped in front of the door of interest. "Have the patients been injured?"

Two nurses stood next to two pushchairs occupied by severely burned men wrapped up in bandages and glistening with burn cream. "No damage to the patients, Matron. We got them out in time."

Sickness twisted in Alec's gut. Like a man facing the gallows, he moved to the open doorway and choked back a string of curses. The far corner of the ceiling had caved in with a gush of water spilling across the floorboards. Glimpses of the sky poked through the hole and offered the perfect view of the broken gutter dripping its watery destruction. The gutter would have broken and redirected its spewing some time ago to saturate through the wood and plaster, leaving enough evidence as warning.

Alec rounded on Matron Strom. "Why was I not informed of the leak before it was too late?"

To her credit, the matron didn't appear the least bit ruffled. "This room has been unoccupied until yesterday when two new patients were moved in. Otherwise I would have arranged different rooms for them and alerted you immediately."

He could stand there and argue in frustration all day, but what was done was done. Best to carry on and solve the problem before it got worse. Such as the floor collapsing into the kitchen below. Taking off his jacket, Alec rolled up his shirtsleeves. "Bring a bucket to put under the drain. I need mops and any towels you can muster. Hurry before the water spreads!"

Nurses fluttered like a flock of hens to do his bidding as Matron Strom gave orders to their fleeing backs.

A cool, slender hand touched his arm. Esther. "Oh, Alec. How tragic. The cost in repairs will be staggering."

Yanking the crumpled bedsheets off the nearest bed, Alec dropped to his knees and pushed the sheets across the sodden floor, sopping up the water. Money. Broken gutters. Water damage. A kitchen under threat. More money. Each stacked on him like river stones, weighing him deeper into the drowning current. Another stone and he may slip, never to resurface.

CHAPTER 20

If Lily could have opted to have all her teeth pulled while sitting cross-legged on a bed of burning coals, she would have. Instead she found herself seated between her stoic father and a preening Esther with a dead goose staring at her from its place of honor on the dinner table.

On New Year's Eve, Hogmanay for the Scots, the most unlikely of dinner companions gathered into a room within the family's private wing. The smell of aged wood and disturbed dust lingered in the air — air that should have been refreshed by opening the shuttered windows.

Polished with fresh beeswax, the mahogany table stood on scrolled legs with matching high-back chairs. Besides the fowl, silver platters and bowls boasting the MacGregor crest were laden with potatoes, turnips, flat oatcakes, a soft cheese called crowdie, stewed apples, butter with orange zest, a plum pudding biding its time until it was set alight, and a rather dubious dish Viola had called haggis. It wasn't the unusual name that worried Lily so much as the devious smile Viola had tried to cover when she said it.

At the head of the table, Alec turned to Lily's mother, who sat to his right. "Your daughter informs me that you in America do not celebrate Hogmanay, Mrs. Durham. Are there other customs with which you ring in the new year?"

"Balls. With dancing until dawn." Mother gave a prerequisite nimble to a slice of the goose before sipping her wine. Her sapphire bracelet and matching ring winked in the candlelight. "The Astors used to throw the most magnificent gatherings. Only the Four Hundred were invited. A shame the old ways are losing their importance."

Esther dabbed her lips with a linen napkin, then placed it over the ruby folds of her velvet skirt. Her raven hair was swept up into ringlets with a diamond paste comb. A covetous attempt at the small tiara crowning the current Lady Strathem. "I could not agree with you more, Mrs. Durham. If we do not keep to our traditions, we will have nothing left to stand on. I shudder to think what may happen without societal gates in place. Dynasties such as the MacGregors and Hartleys must join together to remain strong."

Was she aiming for proposal number two over appetizers? The blatant delusions knew no boundaries.

Lily rolled her eyes to Viola, who sat across the table. Dressed in dusty pink with a pearl choker and looking more grown-up than ever, Viola offered her a fortifying smile.

Mother glanced down to the other end of the table where Lady Strathem sat bedecked all in jet and shimmering black silk. "Speaking of standing on tradition, I could not help but take notice of a painting along the corridor of our room. *Mademoiselle Guimard as Terpsichore.* By Jacques-Louis David, is it not?"

Lady Strathem pushed at a pile of potatoes with her pewter fork. Presumably Alec had sold all the silver. "I'm afraid I'm not familiar with many of the paintings in this house. They seem to come and go at random." Lady Strathem's gaze cut to Alec. "My late husband had the true eye for art."

"I commend him on his exquisite taste. The Empire style has quite swept the East Coast for all things French."

Lily saw the calculations in her mother's eyes. Without doubt, after the meal she would sidle up to Lady Strathem in hopes of striking a bargain over the painting. Her sweet words and well-placed flattery had garnered them more than one art piece in their New York home, but she didn't understand the force of Lady Strathem clinging to her husband's memory and all that entailed. Perhaps Lily should steer her toward Alec. At least then his family's offerings would go to a devoted patron and not be sold at auction for pennies on the pound.

Poor Alec. He'd put on a brave face to sit as master at a table full of irritable guests when he'd feel more at home in his stables with the comforts of hay and nonspeaking animals. Lily couldn't help but feel proud of his efforts.

He looked down the table and caught her eye. How handsome he looked in full Scottish dress complete with kilt and tartan sash buckled to his shoulder by a gleaming brooch that winked in the candlelight. A sight she would happily grow accustomed to if given the opportunity. She smiled.

The corners of his eyes crinkled in reply as he shifted his eyes to her father. "Have you had a chance to take in the grounds, Mr. Durham? Though it's the heart of winter, beauty is still to be found. Or if you like, I can take you to the best of the coveys.

We've large amounts of grouse on the estate."

"I'm not a hunting man."

"Do you care for horses? Most of mine were appropriated to serve on the front lines, but I've still two who enjoy a brisk walk."

Sensing another refusal based on the principle of not enjoying anything, Lily turned to her father. He was resplendent in black tails and white bib that needed little starching thanks to his already rigid posture. "Lord Strathem has some of the finest horseflesh in the country, Father. There's nothing he doesn't know about them."

Father nodded absently. "I congratulate you, my lord, but my tastes do not extend to equine. If time allows, I prefer a solid book. Biographies mostly."

"Kinclavoch boasts a wonderful library on every subject under the sun. You could spend years in there without touching most of the collection." Lily rested her hand on his sleeve. His gaze flicked down to her gloved fingers for one scorching second. She drew her hand back to her lap.

"We won't remain long enough to bother."

On her other side, Esther delicately cleared her throat. "A pity you should leave so quickly after arriving. Aide Durham's devotion to our British Tommies has been admirable, but I would understand your desire to coax her back to the quiet safety of your own distant shores. Especially after the perilous events —"

"What events are these?" Father's sharp tone cut through the preamble.

Esther dabbed the corners of her mouth with her snowy napkin. "First there was a kidnapping with the culprits still at large, quickly followed by those salacious remarks in the paper about Kinclavoch being unsafe. Then there was that poor Miss Barrymore and the poison ordeal. I wasn't sure if she'd make it."

Mother's wineglass hovered halfway to her lips. "Ethel was here?"

"Indeed she was, madam."

"The honey caused an allergic reaction, not poisoning," Lily said.

Esther's black eyebrow winged up. "Are you condoning the blatant act when Miss Barrymore pointedly said honey was a detriment to her health?"

"Of course I'm not condoning it, but neither can I agree with bloating facts for shock value."

Esther nodded sorrowfully. "I for one still find it shocking that Dreymond would hold a knife to your throat."

429

Father's knife and fork clattered to his plate. "Daughter, what is the meaning of this?"

Mother's glass came down, spilling drops of red wine. "Oh, Lily."

Swallowing back more than a few choice words for the conniver sitting next to her, Lily sought to soothe her mother's distress. "Miss Hartley exaggerates the truth of the matter."

Esther touched a dark lock curling over her ear. "It's hardly an exaggeration when the deranged man attacked you in the kitchen so late at night."

Mother grabbed her chest on the verge of a faint.

Anger blazed in Alec's eyes. "Miss Hartley, please refrain from speaking of such matters at my table where my mother and sister are present." He looked around the table, stopping twice as long on Lily. "Apologies for such unsavory conversation."

Father tossed his napkin on the table. A gauntlet if ever there was one. "Apologies or not, I demand to know what has happened to my daughter. What kind of danger have you allowed her to step into, Strathem? Or MacGregor — or however you style yourself."

Lily reached out to touch his sleeve but

430

quickly withdrew her hand. "Father, it's nothing like that. There have been a few unfortunate happenings, and, Mother, Ethel is perfectly healthy now after her setback with the honey." Lily bunched the folds of her periwinkle satin between her gloved fingers. "Poor Mr. Dreymond. His mind was fragile after his injuries. He would never have hurt me. Lord Strathem saw to that."

"Oh, Lily." Mother's eyes welled up. She pulled a lace hankie from her décolletage and dabbed her eyes. "You were supposed to be far from the danger."

"I can assure you that your daughter is in no danger at Kinclavoch. These malicious attacks were aimed at smearing my name," Alec said in an effort to keep the peace that was fraying faster than a silk thread.

"Why is your name in need of smearing?" Father demanded.

"I'm afraid there's a man insistent on ruining me for his own gain."

"How could this person possibly ruin you by killing Ethel Barrymore? What sort of madhouse have we stepped into?"

Knock. Knock.

"Enter!" Alec's boom startled the room.

Guthrie hustled in and whispered furiously in Alec's ear. Thunder rolled across Alec's brow. He shot to his feet. The chair tipped backward, promptly caught by Guthrie before it hit the floor.

"Forgive me. There's an emergency in the stables." Alec's frantic gaze sought Lily. Without thought, she half rose from her seat. Father's hand clamped around her wrist and yanked her back to her seat. Alec rushed from the room, his kilt flapping against his knees and Guthrie quick on his heels.

Silence quaked in their absence, pressing down like a lead cloth to suffocate the room. Lily stared at the door, wishing with all her might she could follow him. Her every thought carried with him to the stables. His horses. *Please, dear God in heaven, not them.*

Esther leaned close. "So sad when Alec is called away, but then his burdens are many. I look forward to the day when I may help carry them. When I am mistress of this place, he'll not want for anything."

"And yet I remember clearly from that day in the stables him saying he didn't need you." Lily smiled politely to keep the rest of the table guests from knowing how much she wanted to cram her napkin down Esther's throat.

"He will. Much sooner than expected. When he has nothing left, it'll be me he turns to."

432

"What do you mean by that?"

Smirking, Esther turned away, leaving Lily to ponder her cryptic threats.

"Alec will know what to do." Viola's soft voice stole across the fearful emptiness and settled across Lily's pounding heart with reassurance.

Lily nodded. Yes, no one would know better than Alec. Taking a deep breath, she reached for the platter in front of Esther in an attempt to salvage what was supposed to be a celebratory evening. "Mother, have you tried this? It's called haggis."

Hankie still pressed to her face, Mother shook her head.

"A Scottish tradition of sheep's heart, liver, and lungs stuffed into its intestines," Viola offered helpfully.

"In that case, Esther, this sounds perfect for you." Lily tried not to gag as she knifed into the round casing and scooped it onto Esther's plate. "Bon appétit."

Ignoring the dry retching next to her, Lily stared at the door and counted the seconds until she could slip away to the stables.

Alec patted Appin's side. *"Chan fheudar an t-eagal a bheth oirbh."* The simple words to fear not clawed against the terror quaking in his chest. Five hours he'd hunkered down in the stables until the worst of it seemed to have passed. He'd sent Guthrie inside as there was little either of them could do but wait.

He ran a hand over his tired eyes, but it did little to dislodge the memory of finding the animal unconscious on his side and barely breathing. As if he'd simply collapsed, his heartbeat frighteningly erratic. Muscles spasmed, causing the epiglottis to close. Alec had reached into Appin's mouth and pulled out his tongue to help the animal breathe. The hours passed and the mighty muscles ceased their twitching with the breathing slow and shallow.

Cupping his hand around Appin's jawbone, he placed two fingers along the inside of the bone, just below the heavy muscles of the cheek. He closed his eyes and gently prodded for that telltale sign of life. There. A pulse.

"Weak, auld lad." Alec opened his eyes and smoothed his hand down Appin's mane. "But steady and that's something. You best be rising soon. We've too much unridden ground for you to leave me now."

Emotion caught in his throat. From the moment Appin had come into the world, Alec felt a kindred spirit with him. To have his friend taken from him now was akin to removing the thrum of his heart.

"How is he faring?" Lily stood just outside the stall staring in. Soft lantern light pooled around her like a halo, illuminating the worry in her eyes.

Alec cleared his throat against the roughness. "He's no worse."

"That's something to be thankful for."

"Aye." He stood, brushing the hay from his kilt. He'd discarded his formal jacket and sash long ago for the ease of moving about. "You shouldn't be out here."

She stepped into the stall draped in a velvet cloak that looked more suited to attending a theater than a jaunt out to the stables. A hint of sweet rose followed her in. The feminine scent should have clashed with the earthy musk of horse, dirt, and straw, but somehow they melded into a unique harmony. "I couldn't sleep knowing you were out here with Appin. I don't know much about horses but wanted to help if I could."

" 'Tis not much to help with when I don't know the cause. Keeping him warm is the best I can do."

They stood in silence watching the slight rise and fall of the horse's side. Occasionally his leg would twitch or an ear flick as if a persistent fly buzzed about. Appin hated those beasties. None more so than the wee midgies come to feast on him every summer. If only he would let out an irritable neigh as he always did when swatting them off.

Lily's fancy shoes shuffled against the straw-covered floor. Her presence calmed the demented thoughts rallying through Alec's head. "Do you have any idea what could have brought this on?"

Alec leaned his forearm against the low wall separating the stall from Sorcha's. "He's a healthy beast. Always has been. Whatever this is, it's not of natural consequences."

"Foul play, you mean."

"Wouldn't be the first time tragedy has struck. Or threats." The last came out harsher than intended, but he couldn't stop the fear that had seized him when he found out she'd been in his study alone after the ransacking. "You've had too many close calls.

Lily stared down at her toes. "I don't seek harrying situations on purpose."

"Nonetheless they find you."

She looked up, her contriteness now peppered with annoyance. "You sound like Bertie."

She could be annoyed all she wanted.

Trust had built between them, tenuous though it was, and he'd come to understand her as she had him. Yet with understanding came the growing need to protect. The more he learned of her fears and insecurities, the more he wished to shelter her from that which would bring about such troubles. Indeed, she had tried to do the same for him. Only her overprotectiveness could prove fatal.

Alec brushed past her and strode to the end of the empty stalls where a pile of unused equipment had piled up. Digging behind dried buckets of paint and a broken harness, he extracted an aged creepie once used for milking cows. Cows that had long been sent to feed the starving men in France.

"I need to know you're safe. Not to mention the hundreds of others residing here with a madman on the loose threatening to sabotage everything I'm attempting to hold together." Walking back to Appin's stall, he plunked the low, three-legged seat on the ground and brushed the dust from it. "It's all connected. Sit."

Lily gracefully lowered herself to the stool. The edges of her midnight-blue cloak flipped back to reveal the lighter blue dinner gown she still wore. Remembering the glow of candlelight burrowing into her upswept curls and the cut of her dress slipping over her curves with perfection had him wishing to reinstate formal dinners if only to admire her elegance once more. Then again, she didn't need candlelight to prove how bonny she was.

Alec shook away the distracting thoughts and sat once more next to Appin. "Richard Wright would love nothing more than to open his morning paper and read my obituary. I simply need the proof he's behind it all, but he's as slippery as a newborn foal in goose grease."

"I can't believe he would go that far. Both legs broken with your title and estate cast to the winds, perhaps."

"Then who?"

"I'm not sure. Former lover? A lady with slighted affections?" Pink tinged her cheeks as she took great interest in plucking at the silken cord tying on her cloak.

He snorted with laughter. "If those are your guesses, then we're as lost as blind mice in the woods. A woman would not waste her affections on a man like me, saving them instead for a gentleman."

Her gaze snapped up, silken cord forgotten. "You don't know that."

"You don't think I'd know if I had a lover

before? I assure you, that sort of fact does not escape a man's notice." He shifted as a stubborn stalk of straw jabbed the underside of his exposed knee. Readjusting the pleats of his kilt did little to alleviate the tormentor. " 'Tis hardly a matter appropriate to discuss with a lady."

"Because I shouldn't know about such things."

"One of many reasons."

She waved a hand through the air as if to dismiss his words. "I know very well how women work. No doubt you've broken a few hearts, and a wounded heart does not easily forgive."

"Did I say we are the blind mice? Correction: you are the only blind one here if you think any woman has broken her heart over me."

Tilting her head, she grew quiet as she studied his face like one considering the still reflection of a loch. He didn't move lest he ripple the tranquility and forever lose the moment cast between them.

At last a smile curved her lips and she leaned forward. Close enough to reach for his hand. "No, Alec. I'm not blind. Not this time. Not with you. The world is filled with beautiful things that glitter, but after a lifetime of seeing them they begin to look alike. Except for you. Nothing about you glitters and that's what I like best. You've captured me in a way none other could."

A tightness settled in his chest. Not unpleasant, rather an ache to push beyond what was familiar and meet her in a place undiscovered of yet to them both. "You'll find very little around here that glitters."

"Which makes it all the more real."

"I've never been much good with ladies. Always preferred the familiarity of the stables."

"Precisely why I came out here." She smiled flirtatiously before the lightheartedness slipped away. "How long have you known Esther?"

The tranquility suspended between them vanished on the ill omen that was that name. Plucking the wee *sgian dubh* from the top of his wool hose, he split a stalk of hay straight down the middle. "Her grandfather began a coal mining company in the county over some fifty years ago, but it didn't see much profit until her father inherited it at the young age of twenty-five. A few years later he bought an estate near the mine and came with his wife, son, and daughter every summer. I met Esther the first summer they came to stay. Mr. Hartley is one of the richest untitled men in the country."

"With a beautiful, single heiress for a daughter."

"She has her pick of the bucks."

"There's only one stag she has her sights set on."

He grabbed another stalk. "I'm not interested in being anyone's prize target." His blade froze midslice. "Is that what you meant by slighted affections? From Esther?"

He wanted to laugh at the absurdity of her behind the troubling events, but the noise stuck in his throat. Esther was a well-bred young woman to all outward appearances. Highly educated, committee member for several charities, and whose forthcoming dowry would set the king himself up for decades to come. By all accounts, a prize.

And she'd offered it to him.

Esther was the reasonable choice. Her dowry could rebuild Kinclavoch ten times over and preserve its sanctity for generations of MacGregors to come. His tenants would remain safe on their farmland. Viola and Mither would never have their precious possessions sold off again, while the recuperating soldiers could stay as long as they needed with a dependable roof over their heads. Esther's offer was tempting, but what kind of man would he be if he couldn't pull his own fate from destruction with his own two hands? How could he hold his head up with pride knowing it was her money that truly supported him?

A headache throbbed behind his eyes. Too much thinking for his muddled mind to comprehend this night. He slipped his blade back into his hose and checked Appin's pulse again. The same.

He stood and wiped off the straw clinging to his kilt. "You best head inside. It's well on to midnight and I'll not have you freeze out here." He offered his hand to help her up.

Her cool fingers slipped over his palm and nestled in, her small hand perfectly framed within his much larger one. She stood and slowly withdrew her hand, leaving his palm yearning for her touch a moment longer. "Midnight has come and gone. It's closer to one in the morning by now."

"All the more reason for you to be off." Not to mention the temptation her nearness wreaked on his discipline. "I'm glad it's you for first footing."

"Is that another Hogmanay tradition?"

He nodded and stepped out of the stall with her. "The first person to enter a home after the new year is said to bring good fortune. Unlucky as you are being a lass."

Lily's eyebrows shot up in indignation. "I beg your pardon."

"Don't fash. I find it rather agreeable that it's you and not a tall, dark-haired man as custom dictates. Or Guthrie. The last time he was my first foot we had a snowfall that buried us in for nearly a month. Forgot to bring the coal and bread of warmth and prosperity, but he did manage the whisky."

"Alas, I did not bring my sack of coal or other colorful gifts you Scots insist on for good cheer, but I came not empty-handed." She reached into the folds of her voluminous cloak and withdrew a silver package tied with a red ribbon. "Christmas isn't celebrated here in the grand manner we do in America, but I wanted to get you something. Tonight seemed the perfect time to give it to you. Or at least it did before that horrendous dinner."

They stopped at the stable door, which stood ajar. Full beams of moonlight bounced off the white drifts of snow to illuminate the yard with the brightness of a white sun. He rolled down his shirtsleeves against the chill brushing his exposed forearms. "I'm sorry I had to leave you there."

"Never fret. I've had much experience fending off hostile dinner guests. The haggis put everyone off."

Alec winced. "Och, don't insult our national dish. Separates the men from the *Sassenachs*."

Lily laughed and handed him the package. "I shall be more respectful in future. Unless unwanted relatives drop by."

Alec tried not to allow the meaning of her words to settle into the private hopes he held close. Certainly she was glad to see her parents, but did she long for their imminent departure as he did? Since the moment they stood in his hall he'd wanted nothing more than to pack up their trunks and toss them out before they carried Lily back to America. He wanted her here. With him.

Untying the ribbon, he tore off the silver paper to reveal a book. *The Soldier's Guide to Ligament Melancholy: A Study of War and Its Treasons Against the Body.* He frowned.

She pointed to his bad knee. "I was doing a bit of reading, from one of your library books, I might add, about internal strain when there's a bone breakage. Doctors have been studying the wounded soldiers and realized that while the bones may heal, oftentimes the ligaments, muscles, and joints go unnoticed in the healing process. If not properly seen to, a new kind of damage can be wrought. A crippling. They suggest

444

several new methods of treatment that have proven somewhat successful in the short time they've begun administering them."

Alec flipped through the pages. Graphs, charts, and inked drawings of broken and twisted bones. The past twelve years of his life condensed within the words.

"If it doesn't work, we're no worse off than we were before," Lily said softly.

We. When had he ever considered himself in tandem with another? He flipped to the last chapter. *Life Free of Pain.* Never had someone dug deep enough to expose his roots of pain, nor reached down to offer relief. Until her. "Thank you."

"You're welcome. Will you be here all night?" She pulled up the collar of her cloak, her dangling earrings brushing the silver embroidery around the edge. "Of course you will. I expect nothing less of your steadfastness. I'll come back in the morning with prayer of improvement. Good night." She stretched up and placed a gentle kiss on his cheek, the bottom of her lip grazing the corner of his mouth.

He turned his head to catch her lips briefly, grounding himself in the unwavering respite only she could provide. "Good night, Lily."

She slipped out the door and across the

snow-crusted grass. Her rose scent lingered among the patches of warm hay and aged wood, mingling to a new comfort that settled securely about him. A new word, an endearment filled him until he could no longer deny the formation on his lips.

"A ghràidh."

My dear. For that was what she had become to him. Most dear.

CHAPTER 21

"Careful now. I ken well your need to run, but we'll be taking it easy until I know you're in the clear, auld lad." Alec led Appin by the reins around the slushy paddock. The snow had stopped from the night before, but the steely clouds threatened more by afternoon.

The beast had stirred awake around three in the morning. By sunrise the lingering grogginess had finally worn off and Appin had begun neighing to go outdoors. Alec had never known such joyful relief. Yet he was no closer to knowing the truth of what had happened.

"This is what took you away from our table last evening." The statement held no warmth or regard, merely dry fact. Mr. Durham stood on the other side of the white fence dressed in the banking power colors of black and gray, a heavy wool coat, and a bowler hat. Spatterdashes covered his lower legs and shiny shoes.

Alec gave a small tug of the reins, and Appin stopped walking with an irritated toss of his head. "Aye, but I believe he's on the mend."

"Any theories as to the origin?"

Only one that stood out in blatant malice. Appin had been drugged, if Alec had to guess. The hay wasn't moldy, and there were no outward signs of a bite or wound to indicate infection. It was nothing he'd encountered before. "One or two, sir."

Mr. Durham's intelligent eyes, surprisingly the same green as Lily's, probed him for further explanation. Alec gave none. The man's eyebrows narrowed under his round hat. "This place has a way of collecting incidents."

"We're doing what we can, sir. Patient safety is our top priority."

"Only the patients?" That stare.

Alec matched it. "Everyone under Kinclavoch's roof."

Still not blinking, Mr. Durham inhaled deeply and turned to sweep his gaze over the grounds and gray stone turrets of Kinclavoch. "This must have been a magnificent estate once."

Alec bristled at the slight insult. "She still is."

"I would estimate about £20,000 per year for upkeep. Required, that is, not current standings."

"A rather accurate guess."

"I'm a banker, Lord Strathem. It is my prerogative to identify and calculate the approximate worth of an object upon immediate disclosure."

Alec curled his arm around Appin's neck, twisting his fingers into the wiry mane. Who did this man think he was? Scotland was a long way from one of his sterile bank vaults where his boorish manner must never be questioned. "The value of some things cannot be calculated with a chart of numbers."

"In the real world they can. And are." Continuing his irritating inspection of the castle, Mr. Durham clasped his kidskin-gloved hands behind his back. "My business contacts in London inform me that the estate struggles under MacGregor ownership. Outstanding debts and selling of goods. Not to mention a recent sale of property to a Lord Kinnifie."

Alec gritted his teeth. "You are well informed of our circumstances, sir. I wonder at private transactions becoming so apparent."

"A lord facing bankruptcy is not so private an affair within the financial world. Unfortunate as that may be, I had a right to know as my daughter has been here for nearly a year. My associates merely shed light on the details of her circumstantial whereabouts."

"Because you don't trust her to make a sound judgment?"

"I require assurances for her well-being." Mr. Durham's chin dropped a fraction of an inch as if the admission weighed heavily on him. "Lily has always been strong-willed. We thought time in England might curb her ways. To discover her change of address to the wilds of Scotland came as a shock. Imagine my greater surprise to find her residing in a castle in desperate need of repair with the threat of eviction hanging over the roof due to the previous owner's weakness for drink and coin."

Alec dropped Appin's reins and strode to the fence. "You seem to have my facts well in hand, sir. Do you have any further questions that your associates have failed to locate? My shoe size mayhap?"

Mr. Durham turned to face him. His expression, save a twitch of his thick mustache, gave nothing away. "You are a man of honor, Lord Strathem. Or so I have been told. You have done everything in your power to keep your estate from sinking, and despite the enormity of such a task hanging over your head, you have opened the doors to wounded soldiers."

"My suffering is nothing to theirs."

"War is a terrible thing. Something I never wished my daughter to witness, but she has. My only hope is that we have arrived in time to spare her from further distress."

Alec gripped the top rail. Flecks of ice stuck to his fingers, but they melted quickly under the heat of his hand. "Mr. Durham, your daughter is strong. She may have the airs of a genteel lady, but she has a constitution of steel. Never have I seen a woman more intuitive to the needs of others nor so joyful to give them care and kindness. Yet she's never failed to rise to the challenge when hardship struck."

The man's bowler hat lifted slightly with the raise of his brow. "Hardships such as a family friend being poisoned and my daughter being held at knifepoint?"

"Those are aimed at me. Blunt tactics to force me to sell Kinclavoch."

"I am sorry for your troubles, but you can understand my hesitation to allow my daughter to remain in such a place. Why, the Hun may be at your gate before long. This war is stretching further beyond the bounds of safety." For the first time, the flint in Mr. Durham's face cracked. If he looked

451

close enough, Alec dared himself to find a glimpse of a truly concerned father buried under there. "Lily is a young woman of society with high expectations placed on the order of her standing within its realm to secure future generations. The sooner we can return her to New York, the better. For all."

No. It wasn't better for all. Lily had become a part of Kinclavoch, as natural a fitting as the sun in the sky. She had become a part of him. He could not fathom his depth of sorrow if his sun were taken from him. "What if it were her desire to remain here? Her happiness should have some factor in this."

"Happiness in mending broken men? No, Lord Strathem. That is pity."

"With all due respect, I disagree."

The flint fortified back in place. "I cannot allow my daughter to stay in a place of war and destruction. Where the walls crumble around her and the future remains bleak. She may think to find happiness, but I believe there will be nothing but brokenness. Best to spare her this disillusion now."

Alec heard the warning loud and clear like the thudding nail on a coffin sentencing him to a lifetime of darkness. Mr. Durham wanted the best for Lily and an investment in Alec simply did not add up. How many times had he thought that of himself? Too broken to offer significance. Lily had given him significance, but more than that, she'd helped him find it for himself.

"Good morning!" Lily's voice rang through the crystalline air, dissipating the thick drifts of tension. Dressed in her nurse's uniform and a navy-blue wool cloak, she came around the side of the stable with a patient who was missing an arm and sported a bandage around his neck. Her eyes widened in surprise as she looked from Alec to her father. "Father, what are you doing out here? Fresh air has never been your cup of tea."

Unsmiling, Mr. Durham turned at her approach. For a man with his daughter's betterment in mind, he seemed to take little joy in her. A running theme with fathers. "I wished to give our host thanks for last evening's dinner and to inquire after the cause of its unfortunate interruption."

"Appin looks his jolly old self again. Can we expect a full recovery, do you think?" Lily stopped at the fence and held out her hand with a small slice of carrot. The horse trotted over and eagerly gobbled up her offering.

Alec gave the horse an affectionate scratch.

"Aye, already skipping to be off. I'll have him resting most of the day and see how he fares on a walk on the morrow."

"Have you discovered the cause?"

Alec glanced down. "No."

"I hope you do. I can't imagine any more harm coming to this sweetie. Or Sorcha." With a final pat to Appin's head, she flashed a mischievous grin and pulled the man waiting patiently behind her forward. "In the meantime I've brought you a bit of help. This is Lieutenant Wallace of the Fourth Dragoon Guards. Lieutenant, this is Lord Strathem, a rather fine horseman himself."

Forgoing the wear of hospital pajamas, the man had dressed in uniform to brave the outdoors. Alec caught sight of the badge on the man's hat. "Cavalryman."

"Yes, my lord." The man straightened as any good soldier did when professing his career. Alec was surprised when he didn't render a salute to complete the posture.

"Know how to pace a horse?"

"As well as any cavalryman."

Allowing others into his sanctuary was not a permission often granted. Nor was the handling of his horses, but an earnestness shone on the soldier's face as he watched Appin that Alec recognized at once. He found peace with them as Alec did.

Alec unhitched the gate and swung it wide enough for Wallace to slip in. Appin glanced up at the intruder, then went back to snuffling the ground for grass.

"I'll return for you in a while, Lieutenant. Mind yourself not to get trampled." Lily flashed Alec a smile that sent his pulse racing, then hooked her hand around her father's arm. "Come along, Father. Shall we see what corner of the castle Mother has gotten herself lost in? Some of the soldiers need letters written and she has such beautiful handwriting."

Mr. Durham still clasped his hands behind his back. "I doubt your mother has time for writing letters."

"You then?" Lily's laugh at her father's scowl echoed over the yard as they walked away. Her inner light of impish joy never flickered in the face of disapproval.

Alec did his best to drag his attention back to the man before him. Each step she took away felt like a mile of distance spreading between them with her father standing as a roadblock. "How long have you been around horses?"

Wallace stroked a hand down Appin's side as if he held a currycomb. Familiar and practiced. "All my life. When it was time to join up I took my best mount, Comrado."

His face darkened for a moment. "He was shot out from under me during an open field charge. Lost my arm and took shrapnel through the neck. Lucky to have made it out alive. Lucky to be here." Having picked up the discarded reins, Wallace led Appin around the paddock without waiting for instruction.

How Alec would hate to lose all of this. To lose Lily. Was she to serve as the one flash of brilliant light to illuminate his crumbling world before the flame guttered out and he plunged headlong into darkness? He needed her, but Mr. Durham was right. She deserved more than an offering of a leaky roof and its limping master, but mayhap, given the chance he could prove to be worthy of her.

Yet time was not on his side.

CHAPTER 22

"A party? Are you out of your head?" Bertie's glasses slid down her nose. She shoved them back up and continued stacking the books on their proper shelves.

"It's a brilliant idea." Lily gathered up the chess pieces that had been left out and sorted them on the black-and-white checkered board. "The men are climbing the walls from being kept indoors, not to mention their suffering of morale. Have you heard about the latest men brought in from the front? Burns all up and down their bodies from something called a flamethrower."

"Poor devils."

Lily tried not to think on the horror human beings inflicted upon one another in the name of winning a war, but the image of a pig on a spit roasting over an open flame was difficult to dislodge. "Moping around only allows the Germans to further

457

invade our spirits. A celebration is a reminder that the enemy will never defeat our
heart. Or winter's cold or our sanity."

"Your American optimism astounds me at
times." Finished with the books, Bertie re-
arranged the chessboard until all the white
pieces stood on one side and the blacks on
the other as if they all had designated spaces.

"Think of it as an invitation for the British to lighten up." Grabbing a deck of cards,
Lily left the library and traversed the hall to
the patients' ward, where the gray light of a
snow-laden sky filtered through the tall
windows. "You can drop that stiff upper lip
for one evening, can't you?"

"No. It's ingrained, like breathing. One
drop and we all go down."

They maneuvered between the beds with
the practiced ease of ducks among the
reeds. In the back corner, Captain Gibbons
and his new neighbor, none other than
Lieutenant Wallace, debated the merits of
bacon versus streaky bacon. There would be
no winner in this debate as all bacon was
delicious.

"Ready for a game, gentlemen?" Lily
placed the cards on the small table next to
Gibbons, then moved around to the foot of
Wallace's bed.

"No cheating this time." Wallace wagged

his finger at Gibbons.

Gibbons feigned shock. "How dare you accuse an officer of the king of such scandalous acts." His gaze slid up to Bertie, a twinkle in his eye.

Bertie returned the twinkle before she caught Lily watching her. Pink dusted her cheeks. "Ahem. Let's move this bed, shall we?" Taking the head of Wallace's bed, she and Lily slid it over to within arm's reach of Gibbons's and their mutual playing table.

Captain Gibbons was well on the mend thanks in no small part to a certain attentive nurse. They'd all been instructed not to ask him anymore about his ordeal as Matron hoped his memory would soon shed light on the culprits behind his taking. So far, the man only seemed to want to forget it himself. Understandable as it was, Lily didn't want to forget entirely. Not if there was the slightest chance of connecting all the incidents to a single point.

"Why don't you try whist?" Bertie suggested.

"That's an old ladies' game." Wallace scratched at his shoulder where his empty arm sleeve was pinned to keep it from flopping around.

"Snap?"

"Poker," Gibbons offered. A glare from

Bertie resulted in a sheepish look. "Snap it is."

"What do you gentlemen think of a party?" Lily asked. Their gazes slanted to her as if she suggested they ride flying fish through the air.

"Would it involve dancing?" Wallace frowned and held up his slippered feet. "I've two left feet."

"Parties are stuffy." Gibbons shuffled the cards and began dealing.

Lily smiled. "With or without dancing, I know all the nurses would appreciate an occasion to put on their prettiest dresses, which have sadly been neglected in favor of these starched uniforms."

Gibbons's eyes flickered to Bertie, then dropped back to his cards. "Might not be so bad." He slammed his cards down, excitement brewing on his face. "A ceilidh, that's what we need."

Lily frowned. "A what?"

"That's what they call an informal dance here in Scotland. Fewer stuffed shirts, lots of dancing and laughing. My unit came over with the Black Watch and they talked all about it. 'Course they were passing the flask at the time."

"We'll have no flask passing." At Bertie's stern command, the men exchanged disgruntled looks and shifted back to their card game. Bertie motioned Lily away to an empty set of beds farther down. "Logistics aside, I don't think this is a good idea."

"Fun is not a crime. And don't tell me again about your aversion to a lively step."

"It's not that." Bertie glanced around to ensure all the occupants were out of hearing distance and lowered her voice. "How do you think many of these men will feel when invited to a dance when they have no legs to dance?"

Lily shook out a crumpled blanket and refolded it over the edge of the bed. "It's an opportunity for laughing and having a jolly time. No jigging about required."

"What about music? Orchestras aren't that easy to come by these days."

"I'm sure we can scrounge up a fiddle player and a pianist."

"Always with the 'we' as if I want anything to do with your balmy on the crumpet ideas."

"That sounds like a questionable food topping."

"It means another typical Lily idea."

Lily poked her in the side. "In other words, brilliant."

Esther glided toward them with her ever-present clipboard in hand. She stopped in front of Bertie and Lily and marked a decisive line across her paper while staring at them. "Matron doesn't approve of gossiping on the ward."

Bertie met her stare. "We are discussing the dressing of wounds and the use of a tincture of iodine or a flush of saline solution. What say you to the validity of each, Nurse Hartley?"

Esther blinked in confusion. Leave it to Bertie to pull out an obscure reference from a medical journal. "I . . . Those are not the duties of a convalescent nurse. We are for the delicate care and comfort of soldiers transitioning back to active orders."

"If you need musicians for the ceilidh, ask Fergus and Hathaway," Wallace called from his bed. "Don't know how well a set of pipes and tambourine will work together, but it's better than nothing."

Lily nodded. "Thank you, Lieutenant. I'll keep that in mind."

Esther arched a dark brow in triumph as if ferreting out their secret. "You're planning a country dance. With the patients? Do you really think that will work when half of them are missing limbs, not to mention gaining Matron's approval? A foolish idea if you ask me."

"Then it's a good thing we didn't because

it's going to be brilliant," Bertie announced. "Perhaps while the rest of us enjoy the festivities you can spend the wasted time studying in your room. It takes more than a little clipboard to prove yourself a real nurse."

Esther's thin nostrils flared. "How dare you talk to me like that? I am your superior —"

"In what way? Don't say in nursing because we joined the same month, and I know you won't dare to presume societal standing with your family's nouveau riche status."

Esther's mouth gaped open as she sputtered.

Heads swiveled their direction as conversations hushed to a murmur.

"Bertie!" Lily knew of the deeply held English snobbery for money gained instead of acquired through the honest avenue of inheritance, but it only ever existed in silent acknowledgment. Mentioning it out loud was bad form. "I think it's time we readied the medicines for the afternoon round. Come on."

Taking her cousin's arm, Lily hauled her from the ward and into the storage room. She closed the door behind them and leaned against it lest Esther come tearing after them. "What has gotten into you?"

"I don't know." Bertie slumped against a pile of fresh sheets and buried her face in her hands. "It came out before I could stop it. She makes me so angry with her pretentiousness."

"Well, I think you've managed to knock her down a gilded peg or two."

"And in front of the patients." Bertie groaned between her fingers.

"Those men have heard far worse things said in the trenches."

"Not from me! A supposed lady."

Moving away from the door, Lily slipped an arm around her cousin. "You're still a lady, and they know without a shadow of a doubt how much you care for them. One slip in decorum won't tarnish you before their eyes. Just look at all the things I've done, and not once have they tried to tar and feather me."

"That's because you're charming and have the protection of the laird."

A thrill shot through Lily at the mention of Alec protecting her. Now wasn't the time for dwelling on that. She had Bertie's insecurities to bolster first. "Me? Look at you with your dashing captain. Always making eyes at each other. I'm glad Matron removed that privacy screen or I'd have to start sitting back there as chaperone."

Spine snapping straight, Bertie dropped her hands from her face. "Alan is a gentleman."

Lily smiled and tucked a wayward hair under Bertie's cap. "I only hope he's worthy of you. You deserve the cream of life. Now, let's fill these medicine trays before Esther comes in here with her clipboard again."

"Bother her clipboard. She can scratch things all day and I won't give two snaps for it."

"Two snaps isn't what I'm worried about. More likely you bopping her on the head with it."

The corners of Bertie's mouth perked up. She quickly smothered it by grabbing an empty tray and measuring out the needed medicines. "When are you going to ask Matron about the dance?"

Lily stoppered the bottles as Bertie finished and placed them back in the cabinet. "After my shift. By then she'll have had tea and biscuits to soften her up a bit. Then I'll need permission from Alec."

"As if he would tell you no. I believe he'd allow you to paint the castle pink if you batted your eyes at him." Bertie ribbed her.

Lily ribbed her back. "Who's talking scandalously now?"

The day ran along quickly administering medicines, setting up a game of droughts where she tried to convince the players of the superiority of checkers, tidying, folding, and scrubbing. By the time the bell rang for shift change at six o'clock, Lily wanted nothing more than a soak in the tub and then to flop on her stiff bed. Such were the dreams of the naïve.

Before she could put her feet up, she walked to Matron's office practicing her speech about the dance. Lily took a deep breath and raised her hand to knock, but a muffled voice sounded through the door. Esther. Drat. Most likely tattling on Bertie.

Pushing down her instinct to barrel into the room and demand satisfaction for the insults to her cousin, Lily took the less traveled road of maturity and went upstairs to her parents' chambers. Across the hall from their door, the painting *Mademoiselle Guimard as Terpsichore* still hung. Mother had yet to finagle it.

"Entrer."

Lily opened the door and stopped short. Trunks stood open as garments littered the bed. The musty scent of the closed quarters had disappeared under powders and expensive toilette waters. "What's going on?"

Mother glanced up from overseeing the

466

packing of perfume bottles by her maid. "We're leaving."

They'd only just arrived. The time of separation had brought an unexpected sadness and longing to Lily for all things home, but their comfort of familiarity ushered in currents of anxiety as well. For all her time abroad, Lily was changed, and yet some things never would be. It set her on edge.

"When?"

"First thing in the morning. I cannot remain in this inadequate castle a day longer. It is completely uncivilized with a shocking lack of servants and privacy. Not to mention that Lady Strathem, or however she titles herself, can barely tolerate our presence, and I will no longer subject ourselves to such hostility. Thankfully, Cousin Hazel has invited us to stay at Threading Hall until ocean passage is safe for travel."

"Which won't be until the war is over."

"It should've been over months ago. 'By Christmas,' isn't that what they all said? Come spring we'll be bound for home and leave this wretched island behind." Mother blew out an exasperated breath and turned one of the bottles in its velvet traveling case until it met her satisfaction. "Go and pack. Though I can't imagine you brought all

467

your things here with nowhere to wear them. That Strom woman certainly has no appreciation for fashion with her demand for uniforms. Is that what your allowance has been going toward? Those hideous frocks?"

"They're standard issue for nurses."

"Doesn't change their revolting appearance. Don't bother putting them in your trunk."

"I'm not going." Lily folded her hands in front of her apron. The stiff fabric chafed her knuckles, but she'd grown accustomed to it as a knight to his armor.

"Don't argue and do as you're told."

"Mother. You're not listening. I will not be leaving. My life is here." No sooner had she said it than the truth rang through her entire body. Helping the men learn to live and smile again got her out of bed each morning and gave her purpose where she might otherwise have continued drifting along in a state of half meaningfulness. As the men filled her days, it was Alec who filled her nightly dreams and wove them into a new tapestry. One she could not bear to part from.

Mother straightened a ruby brooch on its velvet cushion in the jewelry tray. "Lily, I do not have the patience to deal with your

468

theatrics right now. I have an entire wardrobe to oversee because the last thing I need is to lose a valuable in one of the many cracks running around this room. I'm certain the owners had them especially installed so they might collect what's left after their guests have gone and sell the items for however much they can get."

"Mary." Father's voice held the slightest of warnings from where he sat obscured by his paper. The *London Herald* of all evils.

"No, Philip. That woman is a vulture. She refused to sell me that painting! The daughter, well, I don't know what to make of her. Part ghost, I think she is. And the son —"

"Lord Strathem seems an honorable man."

Mother hiked an eyebrow. "Can you say the same for his intentions concerning our daughter?"

Lily jumped to Alec's defense. "Lord Strathem has no intentions toward me except kindness." A lie, but detailing the way he smiled when they entered the same room or the desire flaring his eyes to deep blue when they stood close enough to touch would not endear Alec to her parents. If anything, Father would be forced to call him out, and he was nowhere near the shot Alec was.

Waving her delicate hand in agitation, Mother turned her attention to a pair of tortoiseshell hair combs. "That's what they all say, but I've seen it before. Several of my debutante friends were sold at auction to the penniless landowners here in England —"

"Scotland," Lily corrected.

"— their family's wealth used to bolster decrepit old estates while the daughters earned their countess coronets."

Lily thought back to the story of Bertie's parents and the hefty bank account her mother had brought to the struggling Buchanan name. They now owned the richest estate in Hertfordshire. "Cousin Hazel is doing well enough."

"Yes, and I have not seen her in over twenty years." Mother's tone softened. Glancing up, she stared hard at Lily, her eyes glistening with more than memories.

Lily swallowed hard at the realization. It was the memory of Hazel's departure from America coming to repeat itself once more that shimmered with fear in her mother's eyes. Lily's heart softened. "Please. I need your help planning a celebration for the men. I thought to ask the villagers to attend as well, and no one knows how to organize a social gathering the way you do."

"Planning parties. That's all you ever think of."

"It's not like that. I want to do this for them. One evening of music might offer —"

"Enough!" Blinking away any reminder of regret, Mother slammed a hairbrush on the vanity. "Our good name is being dragged through the social columns back home stating that Mr. and Mrs. Philip Durham cannot control their headstrong daughter. Men will not want to do business with your father, and I will be cut from all committee functions. Our friends will abandon us."

"Then they're not very good friends."

"Friends among the higher echelon is irrelevant. Powerful connections are what matter, and your antics are severing them from us."

Disbelief throttled the confidence Lily had painstakingly built with each passing day at Kinclavoch. She had come too far to still be considered the flippant girl who had left New York. How could her parents not see the changes she so deeply felt? Were they only ever determined to view her as the little girl in need of their constant guidance and incapable of growing anywhere above their thumbs?

"I am not here on a lark. I admit to not taking my duties seriously at first, but this place and these men have come to mean a great deal to me. It's not about names, or connections, or who next to climb over on the social ladder. The men here have seen horrors beyond belief, and I want to do what I can to help them find beauty again if I can."

"The only thing you need concern yourself with is preserving our good name so potential husbands will make offers. There are several good candidates more than willing to overlook your recent lapse in behavior, not the first tier of Vanderbilt or Fish, but a Bryce or Winthrop should do nicely. Such a connection will keep us in good standing with powerful allies."

"Is that what this is all about? You came to Scotland not out of concern for my well-being, but to drag me back to the marriage market so I no longer reflect poorly on you?"

"Setting up a proper home of your own will squelch any further rumors of unruliness. There will be no more time for gallivanting around, as a husband will ensure you only attend approved functions."

"I do not want a husband like that." Lily's thoughts rushed to Alec as if the mere strength of calling upon him could banish the ropes of distress her mother sought to bind around her. "No woman should who values love and respect."

The skin around Mother's lips whitened as if pinching back a snarl. "Once more your notions prove how little you've matured. Our timing to fetch you could not be more crucial. You will turn in your resignation forthwith and pack your bags immediately."

Fear struck Lily hard. Mother had been this angry once before, and it was the night she'd ordered Lily to England. Lily looked at her father, wishing for once he might intervene, but he remained sequestered behind his paper.

Taking a deep breath, Lily clasped her cold hands tight to keep them from shaking. "You sent me here to discover control over my indulgent actions and I believe I have. Not at first, but I've learned so much over these months. I can make my own bed, wash a dish, and fold sheets. Perhaps these aren't the ways you imagined me being shaped into the ideal woman or acquiescing daughter, but this is who I am. And I'm proud of what I've accomplished."

Mother paled at the mention of menial work. Father's paper lowered an inch to reveal his eyes watching Lily. That tiny action forged her on. "More than that. I've helped people, or at least I'm trying to. These men come here broken in body and mind, and for the first time in my life I've found contentment in helping them discover joy again."

Her pleas shattered on Mother's unmoving coldness. "I daresay they will manage without you. If you continue to defy me in this, your allowance will be stopped. There will be no more money and you will be forced to make your own way in this world without the comforts we have given you. Every door will forever be closed to you. Is that the life you envision for yourself as a young, newly independent woman?"

No, it was not the life Lily wanted, nor one she could fathom. But neither could she slip back into the mold her parents had so desperately tried to craft her into. She'd rebelled against it her entire life only now to find herself carving out a brand-new path. Free of molds and free to reach for a worth far beyond parental expectation and societal rules. To give it up now would be to give herself up.

What of Alec? Such a parting would rend her heart in two, the bits scattered by hopelessness until there were no longer remnants to piece back together. The pieces belonged to him now.

She moved to the window to hide the nearly unbelievable smile creeping over her face. Of all the times for her to realize how much Alec meant to her. And she on the cusp of losing him. Time was what she needed. To stall in hopes of the war's end, to change her parents' minds, to spend one more day with Alec. One day more might summon the courage to tell him how she depended on his strength and how she wanted him to lean on her, not for support but because they were better balanced together.

Concealing her flutter of emotions, Lily turned from the window. "I'm staying."

Mother waved a hand, banishing the thought. "Absurd. You leave with us."

"I am a grown woman and I've made my decision. I don't want to hurt you or Father, but I must do what I believe is right."

"Only a child would consider herself a grown-up before she is truly ready."

Lily fought to control the hurt spiking through her. It seemed no matter the words, Mother only heard what she wanted in order to summon her preconceived response. "When do you think I'll be truly ready, Mother?"

"When your father and I deem it so." Mother dusted her hands together as if to rid the distasteful topic from her person. "Now, you will hand in your notice. Do not think to thwart me again or you will find yourself without an allowance of any sort."

No allowance meant Lily would be forced to live off the royal army's generosity as her position at the hospital was strictly volunteer based with no income allotted. While her needs of food, clothing, and shelter were met at present, the same could not be said after the war. Or heaven forbid, the convalescent home were to close. She would have no means to support herself. She had not the faintest clue how one went about acquiring money. A fate keen to Mother's sense of smug satisfaction to keep Lily under thumb.

Father's paper rattled as he set it down and studied her like a tally column of numbers. "Let her stay, Mary. Until we set sail. A taste of dwelling among the lower class will only stoke her desire to return to the finer style in which she is accustomed and we've now reminded her of."

A backhanded allowance if ever there was one, but Lily wasn't about to quibble with the reasoning. It gave her four to five months to come up with a plan of sustaining herself. The thin foundation of her newly acquired confidence shuddered at the prospect, but she could do it. She had to. The alternative was to crawl back home defeated with her tail between her legs, adding fuel to her mother's bonfire that Lily was incapable of standing on her own two feet.

Across the room Mother calculated the mischievous incidents Lily was likely to create and compared it to the ease of having her under their thumb. Mother despised losing, but she detested dealing with incidents even more.

"So be it. Until spring."

CHAPTER 23

Stepping out of the post office into the foggy grayness, Alec moved out of view of the window and the postmaster's curious eyes and slit open the envelope.

Lord Strathem,
Your recent submission on the story of Lieutenant Wallace has been the most commented-on article our paper has ever printed. Combined with your first story about Left Squint, our readers are clamoring for more straight-from-the-trench tales. We should like to run one with every Sunday edition if this is agreeable to you. Please reply with affirmation so we may discuss payment, and, per your request, we will continue to print as anonymous.

Regards,
P. T. Dobbins
Managing Editor

Alec read it again. And again as the words slowly sank in with euphoric disbelief. They liked his stories. Smiling, he slid the letter into his jacket pocket. A day of victory for the voices too long kept silent. Written from the soldiers' own words, Alec had given them a voice to the world. The payment wasn't enough to restore Kinclavoch to her glory in one whole swoop, but over time he could afford to pay off the creditors and begin much-needed repairs. Not only for the sake of his family, but for the comfort of the Tommies as well.

Walking past the shops, his blood grew colder than the late January chill as he approached Wright's newspaper door. The man had set up a small press and sought out stories from the village and surrounding crofts for a local special edition delivered every Monday, ingratiating himself into the residential populace. It made Alec's stomach sick as the snake bought them one by one.

His breath fogged against the glass window. The blurred puff slowly peeled back to reveal bright splotches of tartan color and paintings dotting the walls inside. Kinclavoch wares. Artwork Alec had sold off months ago to pay for one of the numerous debts. He curled his hand to his side as the urge to punch through the glass and rip it from the walls hissed in his blood. There was a wee bit of justice knowing it was Wright's money being poured into debt charges. If only Alec could forget a part of his soul was lost in the transaction.

A waft of flowers curved over his shoulder. "Aren't bottom-dwellers inclined to darkness rather than plaid?" Lily's face floated in the glass as she stood behind him. Dressed in green and silver with a delicate net fitted over her face, she looked fashionably ready for the streets of London rather than sleepy Laggan.

"Plaid is the garment. This is tartan pattern. MacGregor tartan to be precise."

"He's gone native."

"Only for the sake of lining his own pockets." She stepped up next to him, drawing his attention from the display. Her cheeks were wet and the tip of her nose red. Alec pulled a clean handkerchief from his pocket and handed it to her. "Parents leave, did they?"

Lifting the edge of her netting, she dabbed at the wetness and nodded. "Mother was terrified a flock of sheep would be herded into the compartment with them." Adjusting the net, she smiled brightly. "What a sight that would've been."

Alec's heart had not known a moment's peace since her parents had stepped foot in Kinclavoch, anticipating any second they would drag Lily away from him, never to see her again. He would have filled the train and tracks with sheep to keep that from happening. Their departure now settled, he could breathe easier as she stood with him.

Lily started to hand him back the handkerchief, but Alec shook his head. "Keep it. In exchange for the one you gave me." He held up his hand that had been sliced by the broken shingle. She'd wrapped it so carefully with her delicate hankie. He dare not tell her that he'd carried it with him ever since.

She tucked his handkerchief into her small, matching green purse. "A treasure then."

A tall, dark shadow passed in the window reflection. The air staled at the unwanted arrival of none other than Richard Wright, newspaper tycoon and legacy destroyer. "A treasure at last for the Lord of Kinclavoch. Don't tell me it was the last one you had to give away. A shame, though you must take comfort in handing it to a most beautiful recipient."

"Your flattery is undesirable," Lily said.

Wright flashed his oily teeth. "I appreciate a woman with spirit. Which reminds me, how is Miss Barrymore? I sincerely hope she's recovered from the ordeal suffered while performing for the patients. The *Herald* received dozens of mailbags filled to the brim with letters of concern. It's a wonder she survived the torments of Kinclavoch and the MacGregor hospitality at all."

Alec's hand curled tight. "I won't stand having my home and family insulted by the likes of you. Especially in front of a lady."

Wright sneered. "Does the truth offend, *Lord* Strathem?"

"You should be ashamed to have written such vile things," Lily spat. "It was to have been a lovely night for the soldiers, and your spiteful article cast doubt on everything we're trying to accomplish."

"Your goodwill bores me. Pathetic men lying around in pajamas all day doesn't sell headlines. They should feel privileged to have been mentioned in the sensational article at all."

"I shouldn't have talked Alec out of slugging you."

"Alec, is it? How informal." Cruel delight sparked in Wright's dead eyes as they fastened on Alec. "Much like your shell of a castle these days. Informal and lacking the glory of a lasting legacy. A legacy that now hangs on my walls."

Loyalty in the village ran deep. Not one voice of concern would raise if Alec turned that pathetic waste of bones into a grease smear in the middle of the street. " 'Tis no surprise you profit from my family's misfortune."

"I can state with confidence that the only reason you haven't been driven into the cold by debt is because of my generosity in buying your trinkets."

Words black enough to tar an abyss galloped to Alec's lips. Reining them back with brute force, he took Lily's arm and turned her away before blood was drawn.

"I'll own the whole lot before long. Be sure to eliminate the rabble before I take residence. Can't abide men who've given up pulling their own weight. Like that Gibbons fellow. I hear he has no recollection of his own kidnapping. A pity. The tiniest remembrance on his part would provide me a sensational headline that would serve to drag your name even deeper through the mud."

Spinning around with the fury of a storm unleashed, Alec grabbed Wright's lapels and shoved him against the wall. "I ken well it's you behind every foul happening that's befallen Kinclavoch. Your soul is godless enough to kidnap a helpless man, and I'll see you brought to justice for it."

Wright's eyes bulged as his head rocked against the stone wall. "With what proof do you bring these accusations?" He swatted at Alec's grip. "Everything you have I am taking away from you. Soon you will have nothing left worth taking."

Alec dug his fingers in tighter. "With everything you take, you're digging your own grave. One so deep not even a rat like you can climb out."

"Men like me always land on their feet while you shall land in the mud. My greatest joy will be watching you drag your way through the bog second only to your worthless father's demise."

Lily's small, gloved hand curled over Alec's shoulder. An unspoken temper of his limits. *Enough.*

Alec let go and stepped back, his gaze never wavering from Wright. "Soon. Your end is coming."

Alec marched away despite every bone in his stiff body gnashing for the satisfaction of pummeling the wretch to a bloody stain on the walkway. Lily's arm linked under his, a grateful weight pulling against the anger seething through him like a red mist.

Appin stood tethered to a hitch at the edge of the village. His great hoof pawed the ground as if sensing his master's disturbance. Alec yanked the reins free. Lily stood quietly by, her stillness only agitating him more. His conduct was naught more than that of a brute. "I apologize for what you saw back there."

"There's no need."

"My temper —"

"There's no need. Not with me."

The red mist receded. Alec scoured the area as a new question arose. "How did you come to the train station?"

"Guthrie drove us in the buggy. I told him to leave me here as I'd prefer to walk home."

Home. She said it with a genuineness that tempered his anger and burned it to a different glow. But what kind of home could he offer when he could ill afford to keep it in possession for much longer? "Will you mind the company on the walk?"

"I should enjoy it very much."

Leaving the village with Appin on one side and Lily on the other, Alec inhaled deeply of the wintered woods. The scent of rough bark undercut by dead leaves and crisp pines. It sharpened his lungs, driving his mind to clear itself of rage. Cool and precise like the edges of a loch iced over.

Stuffing her hands into a fur muff, Lily's arm brushed his. "What makes you certain it's Wright? Besides utter loathing."

"Can it not be only that?"

"I'm afraid detesting a person's very being won't hold up in a court of law."

"I don't have proof." Alec guided Appin around a frozen mud puddle and tried to clear away his frustration with facts. "He claims a man like him always lands on his feet, but the incidents couldn't have been accomplished alone. He would've needed help, particularly within the castle on those days he could prove he was elsewhere. Associates are difficult to cover up. What of the nurses? Do you know of any who might be swayed to his side?"

"Most of the girls keep to themselves out of fear of a scolding from Matron. She says the only relationship a nurse should entertain is one with a scrub brush and soap. Everything else is an immoral dalliance."

"What about disgruntlements? Anyone with a personal vendetta?"

"Only Esther."

Alec frowned. "Has she done something to you?"

"Only snide comments and trying to make my workload as difficult as possible."

"She's always been one to swan about in

hopes of praise."

Scattered leaves crunched under Lily's heels. "She has that in spades. Matron believes Esther can do no wrong and she's one of the best nurses we have, second only to Bertie. Yet I find myself on the outskirts of her ethereal spotlight."

"Get on her bad side, did you? Esther's always been a rose with thorns more far-reaching than her petals."

"I blame you."

"What have I done?"

Retracting a hand from the muff, Lily fluffed the gray fur. "Women behave in odd ways when they're rejected."

"I never gave her cause to believe there was an understanding."

"Understanding or not, a woman's genteel manners are compromised when she feels there's a rival."

Alec snorted. Appin echoed the sentiment. "For there to be a rivalry there must be a competition. There is no such thing. I wish to spend time with you. Not her."

She was concentrating much too hard on the fur fluffing. "Is that why you turned down her marriage proposal?"

The incident in the stables. Had Lily been there the entire time? "You were listening. Why am I not surprised?"

Bristling, Lily shoved her hand back into the muff. "I never intended to eavesdrop, but the further the conversation went the ruder I felt it to interrupt. I promise I've told no one."

"Being badgered into marriage is not a prospect worth pursuing. Especially when the eager bride is quick to remind me of my failures from which she alone can pull me. A man must make his own way or he's not worthy of the title."

Lily stopped suddenly. Steady green eyes stared at him from behind the filmy veil. "You prove your worthiness time and again simply by being who you are. I see who you truly are and there is no finer man, Alec MacGregor."

With keen precision she struck to the root of him. That he longed to be seen, cherished, and cared for without the necessity of demands. His abiding loneliness forever chased him. But he couldn't outrun it, not this singular sense of separation from the world. Lily was his tether, anchoring his heart and refusing to set him adrift as the winds of disappointment and change tugged him about.

Emboldened by her words, Alec reached into his pocket and pulled out the letter, handing it to her. No one could understand its meaning more than she would.

A smile curved her lips as she scanned the message. With a tilt of her head, she handed it back to him. "Of course it's wonderful. With you wielding the pen it could be nothing less. Congratulations."

"You were the inspiration." He replaced the letter in his pocket and clicked his tongue to get Appin moving again.

"Nonsense. This victory belongs to you and, more importantly, the Tommies. They're being heard. I merely made the introductions."

" 'Tis not my intention to use their sufferings for my profit, but these stories could save Kinclavoch. Not only for my family, but for as long as the men need to recuperate there. They deserve better than a musty castle. I wish to thank them somehow, but my social attempts at reciprocity are lacking."

The woods thinned as the road turned off to Kinclavoch. Most of the trees lining the drive had long since shed their summer bounty, but a few hearty souls clung to the scraggly branches. A ripple of wind tugged a few loose and spiraled them to the ground.

"A dance." Lily plucked a leaf that landed on her dainty hat.

"No." He said it by pure reaction. The

very word shook to his core with dread.

She didn't bother noticing. "A ceilidh to be precise."

"Even worse."

"Why? Because you can't reel?"

"I'll have you know I'm a braw reeler, but my ego aside, men typically don't work themselves into an excited dither over dancing."

Undeterred by rationale, Lily twirled her leaf. A single performer on the imaginary dance floor of her palm. "They will if they have a room full of nurses doubling as willing partners. Women love to dance. We equate it to romance, so naturally the man who shows an interest is likely to gain our favor."

"Is this for the men or the lassies?"

"The men, of course."

Female thinking. Then again, spending an evening with Lily in his arms was hardly a loss. "I'll think on it."

"Oh, good. We'll invite the villagers too. Make it a celebration for all."

"I never said —"

"Maybe a silent auction with proceeds going to the war effort. People enjoy feeling as if they're doing their bit."

Alec gave up. The dance was as good as planned whether he gave approval or not.

Her joy was difficult to smother, and he found himself unwilling to do so.

Lily slowed as Kinclavoch came into view. Fog pearled around the castle, softening the corners and turrets as if she had risen from the center of a mythical loch. "She's a grand place. I see why you love her as you do."

Pride swelled within him. He'd been determined before not to lose his home, but seeing it with Lily at his side surged a ferocious tenacity to preserve it. Not only for himself, but for what it had become for the two of them. A place to find each other.

Much to Alec's delight, Lily veered away from the front door and walked with him around to the stables. She moved down the row of stalls and stopped as Sorcha stuck her muzzle out in greeting, granting her a friendly pat on her white blaze from Lily's gloved hand. It never ceased to amaze him that dressed in all her finery, she managed to look at home in his rough world.

As Alec secured Appin in his stall, the question that had been burning in his thoughts sprang forward before he could stop it. "Why did you stay?"

"I have work here that I'm happy doing. I stayed for the men, for Bertie." She turned to face him, her gaze steady. "For you."

The admission exploded in Alec's chest,

driving the breath from his lungs as the weight of it settled around him. Not a burdensome weight, rather one he felt every step in life had prepared him to carry and now he could not go on without it.

Yet the guilt of uncertainty anchored about him like a chain, towing him back into doubt. Words of intention too often failed and promises turned to bitter ashes. The pain of her regret was not a weight he could bear.

"Do you not miss your family? Your home? 'Tis far safer in America where you have the familiar things about you."

"Those things no longer seem familiar to me." The veil stirred over Lily's mouth. "Do you want me to go?"

"No. I don't want you to go." And with that, his heart was gone. Forever in her possession as if it had always belonged there. He moved to her and slowly lifted the veil. Bright green eyes, fathomless in their mysteries yet confident in what they beheld, gazed at him. "Stay."

She nodded. Once. It was all the encouragement he needed to lean down and sweep his lips across hers. He poured the chantings of his heart into her possession to do with what she would, yet he yearned beyond all hope that they might echo his. The world hushed around them, privileging them to exist within their own realm of togetherness, and there in the quiet he felt it. Another heartbeat. Not his. Not hers, but an emerging one that wove them together into something new and distinct yet entirely their own. Had his heart every truly beat before Lily? Could it ever beat again without her?

"M'laird, we'll be needin' tae see aboot the buggy's axel. 'Tis leanin' most fierce tae the left — Och, pardon me. I'll just be goin'." Guthrie stopped, snatched the ratty tam from his head, and backed out the door.

Alec glared. "Impeccable timing as always, Guthrie."

"Dinna wear a timepiece," the man mumbled, eyes remaining downcast.

Stepping back, Lily readjusted her veil, denying Alec one last taste of her lips. "No doubt I should, for it would most likely tell me my shift has nearly arrived and I've yet to change. Thank you for the reminder, Guthrie." Lily winked at Alec. His blood galloped as she left.

Tamping down his disappointment, Alec moved to unsaddle Appin. "What's this about the buggy?"

"Aboot time I'd say." Guthrie edged back inside and plopped the tam back atop his head. Gray strands of hair stuck out over his ear.

"I can't think of a worse time for it to break. We may need to haul the household before too long."

"Gettin' on wi' the lass."

Alec's fingers fumbled the horse bit. "There is no 'getting on,' at least not with you stomping around."

Squeezing into the stall, Guthrie took the task of unbuckling the saddle. "Ye should an' quick. She's bonny, canny, and lights ye up like the maypole. I've nay doubt her dowry would set Kinclavoch up fae generations."

"Her dowry makes no standing in my opinion of her."

"Then ye're a fool. Snap her up meself. Leave ye tae that Hartley lass."

"May we dispense with the relationship advice and turn our attention to the tasks at hand?"

"I'd rather discuss women."

So would Alec, one in particular, but not to the tune of Guthrie's waggling eyebrows. Finishing with Appin, Alec promised to return after a change of clothes. Climbing under and all around the buggy always resulted in grease marks and tears on his somewhat limited wardrobe. He slung his jacket over his arm and entered the house through the back door, then turned toward the stairs that went straight up to the family's private wing.

Matron's voice rang down the corridor as his foot hit the second step. "Now, an unofficial announcement for a night of entertainment."

Lily's dance. She'd wasted no time in securing permission. Half smiling, Alec slipped down the hall to where the nurses stood in a row before Matron. Lily stood at the end still dressed in her outfit from earlier. A shame she'd have to trade it in for that shapeless sack called a uniform. She had too lovely a figure to hide.

"In a few weeks' time, we shall be holding a dance —" The nurses tittered with excitement. "Quiet! A dance for the men and the local villagers to attend for an evening of frivolity. I don't customarily encourage such things, but I'm willing to forgo my inclinations on behalf of our patients."

Lily's expression pinched with confusion. She glanced down the line at Bertie, who shrugged. Was she not delighted with the swift placement of her idea?

"Every nurse will be divided into a team for preparation. Nurse Hartley will oversee the teams and any other planning required, along with Aide Durham. Further questions?"

A hand shot in the air. "Must we wear our uniforms?"

Matron's lips pinched together as if responding went against every personal conviction. "You will be permitted to wear civilian dress if you feel the need to do so. This one night only."

The nurses leaned against one another with dramatic sighs and girlish laughter. Except Lily. She stood stock-still with disbelief rippling over her face.

"Lord Strathem." Esther slipped between the other women and glided toward him. "A marvelous idea for a party, is it not? Just the thing we need to bring a little life into Kinclavoch. Your mother was such a dear to give her permission."

"You spoke to my mother?" For claiming to loathe anyone near their private wing, Mither was doling out the guest invitations with aplomb.

"I would have preferred to discuss the matter with you, but you were nowhere to be found. Busy man. Perhaps you can go over the details with me? I would so much appreciate your opinion." She slipped her hand around his elbow as natural as could

496

be. "Now, for decorations I was thinking —"

"The ceilidh is Lily's idea. All decisions should be hers to make." Across the hall Matron Strom motioned to Lily down the corridor where her office was situated. With a fleeting glance over her shoulder at Alec, Lily followed Matron out of sight before he had a chance to speak with her about her apparent confusion.

"Truly I thought Aide Durham had approached Matron Strom earlier when I went to her office to offer my services for the planning, but it was apparent by Matron's shock that Aide Durham had not done so. I was quite embarrassed at having broken the news before its original bearer had the opportunity. My enthusiasm is to be blamed." She ducked her head demurely to the side as pink stained her cheeks. "Matron was forgiving of the blunder and thought it a grand idea to name Aide Durham and myself as co-hostesses in a reprise of our partnership from the Christmas festivities."

"The festivities where Miss Barrymore was poisoned?"

"Yes, poor lady," Esther murmured, brushing horsehairs from his sleeve. "Though I'm referring to the beforehand preparations. In a gathering of this importance, I believe two heads are better than one. And I do know the local expectations better than she."

Alec slipped his arm from her grasp as a sense of injustice rippled through him. "I believe Miss Durham should prefer to make her own decisions since the party is her idea. Excuse me." Turning on his heel, he marched up the stairs to his mother's chamber.

"Is there a reason for this disturbance?" she inquired after biding him enter. Stuffy as always, the confining room was filled with elegant bric-a-brac of days gone by.

"You gave permission for a dance to be held here."

"Hmm? Oh, that. Esther Hartley approached me this morning. She wanted to do something for those men you keep down there. Why, I can't tell you. Ungrateful for everything we suffer due to their presence." She flicked a glance up from her needlepoint. Always red roses. Like the kind she laid on Father's grave every year. "The expense better not come from our pocket."

Alec took a deep breath to keep calm and immediately regretted it. The slow decay of books, flowers, clothes, and a life assaulted his nose. "Why was the matter not brought to me before permission was granted?"

"I believe I am still allowed a say in this

house. Its running was in my command long before you took it."

"Not once in the past six years have you shown any interest in what happens at Kinclavoch."

She slapped the needlepoint onto her lap. "Perhaps it's time I do now that half the country is privy to our affairs with thanks to Richard Wright laying them bare in blackened ink."

The summoned calm fled Alec as swiftly as a blue sky from a roiling thunderhead. "Any time something bad occurs that man is shifting on the edge. Why is that? What happened that night Father threw him out that left you in tears? And why does he have your coming out portrait?"

"My portrait?" Mither's face paled like dried chalk. "Have you sold that to him? He begged to have it that night your Father threw him out. As if I would ever deign to become another possession of his. He always wanted whatever your father had to the point of obsession."

The pieces clicked together in an instant. The frequent calls, setting up shop in Laggan, imploring gazes drifting up the stairs as if Mither might be standing there. Alec had been too occupied with keeping everything from crashing down to see the delicate dance of unrequited love spinning in the shadows.

"That's why he so desperately wants Kinclavoch." Love. Passion. Obsession. Nemeses to mankind's rationale since the dawning of time. It drove a man to the highest of pinnacles and the deepest of pits without a care to the scars it leaves upon the soul, forever to bask in the attained glory or succumb to the bleakness. "He wanted you before, and when you rejected him he attempted to seize the next best thing out of revenge."

"And now you've gone and laid our tragedy at his feet. You did, of course you did. So desperate for money. The mismanagements have gone on far too long. You've all but ruined us. If your father —"

"Father ruined us. I've done the best I can to salvage our misfortunes, and your constant defense of him serves you no credit."

Her eyes shot wide. "How dare you speak to me in that manner?"

Alec bowed his head in regret. No matter the provocation, she was still his mother and deserved the respect that position afforded. He'd tried so hard to heal the gap between them, but there had never been much room in her heart for anyone beyond Father.

When he died, any remaining sentiment shriveled to encapsulate his memory alone. "Forgive me. I mean no disrespect."

"Didn't you? To his memory?"

The accusation lashed his wounds. Old and scarred over, but the pain cut them quick. "I've no wish to argue, Mither."

"Then why did you come in here if not to accuse and quarrel? Asking me about past affairs that do not concern you. You do test my nerves. You and your sister both." Casting aside her needlepoint, his mother crossed to her vanity and uncorked a small bottle. She dribbled a few drops onto a hankie before lying down on her bed and holding the hankie to her nose.

Alec eyed the dubious bottle. He'd never seen it before. "What have you got there?"

"Ether. For when my headaches come." She glared at him and breathed in deeply. Light filtered through the high-arched windows and set the crimson velvet bed curtains afire, wreathing her pale face with a red glow. Her eyelids fluttered closed. "Helps me . . . forget."

Alec moved to the bed and looked down at the sleeping form of the woman who had born him. A woman he'd known his entire life who yet existed as a stranger. Taking the hankie from her hand, he hesitated a moment before leaning down to place a kiss to her cheek. And stopped cold. That sweet smell on her breath. Identical to the night Appin was sick.

A chill prickled the back of Alec's neck.

Hurrying to his chamber, he grabbed the book Lily had gifted him and flipped to the chapter on sedation. *Chloroform. So also named Methane Trichloride and Ether. Colorless, sweet-smelling liquid used as anesthetic, euphoriant, and sedative. May produce permanent death in cases of overdosage.*

Alec closed the book with trembling fingers and sank wearily to the edge of his bed as the impossibility confronted him. All this time he had shot guilt straight at the one man bound to bring about Alec's demise.

Never did he think to look closer to home. To his own mother.

CHAPTER 24

"Did this really come from Paris?" Viola twirled in her confectioned dress of pink lace in front of the mirror.

Lily adjusted a ruffle on the hem and stepped back to admire the transformation of the girl into an elegant young woman. "It's three seasons old, but no one will notice such a trivial detail when they see how beautiful you look."

She circled her cousin with a critical eye. Becoming a lady's fashion designer or dresser had briefly crossed her mind as a means for income, but she'd quickly lost faith in the prospect, as knowing how to dress well and knowing how to design well were two entirely different avenues of expertise. "As does Bertie. So nice to see you out of starch."

Bertie glided her hand into the elbow-length depths of an evening glove. She wore a rose-colored gown with delicate gold beading and a square neckline that showed off a diamond choker to perfection. Her thick brown hair was piled on top of her head and secured with diamond-studded pins.

"I'd nearly forgotten what real fabric felt like." She ran a gloved hand down the sleek lines of her skirt before reaching up to her glasses. A thin crease puckered her brow. "If only I didn't need these."

Lily pulled her hand away and squeezed. "I happen to know a captain who thinks very highly of glasses. I may have also heard that he's been practicing the waltz because a certain nurse adores the dance."

"Who told him that?"

"I did, of course."

"Cheeky."

"My dear cousin, it is my intent to have you engaged by the end of the evening. It is as simple as that."

"You can't say such things!"

"Don't tell me you haven't thought about it."

Bertie seized a pillow and shied it at Lily.

Lily ducked and the pillow sailed harmlessly by to land on the floor. "Careful! It took me an hour to fashion this updo. I'll not have you scrunch it due to feigned shock." A talent for hairdressing was not to

504

be her source of income either unless her skills dramatically improved in the next four months, which was highly doubtful.

Viola rushed between them and clapped her hands as Bertie grabbed at an empty hot water bottle. "Ladies! No more mussing. It'll make us all late and a certain brother of mine would hate to be kept waiting." She looked pointedly at Lily.

Heart pattering at the thought of Alec dressed in his finest, Lily moved to the dresser and dabbed perfume behind her ears and along her décolletage. "It is a woman's prerogative to keep a man waiting. At least for a few minutes lest he think she had nothing better to do than wait eagerly for him."

"But you are eager to see him?"

"Yes." Excitement blushed up her neck and onto her cheeks. If she didn't calm down, she'd turn blotchy. An unappealing prospect. Smoothing the front of her dress, she spun around. "Is it vain to ask how I look?"

"When has that stopped you before?" Bertie grinned and pushed her glasses securely on her nose.

With deliberate slowness, she and Viola circled Lily muttering and nodding. At last they stood back with concealed expressions.

Lily couldn't take the silence. "Verdict?"

Viola cracked first. "Enchanting."

Enchanting. A description that delighted every sense of feminine happiness. Lily twirled and the periwinkle chiffon floated around her ankles like airy whips of cream. The iridescent underskirt shimmered in the candlelight as if a rainbow danced beneath while sheer sleeves fell off her shoulders like wings. A delicate twining of sapphires and silver strung around her neck with earbobs to match. She'd spent a great deal of the afternoon curling and puffing her hair until it floated around her head with sapphire combs holding it in place. She felt as if she'd stepped from a magical garden.

Pulling on her gloves, Lily moved to the door. "Let's not keep the men waiting any longer."

Unlike all the other balls she'd attended, this ceilidh caused her heart to pound beneath the intricate embroidery of her dress. Every sense was heightened by the blood rushing in her ears, her shallow breathing, the tingling of her fingers inside her tight gloves. She'd hated the gloom of these corridors, but tonight it was like walking through the darkness backstage with every ticking second drawing her closer to the moment she'd been waiting for. The lively strand of a violin skipped its way up the stairs to herald what awaited them. But music and dancing weren't what Lily anticipated.

Descending the stairs to the second landing, warm light bloomed from the great hall below. The violin was joined by more strings, a harp, and a few other instruments she had difficulty picking out beyond her drumming heartbeat. She looked all around, but the landing was empty.

"Let's go down," Bertie said.

Lily shook her head. "No, I'll wait a moment. You go ahead."

Bertie and Viola swapped smiles and continued down the stairs to the party. Lily took a shaky breath and peered around the darkened landing once more. Again. No familiar form materialized. She touched an uncertain hand to her hair. Had he changed his mind?

"You've no need to assure yourself of how beautiful you look."

At the sound of his voice, Lily twirled around, her skirt swishing around her ankles. Alec stepped from the shadows and quite naturally stole her breath. Resplendent in a kilt with a length of plaid secured over his black Jacobean jacket, snowy white shirt, sporran, hose, and brogues, he looked every inch the laird he was born to be.

He stopped in front of her. A smile — no, something more than that, as if a light from within — melted across his face. "You are . . . stunning." He swept a low bow. "Your servant, ma'am."

Lily sank into a curtsy and rose to meet his gaze. She held out her hand and he took it without question to lightly kiss her fingers. Her heart filled so much with him that she dared no longer call it her own.

With a smile broad enough to shame all others, he tucked her hand into the crook of his elbow before sweeping his arm to the stairs. "Shall we?"

It was the longest flight of stairs Alec had ever taken in his life as over a hundred pairs of eyes watched him descend with Lily. Guiding her off the stairs, he nodded to the gathered patients and nurses along with the invited villagers. Dressed in their Mac-Gregor colors, they beamed with pride. They deserved this celebration as much as the soldiers.

"Thank ye for inviting us, laird."

" 'Tis a pleasure to be celebrating in yer halls. Ye've given us a bright spot in our dreary days."

"Proud we are to see the castle serving

the Tommies."

Alec thanked them all for coming. He should have done this a long time ago.

He led Lily and the congregation to the ballroom. Stuffed with old furniture, locked away, and forgotten, the heavy doors had been thrown open to a grand splendor of polished wood and windows. Silver chandeliers dripping with crystals suspended from the coffered ceiling while dozens of mirrors lining the walls reflected their prisms of light. Musicians tuned their instruments from the gallery, and a fireplace that was large enough to fit two standing horses blazed with a bonfire along the far wall.

Alec was speechless.

"Do you like it?" Lily's hand tensed on his arm, waiting for his answer.

"I nearly forgot how magnificent the place could be." He gazed about in wonder at the transformation under Lily's guiding hand. She'd spared no expense of attention with every corner shining from her careful ministrations. Gone were the gloominess and hollow sounds of merriment left to decay in the past, her touch harkening a new era of joyful beauty.

"When you've kept it locked away for so long the magnificence tends to lose itself under mountains of cobwebs and dust. A shame really. A room like this is made to be enjoyed."

"The heating alone requires the attention of five men. Besides, we haven't much use for it anymore."

Reaching up, she smoothed a hand over the pleats in the plaid across his chest. Warmth trembled around his heart. "You do now."

His eyes roamed over the golden hair, the skin that shone like a pearl, the tinge of rose to her cheeks. "Aye, that I do."

The room filled out around them, leaving the polished walnut dance floor unoccupied. Expectant eyes settled on them.

"What are they waiting on?" Lily whispered.

"The laird." Dropping her arm, Alec turned to face her and bowed. "Will you honor me with the first dance?"

"My pleasure." She slipped her hand into his as the music started.

" 'Tis a basic waltz. Follow me for the changes." Alec stepped to the left, back, right, and forward in a small box, then half turned them so they were back-to-back. Another half turn brought them facing once more.

Lily kept in step with him, only hesitating a second as he turned them back-to-back.

510

She moved with the grace of water, her hand light as a petal in his as he guided her around. Other couples moved to the floor in joining steps, but Alec and Lily held center sway. She moved as one with him, perceiving what he wanted with only the slightest pressure from his fingertips. With each twirl away from him, Alec counted the seconds until she spun back into his arms and fitted herself into his welcoming embrace.

The dulcet notes plucked to an end. With deep regret Alec let go of Lily's hand and clapped with the other dancers. " 'Tis my duty to ask Matron Strom for the next dance."

"If you can pry her away from Guthrie. They seemed to make quite the pair."

Alec glanced across the room in time to see his man nipping from a flask as Matron turned her back. "I'll see you to my sister first and not leave you stranded alone on the floor." He offered his arm, which she accepted. Leaning down, he brushed his lips against her ear. "Though I would gladly spend the entire evening with you."

Her gloved hand curled over the top of his. "As would I."

A man had the gall to appear in front of them and bow shortly. Dressed in army khaki, there was no mistaking that eye bandage. Left Squint. "May I ask for this dance?"

"Of course." Lily's hand slipped reluctantly from Alec's and transferred to Left Squint's arm. A glance over her shoulder at Alec sent a curl slipping over her ear. "Don't fill up your dance card too quickly."

With your name only. It wasn't difficult to imagine a piece of himself leaving with her as she took her place in line for the *Dashing White Sergeant* dance. Tearing his attention away before getting walloped in the face with an errant elbow, Alec ducked through the crowd and ran into a swarm of feathers.

"Pardon me," he said, sidestepping the airy creations intent on floating in his mouth.

A gloved hand landed on his arm. "Ducking out so soon?" Gowned in black and white with black plumes dancing in her dark hair, Esther stood before him shimmering like a regal swan in candlelight. "A shame. This tune is one of my favorites."

"Forgive me, but I've promised Matron Strom a dance."

"It seems someone beat you to the opportunity."

Scanning the crowd, Alec spotted Matron Strom whisking around the floor with the old postmaster. Esther's delight to dance heightened, and Alec didn't wish to fail her an invitation. "Shall we?"

He led her in the reel as they circled about with two other couples. Across the room, Lily had joined another circle as Left Squint tried to spin her the correct way and failed miserably much to Lily's laughter.

"Smiling becomes you," Esther said, drawing Alec's attention back. Light as feather, she danced as airily as one of the bobbing plumes in her hair. More than one villager nodded approvingly in their direction.

He clasped her hand and ducked under an approaching couple's arms. "It's a good night."

"In all our years of acquaintance I've yet to witness you in such light spirits. When not on a horse, that is. Perhaps Kinclavoch should host more celebrations if only to see its laird carefree. After all, you set the example for the entirety of the surrounding lands and populace."

A rather poor example he'd set at that. Locking himself away in this lonely castle. Failing to provide a stable presence to those who might look to him for a guiding hand. Shutting out the community that had known him since he was a bairn by deciding they would not wish to be tainted by his physical blemish nor his family's dark history. It was time to release his insecurities and be the man and laird he truly wished to be.

Faces whirled by. All having a braw time, but struggle had etched its way into premature creases. Ladies dressed in mended fashions, white hairs sprouted from gentlemen's heads, and soldiers sported coats with empty sleeves. The war had claimed sacrifice from them all in different manners. Peace couldn't come swiftly enough.

"The only celebration I'm in favor of hosting next is the end of the war," Alec said.

"Huzzah to that." Her gown brushed his legs as she spun. "Though I should hate to see all hope of splendor leave this place once the soldiers do."

All cheer he'd managed to gather plunked to rocks in his stomach. Could an hour not pass when he might enjoy the occasion without dwelling on his misfortunes? "Your concern is admirable, but I am Kinclavoch's guardian. As such, I will see to its needs."

"Who will see to the needs of its guardian? The MacGregor name is proud and should serve as a herald of status in the county. Not be relegated to pages of dusty history and cobwebs." Her dark eyes pooled with concern. "As lord of this estate you deserve your honor."

Was that what she thought? Only with a title was his integrity worthy of gathering notice? "My honor roots deeper than a title. It's in the love and caretaking of this land and its people."

They linked arms and wove in and out with Esther's feathers a constant irritating companion to his cheek. "Your principles are what I most admire about you, but there's a stubbornness clinging to them. Have you considered what will become of this land and people if you are forced to remove yourself from them? If Wright has his greedy way?"

"Of course I have. The outcome plagues me day and night." Several heads turned their way as the force of his words crackled over the music. Perfect. One of the few times for his doors to open to others, and he was ensuring they all witnessed an ill temper.

"It doesn't have to." Ever calm and collected Esther remained unruffled. "Have you thought further on my offer?"

Only in the barest moments of dejection had he allowed himself to consider the temptation. To free himself of debt, to rebuild Kinclavoch, save his family from destitution, and earn his way in the war effort by giving the Tommies respite. A logical man wouldn't hesitate, but he didn't claim logic when it came to these matters dear to his heart. He caught sight of Lily across the room, her effervescence and joy brighter than any candle in the grand room. Aye, matters dear to his heart. "I'm sorry, Esther. You're a lovely woman with every quality a man could want."

Her eyelashes fluttered down. "Every man, it seems, but you."

The song twanged to an end. And so, too, did their dance. Alec guided Esther to the edge of the dance space as the reeling groups drifted apart to form new partnerships for the next set.

"I must take care of my own on my own terms or I can no longer call myself worthy of the title laird." Alec took a deliberate step away from her. "If you'll excuse me, my sister is in need of attention. Shall I find you another partner?"

"How polite of you. First a smile and now civility. Will wonders never cease this eve?" Smiling a little too brightly, Esther snapped open a lacy black fan and waved it rapidly in front of her face. The force of the air stirred the feathers atop her head into a tizzy. Taking a deep breath, she slowed the fan to a more languid pace and smiled at him as if nothing were amiss. "Thank you for making your decision clear. There is nothing a lady detests more than to be kept waiting."

With a swish of her fan, she turned, and the crowd parted like the Red Sea for her sweeping departure. In a slightly more agitated state than when he'd first begun the evening, Alec wove in the opposite direction to his sister, who sat off to the side with Bertie and Captain Gibbons. "Where is Mither?"

"Not coming." Viola worried the pale-pink lace on her skirt. She'd grown years of elegance in one single night. "Pleading a headache."

Alec had barely spoken to his mother since finding that bottle in her room. She'd kept herself locked away in protest of the impending frivolity, and he was nearly glad of it. Night after night he lay awake forming words to say to her. But what does one say when suspecting his own mother of poisoning a beloved horse?

"It's a lovely party, Lord Strathem," Bertie said. Seated next to Viola, Alec might not have recognized the bonny woman if not for her glasses. And the doting attention of Gibbons, who had yet to take his gaze from her. "I do believe the entire village of Laggan is in attendance and pleased as punch to express their gratitude in person to the men fighting for our beloved country."

Not one corner of the room wasn't filled with a familiar face, several he'd not seen in years. Laughter flowed, feet tapped, and new acquaintances made as plaids and army khaki mingled in celebration.

"It's good to ease their cares for a night."

"Bertie, have you danced once?" Like a sash of silk, Lily slipped next to Alec with a crystal glass of punch in her hand. The imbalance that had persistently trailed him for part of the evening righted itself at her nearness. "And don't tell me you don't know the steps because you taught me a few of them last summer."

"You know how I totter about." Her cousin sniffed with righteousness, but her lashes fluttering Gibbons's direction gave her away.

Thankfully the man knew when to take a cue. He jumped to his feet and smoothed down the front of his tunic, then held out his hand. "Honor me with a dance, Miss Buchanan?"

Red blushed to Bertie's cheeks, matching the color of her gown as she placed her hand in Gibbons's. "A pleasure."

Lily took Bertie's vacated seat and sipped her punch. "Mmm. This tastes good, but I can't quite place that flavor."

Alec's attention whipped to the punch bowl and Guthrie loitering suspiciously close. If he'd taken the notion of spiking the refreshments — no. His man would be ladling cup after cup if that were true. Alec relaxed a fraction and turned back to the ladies. "Many of the locals add a drop of heather honey to their drinks. Could be what you taste."

She sipped again. "Hmm, maybe." It wasn't convincing enough to clear Guthrie from the possibility.

A harmony of fiddles and a pennywhistle stretched across the hall, plucking ears and tapping feet to the newly minted strain of "Scotland the Brave."

"*The Gay Gordons.* Your favorite," Viola said.

The notes swelled in Alec's chest as each beat thrummed his pride. A new song it may be, but the sentiment was centuries ingrained. "Aye. Will you dance it with me?"

Viola shook her head. "You know I don't dance. I'm content enough to watch. Take Lily." Alec started to protest at leaving her alone, but she shooed him away. "Hurry before you miss the beginning."

Taking the allemande hold, they marched in step, then turned and marched backward with the other couples. A few steps more to the front and Alec twirled Lily, sending her skirts floating.

"Why is this your favorite?" she asked.

He curved his arm around her in waltz form. "It's one of the few where you've only the one partner. 'Tis always a lad's prerogative to have a lady's sole attention when he's learning the steps."

"Only when he's learning?"

"And every time after." Alec laughed and turned them around. His knee twinged, bringing a grimace. "After my injury it was also the easiest on my temperamental knee. Mither didn't like me sitting out. Wasn't a good image for the family."

Another spin and the pain rippled down his leg. He'd been using the hot and cold compresses combined with massage as suggested in the book Lily had given him. Surprisingly, the methods worked and he was able to walk without his cane for longer periods of time, but dancing seemed to add a new layer of strain he was unprepared for.

Laying a hand on his arm, Lily leaned up to his ear. "All this spinning about is making me dizzy. Would you mind if we stepped out for a bit?"

The woman could spin on a top for hours and never tire, but her sweet lie out of consideration for him was all the excuse he needed to sweep her off the dance floor and outside to the terrace overlooking the garden. A bright moon bathed the night in silver as the crispness of winter lingered in the air.

"Much better. I can breathe again without the crush of people stamping on my toes." Lily's gossamer sleeves fluttered about her shoulders as she strolled across the limestone. Moonlight bathed her skin in ivory, skimming over the shallow dips of collarbone and smooth plane between shoulder blades. If he fit his hand just there, would it be warm or cool to his touch?

Alec clasped his hands behind his back before temptation got the better of him. "Ceilidhs traditionally started with storytelling and a wee bit of singing. The community would gather into a house or a hall, some so small that the bairns would crawl into the rafters to get a better look. The stories would go on for hours while the womenfolk wove ropes of heather. Dancing wasn't as common as it is now."

"I've enjoyed every minute of it."

"Despite the idea being stolen from you. Why did you not say something?"

"Because it would've looked like I was grasping at attention again, and the recognition wasn't worth the exertion." She rubbed her bare arms as her skin pebbled in the cool evening air. "There's something you never thought to hear me say."

Alec unclasped the wool plaid from his shoulder and wrapped it around her. If possible, the MacGregor red and green made her more beautiful. "You surprise me at every turn, my lady."

A tempting smile curved her full lips. "You are the man of surprises. Who would've known there was a dancer beneath all that gruffness?"

"Scots are taught at a young age to reel. So many of our traditions were stripped away after the Rising of the '45. Our dress, our language, our land. One by one we've tried to resurrect them. It's a part of us that refuses to die."

She moved to the edge of the terrace and leaned against the railing. "The more I learn about Scotland, the more I fall in love with it."

" 'Wherever I wander, wherever I rove, the hills of the Highlands forever I love.' Rabbie Burns was a man who knew what he was about with words." Alec joined her at the rail. The garden lay thick and unmoving as a carpet put to slumber by the cold, receding from them until it melded into the darkness of the woods. The scent of hardy pines lingered faintly in the air, but soon the flowers would awaken to spring and fill the outdoors with their fragrance.

"It's deceptive, this landscape," she said. "The jagged mountains, the windswept moors, freezing waters, and less-than-appealing food. They all serve as a gauntlet of sorts. Overcoming the ruggedness sifts out the rubble to reveal the truest of hearts. Who could not love something that fights with such ferocity to protect the beauty within?"

Lily shifted closer to Alec. Her rosewater scent drifted under his nose, tantalizing him with the promise of warm days to come, but it was her words that held him spellbound. Much of his life had been wrapped in a harshness chiseled from the elements howling against him. None had dared broach the severity before as they remained at a sheltered distance. Lily held no such reservations. She scaled the insurmountable peaks of his disposition to lay claim at the summit and declare it beautiful. Dare he hope that this woman for all her grace and life spoke of the single word beating in his heart? A single word that began and ended with her.

"Do you mean that, Lily?" His voice was

hoarse as anticipation dragged through him like a serrated blade. With one word she would give him life or death. Too long he'd dragged the borders of death.

Facing him, her gaze swallowed him whole yet pinpricked to the very core of his being. She nodded.

Grasping her arms, he pulled her roughly to him. "I am a man of simple conveniences, but 'tis the inconveniences that have come to matter most to me. You are the most extraordinary inconvenience that has ever happened to me." He lowered his forehead to hers. "I find I seek my heart more these days, for that is where I find you."

Her soft breath stirred against his cheeks. "As I have found you. A treasure that has been worth the ferocity of battle."

"Àrd-Choille."

Alec dropped his mouth to hers and poured the hidden places of himself into her keeping. She answered back with a matching urgency of risk and promise. Lily touched every part within him, setting him alight with a consumption he had no will to control. The softness of her lips, the scent of her hair, and the moldable fit of her in his arms were beyond anything he had ever known, stretching the limits of his world while precisely narrowing it to a pinprick of existence balancing on the beating of their hearts.

In that moment with her arms about him and the night belonging only to them, Alec let go of the fear holding him back. Lily's lips curved against his in a smile and caught him.

A distant rush of noise vibrated into Alec's ear. With great reluctance, he pulled away but kept his arms about her.

Lily laid her cheek against his chest. "What does *Àrd-Choille* mean?"

"Hmm?" Alec's brain fumbled through the haze for words as he brushed his fingers over the nape of her neck. "Oh, it means high wood, the place where the clan would gather in times of war and decide what was to be done."

"You give a war cry before kissing me?" She giggled. "How romantically Scottish of you."

"If you know anything about our history, then you should well understand that only battle and women thrive in our blood."

Lifting her head, Lily gazed up at him, then shifted to a point over his shoulder. "Do you see that?"

"Where?"

"That light. In the sky."

Alec tilted his head in the direction she

525

indicated. Around the east side of the house, where the stables were located, a bright orange light glowed against the blackened sky. Alec's stomach heaved as the doors crashed open on the terrace to a panicked scream.

"Fire!"

CHAPTER 25

Flames crawled up the sides of the stables. Demons of fire spat and leaped onto the roof, devouring the slate tiles with greed as each bite fueled their destructive hunger. Figures raced out of the castle, grabbing buckets and whatever else they could find to fill at the water pump. They formed a line and tossed the inconsequential water onto the flames with sizzles of hopelessness.

Lily stumbled to a stop in the yard as Alec sprinted ahead of her. A scream crackled from within the fire. The horses!

Flinging a bucket of water on the door, Alec wrenched it open. Black smoke poured out. Throwing his arm over his mouth and nose, he dove inside.

"Alec!" The scream ripped from Lily's throat.

"Where's he gone?" Lieutenant Wallace appeared at her side.

"The horses." Lily's feet picked up pace,

carrying her to the stable door through which Alec had disappeared.

"Stay here! I'll go —" Black smoke belched out and suffocated them.

The air choked Lily's lungs as she turned away in frantic search of clean air. A shrill horse cry echoed from the smoking innards of the stables. "Alec!"

The world droned around her, punctuated with sharp sizzles of water and cracks of wood. Voices muffled in her ears and the pouring heat stung her eyes. Nothing mattered over the hammering of her heart. *Alec. Alec. Alec.*

Orange burned the blackness from the night sky as more buckets emptied water on the conflagration. Support beams bowed and splintered. Piles of hay blazed yellow with the white hearts carved out.

Hands grabbed Lily and hauled her backward. She kicked against them. "Let me go! I have to find Alec!"

"Where is he?" Guthrie.

"The horses are trapped." She wriggled out of his hold and moved back to the door. She couldn't stand out here doing nothing — a sob strangled up her throat — not while he was in there. "I have to —"

Pounding sounded at the far end of the stables where the flames were beginning their murderous feast. The side door. Racing around, Lily fumbled with the gate latch to the paddock. The doors bulged as something beat against them from the inside.

Crack!

The doors kicked open and out raced Sorcha and Appin. Eyes wild, they skittered around the paddock snorting and stomping. Wallace vaulted over the fence and ran to the panicked beasts. A figure stumbled from the doorway.

"Alec!" The gate latch slipped through Lily's fingers. Blast these gloves!

Guthrie unfastened the lock and the two of them raced forward to catch Alec as he fell to his knees. Looping their arms under his, they dragged Alec to the far side of the paddock and propped him against the fence.

Unable to hear past the blood pounding in her ears, Lily gave him a quick examination. "Are you hurt?"

Alec wheezed and shook his head.

Lily took his blackened face between her hands and searched for injury. "Burns?"

Again, he shook his head. She examined the exposed parts of his skin, his hair, his clothing. There. The edge of his kilt and jacket singed. But he was alive and unharmed.

Pushing away her hands, Alec staggered

to his feet. "The horses."

"Wallace has them well in hand." Lily choked back the angry words clamoring to her lips. Angry words propelled by fear. How dare he rush into a burning building? He might have died! Gone like that before her very eyes. She took a shaky breath. Alec would not be the man she adored if he hadn't done what he did. Putting the welfare of others, his animals, before his own safety. Stupid man!

Fire mirrored in his eyes as he stared at the burning stables. His mouth set in a determined line. "Stay here. Guthrie. With me."

Before she could protest, Alec and Guthrie ran to grab buckets and join the crowd of patients and partygoers desperately trying to control the fire. White-hot flames engulfed the building. Sparks shot through the air like demonic heralds of burning triumph. There was no defeating it now. Alec's strong figure cut through the buckets of water to save the surrounding areas. At least that they could hope to control.

"Nurse. A hand!"

Tearing her attention from Alec, Lily hurried over to Wallace as he tried to keep both horses under control.

"Let's get them to the outer paddock.

Away from this heat," he said. "Go unlatch the gate there and I'll try to herd them in."

Lily did as instructed and swung the gate wide, but the horses refused to move. She hurried to Sorcha and held out her hand in calm greeting. The mare eyed her with panic. *"Chan fheudar an t-eagal a bhith oirbh."* Alec had muttered the soft command to not be afraid many times. "Come, *mo maise.*"

With coaxing and soft utterings, Sorcha walked into the next paddock followed by Appin. They kept the horses calm as the battle raged on. A losing battle with no casualties, save the building itself, which burst into a fireball. The crowd could do nothing but stand back, helplessly watching its collapsing death.

What seemed a lifetime later, the black flames turned to wisps of ash charcoaling the predawn light. Pockets of fire crackled amid the ruins. A variety of metals from bits, stirrups, pitchforks, and lantern handles glinted among the crumbly ash. A scattering of villagers stood like smudges on the grass, holding buckets in their hands and shaking their heads with disbelief. A loss to one of them was a blow to them all. A loss to the laird proved a grief too heavy to bear alone, and so they waited in solidarity to shoulder it together.

Lily picked her way across the yard. Fallen ash covered her shoes and turned gritty against the dewdrops crystallizing the grass. She scanned the soot-covered faces, seeking only one. Looking toward the paddock fence, she found Alec and Guthrie sitting on the ground, arms dangling over their knees and buckets discarded next to them.

At the sight of her, Guthrie grumbled to his feet and shuffled forward. The edges of his kilt were singed too. "A grave day, lass." He clapped her on the shoulder and ambled off to speak with the villagers.

Kneeling behind Alec, a thousand words of grief assailed her, but none carried the absolute heartache welling inside her. She wrapped her arms around him and tucked her chin against his shoulder, holding him. He stared vacantly at the blackened skeleton before them. The exhumed bones of his pride and joy ripped from life. His body was rigid, muscles taut under his now gray shirt — the jacket having been discarded at some point — yet the bones within him seemed to sag as if the strength long supporting them had gone out.

"How?" His voice cracked.

"I don't know, my darling."

His blackened hand curled over hers. A wisp of ash floated through the air, tumbling in delicate movements like a dancer in water. Its smoky body twisted as if gasping for air and landed on the grass between Alec's feet. Bit by bit, the ash crackled and melted to nothing.

Alec turned his head to look at Lily. Dirt and soot streaked his face. "The horses?"

"Safe. Wallace is taking care of them in the far paddock." Lily stroked a burnished curl away from his forehead. "What were you thinking going in there? You scared me to death. If something had happened . . ." Tears clogged her throat. She squeezed her eyes shut to keep the burning at bay.

" 'Tis all right, *mo chridhe*. It's all over." Cradling her face, he brushed his lips over hers and each cheek. "I'm not as reckless as you make me out to be."

Expression shifting to granite, he surged to his feet and stalked to the ravaged stables. He kicked aside charred wood and scored stones with the intensity of a man on the hunt. Lily followed him, the tattered ends of her gown trailing in the black grass. Her beautiful creation ruined beyond repair, but it was nothing compared to Alec's loss.

"It couldn't have started on its own." He moved around, eyes searching. "The lanterns weren't lit."

"Maybe one of the guests came out with

one? Wanting to see the horses. Or to smoke."

Fury flashed across his face. She knew precisely what whipped through his mind. How dare some careless act endanger his animals? It was a sin nearly as unforgivable as someone bringing harm to his family. Crouching, he flipped over a stone that was once part of the wall and dug through the rubble until he extracted a glass bottle. Or what was left of one with tiny fragments of cloth melted to the rim.

Horror curled through Lily's stomach. "That looks like one of the bottles we use in the ward to store rubbing alcohol."

Alec stood, holding the guilty remains. His fingers trembled as if he restrained himself from crushing it in his bare hand. "Arson."

"You think this was on purpose?"

"How else can you explain it?"

Lily glanced all around, desperate to find evidence to the contrary. Who could prove to be so hateful as to commit such a horrendous deed? "I-I don't know."

"Aide Durham!"

Lily turned at the sound of Captain Gibbons shouting her name as he ran around the corner of the castle. His clothing, once shiny from the ball, now was smudged with ash and . . . wet shoulders?

"You need to come with me. At once." Out of breath upon reaching her, he shoved a yellow telegram in her hands. "It's Bertie."

A new kind of fear gripped Lily as she took the telegram. She'd seen them before, often delivered to the patients with brothers, fathers, or cousins serving. It was never good news. With shaking fingers, she unfolded the paper and scanned the black words.

Elizabeth

Reggie KIA. Stop. Come home at once. Stop.

Mother

Reggie. Bertie's brother. Their father's pride and legacy, killed. Lily's vision blurred. "Where is she?"

"Matron Strom's taken her to your chambers. I was with her when the news came."

Spinning around, her heart sought Alec. "My cousin, Bertie's brother, has been killed in action. I have to go." Tears slipped down her cheeks.

His mouth convulsed. "Go."

"Alec, I'm so sorry."

"Go."

Clutching tight his plaid still wrapped

around her shoulders, Lily ran back to the castle, its gray stone facade impervious to the sorrow playing out among its grounds. Nearing the door she caught sight of a pale face floating in the glass from a third-story window.

Edwina MacGregor, the dowager Lady Strathem, watched it all without a hint of expression.

"I am sorry for your family's loss and wish you the best in your time of mourning." Tiredness smudged under Matron Strom's eyes. Her movements were a full second slower than normal, but it was the only hint of the difficult night before, during which she had managed the care of a dozen villagers with minor burns. "Nurse Buchanan will be greatly missed. She's a fine nurse, and if ever she wishes to return there will always be a spot for her."

Lily nodded as she stood in the middle of the room. Dressed in a traveling suit of light blue, she had opted for a small hat that did well enough to disguise her hasty coif, to say nothing of the smell of smoke still lingering in the strands. "Thank you, Matron. I'll be sure to tell her of your generous offer, though I can't say if she'll return or not."

"She has a strong constitution and is only suffering now what a great many of our citizens have already endured. But endure we shall."

At one time Lily might have thought the old dragon's words bitter and unfeeling, but she now saw them as the compliment they were. It was a terrible blow, but Bertie was strong. She would pull through, and Lily would be there to help her. "I only hope to offer what comfort I can."

Matron rifled through a file. "You have not told me if you'll be returning, Nurse."

"I . . . Well . . ." Lily's drained brain stumbled over Matron's respectful use of the title nurse. "I don't wish to presume my services are still needed."

"Because you think I don't like you."

"No, I don't think you do."

Matron assessed her for a solid minute before replacing the file and coming around to the front of her desk. No barriers between them now. "In that you are correct. When you first came to hospital, I considered you the worst thing to befall the uniform. You stand out, you fail at assignments, you fraternize with the patients, and you have the extraordinary talent of being precisely where you do not belong. In other words, you do not belong here."

Her sparse eyebrows lifted in punctuation. "However, you have proven a work ethic by trying. The men are cared for and, dare I say, quite happier since you've come on the ward. In short, you have tended them not only in body but in soul as well. A task equally important to that of mending bones."

Lily's ears rang with the unexpected compliment. "I know I'll never be as good as Bertie, but I'm humbled to have helped in what way I could."

"It's not often I'm proved wrong, but in this case, I shall forgo the entitlement."

"Thank you, Matron."

Nodding, the older woman retreated behind her desk and resumed her seat with a fresh stack of paper. "Why didn't you come to me first about the dance? Or at least correct the situation when Hartley claimed it as her own idea?"

"How did you know?"

"No one else could have dreamed up such a ridiculous event and had the laird himself give his blessing. You have many friends on the ward. They all wished to see you recognized for your contribution."

Lily knotted the strings of her handbag between her fingers as the weight of that statement settled. "Not long ago I might have needed that recognition. However, I was only too happy to see them enjoying themselves, no matter who introduced the idea."

"And there is the woman I had hoped you to be all along." Was that the ghost of a smile at the edge of the old dragon's mouth? "Now, go. I have papers to file. No doubt HQ will be all over last night's fire, and I can't say what that means for us."

Crossing to the door, Lily stopped and looked back. "I'd like to return, if you'll allow me. Once I see to my family and they no longer need me."

"The door will be open for you."

Leaving Matron's office, Lily hurried into the great hall. She and Bertie needed to leave in the next ten minutes if they were to catch the noon train to Threading Hall, but Lily had yet to see Alec since leaving him by the stables. She hurried outside to the grisly scene, but he wasn't there. Had he returned inside to change or buried himself in his office? She walked to the front of the castle, where Guthrie waited in the buggy already loaded with her and Bertie's trunks.

"Best get goin' if we dinna wish tae be late," he said. Somewhere he'd found harnesses to hitch the horses to the buggy.

Wallace had done a splendid job in calming them.

The front door opened and Bertie trudged out, escorted by Captain Gibbons. Dressed in the simple traveling suit she'd worn all those months ago for their arrival at Kinclavoch, when the world was full of possibilities, she'd wilted into a shell of herself. Gibbons helped her into the buggy and stroked her hand as he spoke softly to her. Bertie didn't respond as she sat on the bench with her head down.

"Ready, lass?" Guthrie called to Lily.

"A moment." Where was Alec? She hadn't told him they were leaving, and no way was she boarding a train without saying goodbye. Lily picked up her skirt and readied to charge back inside and shout his name from the bottom of the stairs.

He stalked around the corner of the castle. Shoulders tense and mouth pressed tight, he'd changed into a light-blue shirt, gray trousers, and dusty boots that came to his knees. His auburn curls bounced with each step he took. Each step looked as if he marched to a gravesite.

Lily flew to him and threw her arms around his neck. "I tried to find you earlier. I'm so sorry to leave you now, but I have to go to my family. Bertie needs me."

Alec grasped her arms and gently pushed her away. Melancholy singed the blueness from his eyes. "She does. As does your family."

"Will you be all right?"

"There's more for you to worry about at present than a burned building."

"I'll write when I can." He nodded solemnly as his gaze pinned her to the spot like an invisible lance. She nearly flinched from the intensity. "I'll come back. I promise."

"There's no need for promises. Go, before you miss your train."

Promises, desires, and dreams flooded the space between them, each second pushing their precipices further apart. Lily grappled to hold on to the moment before their separation was irrevocable. "Alec, I'll return."

"Don't."

The pain of betrayal in Lily's eyes cut Alec to the very core of his breaking heart. He couldn't have her here, not now when she was desperately needed by her family, and he had nothing to offer but the ash of once-upon-a-time dreams. To ask her to stay, to ask her to return to him would forever stain her with his failures. For the love he bore her, he would not contemplate such selfishness.

He had mastered locking himself away, and how much simpler it all would have been had he the strength to do so despite her. But his strength had failed, and she'd stolen into his melancholy heart, giving him hope that he wasn't fated to loneliness. Fate was a cruel mistress. Promising one thing while planning another. He should've learned a long time ago that happiness was not his intended destiny. His was a destiny he would not bind Lily to. No matter the pain he felt or was forced to inflict, for she would leave him no other way.

"Do not return here."

"Alec, you don't mean that. I know you don't. Last night was a dreadful shock. We've barely had time to sort out the situation and decide —"

He stepped back as she reached for him, leaving her fingertips to brush the front of his shirt. If he allowed her touch, his resolve would crumble. "I've made my decision on what's to be done, and I ask that you not return."

"If you're concerned that it may be unsafe, I don't care. As soon as I've seen to my family, to Bertie, and know she's well enough on her own, I'll come back to where I belong. To you."

Her words pierced the broken pieces of his heart, bleeding to the ground between them with his love. "You do not belong here. You never have. Not playing nurse, not planning parties, or pretending to be my sister's friend. And certainly not with me. It was a distraction, nothing more, and one I can no longer entertain when there are more pressing matters demanding my attention. Return to America and your ballrooms filled with stuffed shirts and easy living. There is nothing here for you." All that remained of his heart was dry and brittle. It had to be.

"Is that what you think I am? A distraction."

"Have I not said as much? Do you wish me to torment you further with the truth?"

"No, I believe you've said quite enough." Tears pooled in her liquid green eyes as all that might have been slipped away from his grasp. "To think I gave you my heart."

"I never asked for it. Then again, you've a bad habit of pushing in where least desired." He stepped away and clasped his hands behind his back, wringing his knuckles until the bones cracked. He forced away any telltale emotion behind his shuttered expression. "Go."

Lily climbed into the buggy next to Bertie and clasped her hand as Captain Gibbons relinquished his hold on the other and stepped back. With a click of Guthrie's tongue, the contraption jerked into motion. Lily turned, gripping the seat back with white fingers with a wilting expression that would torment Alec the rest of his miserable days.

He stood so stoically against the cold stones of Kinclavoch that he might have become a part of it. If he dared to move, the dam of emotion would break free and fly him down the road after her. The unfamiliar tug of a tear stung the back of his eye. He trained his focus on the buggy as it drove farther and farther away. The tear slipped, blocking out the last image of her before she rounded the corner and his world disappeared from view.

CHAPTER 26

April 1916
Hertfordshire, England

Lily sat on the cushioned window seat of Threading Hall's front parlor and gazed out over the manicured lawn washed out by the milky sun. Perfectly trimmed boxwoods hedged pebbled paths that had been raked into level submission. Orderly, quaint, beautiful, and boring. No sprigs of heather, no bursts of yellowing broom. No Kinclavoch.

The door opened and in slipped Lord Fowley's butler. He carried a silver delivery tray to where Bertie sat in a Queen Anne chair with a book forgotten on her lap.

She barely glanced up to take the message from the tray. "Thank you."

"Anything for me?" Lily asked, dreading the answer she'd come to expect.

"No, miss." With a dignified bow, he left as silently as he had come.

The familiar ache settled in Lily's stomach. She'd written a letter to Alec every week for two months, but not once had he replied. For weeks she'd tried convincing herself that their parting words had been a terrible dream brought on by the fire tragedy, that Alec could not have meant what he said. Not after he'd called her *mo chridhe.* My love. Yet his silence far outspoke any words. The ache in her stomach tightened to a knot.

Bertie sighed and traced a finger around the edge of the envelope.

Lily pulled out of her own misery and uncurled her legs from the cushion. "Aren't you going to open it?"

"It's from Joan."

Reggie's poor fiancée wrote every week like clockwork in hopes of one more story about her lost love. One more tie to the family she had almost been a part of. It was sweet but draining for Bertie and the emotions she had struggled with since receiving word of her brother's death nearly two months ago.

Rising from her chair, Bertie crossed to a vase of flowers and fluffed the drying tulips. The entire house was littered with flowers from neighbors and acquaintances sending their condolences until the chambers and halls were filled with the decaying scent, but Lady Fowley refused to discard them. They served as reminders for her dear boy.

"I'll be leaving soon," Bertie said.

"A stroll around the garden? Or a walk to town? I know your father claims it's a long walk, but it'll do us both good."

"No. I mean leaving Threading Hall." Bertie plucked a leaf from a chrysanthemum and methodically tore it to strips. "I can't stay here another week. This house suffocates us all. Mother and Father barely notice . . . Well, my presence makes no difference."

Stricken, Lily came off her seat and crossed the room to her cousin. "Don't say that. Of course you bring them comfort. You're their daughter, Bertie."

Bertie lifted a shoulder wreathed in black crepe. Its severity drew the color from her face. "Be that as it may, I don't belong here. Not anymore. Reggie will always be in my heart, but he's not the sole occupier and I must follow that."

The knot in Lily's stomach doubled. Over the past two years she'd come to depend on Bertie as more than a cousin. She'd become a raft of safety and sensibility in this unfamiliar territory, and Lily could not bear the thought of losing her. "Where will you go?"

"London, first. Hospitals there are in desperate need of nurses. Then hopefully to France when Alan receives his orders to return to the lines." Bertie dusted the dried leaf bits from her hand.

"You can't follow a man to the trenches."

"As his wife, I will be where he is."

Lily's mouth slacked open. "His wife!"

A smile lifted Bertie's mouth. "He's arriving here a week from Tuesday to speak with Father. With or without a blessing, we'll be married as soon as the banns are read, though Alan is hoping to procure a special license that will allow us to marry sooner."

"I don't know what to say."

"A first." Bertie's smile fell flat. "Say you're happy for me. That you understand. The world is filled with sadness. I need to find joy. Alan is my joy."

Lily's own sentiments jumbled together like a ball of twine. The threads wove together in a complicated shape that kept her upright but were now threatening to come undone. What would become of her then? Did it matter so much as the hesitant expectancy emanating from her dear cousin? Bertie deserved her own shining thread of happiness.

Lopping off her knot of selfishness, Lily walked around the table and took Bertie's hands. "Of course I understand and wish you the best of luck and happiness. No one deserves it more than the two of you. I only wish closure was to be found from his kidnapping."

"He wrote the strangest thing in his last letter. His nightmares have returned, presumably because I'm not there to sit watch over his bedside any longer." Bertie blushed. "He recalls a man speaking about Kinclavoch and MacGregors. It was as if the man knew the detriment the kidnapping would cause Alec."

"And no doubt it has."

"Alan wrote immediately to the inspector, whose only response was to add it to their investigation file. Part of me believes the police have no interest in pursuing the matter further."

"Perhaps Scottish law officials consider the case closed once the missing person has been found. Not a very reliable practice, in my humble opinion." Lily tapped a finger to her lips as the possibilities took a darker turn. "Or they have been ordered to stop searching lest the truth come out." Alec. How she wished he were here to talk to about this new information.

An hour later Lily found herself strolling aimlessly in the formal garden splayed behind the house. More hedges trimmed into borders. Pebbles evenly raked. Early spring flowers blooming in organized displays. No spontaneity, no allowance for adventure. Order and discipline reigned supreme. Never had she felt so far from Scotland and its freedom.

Wandering into a small arbor of birch trees with a bird fountain in the center, Lily plucked a fallen rose petal from the ground and set it adrift in the still water. "Be free."

"What freedom might it find there?"

Lily jumped at the sound of her father's voice. He sat on a stone bench tucked between two trees as if in hiding. That morning's paper rested on his lap. "I suppose the freedom of wherever the water takes it."

"Within the confines of the fountain."

"At least it can imagine freedom until it bumps against the edge."

Father shifted his gaze away. "It'll be time to return home soon." A swift, deadly cut to the dangerous topic. "I've contacted business associates in Portsmouth to wire me as soon as arrangements can be made. We can finally put all of this behind us."

"Like the war?" Lily nodded at the newspaper's glaring headline. And not the *London Herald*, she was glad to note. "Or that rebellion starting in Ireland?"

"Blasphemous warmongers. They pick Easter of all times to rekindle a centuries-old feud."

"Is there ever a good time to start a feud?"

With a distasteful press of his mouth, Father folded the paper into precise quarters. "I will inform your mother to start packing. I suggest you resolve to use your time wisely as well."

"I already have."

"Good. I don't need two women fretting over trunks."

"No, I mean I've used my time wisely. To think on things." Lily took a deep breath and met his eye. "I won't be returning to America with you."

Always the color of gray, Father's eyes had the ability to change the tone from winter's cold to a biting steel. At the moment his gaze rang metallic. "We have given you until spring, as you requested. The time is over."

"I asked for time so I might prove to you that I'm capable of making my own decisions. Good decisions, not simply ones that suit me but judgments I can be proud of."

"What does a girl like you need to find pride in? You have been given every luxury in life. You want for nothing. And this is how you repay our generosity? By wanting to decide things for yourself? No. You are too young and naïve to be allowed that kind of control."

Each word cut at her resolve like a fine razor blade that had been sharpened throughout years of use, but she was no longer the little girl determined to run from the pain. If she was ever to solidify her confidence, she must stand her ground.

"In some ways I may still be those things, but I believe I have matured this past year and I am no longer the silly girl you think I am. That's not truly who you wish me to be, is it, Father? Another socialite with air rattling around in her head?"

Father turned away and stared through the wall of branches. Still mostly bare, tiny buds of life had begun to showcase themselves in promise of coming fullness. "Your defiance knows no bounds. Even after what your mother did to send you here."

"Mother and I exist most compatibly from opposite hemispheres. I'm certain the distance has been a relief for her."

"Your mother can be a difficult woman, but she has her reasons. Growing up, her family had very little means. Only when her father worked his way up the steel mills to become one of the richest men in Pittsburgh did she finally taste a life of luxury, but luxury and riches came with a price. A heavy toll of society conformations. She's worked hard to keep us at the top."

Mother had always been discreet about her early life, barely making more than a passing remark about it to Lily, claiming life did not begin until she became Mrs. Philip Durham. Seeing the history so clearly now, Lily could well imagine the reason she struck fear into her mother's heart. "And I'm threatening to topple all she's worked for."

"Yes, but not in the way you think. She never wants to see you diminished to the poorness or pariah status she had to endure for most of her young life. She wanted a better life for you." Father turned to look at her. Gone was the steel, replaced by the soft gray of an afternoon shower. "As all parents do, we only want the best for our children though we may not go about it in the best of ways."

The quiet words echoed in Lily's ear like a gong. She sank onto the bench. "Her idea of a better life and mine do not see eye to eye."

"No, but there are always negotiations for compromise."

"You always told me compromises are for the weak-willed. I don't want to be weak-willed anymore. I want to find confidence in my own accomplishments, and I want to continue working, perhaps attempt a nursing license. Matron Strom said she would be glad to have me back, and I'm certain she would write me a good recommendation."

Father's eyebrows shot up in disbelief. This from a man who never registered shock. "To remain in England? With no allowance, no family to support you?"

"You wanted me to learn responsibility, Father. I have to do this on my own," she said. Who would have thought banishment to be the greatest opportunity she'd ever received? It had taken her to Alec. As much as the memory pained her, she wouldn't trade her time with him for all the gowns and jewels in the world. He was far more precious than those. "My path is here."

One by one, Father's eyebrows clicked back into an unperturbed place as he studied her with the same intensity he gave his business documents. "Does it lead to Scotland?"

Her eyes dropped to her lap as the bolstered confidence from moments before wilted like watered silk. "I thought it did. Once. Now I'm not so certain."

"Is this your fickleness rearing its head, or

is it more to do with a certain lord?"

"He told me not to return."

"That's never stopped you from not heeding instruction before." Father shifted on the bench, his immaculately pressed pants not daring to suggest a wrinkle. "This Lord Strathem, is he a man of his word?"

"Yes."

"Does he put the welfare of others above his own?"

"Consistently."

"To his own detriment?"

"Often." The corner of her mouth tugged up, though there was nothing humorous. It was just . . . Alec. Strong, determined, obstinate, scowling Alec. Most people ran away screaming from that scowl, but if they cared to look closer they would find a man strong in character, determined to do good, and hardheaded for a worthy fight. They would find the man she'd fallen in love with. Scowl and all. "Did he give you reason to believe he loved you?"

"Mo chridhe. I didn't realize how lost I felt until now, when I find myself in your eyes. I find I seek my heart more these days, for that is where I find you." His words haunted her with past longing and surged forth a new wave of sorrow at its loss. "Yes."

Father nodded once. "Very well. It's time

you saw this." He pulled out a copy of the *London Herald* upon which he'd been sitting and handed it to her. The sneering headlines punched the air from her lungs: "Kinclavoch Castle a Danger to All Tommies. Lord Strathem Concedes Long-Coming Defeat. Details on army's response and subsequent sale of castle found on page fifteen."

The paper fell from Lily's numb fingers. Alec was forced to sell Kinclavoch. His pride, his joy, his legacy of honor. Gone. Grief swelled through the broken bits of her heart. Everything he had done to save his beloved home now laid bare in printed ridicule for all the country to mock, or worse, pity.

Taking the paper from where it had crumpled to the ground in a heap, Father smoothed out the edges before folding it into precise quarters. "I ask again, do you think he loves you?"

The swell of grief engulfed her. She turned her face away lest her stoic father bear witness to her drowning. "He pushed me away. After the fire, after the telegram about Reggie, Alec told me to leave because there was nothing there for me."

"And you believed him."

"Think what you will of the Scots, but

Alec is a man of integrity. He does not toss his words about without care."

"Have you not considered that his sudden retraction from you was to save you from sinking with him?"

Far off a bird chattered. The same bird-song she'd heard in Kinclavoch's garden calling to her with wild breezes and heather-clad moors deep in its throat. She'd strolled with Alec in that garden and never felt more at home, but it wasn't the overgrown hedges or leggy honeysuckle that filled her soul with peace. It was Alec.

She didn't need the stone walls of a castle or the fragrance of cultivated flowers in bloom. She needed him, and more than anything, she wanted to be there for him. To share in his loss and carry the pain so he no longer stood alone. Yet Alec would never admit to needing help. His first instinct for survival was to push everyone away. As he'd done with her. The well of grief receded.

"If he is to sink, then I want to be there with him."

"That is precisely my point, and I believe precisely his reason for sending you away. When we care for someone we only want the best for them though we may not go about it in the best of ways." Tucking the vile paper under his arm, he ducked out of the arbor and began walking toward the house. "The question now is whether you wish to swim with your family or sink with him?"

Lily rose slowly off the bench, her decision made without hesitation. "With him, but we won't sink. Not together."

Father kept walking. No argument. No list of reasons why she was wrong. No threats of allowance or severing connections.

"You aren't going to dissuade me?" Lily called after him.

He paused and looked back at her. "If you've decided, then I should like for you to see it through. You did claim to be capable, yes?"

"Yes."

He continued walking. "Good. If nothing else, I expect my daughter to be a woman of her word."

Dumbfounded, Lily stared after him. It was the longest conversation she'd ever had with her father. And what a doozy! Returning to America had been the furthest thought from her mind as her heart continually pulled her toward the wild moors and a man who had become a part of her. A man she missed so terribly.

Had Alec pushed her away to save her

from his ruination? Seemed he still had not learned his lesson on the impossibility of keeping her out of situations in which she had no part. Well, she belonged in this one whether he liked it or not. She belonged with him.

Lily raced in a very unladylike fashion past her father and back to the house. She had a trip to pack for.

CHAPTER 27

Laggan, Scotland

Alec brushed off the last wood shavings from his walking stick. The carving had turned out to be a lily. How appropriate to finish it that day. When all things were coming to an end.

Guthrie stumped into Alec's study, his boots echoing in the mostly empty room. "Be headin' o'er tae the dowager house tae see yer sister and mither settled once I've loaded the last o' the trunks."

"Thank you."

"Want me tae come back fae ye?"

Alec shook his head. "I'll wait for the appraiser to arrive. Hand him the key. I'll walk afterward."

The words clung bitterly to his tongue, but the truth was no longer avoidable as he gazed about his bare study. Nearly every piece of furniture except those too big to fit through the door had been sold to pay an outstanding amount of the debts last month. A week after that the remaining sum was called in to be paid in full by tomorrow at six o'clock. There had been nothing left and no time to scrounge. Selling Kinclavoch was the only solution.

Viola had cried. Mither had gnashed and wailed. And Alec hung like a guilty man drawn and quartered, the rope gradually tightening about his strained neck. Parts of him died each second, the waiting prolonging the agony. Unlike a criminal, Alec would never know the sweet relief of the end. His torment would continue with the home of his family standing as a grim testament to his failure. The lord to lose the MacGregor legacy.

Alec took one glance around his study. He knew every panel, every dent in the floor, the smell of morning and evening on the wood. This room had molded him into the Lord of Strathem. There was no use for it now.

Straightening his shoulders, Alec tapped his thigh to gain Bruce's attention as the dog laid in his customary spot next to the empty fireplace. "Come, laddie. Time to meet our doom." Bruce whined and didn't lift his head. "Have it your own way and stay. The new owner will probably turn this into a frilly parlor and use you as a foot cushion."

Bruce popped up and trotted miserably into the hall. Alec marched out and shut the door behind him without a backward glance. Nor did he gaze one last time upon the empty library shelves where his magnificent book collection once resided, and not once did he look at the grand staircase upon which dozens of MacGregor generations had trod. Only when he passed the sitting room did his feet give pause. A shell of its former glory, it stood as an empty box waiting to be filled. Only the echoes of ghosts now claimed it as not a trace of the Tommies remained. Three days after the stable fire the army had arrived with trucks and packed up the entire hospital, declaring Kinclavoch no longer safe. The patients and nurses were assigned to new homes that weren't as likely to burst into flame or suffer a kidnapping.

A whiff of rosewater drifted under Alec's nose. A laugh whispered in his ear. He clenched his eyes shut. No matter how many doors he locked or backward glances he refused to allow, he could never shut *her* out. Lily had become a part of this place and her absence was keenly felt. Alec opened his eyes and hardened himself to the loss. It was better for her to have left this place with its troubles. Let her find happiness elsewhere for there was nothing here but the ashen memories of what could have been.

Clinging tight to his cane, he made for the back door for a final glimpse of his beloved garden and stable remnants.

"Lord Strathem." The appraiser, a beetle of a man direct from Inverness, scurried down the hall after him. Despite the lack of light, he squinted. "All items accounted for?"

"Aye."

"Do you wish to walk through with me once more? Perhaps consider a few of the remaining items?"

"No."

"Would you consider —"

"No."

"Perhaps it wise —"

"The house, Mr. Innish. That is all." Alec flung open the back door and stepped out.

"Very well. I believe one of the prospective buyers is here with an offer while the other I expect to arrive shortly. I'll finish up the last of the paperwork and meet you around front." Mr. Innish clicked his teeth in beetle fashion and scurried back down the hall before the outside air could swallow him.

Slamming the door, Alec stalked across the stone terrace and down the steps to the grass that swayed dully beneath a gray-blanketed sky. He ground his cane into the dirt. Vultures, these buyers were. Couldn't wait until the morrow before swooping in to seize their prize.

He swept his gaze over the forlorn blooms and shrubbery tumbling through the garden with neglected abandon. Never again would he lose himself on their paths. No more frogs to hunt or fairy rings to make mischief. Time would wrap its immortal hands around this magical place and ease it into the forgotten lands of yesterday. He had loved it as well as he could. Before the pain could buckle his knees, Alec turned away.

A figure emerged from a line of rowan trees thick with tiny clusters of white blossoms. Elegantly dressed in purple and cream with a large hat and veil draped across her face, the woman walked toward him. Alec's heart gave a start. Lily. She'd returned to him. He'd told her to stay away, needed her to remain far away, but in that moment he couldn't bear the separation of twenty yards that kept her from him. He hurried forward. Then slowed. The tilt of her head wasn't right, nor was the curve of her slender waist. There was no swish to her gait. His heart plummeted.

"Hello, Alec." Esther peeled back the veil covering her face and flipped it over her hat. "I knew I'd find you out here."

Alec tried to keep his disappointment from showing. "Needed to ensure everything was in order."

"One last round." Sadness flitted across her face as she glanced over the garden. "My heart weeps for the loss."

"It was good of you to come, but unnecessary. Your hospital work in London is more important than watching a crumbling castle slip further into decay."

"I do not care much for my new assignment in London. Our work here at Kinclavoch was rewarding. It meant something because it was part of our community. There I feel like another fish in the overwhelming pond just swimming to get by. Besides, I couldn't bear the thought of you alone today of all days."

Without thinking, Alec sought the familiar lines and bright red of his stables. But it wasn't there. Nothing was. The ruins had been cleared away, fragments of foul play evidence collected by the police, and the ashes left to an eastern wind. The unbearable pain welled again. "I've had to sell the horses. They deserve peace after nearly dying."

Next to him, Esther fidgeted with her lace gloves. Something she never did. "Come away. You've done enough floundering in the past. Time beckons us forward." Looping her arm under his, she gently tugged him away from the sight of where the stables once stood and the last green whispering of the garden.

They ambled around the front of the castle, each of Alec's footsteps slowing as if reluctant to be parted from the ground it so loved. Bruce kept a sedate pace on the path in front of them, his tail lacking its characteristic wag. "I fought as valiantly as I could, but in the end I've suffered a great loss."

"No one could have fought as bravely as you. I only hate seeing the effort cost you so much. The slandered reputation, the poisonings, the madmen, the fire. All of that horror and tragedy to corner you into submitting to the inevitable." She laid her other hand atop his arm and squeezed. "Still, you would not be the man I admire so much if you didn't fight to the end. A lesser man would have given up long ago."

He resisted the appearance of intimacy between them, craving the closeness of another woman. One that was not to be. One of many things that was never to be for him. "What I wouldn't give to try one day more. To keep the MacGregor legacy from shame."

"Do you sincerely mean that?" She tugged him to a halt. Heavy, dark lashes framed her eyes as she looked up at him with a delicate mix of vulnerability and temptation. "I'm still here, Alec. Waiting. Allow me to give your legacy wings."

Esther had been there all along. The lifesaving rope as waters closed in over his head. Marriage to her would secure Kinclavoch with the blessing of their ancestors surrounding them. No more debt, no more leaking roof, no more selling off precious heirlooms. A home for Viola and Mither to settle into without worry. The mere thought of such a prospect eased the troubles weighing him like bricks. How much more freeing would it be to accept her offer?

True, it would be one of those business arrangements he detested, but choosing Esther was a canny decision. Nothing of his heart would enter into the deal. Not that he had that at his disposal to offer. His heart lay in another's possession and would thus remain for he had no need of it without the possibility of having *her* too. She was lost to him. Pain clenched in his chest. He stabbed his cane into the ground as if that futile effort would stab out the agony desperate to undo him.

"Esther." He drove the cane farther into the dirt as the words turned his mouth to ash. He'd tried to stand on his own, but this wasn't about him any longer. With his heart gone, his head took free rein to the only course left.

She leaned in, hope flitting in her eyes. "Yes?"

He opened his mouth. Words failed as if he tasted their wrongness.

Movement over her shoulder drew his attention. And immediate wrath. *I should have known he'd slither in for the final kill.*

Richard Wright stepped from a fashionable Rolls Royce parked in the drive. He had the nerve to look calm and composed. "Good morning, Lord Strathem."

Rage misted before Alec's eyes. Bruce growled at his master's side. "You're trespassing. Get off my land."

Wright's polished shoes crunched on the gravel as he adjusted the white shirt cuffs circling his slender wrists. Like a bad bawbee turning up, but unlike the Scottish coin there was no value in him past his own delusions. "Hardly trespassing when I'm about to sign as the new owner. In which case I will order you off *my* land."

Strangling his cane with enough force to splinter it, Alec stalked toward him. "I refuse any vile offer you make. I'll destroy this castle brick by brick if I have to before I'll let you set hands on her." He gripped his cane with both hands. If that filth took one ill-advised step forward he'd get wood in his teeth. "Get out."

"A strange way to look at marital vows for that is your only other choice, if I'm not very much mistaken." Shifting between Alec and Esther, Wright's shrewd gaze narrowed. "I'll pay handsomely. A fortune well beyond its worth. Every burden you carry will disappear."

"The only burden I'll be carrying is when I toss you off my property."

A look that summoned the past slipped over Wright's expression. It lighted there for a brief moment of contemplation before morphing into abhorrence. "How similar to your mother you sound. Stubbornness blinding you to a fault. She about your worthless father and you about this pile of crumbling stone. I gave both of you opportunities to see the error in your ways and yet both of you rejected me."

"I know that's why you're here. Your

desperation to buy Kinclavoch is revenge for my mother rejecting you all those years ago. She was too far in love with my father to ever give notice to you." Alec remembered it all. The pleading. The tears. The threats. The haunting had reached through time to wrap its cold fingers around everything he held dear, choking the life from it year by year. "How pathetic you are to chase after a woman who never loved you and now to take away her home because she chose someone else."

Wright's fair skin mottled red, which smeared into a dull rust color under the leaden sky. "Pathetic is the creature standing next to you." Biting off each word, he jabbed a bony finger at Esther. "I shall have you arrested for poisoning and arson."

Esther's poise quivered. Latching determinedly to Alec's arm, she tried tugging him. "Come away, Alec. We've heard enough of his vitriol. He'll stop at nothing to steal Kinclavoch from our hands."

"I have proof she was behind poisoning Miss Barrymore and starting the fire." Reaching into his jacket pocket, Wright pulled out a slip of paper and sooty hankie. "A receipt for the very honey the police found traces of in Miss Barrymore's cup, and a lady's handkerchief found near where the fire had first been set."

A bevvy of curses filtered through Alec's head. English, Scottish, and Gaelic, which never disappointed when it came to vivid expression. He gritted his teeth to hold them in check. "I've been every day to police headquarters asking after evidence. They've told me the cases are indeterminate."

"That's because you are above bribery where I am not. Though I prefer to call it friendly persuasion." Wright shrugged as if the unlawfulness of such a deed bothered him not in the least. "I'm a newspaperman. I know who's ripe for picking a juicy story, and one of the lowly coppers was looking to make a few extra coins for his cooperation in loaning me the items."

Holding back a new string of curses, Alec took the items and scanned the purchase order. One item of African bee honey purchased the day after the actress arrived and signed by E. E. H. Sickness roiled in his gut as he traced his thumb over the same initials on the charred hankie. "Esther Ernesta Hartley."

Esther blinked once. Twice. Her thick fringe of lashes batting down in incredulity. "You honestly don't believe I would ever think of harming anyone, do you? These are terrible, terrible lies brought forth by a man who earns a living selling lies. It's only to his advantage to discredit me in your eyes." Her voice rose with each word until ending in a shrill squeak.

Numbness descended like fog, muting the inferno of anger threatening to consume them all in its explosion. The sensation pushed Alec beyond the boundaries of himself as if the happenings were too far removed and unreal to be believable. With deft movements he unhooked himself from Esther's hold and took a deliberate step back. "Do these items belong to you?"

Flicking a distasteful glance at the questionable items, Esther dismissed them with a wave of her hand. "He must have forged them. Rolled the handkerchief around in a fireplace and had some poor laundress stitch my initials on it."

Wright scoffed. "Entirely too much trouble when you so aptly provided the proof for me. The clerk at the grocer is willing to swear in court that you are indeed the buyer and signer claimed on the receipt. The hankie was a bit more difficult to use as proof, outside of your obvious initials, until the investigation team detected traces of ether."

"An ether bottle was used to start the

fire." Alec examined the hankie. Loose fibers made a ring in the center. The ether fragments found in the rubble had bits of cloth stuck to the rim. Fibers that matched the hankie. The numbness shifted. Sparks of anger shot through the fog. "You weren't seen at the fire. Or afterward. Can you explain how this got there?"

As long as he'd known her, Esther had always been the picture of elegance and composure. Any amount of fluster was always quickly smoothed over with good breeding, but this day, no matter how hard she tried smoothing the cracks fissured into her expression, they exposed the uncertainty wavering beneath.

"I . . . someone must have stolen it. The true culprit behind all of this. Alec, do not allow him to twist these accusations against me."

Her pleas raked against the mounting truth. Alec ignored her as he turned the hankie over in his palm. A bit of horse oats clung to the back. "These items must be returned to the police for a proper investigation. I'll not allow blackmail and bribery to falsify reports any longer."

Wright buffed his nails against the lapel of his tailored jacked and shrugged. "Return them if you like. I'm no longer in need of them. My point has been well made."

The sound of an engine rattled far down the drive, and in a matter of seconds a tilting Model T rumbled into view. What now? Two figures appeared in the front seat, one wearing an army officer's peaked cap and the other . . . Alec's throat went dry as he spotted two fancy feathers sticking out of the window.

Before the auto pulled to a stop, the side door flung open and out bounded Lily with hat feathers bouncing. Lifting her rose-colored skirt, she raced toward Alec.

"What is *she* doing here?" Esther hissed. "She's supposed to be halfway back to America."

A few yards away, Lily's run slowed to a halt as Esther's father, Mr. Innish, and Guthrie walked out the front door. Her confused gaze sought Alec's before sweeping to Wright and Esther and the obvious chaos heaving between them. "What's happening?"

It was then Alec saw it all as clearly as lightning striking across a thunderous sky. Esther's caged reactions. Lily's threatening appearance. Wright standing to gain it all in one fell swoop. Taking Esther's hand, he pressed the handkerchief into her pristine gloved palm and curled his fingers over the top.

"The honey. The ether, which not only started the fire, but was likely used to poison my horse." He swallowed against the vehemence burning his throat. "Each disaster forcing me past the point of no return where I would have no choice but to sell to the one man I vowed never to hand ownership to or agree to a marriage contract with the very woman who promised to save my estate all while plotting my downfall."

"Alec, please." Fear widened Esther's eyes, releasing the truth that she'd concealed for far too long. He saw it now. Ugly and raw and brimming with misguided intention.

"Do you deny it?"

"I deny ever wanting harm to befall you. Surely you can see how I've tried to save you from your own stubbornness and pride? What good will your pride be when you lose everything you've worked so hard to keep? I had no other choice to make you see sense." Somehow the glistening of fear in her eyes glided to shades of righteous haughtiness. A superior expression to claim the ends justified the means.

The shreds of numbing fog evaporated. The barrier gone, Alec's anger raged. "Peo-

575

ple could have died!"

"But no one did. Not even when Drey-mond put a knife to her throat. That was the closest it ever came." Eyes popping wide, Esther slapped a hand over her mouth. It was too late. The damage was done and her guilt complicit for all the world to witness.

"You told him to threaten me?" Lily stepped closer to Alec, which inadvertently was within striking distance to Esther. He'd never witnessed two women having a stramash outside of gilded insults, but if it came to fisticuffs his money was on Lily. Or would be if he had any.

Sensing her predicament, Esther took a step back. "I . . . not in so many words."

"Daughter, what have you done?" Cheeks high with color, Mr. Hartley grabbed Esther by the elbow and spun her around to face his wrath. "Drive me all the way here under the impression I was to purchase a castle as part of your dowry only to discover sabotage in the most heinous of crimes. You bring shame on our house!"

Esther's haughtiness wilted in a wash of tears. The veil fell over her sagging head, muffling the sound of sniffles. In her own mind she thought what she'd done was for the best, and while Alec might have forgiven the slights effected on him, he could never pardon the danger she'd inflicted on his estate and those within it.

His ire smoldered among red-hot coals, seething for release. By sheer willpower to remain calm lest he do something unforgivable, he *smoored* the fires of temper. "Guthrie, escort Mr. Hartley and his daughter into the sitting room. Ensure they don't leave. Then ride to the village and inform the inspector. Bring him about at once."

The veil rippled over Esther's face, obscuring her features into a softened blur. Masking the truth beneath. "Alec, is this what you truly want? Without me Kinclavoch will go to him."

Alec nodded to Guthrie. "Take her."

Taking her arm while Mr. Hartley held the other, Guthrie escorted the weeping heiress inside the castle she sought so dearly to have but would never hold for her own. How Alec would welcome the numbness now, to be swallowed into the thick grayness obscuring the sky and washing the earth in dullness.

But there was Lily before him. Fresh as dew and bright as spring in the color of roses beckoning him not to disappear. He sensed her hesitancy, but she smiled and he felt as if the sun had finally burst to life.

Until the black cloud scuttled in.

Wright cleared his throat as if having finished a drama he found less than worth his attention. "An amusing morning to be sure, but with the theatrics out of the way, I'd like to get on with the signing. Innish, bring the papers."

The appraiser, who had remained motionless on the front steps during the performance, roused back to life and clicked his heels into action, scurrying toward his auto where a tower of precarious folders teetered on the front seat.

"You're daft if you think I have any intention of signing to you." A deep growl rumbled in Bruce's throat. Alec placed a commanding hand on top of the dog's raised hackles.

"You have no choice. No other buyers are coming. I've made sure of that. This is an exclusive contract offered to me alone."

"No."

"Do not make me regret my leniency to you as your mother's son. I will win. Of that you can be as —"

A ball of khaki launched itself at Wright, driving him to the ground. Captain Gibbons knelt on Wright's chest and punched him. "You! I know your voice. I hear it in my nightmares. All those days trapped in

578

that shed, blindfolded, but oh yes, I remember your voice." He drove his fist into Wright's nose again. Blood spurted.

Wright gasped and struggled to throw the soldier off. "Unhand me, you wild swine!"

Gibbons held his fist inches from Wright's mouth. "Say one more word. I dare you."

Bruce circled Wright's head, teeth bared, a warning deep in his throat. Wright thrashed to get away from the animal. "Call your bloody beast off! If he takes one step closer, I'll have him destroyed."

"Funny thing about border collies, they're not known for aggression unless provoked. Or their master is threatened. I once watched him rip out a wild boar's throat after it charged me while hunting. Most vicious piece of work I've ever witnessed." Alec squatted to Wright's eye level. "You wouldn't make it off the ground fast enough to stand a chance." Patting Bruce on the neck, Alec stood. "Captain Gibbons, take your hostage to the wine cellar and lock him in. He'll be secure enough until the inspector arrives. Bruce, follow."

Gibbons hauled Wright to his feet. Blood ran down the newspaperman's nose and dripped onto his pressed shirt. With the slump of his shoulders and shuffling of his dirt-caked shoes, one would never take him for the slick London tycoon.

As Wright stepped past, Alec reared his fist back and slammed it into his face. Wright's head snapped back, but Gibbons held him upright.

"The only time I want to see your face again is behind bars." Alec flexed his knuckles to cordon off the anger surging through his veins. Pale and rooted to the spot, Lily watched him. "I'm sorry you witnessed that."

"If you hadn't punched him, I would have."

A half-hearted smile quirked his mouth. It immediately fell flat. Too much had passed between them, but now was not the time to sort it. He had other accounts to settle first. He started for the castle door. Before crossing the threshold, he glanced back at her. "Wait for me?"

Lily nodded. "Always."

Alec shut his study door behind him and quietly leaned against the solid wood. "It's done."

Lily turned from the window. She'd removed her hat and gloves and discarded them someplace. A mixture of sadness, resolve, and understanding passed across her face.

"The authorities have taken Wright and Esther into custody and will return tomorrow for further questioning. I suspect they'll wish to speak with you as well."

She clasped her hands in front of her skirt. "Have you truly lost Kinclavoch?"

His hour-long conversation with the police still rang in his ears as unbelievable as when he'd first been told. "Funny thing that. Wright bought all the outstanding debts from my creditors and then called them in with a deadline for tomorrow evening. It seems that with his impending sentencing of guilt, he's been forced to decline all further payments. According to the law, a refusal of payment considers the debt paid off. Kinclavoch remains mine, debt free."

"Alec, that's wonderful!"

Beaming with delight, she started toward him, but Alec turned away and walked the length of his built-in bookcases. Pages filled with generations of knowledge all gone. Just as he'd thought she was. He'd locked the pain in his heart, forcing himself to forget its existence, but a word, a memory, a sudden turn on the stair, and the pain would beckon him to its domain. Down he would spiral, helpless to fight against it as it was the only way he could be near her. The pain was a part of him, and he had no wish to release it as it too easily distracted from the want in his heart.

Yet here she stood, eager to rush to him and all he could do was keep her at arm's length. One touch would rip open the pain and out it would spill. He had not the strength to endure it again.

Keeping his gaze from her, he moved farther down the bookshelves, fingers running along the worn wood with bits of dust outlining the shapes of books. "What is Captain Gibbons doing here with you?"

"I — Oh, we met at the train station." Her voice fell flat. Without turning, Alec imagined the disappointment on her face as she tried to comprehend his remoteness. "He's on his way to see Bertie in Hertfordshire, but his train doesn't leave until this evening. He offered to escort me to Kinclavoch, and we borrowed the postmaster's auto. I think it was an excuse to hear about Bertie. They're to be married, you know."

Married. The word was a punch in the gut. "No, I didn't. Nor did I realize Gibbons was still local after all the patients were transferred."

"He was discharged from hospital yesterday and only came to Laggan to inform the inspector of his new orders should more questions arise about the kidnapping. Fate is odd in that regard."

Alec felt her eyes on him, begging him to turn and look at her. Pain rattled in his heart. "I'm sorry you've come all this way with the hospital gone. No doubt you'll be off to America soon."

"I'm not going to America."

His heart thundered. "No? Well, mayhap you can contact Matron Strom and see if there are nurse openings elsewhere."

"The hospital isn't why I've come."

Don't ask why. Let her think nothing lies between you and make her leave before regret is insurmountable. Alec's fingers pressed hard into the shelf. "Then why are you here?"

"I came because I thought you might . . . Perhaps I've misunderstood." Her shaky breathing filled the room. An echo to the trembling in his bones. "Would you like me to go?"

"No, I don't want you to go."

"If I've misjudged a sentiment between us that you don't return, then —"

"There isn't one thing in this world that I want more than you." He finally turned and looked at her, every vulnerable fear on display. He had always hurt the ones he cared most about, not out of spite but in his need for self-preservation. What was there

583

left of him to preserve? He was a hollow man. "But I am not a whole man and therefore undeserving of you."

Tears filled her eyes. "You are all the man I need, and I will take you no other way."

Alec inhaled a shuddering breath. So many years he'd wasted in the barrenness of winter, but she brought forth the spring. Renewal, purpose, and hope.

He edged away from the bookcase, away from safety. "Do you mean it, lass?"

She matched his steps and didn't stop until they were a hand-breadth apart. The universe and its heavens and all that rotated within them narrowed to the point of inches between them.

"I never meant to fall for you." Her hand slid up his chest to cup his cheek. Soft and cool, her touch lit a flame within him. "Lord knows you made it increasingly difficult, but here I am. Head over heels."

"If you start tripping, we'll both need a cane. A fine pair we'd make, *mo chridhe.*"

Alec's uneven breathing matched hers as his lips covered the last remaining inches of emptiness, and a new heaven burst to life at their meeting. Her arms came about him as she pressed tight against him, a promise never to leave again. Alec responded with all the passion and vows of his heart. Never to be parted again.

An hour, perhaps minutes passed. Time was difficult to determine in their new world. Lily gazed up at him, a slow, satisfied smile curving her lips. "*Mo chridhe.* My love."

He stroked a finger down her cheek, marveling at how complete it felt to hold her. "The actual translation is 'love of my heart.' For that is what you are to me, yet infinitely more precious."

"Is there Gaelic for that?"

"No. There is no single word that conveys the whole of my meaning, but I shall call you my Lily and you shall know its significance." He touched his forehead to hers and breathed in her nearness. His heart, at last, content. "My Lily."

Smiling, she brushed her lips to his. "My Alec."

EPILOGUE

June 1918

Lily tilted her hat to the side to shield her eyes from the afternoon sun as her son waddled through the heather. "That's enough, darling. We have plenty to give Auntie Viola and Gran."

"Gut-gut." Robert Roy Philip MacGregor reached out a chubby hand and uprooted several of the slender stalks, dislodging most of the delicate purple flowers in his enthusiasm. He grinned and held out his collection.

"Oh yes. I suppose Guthrie needs a few sprigs as well." Lily tucked the flowers into her basket, then scooped him up in her other arm and walked down the garden path to where Viola rested on a bench beneath a towering silver birch.

"La-La!" Robert squealed and raced straight into his aunt's sweep of white skirts with Bruce clipping at his heels.

"I see he found you," Lily said.

"Of course he did. Didn't you, angel? Just in time for tea with Gran." Viola cooed and rose from her perch on a bench, sketchbook in hand. "You'd like some cakes, wouldn't you? Maybe a few scones and jam?" She tapped Robert on the nose and he giggled with delight.

The dowager Lady Strathem was still enshrined in her mourning clothes and had worn a decidedly heavy veil to Alec and Lily's wedding. She spent most of the ceremony glaring at Lily's parents, who had remained in Scotland long enough to attend the event. It was the birth of their son, Robert, that brought out a part of the woman that had been shelved far too long — her heart. Matters still remained rocky between Lady Strathem and Alec, but the little boy had ushered in the beginning of healing between them.

As for his grandparents, who resided safely in America once more, they sent letters and gifts from time to time all laced with formal cordiality. Mother had accepted but not entirely welcomed Lily's decision to marry a foreigner when she could have had her pick from New York's cream. Lily had told her she'd rather have parritch with Alec than cream with any other man.

"The post came. A letter from your editor," Viola said, handing her a single envelope.

Their editor at the *London Herald*. A twist of justice. After Wright's arrest and sentencing his share brokers dropped him like a pinched shoe. Alec had scooped up the newspaper for mere pennies and hired the injured Tommies who had difficulty finding jobs. The paper earned them a handsome profit, and the column "Straight from the Trenches" had become the most popular in the country.

While Wright drudged through his ten-year sentence at Bedford Prison, Esther had been admitted to Holloway Sanatorium, which provided private care for the mentally ill. Her father had written to the MacGregors once to state that while Esther was doing well, her delusions persisted with no remorse for her actions. The report saddened Lily, but as Matron had often said, not all could be saved.

Lily pocketed the letter. "Anything else?"

"Nothing from Alec." A sad smile flitted across Viola's face. "Join us for tea?"

"You two go on ahead. I'll join you shortly."

As the two conspirators scampered off to the promise of sweets, Lily meandered down another path overflowing with colorful blooms and came face-to-face with the statue of Rob Roy MacGregor. "Still missing your arm, I see. Sorry we couldn't repair that for you, but we hope naming our son after you makes up for it in some way."

As the new Lady Strathem, she had used a healthy portion of her dowry to restore Kinclavoch to its former glory. It had taken her months to track down and purchase several of the family pieces that had been auctioned off and return to them to their rightful places within the castle. Some pieces would remain missing forever, but it was a good start in rebuilding their history while investing in their future and the generations of MacGregors to come. The most delightful returns had been Appin and Sorcha, who took to their newly built stable as if they'd never left.

She stared hard at the statue, trying for the millionth time to find traces of Alec in the solid face and once more turning up empty. "Perhaps not in looks, but it seems the MacGregors all have battle in their blood."

For so long Alec had cursed his leg. Until the army became desperate enough to take on all men under the age of forty-one. A bad leg was no longer a concern. Three months after Robert was born, Alec's orders came. He'd shipped off to France on a rainy Sunday morning, and they hadn't seen him in over a year. The last she'd heard, his regiment had been transferred to St. Quentin for a big push. That was two months ago.

Lily sank to the soft grass as the heartache threatened to undo her. Most days she was able to hold it at bay, but on others it became difficult to breathe without her husband. Their brief time together as man and wife had been filled with discoveries and exquisite passion, but it wasn't enough. She would never have enough of him, not even when their silver years set in the twilight of their lives.

"What's this? A bonny lass sitting by herself. Come give us a smile, *mo bhean bhrèagha.*"

My beautiful wife.

Lily jumped at the sound of his beloved voice.

"Alec!" She launched herself toward her long-awaited husband and backward they tumbled into a heap. She peppered his face and throat with kisses. Only when she pulled back a fraction of an inch to kiss him again did she notice the grimace on his face. "What's happened? I know I'm months out of practice, but my eagerness should more

590

than make up for — What's happened to your arm?" She rocked back and at last took in the sling cradling his right arm.

He propped up on his good elbow. "Dislocated shoulder. Got kicked by a horse."

"No!"

"Then stepped on."

"Alec!"

He sat up and adjusted the cotton strip looping around his neck to keep the sling in place. "Nearly pulverized my kidney. Cannon blast went off and spooked the horse. He reared back, throwing me . . . and, well, I've a nice set of hoofprints to commemorate the event."

"How ironic to be trampled by the thing you love most."

"You are the thing I love most." He stroked a finger down her cheek, stopping just shy of her lace collar. "Our son?"

"Walking and babbling." Lily leaned in to his touch. "Are you home for good?"

Alec shook his head, attention fixated on the ripples of her skin left in the wake of his touch. "I have orders to return, but it'll be to the reserve lines. The brass are finally realizing how useless the cavalry is against these modern guns." He looked up. The rich blue of his eyes mesmerized her, drawing her in to their promising depths. "Let's not

591

talk about that."

Lily's breath caught in her throat. "Let's not talk at all."

Cupping her face, he kissed her. Once for separation. Twice for reunion. Three times for delights to come. "My Lily."

ACKNOWLEDGMENTS

When a novel begins, It's often no more than a spark in a writer's imagination. If the writer is very lucky, the spark catches and flames to a bonfire of possibilities, but this bonfire could never burn so bright without others to help fan it along. When this idea first sparked as a WWI Beauty and the Beast retelling, a very carefree young lady twirled across the page with a mischievous laugh and the intent to flip the world on its ear. She might have succeeded if not for a laird brooding in the shadows. Wary of one another from the start, they can't help but be changed by the influences in their life and, thereby, their stories made that much richer. The same is true of any novel and the people it takes to make it special. The richness, I mean, not the wariness.

To my publishing family at Thomas Nelson who brought me in with welcoming arms. Y'all are so amazing to work with and have pushed my stories to heights I could only once dream about. Kerri, Margaret, Amanda, with a special shout out to Jodi and Jocelyn who took my words and coaxed forth the sparkle from the mire. I hope the next time I'm in town we're not ducking from tornados.

Mary, thank you for reading that early draft and reassuring me it was a tale worth telling. And Kim, as always my magical unicorn who never lets me get by with a boring plot.

At the end of the day, words could never be written without the love and support of my little family. Miss S whose endless imagination is a thing to behold and still thinks her mama writes the bestest books in the whole wide world. And Bryan, who offers me everything good and joyful to be found in this life, most importantly, love.

DISCUSSION QUESTIONS

1. It took Lily crossing an ocean to an inside perspective of war to change her frivolous ways. Would she have found maturity had she remained in New York under her parents' thumb or was her exile truly the best thing to happen to her? Is it the major events or the minor events in life that change a person the most?
2. Alec's legacy is also his greatest burden, that of his home, Kinclavoch. Was his struggle to keep his family's estate one worthy of pursuit or should he have accepted his limits and sold it? Was his pride misplaced in forging on?
3. If you were the heir to a crumbling estate and desperate to save it from ruination, would you modernize by taking on a more common job, sell off all the family belongings, or find a rich spouse in a time where love didn't often go hand in hand with marriage?

4. During the Great War, hospitals were overwhelmed with the number of wounded soldiers and so many private homes were opened for their convalescence, particularly the larger estates such as Highclere Castle, the real Downtown Abbey. Would you open your home to convalescing soldiers for the duration of a war? Why or why not?

5. Given Alec's medical disqualification from the war, he sinks into a deep depression. What advice might you give him when his pride and manhood are under attack?

6. Lily was often criticized for not acting serious enough in the convalescent home. Was she right to bring in a spot of fun, or she should have tried harder to perform her assigned duties better?

7. During the war, the soldiers often lived a different experience than what those back home believed. Should the public have been made aware of what it was truly like in the trenches, or should they have continued on believing that there was far more good than bad for the fighting men? Is ignorance truly bliss?

8. This is a classic story of opposites attract as Alec's darkness rebuffs Lily's lightness. By the end, do they complement one

another or not? If so, how?

9. Lily represents the heart while Esther represents the head, both of which Alec has to consider. Have you ever been tempted into a relationship for practical reasons rather than authentic feelings?

10. Known for his stubbornness, pride, and brooding worthy of a tormented wind-swept moor, Alec is hardly a delight at first acquaintance. Could you fall in love with such a man?

ABOUT THE AUTHOR

With a passion for heart-stopping adventure and sweeping love stories, **J'nell Ciesielski** weaves fresh takes into romances of times gone by. When not creating dashing heroes and daring heroines, she can be found dreaming of Scotland, indulging in chocolate of any kind, or watching old black-and-white movies. Winner of the Romance Through the Ages Award and the Maggie Award, she is a Florida native who now lives in Virginia with her husband, daughter, and lazy beagle.

Learn more at www.jnellciesielski.com.
Instagram: @jnellciesielski